W9-BTA-715

From author Thea Harrison comes the latest story in the New York Times bestselling Moonshadow trilogy....

Kidnapped while on tour, musician Sidonie Martel is transported to the mystical land of Avalon. A human without magical ability, she is completely vulnerable to the deadly forces surrounding her.

When she defies her captors and refuses to share her music, an act of violent cruelty leaves her broken, her ability to play silenced, maybe forever. Her only hope is a whisper in the dark, gentle hands that offer healing, and a man who refuses to show her his face yet who offers advice she dare not ignore.

One of the most feared and powerful sorcerers in history, Morgan le Fae serves a Queen he despises, Isabeau of the Light Court. Once a famous bard and an advisor to kings, Morgan has been enslaved to Isabeau for hundreds of years, acting as enforcer and the commander of her deadly Hounds.

Sidonie's music touches Morgan in places he had abandoned centuries ago, and her fiery spirit resurrects feelings he had believed long dead. For Sidonie, trapped in captivity, passion offers a comfort she cannot resist.

But Isabeau holds Morgan bound in magical chains that only Death can break. *And in the court of a cruel, jealous Queen, the only thing that burns hotter than love is revenge...*

Praise for Moonshadow

"*Moonshadow* is exactly what I expect of a Thea Harrison story, a stay-up-all-night read. Marvelous characters, lots of action and romance, and just the right touch of humor. This one goes on my keeper shelf. I loved this book."

~ Patricia Briggs—#1 *New York Times* bestselling author of the Mercy Thompson series

"*Moonshadow* hits all the right checkmarks on my must-have paranormal romance list: an Alpha hero, a heroine who kicks butt, worldbuilding that just keeps getting better, and a steamy plot that pulls me in from the first page!"

~ Carrie Ann Ryan—*NYT* Bestselling Author of *Wolf Betrayed*

"I loved this book. *Moonshadow* is Thea Harrison at her finest. I haven't been this excited since *Dragon Bound*!"

~ Kristen Callihan—*USA Today* bestselling author

"A brilliant new chapter in an enthralling saga! *Moonshadow* kicks off a new trilogy in Thea Harrison's fantastic *Elder Races* series. With a compelling heroine entering this world, this is a perfect place for readers to step into the ongoing story. The hero is intense, the heroine clever, and the sexual tension sizzling. Can't wait to find out what happens next!"

~ Jeffe Kennedy, Award Winning Author of *The Twelve Kingdoms* and *The Uncharted Realms*

"I'm already addicted to Thea Harrison's new world of Arthurian alpha warriors—especially after an American kick-ass heroine with serious magic powers teaches them a lesson about 21st century women!"

~ Eloisa James, *New York Times* bestselling author of *When Beauty Tamed the Beast*

"Scorching chemistry, perfect pacing & memorable characters sent me on a roller coaster ride of emotions! I want to live in the Moonshadow world."

~ Katie Reus, *New York Times* bestselling author of *Breaking Her Rules*

"*Moonshadow* is a beautiful book and exactly what I needed— hot romance, wild sex and a happy ending. Please don't miss anything written by Thea Harrison. She is a wonder."

~ Ann Aguirre, *New York Times* bestselling author

"Thrilling and deliciously sexy, *Moonshadow* is a smart, action-packed introduction to a new adventure in Harrison's complex and compelling Elder Races world. Intrigue goes hand-in-hand with an addictive romance that will please new and established readers alike. I can't wait to see what comes next."

~ Elizabeth Hunter, bestselling author of the Elemental Mysteries series

"A breathless, rollercoaster ride of a tale, complete with a fierce, capable heroine and a powerful hero worthy of her in every way. The bonds of love, trust, and friendship are stretched and sometimes snapped in a war of attrition that crosses time and worlds. Thea Harrison blows the doors off with some rollicking good storytelling in *Moonshadow*."

~ Grace Draven – *USA Today* bestselling author of *Radiance*

Spellbinder

Thea Harrison

Spellbinder
Copyright © 2017 by Teddy Harrison LLC
ISBN 13: 978-0-9981391-4-2
Print Edition

Cover Photo-illustration © Gene Mollica Studio, LLC

This book is a work of fiction. The names, characters, places, and incidents are products of the writer's imagination or have been used fictitiously and are not to be construed as real. Any resemblance to persons, living or dead, actual events, locale or organizations is entirely coincidental.

All rights reserved. No part of this book may be used or reproduced, scanned or distributed in any manner whatsoever without written permission, except in the case of brief quotations embodied in critical articles and reviews.

Chapter One

MORGAN STRODE INTO the Queen's private audience chamber, sweeping the room with a sharp gaze. It had become a way of life to automatically look for threats.

There was one enemy waiting for him.

The Queen herself.

Isabeau stood with her arms crossed, watching him with the deadliness of a coiled snake. She wore a blue silk dress that matched the blue of her eyes, and her long golden hair flowed in immaculate curls down her back. She was careful with details like that.

A gold chain looped the slender circumference of her waist. The chain was enchanted so that it was virtually unbreakable. She had ordered Morgan to make it. A scabbard made of ancient black leather hung from the chain.

The hilt of a knife protruded from the top, wrapped in the same humble, worn black leather as the scabbard. Deadly Power pulsated like an ebony supernova in Morgan's mind whenever he glanced at it.

Isabeau never met Morgan without wearing

Azrael's Athame, not since she had captured him. She didn't dare. Without Death's Knife to control him, she would become his prey.

How he longed for her to be his prey. No matter how many centuries passed, that longing never ceased. It had become his purpose for existing as everything else had faded away.

He eyed her impassively. While she remained armed whenever he came into her presence, his greatest, most effective weapon against her was calm, bland indifference. It gave him a cold pleasure to know she hated his indifference almost more than anything.

"Shut the door," she ordered. Raising one eyebrow, he did as she ordered. Private audiences with Isabeau almost never went well, but then he had expected nothing else.

As soon as the thick door settled into place, she grabbed a priceless antique porcelain bowl and flung it at him. Casually, he stepped to one side, and the bowl sailed past him to shatter against the paneled wall.

"I can't believe you let Oberon's bastards find a way back to Earth!" she raged. She tore at her own hair, her beautiful face suffused with fury. *"How could you do this to me?"*

"Because as we know," he murmured, "it's always all about you, Isabeau."

There was no reasoning with her when she got like this. The Queen of the Light Court couldn't bear to be crossed or disappointed in any way. When everything went the way Isabeau wanted it to, she was all sweetness and flirtatious, pretty smiles.

When things didn't work out the way she wanted, she flew into uncontrollable rages. She became convinced everything that happened, even the most arbitrary act of fate, was a personal attack against her.

She had destroyed the image of immaculate beauty she had worked so hard to achieve. Her tousled hair parted enough that he caught a glimpse of fury in those lovely blue eyes.

Lunging forward, she raised one hand to strike at him. He strode forward to face her. Pain flared at the sudden movement, and he pressed one hand to the fresh wound in his side.

"Be careful, Isabeau," he said gently as he looked down into her face. "Remember what happened the last time you hit me."

She had struck him only once, and in retaliation, he had cast a blight over Avalon's farmlands and ruined an entire harvest. That had led to a winter so bitterly lean even those at court had felt it, and Isabeau had been forced to dig deep into the crown's coffers to import enough food so she could still have the luxuries she loved and her people didn't starve.

She had since forbidden him to take such action against her, but if he had found a way once around the terms of the geas that bound him, he could do it again, and she knew it.

Fear flared in her eyes, and she gripped the hilt of

the Knife. She had disemboweled people who had disappointed her far less than he had just now.

But it took a major act of strength to draw Azrael's Athame, let alone wield it, and she hadn't done so in a very long time. To the best of his knowledge, she had only drawn it once.

He watched with clinical interest. Did she have it in her to draw the Knife again? In a way, it didn't matter. The single time she had drawn the Athame, she had struck him with it, and once was all it had taken to trap him.

Her fingers clenched, but the Knife remained in its scabbard. She snarled, "You said it would be impossible for them to reach Earth."

"Clearly," he replied sardonically, "I was mistaken."

"What happened?!"

"The knights of the Dark Court converged on the old Shaw manor. Even though the house had been built on a broken crossover passageway, somehow Nikolas Sevigny and his human witch found a way through to Lyonesse. They brought hundreds of troops back as reinforcements. I didn't think it was possible, and I don't know how they did it, but if they could break through using one broken passageway, they might be able to figure out how to use the other broken passageways as well."

"Why didn't you stop them!"

"I tried, but I couldn't," he snapped. "I'm not familiar with the magic they used. If the witch has an affinity for passageways, they might even be able to find the ones I've shrouded with cloaking spells—including the hidden Light Court passageways. Face facts, Isabeau. Lyonesse is no longer cut off from Earth. The tide of this war has shifted, and it is not in your favor."

"You should have killed her! Why didn't you kill her?!"

He raised an eyebrow. "I had no such orders to kill an American."

"Yet you knew she was responsible for this!"

"Incorrect. I suspected she *might* be responsible. Much of what I just told you is speculation. I don't know anything for sure."

Like a bird of prey, she swooped away to pace the room. Then she whirled and stalked back to him, lifting her rage-distorted face to his. She hissed, "I should tear your heart out for this."

His lips pulled back in instinctive, feral reaction to the threat. He met her gaze, and she saw something in his expression that made her recoil.

"You could try," he growled. "And even if you succeeded, see how long you survive in this war you created when you no longer have me to compel."

She loved the control she wielded over him, but at the same time, she hated that she feared him. She hated the fact that she needed him. It was virtually the only thing they agreed upon, because he hated it too.

He watched her struggle with conflicting emotions.

She ran her gaze down his figure, and the expression in her lovely eyes changed. She was one of the most beautiful of all the Fae he had ever met, but her beauty left him cold. After she had trapped him, she had never bothered to hide her true nature around him. He knew all too well the deadly creature that lived behind the charming façade.

Abruptly, she rapped out, "You demanded an audience with your Queen while you're still filthy and bleeding. What's wrong with you? Why aren't you healed already?"

He sighed. "I'm not healed because they shot me with silver arrows, and silver is anathema to a lycanthrope. I barely got away as it was. If I hadn't had a lycanthrope's speed, and if I hadn't stowed a car nearby, they would have caught me."

She gestured at his side. "So heal it!"

"Magic spells don't work on these wounds, and I can't heal at an accelerated rate. I can't shapeshift while the silver is in my system, and my ability to cast magic is dampened." Gritting his teeth, he added, "And I'm here because you ordered me to give you an update as soon as I possibly could. This was the fastest I could arrive."

He had to follow her orders to the letter. That was the nature of the ensorcellment she had trapped him in. He had warned her before to be careful how she worded her orders to him, but the stupid bitch never learned.

One of these days her utter self-absorption and impetuous carelessness might very well end his life. He lived in hope for the other possibility—that a carelessly worded order from her might give him the chance to end hers.

Rage and frustration took over Isabeau's features again. She spat, "What use are you like this? Get out of my sight. I don't want to see you again until you're fully healed."

He froze, not quite believing what he had just heard. Isabeau was Light Fae. She had no real understanding of how long it took humans to heal from serious wounds, and he had once been human. His supernatural attributes were of no use to him in healing wounds made by silver. He would have to recover the slow, hard way. The human way.

Lowering his lids to hide the flare of triumph in his eyes, he murmured, "As you command."

Her gaze darted around the room and fell on a marble figurine. She swept it up and flung it viciously at his head.

He ducked his head to avoid the figurine while his mind raced. He barely noticed when she stormed out of the audience chamber and slammed the door.

If Isabeau's temper cooled enough to allow her to think, she might realize what she had done. He had to leave before she could find him and rescind her impetuous order.

Tightening his lips against the vivid, tearing pain in

his side, he wended his way through the castle, using magic to avert attention from his presence.

Normally his Power flowed like an abundant, nearly inexhaustible river. With the silver poisoning his system, he could barely manage enough for the avert spell.

He didn't stop at the infirmary to get medical attention or bother going to his rooms to pack clothes. He was too intent on leaving Avalon as quickly as possible.

At one point guards ran down the hall. He heard them coming in time to step into an alcove. They might have been looking for him, or they might have been sent on some other urgent task. He didn't know or care, and he wasn't about to risk finding out.

I don't want to see you again until you're fully healed.

As long as he avoided hearing a countermanding order, he would have weeks of freedom, something he'd never had under the unending yoke of Isabeau's geas.

Weeks.

His imagination leaped ahead, racing through possibilities.

If he could acquire another injury before he was fully healed, he might be able to prolong this hiatus, perhaps even indefinitely. Unfortunately, he couldn't reinjure himself. Long ago, she forbade him to commit any acts of self-harm.

What if he found someone else to strike the blow for him? Someone he could trust to wield a silver weapon without killing him?

Would the geas allow it? He was sure as hell going to find out. If the geas would only let him, he would happily stick a silver knife in his own gut repeatedly to avoid returning to Avalon and living as Isabeau's slave.

He could gain time. Time to himself.

Time to research ancient texts and learn everything he could about Azrael's Athame. Time to see if he could work around the magical restraints that bound him and still find a way to destroy Isabeau and Modred.

The geas wouldn't allow him to destroy them himself—Isabeau's long-ago first order had forbade him to harm either her or Modred—but what if he could set in motion certain events that would destroy them for him?

As for the wound… life was full of pain. He would deal with it.

First, however, he had to leave Avalon.

His strength ebbed in a slow, steady trickle. Pausing only long enough to tear off strips from the bottom of his jacket, he folded a pad of material over the wound and tied it in place. The cloth was soon soaked, and he reached the closest crossover passageway in a haze of blood loss and pain. The guard at the passageway had been doubled, and conviction solidified.

They were looking for him. He had to wait until nightfall, and then he used the last of his magical strength to cast a sleeping spell over those on duty. When the guards were stretched out on the ground and snoring, he eased past them.

Into the passageway, to England, where the cool of a rainy summer evening greeted him. Morgan had money and resources on Earth. Cars, safe houses, and go-bags packed with credit cards, clothes, weapons, and necessities.

Nobody would be able to find him. Not unless he wanted them to.

By the time he reached the spacious country home of a doctor he kept on retainer, he had turned feverish and the insides of his lungs felt raw.

It was late, and he had to pound on the front door before lights came on downstairs. The doctor himself, a lanky human with receding hair and a nervous expression, answered the door.

"You can't show up on my doorstep at all hours of the night!" the doctor exclaimed. "My wife doesn't know anything about our arrangement."

Morgan's lip curled in a feral snarl, and he had to restrain his response. His lycanthrope abilities might be dampened for now, but the instincts weren't.

"You want to end our arrangement, fine," he snapped. "I'll stop paying your retainer—after you treat me."

"Who is it, Giles?" a woman called from above a flight of stairs.

The doctor raised his voice. "No one, darling. Just someone asking for directions. Go back to bed. I'll be up in a few minutes."

"All right." Footsteps receded.

Morgan had locked his knees to keep from falling over. He had used the last of his magical ability when he had cast the sleeping spell on the passageway guards, so he had a Beretta tucked into the waistband of his jeans.

A fine tremor ran through his muscles as he waited to see what the doctor would do. He didn't have the resources to find medical treatment elsewhere. If he had to, he would use the gun to compel the doctor to treat him.

Giles turned back to him. "No need to stop the retainer," he muttered, avoiding his gaze. "Next time text me, and I'll meet you somewhere. Don't come to my house, for God's sake."

Morgan began to unbutton his shirt. "Let's just get through this. We can discuss details of any future arrangements later."

Giles led him to a large farmhouse kitchen that had been stylishly updated, and as Morgan sat on a stool at one end of an island, the doctor eyed him much as Isabeau had. "Wounds made with silver?"

"Yes." Lycanthropes might heal with supernatural speed, but sometimes injuries still needed attention. Broken bones needed to be set correctly—or often rebroken and set—and wounds made with silver needed treatment just like a human's injuries would. He shrugged his good arm out of the sleeve. "After you clean the wounds, I need stitches, pain medication, and antibiotics."

"Don't tell me how to do my job." Despite his irritated response, Giles proceeded to do just as Morgan had said.

He cleaned both wounds, gave Morgan a shot for the pain and another shot of antibiotics. After he had stitched and bound the injuries, he left the kitchen. Morgan scooped up his lacerated shirt and jacket and followed the doctor into his office, where he watched Giles unlock a cabinet tucked in one corner.

Giles pulled out bottles and turned to him. "I'm giving you two pain medications. One is a narcotic, so use it sparingly. Take the full course of antibiotics until they're gone."

"Understood." He eased his way back into the shirt.

Giles eyed him with a frown. "I don't like this," he said abruptly. "That wound in your side is especially concerning. You should be on an IV in hospital."

Morgan took the bottles and tucked them into the pockets of his jacket without replying. The less Giles knew, the less the doctor could do to betray him.

Whatever else Giles was, he wasn't a stupid man. The doctor muttered, "The trouble you're in—it won't be coming here, will it?"

"I don't know." Morgan turned away. If he'd had a drop of Power left, he would have spelled Giles to forget his visit, but he was bone-dry on magic, and he would only get it back with rest and healing. "Most likely not, but anything's possible. You might use some of that exorbitant retainer I pay you to take your wife on holiday."

The doctor trailed behind him as he strode for the front door. The last thing Morgan saw of the doctor was his pale, frightened face as Giles stood in the doorway and watched him climb into his Volvo.

So many people had looked at Morgan with that same frightened expression over the centuries that he had grown immune to it a long time ago. Putting the car into gear, he reversed down the long, winding drive.

Then he drove until exhaustion forced him to stop. Finding a quiet, out-of-the-way place to park, he slept in the car, and when morning came, he bought coffee and a hot breakfast and drove until he again couldn't go any farther.

Morgan had plenty of safe houses, but he didn't go to any of them. Instead, he kept traveling north until he reached Glasgow. Only then did he search for a place to stay.

He checked into a hotel in the stylish West End area—some place big enough that he could get away with unusual behavior—and used one of his alternative IDs along with a new, unused credit card to pay for a week's stay.

When he finally carried his bag into the hotel room, he kicked off his boots, shed his clothes, set out a Do Not Disturb sign, and fell into bed, where he slept for thirty-six hours straight.

The next several days passed in a blur. He slept, waking only to take the medications, order room service, and wolf down food.

The fever broke after the third day. By the fourth, he felt a trickle of magic return, the flow of Power steadily increasing. On the morning of the fifth day, he appeared downstairs in the dining area for breakfast, clean and freshly shaven, albeit moving somewhat stiffly.

The fever and his own inhuman metabolism had worked to hone his features. He knew he was leaner and harder-looking, not quite so pleasant and therefore not nearly as forgettable, so he went out of his way to be agreeable to the waitstaff.

After breakfast, he stopped at the hotel office to tell a brief story of recovering from a bout of flu, to request his room be serviced, and to pay in advance for another week.

The manager was more than happy to oblige, and oh dear, the flu! She was sorry to hear Morgan's visit to Glasgow had gotten off to such a poor start, and was there anything else she could do for him?

He told her mildly no, he didn't want for anything, and everything in the hotel was perfectly lovely, thanks. To keep up the appearance of a man on holiday, he paused in the front hall to collect all the pamphlets on sightseeing tours and local attractions, then left to walk to the nearest café, where he ordered a coffee and settled at a corner table to pass the time while his room was cleaned.

He could sense a few of Isabeau's Hounds searching for him. They were trapped in the same immortal geas he was, like monsters captured in amber, their lives frozen in the moment they had been taken.

In the usual course of things, Morgan was their captain. The Hounds were his to command in her majesty's service. Now they were hunting him, to fetch the Queen's wayward captain back to her.

Mentally he ran through his actions since he had left Avalon. The rain had been on his side. Any trace of his scent would have been washed clean. They would check with Giles, along with every other physician and safe house they had a record of him using.

But he had told Giles nothing, and in any case, the doctor had probably taken Morgan's advice and gone on holiday with his wife. And Morgan had driven much too far for the Hounds to have any chance of picking up his scent trail anywhere.

He was unaware he had settled into complete stillness until he caught a few sidelong glances from a young couple sitting at the neighboring table. In an attempt to appear more normal, he riffled through the pamphlets he had set beside his coffee cup.

One caught his attention. Indifferently, he ran his gaze down the page.

The title *Wildfire* sprawled across the top. Underneath, there was a large glossy photo of a woman's silhouette on a stage. She had been captured playing a violin in front of a crowd, her body as taut as the bow she gripped in slender fingers. Various quotes of praise followed the photo.

The *Standard*: "Genre-bending."

Rolling Stone magazine: "Simply transcendent."

The *Telegraph*: "Sidonie Martel took my breath away!"

A sliver of Morgan's attention engaged.

But mostly it did not. Once he had been a famous bard in his own right and an advisor to kings, but it had been many, many years since he had played any kind of music.

The desire to play had been burned out of him by the geas, and as the desire to play had faded, so too had his desire to listen to music for pleasure. He had never heard of many modern singers and musicians. Sidonie Martel's name meant nothing to him.

Still, there was something about the photo that held his gaze. The woman's stance, her tension, vibrated off the glossy page. She was so full of passion. His mouth twisted in a self-deprecating smile. He couldn't remember the last time he had felt such bright, creative joy.

A young woman at the neighboring table leaned toward him. "Can't help but notice the pamphlet you're holding," she said in a friendly tone.

Morgan's gaze lifted. "Indeed."

The woman grinned at him. "If you're thinking of going, you should try to get a ticket. We went last night, and it was amazing."

"True, mate," said her companion. "We'd go again if we 'ad the quid."

"Thank you for telling me." The hotel staff had to be done with his room by now. Taking a last sip of his coffee, he gave the couple a pleasant smile, and as he exited the café he set the stack of pamphlets on a table by the door.

Walking back to the hotel, he assessed his injuries. The wound in his biceps was lighter and would heal faster, but the arrow he had taken in the abdomen had gone deep and would take longer. It lay burning in his side, the nagging pain a constant reminder of its presence.

How long would it be before it healed enough for the geas to kick in? Two more weeks? Three? He needed to try to find someone willing to stick a silver knife into him before then, or he would be forced to return to Isabeau's side.

He already had silver weapons, so that wasn't a barrier, but he couldn't approach any of his usual contacts, not with the Hounds searching for him. He had to recruit someone new.

As he entered the hotel, his gaze was drawn to the table of pamphlets, and the *Wildfire* photo leaped out at him again. This time he paused, head cocked.

He might find a few possibilities worth exploring at the concert. Like his physical strength, his magic was not yet at full strength, but with the right nudge and a subtle spell of persuasion, he might be able to engage someone's interest and discover just how far he could push the geas before it intervened.

He took another pamphlet with him up to his room, and a quick phone call informed him that night's concert wasn't sold out. The performance started at seven. He bought a ticket, rested until it was time to leave, and then took a taxi to the large arena at the Scottish Exhibition and Conference Centre.

As he filed meekly to his seat, just one more man among many, the crowd's electric, happy anticipation washed over him. It left him unmoved.

Looking around, he took note of the various individuals who seemed like they might be worth approaching—a rougher-looking male working the ground crew near the stage or perhaps the few blokes lounging near the exit.

His sensitive lycanthrope nose had caught the scent of drugs as he'd strolled past them, but as he ran his gaze over his potential prospects, he felt no urgency. The night was young. There would be a concession break and time afterward to make contact if he wanted, and in any case, it wasn't necessary for him to find someone that evening.

Even though the photo had been of a woman with a violin, the apparatus on the stage looked like the setting for a rock concert. Ah well, the *Standard* had promised something genre-bending. Bored, he stifled a yawn.

There was a warm-up band. Everyone around him

appeared to enjoy it. His sensitive ears felt assaulted, but he endured.

When the opening act finished and the lights dimmed, a few invisible entities flowed into the concert hall. Morgan's attention sharpened. He tracked the entities with his magic sense as they settled at either end of the stage. Most of the crowd would never know they were there.

More Djinn flowed in until the arena felt charged with the thunderous impact of their presence. There was little that Djinn adored more than music. The presence of so many was high praise all on its own. Despite his ennui, a sliver of curiosity brought Morgan to his feet along with the rest of the audience.

With an explosion of color, the lights flared, and the crowd roared as *she* blazed onto the stage. Other people followed her, a drummer, a bass guitarist, along with more musicians, but they faded into the background as *she*, the woman carrying a violin and a bow, captured everyone's attention.

Even Morgan's.

She didn't so much walk onto the stage as dance across it. Or maybe she stormed it. As she conquered the space, seeming barely connected to the ground, she carried so much energy she felt larger than life.

Instinctively, he double-checked his impressions. Even though she wore three- or four-inch heels, the top of her head came to the nearby drummer's shoulder. She had to be small, no more than five foot two or three.

His gaze lifted to the large telescreens, although he barely registered her features. She was pretty, or appeared to be, but she was wearing so much stage makeup every feature was accentuated, and it was hard to tell what she really looked like. He got the impression of high cheekbones, a full mouth, and perhaps a touch of Asian ancestry in long, elegant eyes.

Then she tucked her violin against her neck and lifted her bow. Expectant silence swept the arena. She began to play.

The first strains raced after each other like hawks lunging through the air, and all Morgan's ennui fell away. His hatred for Isabeau, the wounds, and his untenable situation were forgotten, all his emotional distance shredded.

He didn't welcome it. Part of him went into shock. That part of him hated it, hated *her* for doing it to him.

He still felt passion, but long ago his passion had turned dark and tinged with crimson. It had died down to a single thread, a burning desire to destroy those who had laid waste to his homeland and had enslaved him. That had become his mission in life.

This. This buoyant crescendo of sound.

It had no place in his life. He had other things on his agenda. Important things, blood-drenched things he had longed to do for centuries.

He had no room for this music. *No time for it.*

Yet he couldn't shake the hold it had on him.

She was everything the quotes promised, everything and more. Transcendent. Genre-bending. Her music ran through him with electric energy, more joyous than anything he could remember and more painful than silver. No wonder the Djinn flocked to listen to her. He didn't think there had been a musician like her in generations.

He didn't sit. None of them did. For the duration of the entire concert, his attention stayed riveted on her enlarged image, and when it was finished, he felt emptied, wrung out.

He didn't try to make contact with any of the likely people he had marked earlier. Instead, he made his way to his hotel, and as soon as he was back in his room, he called the ticketing agency to book another of her concerts. And another.

While he called, he ran a Google search on Sidonie Martel on his phone. Of French Canadian and Vietnamese descent, she was thirty years old and a graduate of Juilliard. Five of her albums had gone platinum, and she had won three Grammys.

He stared at the headshot posted on her website, at the high cheekbones, the spark of intelligence in her long, elegant eyes, and that full, sensual mouth. The impact of her personality leaped off the screen at him. Her thick black hair fell in a straight waterfall past slender, shapely shoulders.

When he tried to buy a ticket for a fourth concert, the ticket agent told him, "Sorry, that's the last concert she's doing in Glasgow. I'm afraid her next one will be in London."

"Is it sold out yet?"

"Not quite, but close. Most of her European tour is sold out."

Tapping his fingers on the table, he surrendered to this new, unwelcome obsession.

"I'll buy a ticket for every concert of hers that's still available."

Chapter Two

S IDONIE HAD A stalker. Another one. She could feel
it in her bones.

As she went for her early morning run through
Hyde Park and Kensington Gardens in London, her
security detail kept pace beside her. They were two big
strapping males, extremely competent magic users, and
ex-Navy SEALs. Nothing at all conspicuous about that.

Sid's mother had immigrated to Nova Scotia from
Vietnam as a young adult. If her mom had still been
alive, she would have been torn between pride and
disapproval at the direction Sid's life had taken.

She would have been very pleased Sid's career had
advanced far enough that she needed bodyguards,
although she would have wished that Sid maintain a
more discreet appearance. She also wouldn't have
approved of Sid's departure from strict classical music,
but she would have been delighted that so many other
people enjoyed it.

In any case, conspicuous or not, the security detail
was a necessary evil whenever Sid went on tour. She
was not the most famous musician in the world, not by

any means, but she did attract her fair share of weirdos.

"I don't like the fog," Vincent said on her right as he scanned the surrounding area.

He had to talk out loud, because Sid couldn't telepathize. She was a "deadhead," the slang term for a human who didn't have any spark of magic.

While she didn't have any proof of a stalker, there was nothing extraordinary about her sense that someone was watching her. It was a feeling in her bones, the prickle at the nape of her neck when she was sure someone was watching, even when she was alone or when there was supposedly no one in sight. Just good old human intuition.

"Oh yeah?" she said as she glanced around too. They had been running for a while, so her voice came out breathy and short. "I kinda dig it. It's a proper London fog. Gives everything a spooky, otherworldly feeling."

"It also obscures line of sight," he said dryly.

She frowned. The last thing she ever did was cause problems for her security. They cost a fortune, and they knew how to do their jobs.

Vincent had been head of her detail for the last five tours, and he had caught both the other stalkers. The first one was still serving jail time. Vincent had scared the second one badly enough he had gone back to his home in Texas and, last they had checked, hadn't left again.

They approached the Albert Memorial, Queen

Victoria's loving tribute to her husband. The top of the tall spire looked spindly and somewhat insubstantial in the gray, wet morning. As Sid glanced up at it, she asked, "You want to head back to the hotel?"

"No," he said after a moment. "We're good for now. But if it gets any thicker, I think we should probably turn back."

"Sure thing." She bit back irritation to keep her reply sounding easy and reasonable.

It was all an act for their benefit. Her OCD tendencies kicked in when she was on tour. Really bad OCD. The strain of the schedule and constantly performing onstage did things to her head, and the result wasn't exactly pretty.

She *had* to get her three-mile jog in. She *needed* to eat the same thing for breakfast every day. Her shoes were always lined up the same way in every closet in every hotel, her clothing organized by color and type, and she had a separate piece of luggage for the pillow she brought from home. She couldn't go to sleep unless her violin was in the same room with her, and she needed to rehearse three times in every venue before she performed. Anything less than three times was unacceptable.

She made a face at the statue of Prince Albert as they passed him. It was no wonder she was single. She was just as weird as any weirdo she had ever attracted.

Abruptly, her perspective shifted as what Vincent had said sank in. Now, instead of enjoying the cool, thick fog that wreathed the park, she saw how it obscured the nearby bushes and how the path they were currently on seemed to disappear up ahead into a formless, filmy white.

She slowed to a stop, and Vincent and Tony slowed along with her. The two men didn't chitchat when they were out, which was one of the things she appreciated about them. While they were friendly enough, and she liked and respected them, they weren't friends.

They were doing a job they took very seriously, and they did it well. Usually their professional demeanor allowed her to disappear into her own head. Now she glanced from the men's casual, alert stances to their foggy surroundings and frowned again.

After a moment, Vincent angled his body half toward her while he continued to survey the surrounding area. He asked in an easy tone, "Anything wrong?"

She scrubbed at her face with both hands. This blasted tour was getting to her. Why had she listened to her manager, Rikki, and booked so many concerts? It would be months before she got home to New York.

She loved living in New York. It was one of the most diverse places in the world, and she felt she could relax and disappear into anonymity in the sprawling city.

When she was on tour, she lost that relaxation and sense of belonging. She wasn't good with people. Growing up *hapa*—a slang term for someone who was part Asian, part Caucasian—had often left her feeling like she didn't fully belong in either culture.

Added to that, she had spent most of her childhood practicing and studying music, not playing with other kids, and neither her perfectionist mother nor her academic father had considered social interactions relevant or necessary.

As a result, she had developed a reserved personality. It was hard for her to break free from that early conditioning, and often she needed to strategize on how to relate to people.

Constantly having to think things through like that was exhausting. She could never just relax and play cards with the rest of the band and the ground crew. When she was on tour, the only time she really enjoyed was when she immersed herself in her music.

And she willingly went through all of it—the strange beds, the isolation, the unending pressure—so that she could pick up her violin and play.

How was she supposed to respond to Vincent's question? *You know nothing,* her mother would have said. *So don't complain. Say nothing.*

Before she could overthink her impulse, she forced herself to confess, "I think I've got another stalker."

His gaze snapped to her face. "Why?" he asked. "You get any mail? See anything?"

"No. And no, or Julie would have told us." Julie, Sid's publicist back in New York and her best friend, handled all her email and mail.

"Then what happened?"

Giving up on the morning jog, she sighed, turned, and started walking back to the hotel. Smoothly, the men changed direction and kept pace with her. "You're going to call me neurotic or crazy, but nothing has happened. I just feel it in my gut. I can sense eyes watching me, when nobody should be watching. I'm not talking about the concerts—everybody's watching me at the concerts." She groaned. Maybe she should have listened to her mother's voice in her head. "I sound crazy even to myself. Forget it."

"No way," Tony said, taking a step closer as he flanked her side. "We take instinct seriously."

"How long have you felt this way?" Vincent asked.

She glanced from one man to the other. It rattled her that she had voiced her concern and they were treating it like a real threat.

She had to think back. Had she sensed anything while they were in Glasgow? She couldn't remember. Hesitantly, she replied, "Since we got to London, I think."

"Okay." Vincent paused, thinking. "Tonight's your last performance in the UK. Instead of leaving for Paris in the morning, why don't we leave after the concert? We can slip away from the arena when you're done and let the rest of the band drive to Paris tomorrow as planned. Maybe this one is geographically focused, and we'll shake him off when we get to France."

She frowned. She tried not to travel separately from her band. It was hard enough for her to build a rapport, and traveling separately could create distance between them and cause unnecessary tension, but she couldn't see how it would hurt this once.

"Sure," she said. "Let's do it."

"I'll see if I can get us flights. Better yet, maybe I can charter a plane. Tony will slip your bags out of the hotel this afternoon." Vincent smiled at her. "It's going to be okay."

Sidonie smiled back, feeling a brief twinge at the wedding ring he wore. If Vince hadn't been married, she would have been interested in him, but his wife, Terri, ran the security agency and was the nicest, most genuine person, just as he was. They were the real deal too, happily married and utterly devoted to each other.

"Thanks, Vince," she said.

"You bet." He gave her an easy smile. "I'm glad you said something."

She hesitated. "You haven't noticed anything, have you?"

"No, but as Tony said, we take instinct seriously, and you're not emotionally needy. You're not trying to draw attention to yourself. We've worked together for quite a while, and this is the first time you've ever said anything like this to me."

"Okay, good." Having gotten that off her chest, she picked up the pace again, and they finished the rest of the route back to the hotel at an easy jog. She might not get a full three-mile run that morning, but at least she did feel better.

Successful concert tours took hard work, determination, and stamina, and they were only a third of the way through this one. That was just long enough for her to start questioning her life choices.

Still, after finishing in the UK, the rhythm would break for a short time. They had a few days' rest planned in Paris, then the requisite three rehearsals in the new venue before starting the next round of performances. She couldn't wait to get the next leg in the journey behind her and arrive in Paris so she could relish those few days off.

After Tony and Vincent left her at the door of her suite, she had lunch delivered, ate, and packed. Then she called Julie while she lay facedown on the bed. When Julie picked up, Sid asked, "What are you doing?"

"I just ate a big breakfast of bacon and waffles with whipped cream and strawberries," Julie told her. "I've got this huge pile of work I need to do, but I can't move. I needed someone to wheelbarrow me into the office."

"I want bacon and waffles with whipped cream and strawberries." Sid sighed. "Or a giant bowl of pho."

"So order takeout," Julie told her unsympathetically. "You've got two huge strapping guys at your beck and call. Make one of them run out and get you some pho."

"I can't," she groaned. "I'm performing tonight. If I get too full, I won't have any energy onstage."

She could hear a smile in Julie's voice. "I bet you ate your oatmeal like a good girl this morning, didn't you?"

"Of course I did. I'm telling you, I have to eat exactly the same thing every morning," Sid told her. "It drives me crazy."

"One of these days I'm going to come join you," Julie warned. "I'll drag you out to breakfast, and make you eat something shocking, like scrambled eggs."

"Yes!" Sid exclaimed. "Break me out of this nonsense… as long as I can eat oatmeal."

"You're hopeless! Listen, I've got to go. I need to, I don't know, make calls and answer emails or sleep off this breakfast coma."

"Okay." Sid flopped over to stare at the ceiling. "You could always fly out to Paris for a day or two. We've got that short break coming up."

Julie's voice warmed. "That's a great idea! I'll check flights. It would be so much fun to hassle you into trying a different breakfast in person. Listen, I know you don't like to read reviews, so I want to tell you— you're doing good, kiddo. Really, really good. I'm reading all of them, and there's nothing but rave reviews. They're loving this new album."

Pleasure felt light and warm, like sunshine on her skin. She smiled. "Thanks."

Shortly after she hung up, Vince texted to let her know he had chartered a plane that would be waiting for them after the concert. They would travel by car to a small, business-oriented airport called London Biggin Hill.

She chewed her lip as she read the text. The only airports she knew in the greater London area were Gatwick and Heathrow, but she was well acquainted with using smaller airports that ran private charters. The arrangement wasn't unusual, just more expensive, but Vincent wouldn't have booked it if there had been any commercial flights available.

She sent a reply approving the plan, and then she took a few minutes to text her band to tell them she would be going ahead to take care of a few business matters, and she would see them in Paris. The texts they sent back were easygoing and untroubled, and she smiled as she read them. The group she had gathered for this tour was a solid one.

Afterward, she forced herself to lie down and take a nap. Since they had decided to leave directly after the concert, it was going to be a long night.

That evening at the concert, the preperformance buzz ran through her veins while the warm-up band played, and she had to work at restraining herself until it was time to step onto the stage. While she waited for them to finish their last number, she looked over the crowd from the wings.

With the hot, bright stage lights, she couldn't see any individual faces, but still a sense of conviction ran over her skin like ice water. Her stalker was in the audience. She could feel it. Feel him.

Hardly breathing, she poked at the certainty. He was there, unmoved by the music, and his sense of purpose was almost palpable. The comfort she had gleaned from talking to Vincent earlier evaporated, and gooseflesh raised on her bare arms. She shivered.

The noise from the crowd shifted and rose in volume, but she hardly noticed. Only when her drummer, Dustin, tapped her on the shoulder did she jump and come back to herself.

He leaned forward, eyes sharp, and said in her ear, "Showtime, Sid. You okay?"

"Yeah, I'm good," she told him. With an effort, she shook off the pall that had fallen over her, gave him a grin, and strode onto the stage. A waft of air brushed her cheek, and she looked up to catch sight of a transparent sketch of a face that smiled down at her as it drifted by.

The Djinn had come again. This one had materialized just enough so she could see it. They had bargained with her to attend her concerts, and she now owned a wealth of Djinn favors.

Smiling, she nodded at the strange creature, and the pale outline of its face faded. Then she raised her violin and bow, and the music rushed in like a tidal wave and swept her away.

It always took her away. It transported her to a place of such piercing purity, such raw transcendence, that it filled up her veins and flowed out of her like liquid fire.

She never questioned her life choices, not when she was flowing with the music. Never questioned the years of sacrifice, the harsh regimen, study, and diligent practice. She never felt lonely or worried or afraid because the music was everything, her lover, friend, and family, and her most demanding, invisible companion.

She fed it, and it fed her, the energy running back and forth, building into a towering edifice of sound, her unique citadel of radiant vibration.

Nobody else could reach that radiant citadel. Nobody could touch it. They could only glimpse it when she played, only hear it because she allowed them to.

After a timeless period, suddenly the concert hurtled to an end. The high, transcendent peak of energy had been achieved, the last strings played, the final notes piercing the silence.

Sweat pouring down her neck, she glanced sidelong at either end of the stage. As if on cue, the Djinn materialized enough so she could see them. They smiled and bowed to her, while the audience gave her a standing ovation.

Afterward, it took some time to extricate herself. Flowers were delivered, the manager of the arena wanted to thank her, and three of the band members had things they needed to discuss before she left. She attended to all of it while the remnants of the fire still ran in her veins. It was only when Vincent and Tony urged her away that tiredness began to sink in.

The car was waiting at the back entrance. Tony

rode in the front, while she rode in the back with Vincent. The driver took them out of the arena and down unfamiliar streets.

Letting the men's quiet, easygoing conversation wash over her, she leaned her forehead against the window and blinked tiredly as she watched the scenery go by—neighborhoods and clusters of shops interspersed with areas of dense greenery.

Even though it was high summer in England, the fog on that cool, damp day had never truly lifted. Now it seemed alive as ghostly tendrils flowed over the road. The time had slipped to well past midnight, and traffic on their route was almost nonexistent.

Sleepiness tried to take over, but she fought it. She would only have to wake up again in twenty minutes or so once they got to the airport, and then any chance she had of sleeping would be ruined for the rest of the night.

Despite her best efforts, she must have dozed. Sudden cursing tore away the peacefulness that had shrouded her. She jerked upright.

An immense black horse filled the windshield in front of the car. As it reared, fire danced in its mane and sparks shot from gigantic hooves.

The driver yanked the wheel sideways, brutally hard. Vincent shot out an arm to brace her as they were both flung sideways. Tires screeched. The car hit a curb and rolled down an incline. Pain flared as the seat belt bit into her shoulder and breasts. She tried to find something to hang on to and grabbed the door handle.

Not only was the driver cursing, so were Tony and Vincent. Her ears were filled with their rough voices, with the sound of a scream.

The horse? Had they hit it?

Metal. It was the metal from the car, screaming as if it were alive.

The world upended, then upended again, whirling outside the windows in an insane kaleidoscope. Then the ground slammed into the car with a gigantic crunch. Pain flared again as she struck her head on something, and everything went black.

DIM AWARENESS RETURNED as fresh, damp air blew across her skin. Traveling across the bumpy ground caused everything in her body to throb with pain. Someone was dragging her from the car.

From the wreck.

Someone…

Blinking at the wetness that streamed in her eyes, she tried to squint up at the person who gripped both her wrists.

Whoever he was, he wasn't human. He was perhaps her height or a little taller, and thin, with a narrow chest, spiky, nut-brown hair, and a thin, triangular face.

It was a feral face, and he had wild, feral eyes that burned with determination.

She coughed wetly and tried to speak. "Vince—Vincent. Tony. The d-driver."

"Unconscious, but they'll live," the creature said. "So will you."

"The horse?"

"Untouched."

She coughed again, spat blood, and whispered, "Thank you for helping."

"That's not what I'm doing." He touched her forehead with a forefinger. She focused on his hand. He had too many fingers. "Sleep now."

Unconsciousness spread through her mind like black ink flowing over a canvas.

PAIN BROUGHT HER awake, the pain of bruises being rhythmically jostled, while blood pounded in her head. She was riding on the back of an immense black horse. Rather, she was lying on the back of a horse as it galloped along the countryside.

She tried to make a noise, tried to move. Rough abrasion bit into the skin at her wrists. She stared down in disbelief. Her hands had been tied to a rope that looped around the horse's neck.

That couldn't be right. She had just been in a car accident. She couldn't be riding on the back of a horse. It had to be a hallucination, or maybe she was dreaming.

Consciousness slid away.

WHEN SHE WOKE again, her head still dangled at an odd angle, and her neck hurt. Everything hurt. Around her lay a quiet, cool forest wreathed in night.

Someone carried her in thin, strong arms. She tried to move, but her hands and ankles were bound. A new, sharp spike of pain dug into her head, over her right eye that was gummed shut. Despite the persistent dizziness and disorientation, panicked conviction settled like ice in her bones.

She was being kidnapped.

Angling her jaw, she moved her mouth experimentally. She wasn't gagged. If she was anywhere near London, there had to be houses… some kind of neighborhood nearby. Drawing in a deep breath, she tried to scream.

The sound came out in a breathy, thin mutter. "Help me."

The person carrying her looked down at her. She caught a shadowed glimpse of a wild, inhuman gaze as he remarked, "You just won't stay asleep, will you?"

"You can't get away with this," she croaked. "Let me go."

The creature lifted his head and looked straight ahead. He said grimly, "I'll get away with it."

This time when the world grayed around her, she didn't go fully under. Cotton wool filled her head, which ached abominably.

I must have a concussion, she thought dimly as she struggled to come more alert. There was a reason why she couldn't black out, some kind of danger. She had to remember.

As if from a great distance, she sensed when they came to a stop. Full awareness returned as the creature set her down on a hard, rough surface. Cold dampness seeped into her jeans, and she could smell rich, loamy dirt. He had laid her on the ground.

When he left her for a time, she struggled wildly against her bonds, but she was too securely tied. When he returned, he lifted her head and shoulders to wipe her face with a wet cloth that smelled dank, as if it had been dipped in a river.

As he cleaned away the gummed blood around her eyes, her vision became clear. She looked around. They were in a clearing, and over the tops of nearby trees, the darkness of the night sky had begun to lighten.

Panic skittered like mice running over Sidonie's skin. It had been a long time since the accident. Hours. How far had they traveled by horse? Where were they?

Was she even in London anymore?

Suddenly the pain in her head lessened, and she could think again. A tingling spread through her body and other aches eased. While she might not have magic sense, she'd had magically based medical treatments before. The creature had thrown some kind of spell to heal her.

That had to be a good sign, didn't it? He couldn't mean to slaughter her here in the woods if he cared enough to heal her.

Looking up at his strange, shadowed face, she said, "You were the one. You were stalking me."

"No," he said. He set aside the cloth and gathered her into his arms. "I was stalking someone else. I found him in Glasgow and started to follow him. When he came to London, I followed him there too. He kept going to your concerts, and it was unusual. Unlike him. For some reason, you… matter to him. So I took you."

She tried to follow what he was saying, but while he spoke English clearly enough, he sounded insane. "But why?"

His face twisted, and tears began to spill down his cheeks. He rocked her and sobbed. "Because you're perfect. You're so perfect I couldn't have found a better weapon if I had tried."

"I'm no weapon," she whispered, staring. "I'm just a musician."

"I'll give you to her, and she will be *horrible* to you. And that will matter to him. With you, I'll drive a wedge between them so deep it will tear them apart. And they need to be torn apart. You have no idea the damage they've caused or how many people they have killed over the years. You have no idea the kind of damage *she* did to me. If she isn't stopped, she'll target a friend of mine, and I will not let anything happen to my Sophie."

Killed?

Sidonie was tired and cold, damp, and so scared that tears began to leak out of the corners of her eyes as well. This creature wasn't human. He wouldn't think in human terms. Maybe he really was crazy. Did he even recognize he had committed a crime?

Even though it was futile, she twisted her hands, trying to find purchase against the cords that bound her wrists as she forced herself to say in a soft, cajoling tone, "Can you please listen to me? Just listen. Whatever you're planning, I can see it matters deeply to you, but you don't have to go through with it. You have time to rethink everything, and—and I'll help you. I promise. But you have to let me go first. I can only help you if you let me go."

The creature's gaze focused on her. There was so much emotion in his strange eyes, so much grief and rage, it held her transfixed. "I don't expect you to forgive me."

Renewed panic jolted through her. "There's no need to talk like that. You haven't gone too far yet or done anything that isn't fixable. We can—I can—I have money. Resources. Whoever your enemy is, we can go after her together."

What the hell was she saying? She had never "gone after" anybody before in her life. Her worst enemies had been rivals at school, and her biggest battles had been won through music competitions and grades.

But she could tell by his stony, unmoved expression that nothing she said was getting through to him.

What else could she promise? The need for revenge was driving him. She ran through all the famous revenge scenarios she could think of, but they were all based on fictional characters. Dropping that idea, she focused on another one.

His friend mattered to him.

"You're worried about your Sophie," she said rapidly. "We can get protection for your friend. I have contacts with a good security company."

His gaze met hers. "Did they protect you from me?"

Her breath caught. Before she could come up with another argument, he wiped his face with the back of one hand and drew out a knife. As her panic escalated, he used the knife to cut a strip of cloth off the bottom of her shirt and forced it between her teeth as a gag. The tears still streamed down his face, but his expression had turned stony with resolve.

"Listen to me," he said harshly. His strange gaze was lit with a feverish light. "Take my advice for what it's worth. Don't tell her about me, or why I took you. If she considers you a threat, she will have you killed— or if she thinks you have any information that might be useful to her, she will do much worse than have you killed. And if you're smarter than me, if you have it in you to bow to her will and pander to her every whim, it will go easier for you. Because even though I regret the need to do this, you are only one person and your sacrifice will mean so much to so many. I'm afraid *you're going to have a tough time now.*"

Chapter Three

S ID HAD FALLEN into a nightmare so strange she had no idea how to dig herself out of it. As she stared, the creature eased her away, stood, and his body shimmered and disappeared, to be replaced by a gigantic, thick creature with tiny eyes and skin the color of gray rock.

He had shapeshifted into a… a… troll?

As a human deadhead, she knew almost nothing about magic other than what she read in magazine articles or saw in the news. But from what she had gleaned from idle conversations with others, she was fairly certain of one thing.

It took tremendous Power to shapeshift into a shape that was either bigger or smaller than the original person. The two-natured Wyr accomplished the shift the most easily, as their animal forms were literally second nature to them.

But whatever this creature was, he wasn't Wyr, and this troll was so much bigger than the creature that had carried her through the forest it meant he had Power, a lot of it.

Realization flared. He had probably been the black horse that had caused the accident and carried her to this unknown place. The kind of deliberation that had gone into her kidnapping was chilling.

She shrank back as the huge troll bent over her, but tied as thoroughly as she was, there was nothing she could do to stop him from picking her up again.

He trudged ahead, following a narrow footpath that wound through the woods, until Sidonie could smell a hint of woodsmoke on the breeze that blew gently through the trees. Soon he stepped into a large clearing that held several buildings—a long, larger building and a few typically English-looking cottages.

Her view was obstructed, and it was making her crazy that there was literally nothing she could do about it, but she could hear a sudden flurry of movement, a sharp exclamation, and as she craned her neck, she saw they had been surrounded by several tall people.

The newcomers weren't human any more than the creature that had kidnapped her. They were dressed in dun and green uniforms, colors that would disappear easily in a forest, and they had weapons. Some of them carried both guns and swords.

Sid took in the hard, wary expressions on their angular faces along with the signature golden blond hair they all shared, but it was only when one of them turned to shout an order to the others and she caught a peek of one pointed ear that she could place their race.

They were Light Fae.

"What are you doing here?" the Light Fae male asked sharply.

The fake troll came to halt. Without warning, he dropped Sidonie. Unable to do anything to break her fall, she groaned as she made bruising impact with the ground.

The troll said in a deep voice that sounded like grinding rocks, "Tribute for the Queen."

Forcing herself to breathe evenly, Sidonie latched on to the word.

Queen. The Queen must be the female the creature had referred to. She would be Light Fae, like her soldiers. One of the Elder Races.

The Elder Races were magical creatures that lived alongside humans, with demesnes that often overlaid human boundaries. Then there were Other lands that were connected to Earth by a series of crossover passageways. Most modern technologies didn't work in Other lands, which were intensely magical places, but she had read interesting articles on the inventive ways people had adapted many modern conveniences.

As a nonmagical human, Sidonie knew only the basics of Elder Races politics and terminology, mostly concepts she had gleaned in school. She had once been invited to play a concert for Niniane Lorelle, the Dark Fae Queen in the Other land of Adriyel that had passageways connecting to Chicago.

While that Queen had been willing to pay an

exorbitant amount to make up for the time slippage between Adriyel and Earth, Sidonie hadn't been able to work the trip into her upcoming schedule for the year, so she had reluctantly declined. The charming and persuasive Dark Fae ambassador had wrangled a promise out of her to consider the trip in the future, but they hadn't yet agreed upon a date.

In Great Britain, there had to be any number of Elder Races, demesnes, and their individual rulers, but Sidonie only knew of one Light Fae Queen—Queen Isabeau of the Light Court.

While the thoughts raced through her mind, she waited for the Light Fae leader to denounce offering a *human being* as tribute for anything.

Instead, the male said impatiently, "What's this? The troll clan has already offered its tribute. We received the shipment this morning."

Wait, *what*? No denouncement? This was utter insanity. Nobody offered a thinking, living being as tribute, at least not in modern society as she knew it. Outraged fury pounded under her skin, and she chewed on her gag as furious words piled into rocket launchers in her head, readying for ignition.

The troll rumbled, "We was gonna add this 'un in, but we got her late. Plays music real good."

"And now, thanks to your bumbling, she's seen this encampment. But she's a musician, you say?" The Light Fae male looked down at her and heaved a sigh. "Oh, very well. Next time keep your tributes to items that are easier to transport." As he turned away, he ordered one of his men, "Put her in a holding cell until we're ready to leave."

One of the men hauled her to her feet. The fake troll gave Sidonie one last inscrutable look then turned away. She watched his massive figure amble back into the forest the way he had come.

As the troll disappeared, Sidonie thought, I won't forget what you did to me. She turned to study the Light Fae leader's features. I won't forget any of you.

I don't know how, and I don't know when, but you will regret doing this to me.

I will make sure of it.

AFTER THE TROLL disappeared, the soldier slung her over one hard shoulder and carried her along a path to another clearing with more buildings. Then he put her in a primitive prison cell, with honest-to-goodness bars, a rough cot, bare stone floors, and a dirty, horribly basic latrine that offered no privacy whatsoever. She had a small, high, barred window that let in sunlight but gave no real view outside and nothing else.

At least the Light Fae soldier untied her wrists and legs so she could move around. As soon as her hands were free, she had to fight the urge to hit him. The violent impulse might bring short-term relief to the rage and fear beating through her veins, but in the end, it wasn't a strategy that could go well for her.

Instead of giving in to her feelings, she stood rubbing the circulation back into her wrists while she watched him lock the cell door.

I'll remember you too, she thought.

After he left her alone, she looked around. The cot was made of some kind of crosshatched leather strung tight on a frame. No pillow, no blanket.

There was no running water, and apparently no electricity or heat either, she saw as she glanced at the ceilings that were bare of any light fixtures. This place was strange and disturbing, almost as if it had nothing to do with the modern England she had been visiting only just yesterday.

Her hands prickled painfully as circulation increased. Giving up on her wrists, she rubbed her arms in an attempt to generate some warmth. Even though the day had turned sunny, the thick cover of trees kept the temperature mild, and the walls of the building were constructed of thick stone that emanated a damp chill.

She was glad she was still wearing the soft cashmere hoodie, jeans, and sneakers she had slipped into for the drive to the airport. Thanks to her kidnapper, the T-shirt under the dirt-streaked hoodie was ragged, and her jeans were smeared with grass stains and blood, but if she were still wearing the thin spandex outfit she had worn for the concert, she would be freezing her ass off.

Her kidnapper had said Vincent, Tony, and the

driver would live, and she didn't think he had lied to her. He had said scary, crazy stuff, but as far as she knew, no falsehoods.

"Buck up, Sid," she whispered. "Vince and Tony will be looking for you."

At least they would be looking as soon as they were able to. How badly had they been hurt in the crash? How long would it take for the news of her disappearance to hit the tabloids?

Some time ago she, Vince, and his wife, Terri, had talked through strategies for a variety of extreme scenarios.

In the event of her disappearance (how they had chuckled at the unlikelihood of that), the security company was authorized to offer a reward for any credible information on her whereabouts.

They were also authorized to conduct transactions, in case she had been kidnapped and was being held for ransom. After the first two stalkers, she had taken Vincent's advice and now carried an insurance policy that would cover any ransom up to five million dollars.

So they had mechanisms in place to handle almost any situation, but none of it brought her any comfort, because what had actually happened was completely outside any scenario they had discussed.

They had no protocol in place for how to deal with crazy magical creatures bent on enacting an elaborate scheme of manipulation and revenge. No protocol to handle something like this.

Human trafficking was a crime that mostly involved victims who were too poor and vulnerable to protect themselves against it. Life had skidded so far off the path of anything that seemed remotely feasible she felt utterly adrift and more alone than she had in years.

Someday I'm going to look back at this, she told herself. And while I'm never going to laugh at what happened, I'm going to be grateful I made it through alive. Someday this experience is going to be in the past, and I will know what it feels like to seek revenge myself.

As foreign as the concepts were to her, nursing her anger was far better than sinking into depression or giving up. They gave her something to focus on, somewhere to direct her rage.

Desperate to take some kind of action, she started counting the strips of leather in the crosshatched cot. There were twelve strips in length and thirty-six strips across. Anxiety knotted her stomach. Had she counted right? She started over. Twelve and thirty-six.

Then again. Twelve and thirty-six.

Maybe she needed to touch them to be sure. Compelled forward, she moved her fingers along the crosshatching, whispering to herself as she counted. After going over the leather strips fifteen times, she pressed both clenched fists to her forehead and forced herself to step away from the cot.

If she thought going on tour was stressful, it was nothing compared to this. To try to distract herself from getting trapped in more OCD behavior, she studied the details of her surroundings more closely. Goose bumps rose along her arms.

Everything looked... historic. Was that the right word?

Walking over to the bars of her cell, she ran a finger experimentally down one. The slightly rough surface disturbed her more than anything. They were strong, well made, and sturdy, but they had not been generated by modern machinery.

There were fourteen bars.

Fourteen.

Fourteen. *Agh!*

She tore herself away from them, stepping back to turn in a circle. The lock on the cell door, the cot itself, the window—none of it looked sleek or mass-produced, or as if it had come from the industrial age.

She felt as if she had almost traveled back in time, or... or as if she wasn't quite on the same Earth she knew anymore.

As if she wasn't on Earth at all, anymore.

Her throat closed as panic threatened to set in.

What would it be like to travel through a crossover passageway? She had always wondered, but she didn't know. She had read stories of how deadhead humans experienced crossovers, but she'd not yet visited an Other land herself. She had thought her hypothetical trip to Adriyel might be the first time.

Since she had no magic, she couldn't make a

crossover passage on her own. A deadhead had to be touching someone with magical ability in order to make a crossing, and she had always known she would have to rely on someone else with magic to walk her through the passage. The most common way was to hold hands.

The stories told of a strange, surreal experience as travelers watched everything around them change while they traversed a passageway. But would she have had that experience if she'd simply walked from the middle of one forest clearing to another?

The soldier had thrown her fireman-style over his shoulder, and her head had dangled upside down. It hadn't exactly been a priority for her to study her surroundings closely as he'd carried her down the path. She had been too busy staring at his ass and wishing she either had the courage or the lack of sense to bite him.

If he'd carried her along a passageway to an Other land, they didn't need to put her in a cell, because she didn't have the ability to get back to Earth on her own. She couldn't contact any of the Djinn who owed her favors—without telepathy, she could only reach her Djinn contacts by phone, and even if she still had her cell, phones didn't work in Other lands.

Suddenly she could no longer fight back the rising panic. Rushing to the cell door, she shouted, "Hey! *Hey!* Do you realize how many crimes you're committing by putting me in this cell against my will? You can't keep me here—I'm a Canadian citizen!"

No one came. As she paused, a deafening silence pressed against her eardrums. As far as she could tell, she was the only one in this horrid little building. They didn't care enough to respond, and that frightened and enraged her more than anything.

Hours passed. Finally her own body's needs forced her into using the latrine. She did so quickly, in case someone came, and afterward she flung herself onto the cot. From there, she counted and recounted the bars in her cell door and watched the light from the high window shift and eventually dim.

Her violin had been in the trunk of the car. Was it all right?

That violin was her most treasured possession. Crafted by the famous French luthier Jean-Baptiste Vuillaume, it was nearly a hundred years old, and acquiring it with her own hard-earned money had been one of the biggest triumphs of her life.

She wanted to ask one of the more Powerful Djinn who owed her a favor for a much rarer Stradivarius, but she hadn't yet worked up the nerve, and in any case, that wouldn't feel the same as it had felt to buy the Vuillaume for herself.

She chewed her lip bloody as she fretted about her violin, but there was nothing she could do and no way to get any answers.

Eventually hunger set in, along with boredom, cold, and exhaustion. She curled herself into a small fierce ball as she worried at her dilemma like a dog gnawing at a bone.

While her kidnapper had made Isabeau out to be dangerous, even cruel, how much could Sid trust of what he had told her?

He hadn't been impressed when she'd mentioned she had money, but maybe the Queen would feel differently. Almost everyone liked money, and they liked accruing more of it. The possibility of collecting five million dollars in ransom should mean something, damn it. The insurance certainly cost enough.

And who had her kidnapper been stalking? She knew nothing about Isabeau and the Light Court, other than the fact that a Dark Court existed as counterpart to it. Her kidnapper hadn't mentioned a name—just referred to *he* and *him*.

Whoever *he* was, he liked Sid's concerts. She might find an ally in him.

She had to face some cold hard facts. If she really had been transported into an Other land, she might find it hard to get justice for her kidnapping. The demesnes on Earth cared far more about interactions with human societies, but the demesnes from Other lands had a much greater degree of self-reliance.

If nothing else though, perhaps this male could help her cross back over to Earth and go home again. That was the most important thing.

As night came and her cell fell into darkness, the air chilled even further. Thirsty now, very hungry, and shivering from the cold, she thought she would never be able to sleep, but eventually she slid into an uneasy, miserable doze.

A sharp clang of metal against the bars jolted her awake. Heart pounding, she stared around her, disoriented.

"Awaken, human."

She focused on the Light Fae male on the other side of the bars. She hadn't seen him before. He carried a beaten metallic bowl and a cup that he shoved through a space at the bottom of the bars. She asked, "Can I talk to someone in charge?"

He threw her an indifferent glance. "You'll be talking to someone in charge soon enough. Eat. We leave for the castle shortly."

Castle? She would bet her next year's salary he wasn't talking about any castle on Britain's list of historic sites.

Swallowing in an attempt to ease her dry throat, she asked, "Are we in an Other land?"

He paused in the act of turning away, gave her a sharper look, then barked out a laugh. It sounded contemptuous. "You don't know? I will pass on the information that you have no Power."

Feeling stung, she ground her teeth. "That doesn't answer my question."

"Yes, human," he said impatiently. "You are now in Avalon, and you are subject to our laws, our Queen. The sooner you come to terms with that, the better things will go for you."

With that, he strode out, leaving her staring after him. The ground felt unsteady underneath her feet as the enormity of what he had said rang in her ears.

She really was no longer on Earth. Not only had she been transported to an Other land, she was in Avalon.

Avalon, the land of apples and faerie, fabled for its beauty and danger. She had remembered that Isabeau was a monarch of the Light Fae, but she had not even realized that Isabeau was Avalon's Queen. Her knowledge of the Elder Races demesnes in Great Britain was that sparse. Angry at her own ignorance, she clenched her fists.

And without any magic, she had no way of getting home, at least not without help. Much as she hated that guard for his scorn, he had a point. She was going to have to lose that ignorance and learn as much as she could, as fast as she could, if she had any chance of coping with her new reality.

She was still shaking as hunger compelled her to go inspect the contents of the metallic bowl. Inside there was a plain hunk of bread and a piece of hard cheese. The cup contained water. Carrying both to the cot, she ate every scrap, and she drank all the water too.

After eating, she had barely finished taking care of some private business when the same guard strode to her cell door. As he unlocked it, she said, almost conversationally, "I was kidnapped and brought here illegally, you know."

"Out," he said as he stood back and held her cell door wide. He didn't tie her up or threaten her with any other kind of confinement.

He didn't really have to, did he? Simmering with fury again, she strode out. "Do you have any reaction to what I just said?"

"Not my place to have a reaction. I just follow orders." He put a hand at her back and shoved her so hard she stumbled. "Move."

How much evil had been committed by people who claimed they were just following orders? Regaining her balance, she clenched her fists and barely managed to keep from lashing out. If she lashed out, she would get tied up again. She might even get beaten.

That was okay. If he followed orders, he wasn't who she wanted to talk to anyway.

She wanted to talk to someone who gave the orders. That would be the only way to change her situation.

He led her to the back of an empty wagon and made her climb into it. Sitting in one corner, she wrapped her arms around her knees as she watched an entire squadron of guards gather. Most of them had horses, and several drove wagons that were stacked high with barrels and boxes. Some of it, if not all, had to be the real trolls' tribute.

Her kidnapper had known enough about the Light Fae to know when the tribute would be delivered, and where, and he had used that knowledge to insert her into the situation without causing suspicion. The calculation behind that was chilling. He might have cried when he held her, but that hadn't stopped him from planning the details of her kidnapping with precision.

Despite her continued tiredness and worry, she grew fascinated by watching the Light Fae work at assembling a wagon train. She had never seen anything like it before.

If someone gave a signal to start, she missed it, because suddenly a wagon pulled out, then another. Eventually the wagon carrying her as its sole cargo lurched to a start and fell into line behind the others. The guards on horseback arranged themselves at either the head or the back of the train.

For most of the day they traveled through dense, overgrown forest. Quickly growing bored with the monotonous scenery and sore from the constant jostling, Sid counted all the wooden planks in the wagon bed several times over, then she tried to brace herself in the corner to doze.

They took a break at midday, and she got another hunk of cheese and bread, with another cup of water.

In the afternoon, they stopped at a few villages, where conversations occurred just beyond her hearing between the one Light Fae that she had identified as the wagon train leader and others that appeared to be villagers.

After the conversations, some soldiers led people

to her wagon. As they climbed in, she studied them as curiously as they stared at her. Most were young girls, but a few were boys. All were Light Fae, and they were also quite a bit younger than she. Were they tribute too?

She tried talking to them a couple of times, but while they glanced at each other and shuffled uneasily, her attempts at starting a conversation were met with silence. A few of the girls stared unabashedly at her, their expressions filled with such fascinated repugnance, she was taken aback.

As Sidonie glanced around, it dawned on her—she was virtually the only person present who had dark hair and eyes. Also, her skin was pale and creamy, quite unlike the hue of the tanned faces that surrounded her. She might even be the first person these youngsters had ever seen who looked the way she did. Perhaps she was the first human they'd ever seen.

Compressing her lips, she settled into her hard, uncomfortable corner of the wagon and kept to herself after that. The passing scenery might be pretty, but so far, her first impressions of Avalon sucked.

That night they camped by a wide, lazy-looking river, and despite her problems, it was wonderful to get a few minutes by herself at the water's edge to wash. Supper was the same fare as lunch and breakfast. She found a spot close to the warmth of a campfire for the night. Gathering up a handful of pebbles, she curled into a tight ball to keep warm as she counted them, while wild scenarios galloped through her head.

She could steal a horse (she had lived in New York for most of her life and had no idea how to ride a horse). And she could steal weapons (from seasoned fighters who had the weapons and knew how to use them). Then she could race back to the crossover passageway (which she couldn't sense or use on her own).

Then, somehow, she needed to capture and force one of the soldiers there to walk her across to Earth, slip past the troops stationed on the other side, and walk until she made contact with normal civilization.

She had self-defense skills and some knowledge of unarmed combat, but those were all skills she had learned in a training environment. She had never had occasion to use what she had learned in an actual fight.

The likelihood of getting out of the wagon train encampment alive was slim to none, let alone facing the towering list of unlikely events after that. No, her only real hope of getting home again was if she appealed to someone in command.

In the morning, when she tried to approach the commander of the wagon train, a soldier stepped in front of her and forced her to go back to the area where her other travel companions stayed.

Simmering with frustration, she complied. No matter what the time slippage was between Avalon and Earth, her concert tour was almost certainly ruined now. Julie had to be worried sick, and both she and

Rikki would have an administrative nightmare on their hands. Just the thought of it tied Sid's stomach in knots. She'd never had to cancel a tour before.

But despite the amount of time she was going to lose on this journey, it appeared she would have to wait until she reached the castle before she could talk to someone who had the power to release her.

After sorting through her pebbles, she discarded the ones she didn't like and slipped twenty-one small, smooth stones into her pocket. The second day of travel was hot and boring. Focusing on her pebbles, she counted and recounted them, and lined them up in rows on one palm, according to size.

Then according to shape. Then color.

Twenty-one. Twenty-one. Twenty-one.

Toward the end of the day, the wagon train climbed a long, winding incline in the deepening gold of evening light. Sid had made a few more attempts to talk to her young companions without any luck. Resting her head on drawn-up knees, she kept her mouth and nose covered to avoid breathing in the dust kicked up by the horses and wagons ahead of them.

Even as she thought for the dozenth time that surely they had to be stopping soon, a shout sounded ahead, and the wagon lumbered to a halt. Excitedly, the others in the wagon jumped to their feet. As they craned their necks, stood on tiptoe, and exclaimed, Sid stood too, more slowly. Shading her eyes, she looked in the direction everyone else was staring.

The ground fell away from the road in a massive rolling sweep. In the distance, across a rich emerald green land, a huge castle sprawled like a great tawny dragon. Wealth, age, and power were stamped into the stones.

A city crouched supplicant at its feet, and beyond both stretched a sparkling blue body of water.

Unwillingly impressed and intimidated at once, Sid wrapped her arms around her middle. It looked like they were nearing the end of their journey, and she should be talking to someone in power soon enough.

Chapter Four

THE LONG SILVER knife slid home in Morgan's side, slicing through the still healing flesh of the original wound. A spear of pain lanced him. Sucking in a harsh breath, he hunched over as he slammed the other man's hand aside to grab the hilt and yank the blade out. It came free with a gush of fresh, red blood.

The pain made it difficult for him to control his lycanthrope instincts, and the silver from the weapon had not yet hit his system enough to dampen his abilities. He felt his teeth elongate and his face change.

He snarled, "Back off!"

The ghoul who had stabbed him leaped back as if scalded, and his gray face twisted. In an injured Cockney accent, he accused, "'Ey now, that ain't very friendly-like, and after I done you a favor too."

"You didn't do me any favors," Morgan snapped. "I paid you quite handsomely to stick a knife in me."

He could feel the silver's poison beginning to burn through his veins, and his features eased back to normal. He'd kept his Beretta close, in case the ghoul decided to betray him, but the creature looked spooked and ready to bolt out of the alley.

"You is one crazy motherfucker," the ghoul declared. "You didn't say nuthin 'bout bein' no lycanthrope! What if you 'ad taken off me hand for sticking you like we 'ad agreed?"

"I didn't, did I?" He pressed hard to staunch the bleeding. Elation threaded through the pain. The geas hadn't kicked in to force him to protect himself. He had just gained weeks more of freedom. "Let me know if you want to make the same amount next month too."

Greed warred with caution on the ghoul's long, mournful features, and for a moment he looked remarkably like Giles had when Morgan had last seen the doctor.

"I dunno," the ghoul muttered. "What if next time you doesn't manage to control that beast of yourn?"

"Up to you," Morgan said, losing interest in the creature. Having bought himself more time, he could always find someone else to hire for the deed.

"'Ey now, I didn't say I wouldn't." Calculation glittered in the ghoul's eyes. "But I'm thinkin' there may be a price hike for me services. I could use a little danger money as a bit o' insurance."

Morgan coughed out an unamused laugh and didn't bother to reply. He had already paid the ghoul more than enough. Limping out of the alley, he took a careful look around. It was the early hours of the morning, and the London street was deserted.

Walking carefully to his parked Audi, he eased behind the wheel and drove to the rooms he had rented. The small furnished flat was quiet and private, tucked at the end of a mews in a comfortable neighborhood.

When he had initially walked the streets of the neighborhood, he had found no hint of any major Power nearby, and the scents he picked up were mostly human. The location was perfect for his purposes, unremarkable in every way.

As his magical abilities had gradually returned, he had cast subtle cloaking spells around the area that would repel all but the most intelligent and determined eyes from noticing the red front door that led to the flat.

Then he began to gather any texts that were reputed to make mention of Azrael's Athame, even if only in passing. Late one night, he drove to Oxford to slip into the Bodleian Library. One of the oldest libraries in Europe, the Bodleian had an extensive wing devoted to the history, politics, folklore, religions, and magic systems of the Elder Races.

The library was guarded by gargoyles and shrouded in magical protections, but none of the protections were a match for Morgan's skills. He took everything related to Azrael, Lord Death, along with the books that focused on the most ancient magic items.

Between long hours of research, he built an arsenal for himself—casting spells of blindness, creating shields strong enough to hold against a dragon's fire, death curses, flesh corrosion, deadly fireballs called morningstars, charms of confusion, and incantations of havoc that could make armies lose control and fight each other.

He had set them all into magic-quality jewels so when the new injury dampened his magic ability, he would still have ways to defend himself. When he was finished, he had a wealth of weapons at hand, and they all fit into a velvet pouch spelled to conceal the deadly Power it contained.

He had created healing potions too, pouring the precious liquid into small stoppered vials. The healing potions wouldn't work on wounds made of silver, but in his experience, it was always handy to have a healing potion on hand. One never knew when one would need it.

He had also stocked the kitchen with high-protein foods and alcohol, and plenty of medicinal supplies— more antibiotics, bandages, a variety of pain medications, IV supplies, and a metal stand, a double-sided makeup mirror with magnification, and a suturing kit. This time he'd had the luxury to plan ahead to deal properly with this latest injury.

When he arrived back at the flat, he limped to the kitchen, where he had laid out on the table everything he would need after meeting with the ghoul. Easing into a chair, he opened the nearby bottle of scotch, took a stiff drink, then set to work.

The first step was to give himself a shot to numb

the area of the wound. After that, things got easier.

With access to the right supplies, and having the ability to treat the wound immediately instead of suffering from blood loss, he could stitch himself up. He had done it before.

He detached from the chore, watching himself clinically as he tilted the makeup mirror so the magnified side reflected the point of entry where the knife had slid in.

Carefully he sutured himself, and when he was finished, he bandaged the wound. Even though he hated narcotics, he shook out a couple of the strongest pain pills from a bottle and swallowed them with another long pull from the scotch bottle.

Then he slid an IV needle into the vein at his wrist, attached a bag of saline solution, and carried it into the bedroom, where he hung it off the metal stand he'd placed by the bed. Carefully he eased onto the mattress.

As he rested his head back onto the pillow, he smiled in grim triumph.

He had just gained weeks more of freedom. Weeks more of not having to look into Isabeau's eyes or look upon Modred's handsome, hated face. Weeks more to search for possible ways to either break the geas's hold or to find ways to act around it.

Not that long ago, he had longed for just such an opportunity, but he hadn't dared hope for it. Now it was his.

One by one, his muscles relaxed as the medication

kicked in.

In a few days, he could even go to Paris. There was an Elven tome on the seven Primal Powers in the Louvre that was reputed to explore in depth each of the Elder Races gods' many aspects. He needed to examine the book to see if it mentioned Azrael's Athame.

He could walk along the Avenue des Champs-Élysées and breakfast in a café along the Seine. He could attend another one of Sidonie Martel's concerts.

The memory of her impassioned music was like another knife to his middle, filling him with a sweet, piercing pain. With steady focus, he breathed through it.

Life was full of pain. He could handle it.

The narcotics and the scotch did their work. He didn't fall asleep so much as slide into unconsciousness where dreams and memories twisted together like the dark, bare limbs of trees in winter.

"How's this, Morgan? Is this right?" The boy's voice cracked, a harbinger of the man he would become.

"Not like that. Here, let me show you." He adjusted the boy's grip on the sword. "Like this. You're too kind. If you have to pull your sword, then grip it like you're prepared to use it. You don't want to slap your enemy with the flat of the blade. Not unless you want to make him laugh while he kills you."

The boy's grin was bright and abashed. When he

smiled, he lit everything around him. "That's what Kay and I do when we fight each other."

"Kay is your brother." Morgan smiled. "Of course you don't want to really hurt each other."

Then something had happened to interrupt their sparring lesson. Morgan could never remember what. Maybe someone had called the boy's name, and he had sprinted off to handle yet another issue that had arisen with the mantle of new kingship that had settled on his too-young shoulders.

Even as Morgan tried to hold on to the conversation, it faded into the distant past, to be replaced by another dream of an event that had happened much later.

The day had started so auspiciously. The jangle of horse harnesses and the stamp of hooves mingled with dogs' eager barking. The crisp, cold air bit the skin on his cheeks.

Morgan looked up just as the king rode by, laughing at something one of his men had said. Just like his smile, his laughter lit everything around him. Morgan smiled as he always did when he heard it.

He had not yet mounted his gelding and stood casually with the reins looped through his fingers. There was still time. The guests were assembling, and the hunt had not yet started.

"Good morning." The woman's voice came from behind him, and he turned to face a beautiful Light Fae noblewoman who smiled at him. Leading her own palfrey by the reins, she was dressed to ride in warm wool and furs. Jewels sparked at her wrists and graceful throat. "You must be Morgan. The king's merlin, they call you. The famous falcon at his wrist."

"Good morning, my lady." Morgan bowed. "You are correct. I am Morgan. Are you ready for the king's wild hunt?"

"Only Death may lead the true Wild Hunt," she replied as she arched one perfect brow. "And when Lord Azrael rides, no one is ready."

He inclined his head. "True. But in this human court, the king's wild hunt is in honor of Azrael and part of his Yuletide celebration. As such, it should be much more pleasurable for most people than Lord Death's Wild Hunt."

"I love to hunt. I am Isabeau." She extended one slender hand, and when he took it, he scanned her Power. She was a strong sorceress, but Morgan had a rare, fierce talent for magic, and she was no match for him.

If she had been wearing Azrael's Athame, its presence would have burned in his mind's eye, and he would never have dismissed her so casually. But she had been all too aware of that, and she had hidden the knife in anticipation of meeting him. Even then she had plotted her course with meticulous care.

Courteously, he bent to brush the air over her hand with his lips.

"Your majesty," Morgan murmured. He had taken

the Queen of the Light Court for one of her hand-maidens.

As he straightened, a handsome Light Fae male strolled over. As he joined them, Isabeau gestured toward him. "This is Modred, my escort for this morn. We are much taken with your human court."

"His majesty will be glad to hear it," Morgan told her, his voice easy and untroubled. He had been so comfortable then, back when he first gazed upon their doom. "He was pleased when he heard that representa-tives of the Light Court would be visiting, and extremely honored when you chose to grace us with your own presence."

Both Modred and Isabeau turned to regard the king. Something moved in Modred's gaze, assessment perhaps, or calculation. Modred remarked, "He's very young to be king, isn't he? He must be grateful to have you by his side."

Morgan did not reply. His gaze remained on Isabeau as she turned her attention back to him. She gave him a pretty, charming smile. "What I wouldn't give to have a merlin like you on my own wrist."

On the bed in the quiet London flat, Morgan stirred restlessly.

Kill them, he tried to say to the much younger man he had once been, a young man who had come to the height of his own Power just as his young king had come to the height of his. *They are predators looking at the king's courtiers like so many sheep. Kill them before they grow too strong. Kill them while you can.*

But as much as he had tried to find a way over the centuries, he had never discovered how to conquer time so that his younger self could hear when he called out.

And Modred had become the Light Fae ambassador to the king's court while Isabeau laid her plans for Morgan like a spider patiently spinning its web.

He woke in a sweat and lay looking at the shadowed ceiling until he could feel the early morning light grow outside, and the unquiet memories settled into the ancient past where they belonged.

Only then did he stir. To his own sensitive nose, he stank, smelling of chemicals and blood, so he eased himself carefully off the bed and took the metal stand with the IV into the bathroom, where he washed up.

Something, some small noise, made him turn off the faucets abruptly. Holding his breath, he tilted his head to one side and listened intently, but whatever he had heard was gone.

Still, he pulled out the IV needle from his wrist and moved to the bedside table where he had set his Beretta. Then he prowled through the empty flat, checking out windows and opening the front door to look down the length of the mews.

A newspaper lay on the front doorstep. Everything looked quiet and peaceful, just as an early morning should, but when he drew a breath, he recognized a familiar scent—the scent of a creature that had disappeared from Isabeau's court weeks ago.

Someone she had wanted back badly enough that she had sent Morgan to hunt him down and bring back to her. That task had led Morgan to the confrontation with the knights from Oberon's Dark Court, and it had resulted in the injuries that had ultimately set him free.

He had not been as successful as he had thought in hiding his trail. The puck Robin had found him.

The geas shifted uneasily, like the coils of a python sliding around a man's body. Tensing, he waited to see what would happen. Would it force him to obey Isabeau's earlier order to hunt Robin down and bring him back to her? Or would her latest words bear the greater weight?

When the geas subsided, he knew. Her last words to him were the ones that carried the most weight. He was still free, for now.

With a sharp gaze, he studied every detail of the scene—along the rooftop, the shadowed doorway of the shop across the street at the end of the mews—but there was no sign of the puck and no sign or scent of anyone else.

Then he noticed another thing. None of the other flats in the mews had received a folded newspaper. Bending with care, his gun held at the ready, he knocked the paper open. Despite what he had expected, there was nothing tucked inside.

Instead, a black-and-white photo of Sidonie Martel leaped out at him from the front page. Underneath her photo, the headline said FAMOUS MUSICIAN MISSING AFTER CAR CRASH.

A sprawling message had been written in black ink across the paper.

The Queen has her.

The words kicked him in the teeth. Morgan's breathing stopped, then fury roared up in response.

The puck had not just found him. Robin had studied him carefully and struck a calculated blow.

Gathering up the newspaper, he carried it inside and flung it across the sitting room with such force it hit the opposite wall with a crack like a whip. He stalked through the small flat then back again.

No, he thought. By gods, no. *I WILL NOT BE MANIPULATED LIKE THIS!*

After centuries—centuries—he had just won a tenuous measure of freedom for himself, and he had no idea how long he might keep it. If he was going to have any hope of striking a blow against Isabeau and Modred, it was vitally important he continue to follow every avenue of research on the Athame's geas that he could. He could not risk throwing all that away for a stranger.

Unbidden, an image of Sidonie Martel came to mind, along with her joyous, passionate music. She was so beautiful, so toweringly talented.

For those very two things alone, Isabeau would be cruel to her. Robin had known that.

Breathing hard, Morgan ran his fingers through his

hair as conflicting impulses tore at him.

Sidonie Martel means nothing to me, he thought harshly. I enjoy her music, that's all. I don't owe her a thing. Not a blasted thing.

Silence was all the flat gave him in response. After tensely listening to the quiet emptiness for a long while, he strode to the bedroom, pulled out his knapsack, and began to pack.

ONCE THE WAGON train had made its way down the winding road to the castle, it disbanded like segments of a giant centipede falling apart, as various components went off in different directions.

Sid had jumped out of the wagon along with her fellow travelers, but when she would have followed them, a sharp whistle brought her up short.

They didn't put her with the young Light Fae they had collected along the road. Instead, they put her with a large pile of barrels and wooden boxes they stacked in the stables, shackling one of her wrists with a chain to a metal ring that was bolted to a wooden beam.

She was there to be counted as part of the trolls' tribute, she assumed.

Then they forgot to feed her.

As the light of day passed into darkness, then blossomed into the new morning, she drifted beyond fear and simple anger into a kind of incensed exhaustion.

She had enough room on the chain to reach a

bucket that had been set nearby. It was partially full of water that was none too clean, and probably laced with horse spit, but after a certain point she became too thirsty to care. When the water was gone, she used the bucket to relieve herself.

The sound of voices roused her, and stiffly she uncurled from a thin layer of straw that had been her bed. There were three voices, all male, one sounding clearly in command, asking questions while the other two answered. They appeared to be tallying a long list of items.

"Hey," Sid called out, her voice hoarse from disuse. She stood, yanking irritably at the chain attached to her wrist. "*Hey!* What is wrong with you people?!"

Silence greeted her shout. Then came the sound of approaching footsteps, and the nearby doors were pulled open. As bright sunlight spilled in she had to squint and turn her face away.

Three men strode in, led by one tall figure. He stopped in front of her and asked in a cultured, pleasant voice, "What is this?"

The two men behind him shuffled their feet. "Ah, my lord," one of them said as he consulted the papers he held, "this is the trolls' semiannual tribute."

"The trolls gave the Queen a person?" The first male raised one eyebrow. He was richly dressed and handsome, with the characteristic blond hair of the Light Fae pulled into a queue at the nape of his neck, a sharp, angular face, and an ironical gaze.

"I've been kidnapped and unlawfully detained," Sidonie said between her teeth. "I'm a Canadian citizen, and you have me chained up like an animal. No, that's not true. Animals usually get treated much better than this. At least they get fed. I've been here like this since yesterday with no food and only stale horse water to drink."

"Oh, dear," said the man. He turned to look at his two companions. "How did this happen?"

Under his steady gaze, the other two attempted to stammer out an explanation. One forgot to tell the other of her presence. Or maybe she hadn't been added to the inventory. She couldn't have been added, or he would have noticed.

Oh... oh, yes, my lord, it did say so right there on the inventory list: one musician. No magic.

Listening to their excuses, Sid hung on to her patience by a thread. Finally she snapped, "At this point, does it matter?"

The well-dressed Light Fae angled his head back at her. "Why, no. I don't suppose it does."

She held up her wrist. "Will you please unchain me?"

The Light Fae nobleman gestured. "Harkin, if you would, free the lady from her confinement."

One of the other men hurried to obey. As he unlocked the shackle and it fell from Sid's wrist, relief washed over her, leaving her feeling light-headed. Finally she was talking to someone in charge, and what's more, he was listening to her. It looked like this whole, long nightmare might be over with soon.

"Are you really a musician?" the nobleman asked with a smile. "Or did the trolls mess that up too?"

"Yes, I'm a musician," she replied as she rubbed at her wrist. Should she tell him that the troll who had kidnapped her hadn't really been a troll? Or should she heed her kidnapper's warning and stay silent about his part in this debacle?

Watching her with interest, the nobleman asked, "Are you any good?"

She frowned at him. "As it happens, yes, I am, but the only thing that really matters is that I was taken and held against my will. I need to be escorted back to the nearest crossover passageway so I can go home again. If you need reimbursement for the costs of the journey, I can see that you get repaid."

Although really you should take me back on your own dime, with a profuse apology. She managed, just barely, to bite back that acerbic comment.

"I see." The nobleman looked at the other two men. "How close are we to completing a review of the inventory?"

The one named Harkin consulted his sheets. "We're almost done, my lord. Actually, we only have the trolls' tribute left to count."

The nobleman turned to survey the pile of crates and barrels surrounding them. "Well, here it all is, so I'd say we're finished." He looked at Sid. "Come with me, musician."

"Gladly," Sid said.

She gave the other two men a look of pure loathing and followed the nobleman out of the stables. Surely, they would feed her something soon. The last thing she had eaten was the requisite bread and cheese at noon the day before. She felt dizzy and light-headed, unable to concentrate, and her empty stomach was gnawing at her insides.

She had questions she wanted to ask, starting with the nobleman's name and where he was taking her, but he strode through the courtyard to an entrance to the castle, then down a series of passages, at a pace so swift she was hard put to keep up with him. After days filled with stress and an inadequate diet, soon she was too out of breath to speak.

The corridors on their route grew wider and more richly appointed, and they passed servants, uniformed guards, and various other personages who walked and talked together. Several paused to stare at them as they passed, their expressions filled with varying degrees of fascination and distaste, and Sid grew all too aware that she was carrying the filth of several days' journey on her clothes and smelled like a barnyard.

Food first. Then a bath. Perhaps they would give her clean clothes, or at least wash the ones she had. She might even get a bed for the night then a trip back home. She didn't even care if it was the same soldiers who took her back. She just wished very hard for all of it to come true.

At last, the nobleman paused at tall double wooden doors that had been ornately carved and bound with what appeared to be gold. Guards were stationed on either side.

Sid slowed to a stop beside the nobleman and caught her breath. Before she could ask any of her questions, he rapped on one door panel, then opened the door and strode inside without waiting for a reply.

Staring cautiously at the guards, she followed on his heels, stepping into a large, elegant room with high ceilings and tall windows that let in large bars of sunlight that fell across polished, golden oak floors.

Sid looked around, eyes wide, at the brilliant tapestries and paintings adorning the walls, the elegant sculptures, the velvet and mahogany furniture. While she had inwardly railed at the barely veiled prejudice the Light Fae had shown her on the road, the view of the castle in the distance, along with this walk through the interior of the castle, had shown her that she had her own preconceived notions that she needed to shed. This was no provincial demesne. There was serious wealth and culture here and a sense of great, sophisticated age.

A Light Fae woman sat at a large, ornately carved desk, her golden head bent over papers. She was richly dressed, in a yellow gown embroidered with green vines and white lilies, and her long curling hair had been dressed so that it flowed in a profuse mane down her slender back.

The woman barely glanced up at their entrance. She said in an impatient voice, "I'm not having a very good morning, Modred. I have a headache, and I don't appreciate the interruption. What do you want?"

"I'm so sorry to hear that, my love," the nobleman replied in a light tone. "Perhaps I can do something to make your day a little brighter. Here is part of the trolls' tribute. A new musician. Apparently, she has no magic."

At his words, Sid's tired mind stumbled. Wait. His wording didn't sound quite right. She wasn't anybody's tribute—she'd been *kidnapped*.

The woman set aside her pen and stood, looking at Sid for the first time. As she came around the corner of the desk and approached, her beautiful face pulled into an expression of distaste, much like the others Sid had seen throughout the castle.

"No magic?" The woman sounded incredulous. "At all?"

"She didn't respond when I tried to telepathize with her earlier, so I would say none at all," Modred replied.

"Why, she's little better than an animal," the woman remarked. "Also, she's filthy and hideous. Look at the shape of her eyes, the pasty white skin, and that awful black hair."

Sid's mouth dropped open. For a moment, she couldn't believe what she'd heard. She had read that some of the Elder Races didn't think much of those who were magicless, but she had never come face-to-face with such blatant bigotry. The fury that had been simmering over the course of several days began to boil over.

"Isabeau," said Modred, sounding amused. "She's human. She's not going to look anything like a Light Fae, and they chained her up in the stables overnight, so of course she's dirty."

Isabeau was a name Sid was supposed to remember. Angrily she shoved that aside. She snapped, "I have never been spoken to like that before in my life."

"I wasn't talking to you, girl." One of the Light Fae woman's eyebrows rose. "And I didn't give you permission to speak."

"I am not a *girl* or an *animal*," Sid snapped. "And your permission means nothing to me."

"It should," Isabeau said dryly. "It very much should." She said to Modred, "Bring musical instruments. Let us see if the girl has any talent. Perhaps it might offset her ugly looks and poor manners."

Even as the other woman spoke, the pieces came together in Sid's mind. Isabeau. The ornate surroundings, the rich dress, the guards at the door. This was the Queen of the Light Court.

Then Isabeau took a lock of Sid's hair and fingered it, one nostril curled, and all thought of caution or of trying to negotiate a passage home vanished in a surge of rage.

Breathing heavily, Sid knocked her hand away. She said between her teeth, "I don't play music for kidnappers and bigots."

The other woman's expression iced over. "Then you are of no use to me whatsoever." She looked at Modred. "If the bitch won't play her music for me, then she won't play it for anyone else. Break all her fingers. Perhaps that will teach her some manners."

"Consider it done," Modred said, smiling.

Shock jolted through Sid, followed by a surge of terror so powerful it turned her muscles watery.

"Wait," she said. "Wait, please. This has all been a massive, nightmarish mistake—if you could just give me a moment to explain how I got here—there'll be a large reward for my return…"

Suddenly the sound of her voice stopped. She put her hands to her throat and tried to shout, but nothing came out.

"The sound of your voice offends me. I'm done with you, ugly brown-haired girl." Isabeau spared her one venomous glance then turned away. "Get her out of my sight."

"Of course, my love."

As Modred grabbed Sid's arms, she began to fight, all the while screaming silently. Then the guards came into the room and took her away.

Away from the richly decorated corridors. Away from the sunlit windows.

They took her down a flight of worn stone stairs to

a hot, windowless room lit with a fire in an iron grate. There were other things made of iron in the room—chairs, tools, manacles, a cage. A wooden table, along with the floor underneath it, was dark with stains.

No matter how she struggled, the guards who held her were too powerful. One male held her hands to the table, while Modred rummaged through the tools until he found a mallet. Strolling over to her, he smiled at her. "It's nothing personal, pet."

He broke all her fingers, and her thumbs too. When he was finished, they dragged her down into a cold place filled with stone. Unlocking one barred door, they threw her into a room, and the door clanged shut behind her.

Light faded as the guards walked away, leaving her behind in deep shadows and a silence so deep it seemed to be alive.

Shaking, in shock, she crumbled where she stood like a broken marionette and cradled her ruined hands against her chest. The pain was so intense it lit up her mind like reddened stars.

After a time, the spell dampening her voice wore off, and she could hear herself scream again until her vocal chords turned raw and she lost her voice. Then there was silence and she lay curled on her side on the uneven stone floor.

The guards hadn't set the bones after Modred had broken them.

She would never hold a violin again with any kind

of dexterity. She would never be able to play.

The result of all the years of constant devotion to her music was gone, her purpose for living destroyed. She would never again create her unique citadel of radiant vibration, which had been exactly what the Queen had intended.

After that, it didn't matter how long her body managed to survive.

They've already killed me, she thought.

Chapter Five

HER CELL WAS chilly, the stone floor gritty with dirt. A cot stood in one corner, much like the one from the first cell where she'd been held, and from the smell, she guessed that a primitive latrine in the form of a hole in the floor was in the opposite corner.

After a while, the intensegray shadows deepened into inky blackness. Then the blackness receded into gray again.

Some distance away at the edge of her hearing, a creature in a nearby cell moaned and cried. The sound was quiet and tired, as if it had been crying for a long time. There were other noises, shuffling sounds, the drip of water nearby, and sometimes a rhythmic scraping, as if something dragged its body over the stones, pacing back and forth incessantly.

When the blackness turned to gray again, a fierce light came, flaring almost unbearably to her oversensitive gaze. The light came from a torch carried by a guard who shoved a tray underneath the bars of her cage and moved on.

Hours slid away, and when the gray began to

deepen to blackness again, the light came back. The guard took away her untouched tray and shoved in another one.

None of it mattered. She didn't move from her fetal position. There was no reason to. There was nowhere to go. There was nothing she could do. It didn't matter if she was cold. After a while, she stopped shivering. The pangs of hunger had disappeared, leaving her more hollow than before, until her skin felt like an empty shell.

The pain in her ruined hands remained raw and acute, a constant throbbing to remind her of her own stupidity. Her own temper had killed her as much as anyone else had. She had been warned Isabeau was dangerous, and she had disregarded that, allowing her own outrage at how she'd been treated to supersede common sense or self-preservation.

She had always known she had lived a privileged life. She'd had talent, which her parents had recognized when she was very young and had fostered before they had died. She had earned a lot of money in her career, and she'd enjoyed a certain amount of power that money brings.

She'd thought she hadn't taken it for granted, but she had never conceived that one of the consequences of the life she had lived would be to refuse to accept when things didn't go her way until it was too late for her to do anything about it.

How long would it take for her to quit breathing?

Too long, too long. Through half-closed eyes, she watched the blackness come, then despite the cold and pain, she managed to fall into an uneasy doze.

Something roused her. She resented it even as she tried to identify what it had been. A sound? A movement? A new air current she hadn't felt before?

Something touched her.

She jackknifed away and tried to scream, but her vocal chords were still raw and it came out as a hoarse croak.

Hands settled onto her shoulders. Large, strong hands. "*Shh*, quiet! I'm here to help."

She barely registered the whispered words. Panicked, she fought against the hold. Blinding agony exploded as she tried to knock the hands away, and she cried out.

Then her consciousness snapped out of existence, and she knew nothing.

When she came awake again, she did so all at once, awareness rushing in, clean, sharp, and complete, as if someone had thrown a bucket of cold water on her. She had been laid out on the stone, and a large, hard hand covered her mouth. A male hand.

Magic! While she couldn't sense spells, she knew very well what magical anesthesia felt like. She chose it over physical drugs every time she had a dental procedure. Someone had put her under. *What had he done to her?*

She erupted into fighting again, doing everything

she could to break the unknown assailant's grip that held her pinned in place. She slapped and punched him with all her strength, but she couldn't knock him away from her, although when she punched him in the ribs, he exhaled sharply as if she had done serious damage.

"Stop fighting. I'm not here to hurt you!" This time the words came out clenched as if whispered through gritted teeth.

The words barely registered as she realized what she was doing. Realized what had happened.

She had been slapping… punching…

With her hands.

With a sob, she clasped them together, feeling frantically at each precious finger and thumb, hardly noticing the hand that still covered her mouth and muffled the sounds she was making.

Her hands were pain free, whole, fully functional. She could barely take it in.

She fell apart, completely and utterly lost it. Uncontrollable sobs wracked her body, while she kept clasping and reclasping her hands. She could barely comprehend the barbarity of what had happened to her, let alone this miracle that had brought her back to life.

The man who bent over her swore softly. Shifting, he came down closer to her, so close she could feel his body heat. He whispered in her ear, "You don't have telepathy."

She shook her head as tears streamed out of the

corners of her eyes and soaked her hair. Why did everybody care so much about the damn telepathy?

"You need to listen to me," he said, so softly his words were barely a brush of air on her cheek. She scented mint on his breath. "Try to calm down. You must be quiet, do you hear? I am not supposed to be here, and you are not supposed to be healed. Now, I'm going to take my hand away from your mouth. Nod if you understand."

She nodded, and the hand lifted away from her. After that he didn't touch her in any way, but she could still feel his body heat. He was reclining along the floor beside her. Another sob shook through her, and she stuffed her own hands against her mouth in an attempt to muffle it.

Her own pain-free hands.

"Crying's okay," the male told her, again so quietly she had to control herself just to hear him. "That's a sound they would expect, but you're supposed to be alone in this cell. They mustn't hear us talking, and they have exceptional hearing. Understood?"

With an effort, she managed to clench down on the floodgates enough to grit out, "Yes."

"Good. Thankfully, I have exceptional hearing too, and I should hear if any of the guards come close."

"You h-healed me," she whispered thickly. Her body still shook, and the tears wouldn't stop. "Who are you? I can't thank you enough. You saved my life. I thought they had killed me. I can't live without my hands."

The darkness was so complete she couldn't see a thing, yet the soft rustle of clothing told her he had begun to move. The rustle stopped, and for a moment the silence was so intense she almost doubted his reality, her own sanity, until she frantically felt down the length of each of her fingers again and found them whole. Pain free. Limber.

Warm fingers came down over hers and pressed. Turning her hands over, she gripped his hand tightly.

Everything else fell away. Nothing else existed—there was no light, no warmth at all, she didn't know his name, what he looked like, or anything about him, but in that moment holding his hand felt like holding on to a lifeline.

He allowed it, then gently he disengaged. "Can you sit up?"

She nodded and immediately felt silly. "Yes."

"I brought food and water. Not the swill they give prisoners. Clean, healthy supplies."

"A prisoner." She exhaled a bitter cough as she struggled up. It was much harder than she had expected. She was so shaky, she could barely sit upright. "I guess that's what I am. Unless—unless—can you possibly help me escape?"

"No," he said flatly.

The hope had barely been born, and yet that single-word reply felt so crushing she swayed. "But," she whispered through trembling lips, "but you helped me.

You got into this cell, which means you can get out again. Right? You have to leave. You can't be here when the guard comes in the morning. Won't you take me with you?"

"I didn't say I won't. I said I can't. I am... constrained."

She scrubbed at her wet face. "I don't understand."

"I know you don't. Just believe this much: I would get you out of here if I could, and I will help you as much as I can. Here, take this."

Fingers closed over her wrist, making her start. He put something under her fingers. Bringing up her other hand, she felt along a round rim then down the smooth sides. The object felt metallic. "Is this a flask of some sort?"

"Yes. There's soup in it. It's not too hot to eat."

"Thank you," she breathed.

Opening the lid, she held it close and inhaled the rich scent of something meaty. Moist warmth touched her cheek, and suddenly she was so ravenous she could barely contain herself. Cautiously, she sipped at the warm liquid. He was right. It wasn't too hot, and it was unutterably delicious.

Hunching her shoulders, she concentrated everything on savoring the delectable liquid. She had eaten at some of the most exclusive, expensive restaurants in the world, but she had never tasted anything as wonderful as that soup.

Something hard and straight pressed against her

fingers, making her start again. The man whispered, "Sorry. It's a spoon."

She whispered another thanks, took it, and kept the edge of the rim against her lips as she spooned chunks of vegetables, meat, and noodles into her mouth. When she had devoured all the pieces of food, she upended the flask and drank the last of the broth.

He didn't speak while she ate, nor did he move, until again she would have wondered at his presence or her own sanity if she hadn't held the physical evidence of the flask between whole, dexterous fingers.

When she had finished the soup, he touched the back of her hand, slid a light finger down to the flask and took it from her. His actions seemed so confident, it was almost as if he could see her.

She frowned, not liking that thought. She felt completely blinded by the night and intensely vulnerable, and the possibility that he might be able to see her while she couldn't see him was disturbing.

The flask was definitely not from here, which meant he probably had other things from Earth. Could he be wearing night goggles?

"I can't see a thing in here," she whispered cautiously. "But you seem to be able to."

"It's very dark in here, but I have exceptional eyesight too." His reply was calm and untroubled. Confident. "You're mostly a collection of shadows to me, but I can get a general idea of how you're sitting and where you are."

From everything he said she gathered he wasn't human, but that wasn't much of a leap in deduction. She had been in Avalon for days and hadn't seen another human.

While she pondered that, he said, "Here—I have water, fruit, and bread too."

As he talked, he set items in her lap, and she identified each one by touch. One was a water bottle. Another was a small loaf of bread. Unlike the hard, unappetizing bread she had been given on the road, this bread had a crust that broke easily as she pinched a corner of it, and the inside was soft and smelled yeasty. He also set a bunch of grapes on her knee.

After having been without for so long, she felt overwhelmed, and tears prickled at the back of her nose again. She forced them down.

Thickly, she whispered, "This is amazing. I-I don't know what to say."

"No need to say anything. I'll have to take the water flask with me when I go, but you can eat the evidence of the fruit and bread. I dumped out the water cup they gave you on the tray, wiped it out and put fresh water in it. That's safe to drink too. I wouldn't trust the food or drink they give you. It's not very sanitary, and it could make you sick, especially since you're not used to it."

She had eaten so little, her stomach must have shrunk, because the soup had completely filled her up. Still, she rested her fingers lightly on each gift. With real nourishment, she began to feel stronger and more clearheaded than she had for quite some time. Not exactly steady, not yet—the abyss of despair she had fallen into was still too close for that. But still… better.

"You've helped me so much, and I don't even know who you are," she whispered. "What's your name? Where are you from?"

He took in a deep breath. Like everything else, it was a quiet sound, but something about it made it seem as if he braced himself. "I can't tell you that."

She considered that. "Can't?" she asked. "Or won't?"

A small silence fell. Without sight, everything felt extra weighted, especially significant.

Then he replied, "Won't."

That shook her. She wasn't even sure why it rattled her so, but it did, and her imagination careened from thought to thought like a car hurtling down a mountain without brakes.

Why wouldn't he tell her his name? What was constraining him from helping her to escape? Who was he? Why was he here?

She had relaxed with him, and all because he had healed her hands. She had eaten the food he had given her, but what if it had been drugged or poisoned? What if he worked for the Queen, and this was all an incredibly cruel ploy? What if—what if—

What if they had healed her fingers only to come back and break them again?

The blackness pressed down all around her. Suddenly it felt crushingly heavy, almost as if it were a live creature intent on suffocating her. Her breathing turned short and ragged as panic closed her throat.

"Easy there," he whispered.

Fingers touched the bare skin of her forearm. Flinging the food and water bottle, she scrambled blindly away from him, scuttling on hands and knees. Pain exploded in her head and one shoulder as she slammed into something hard. Reeling back, she reached forward with both hands and felt rough stone. She had run into a wall.

Firm hands came down on her shoulders. The man whispered, "Stop before you seriously hurt yourself."

Still in the middle of panic and driven by instinct, she slammed her elbow back, collided with hard, packed muscle, and twisted away from his touch.

He emitted a quiet, strangled moan. It sounded odd enough that she paused uncertainly, but this time he didn't follow or try to touch her again. His breathing had turned ragged.

After a moment, he gasped, "I understand you are… under extraordinary stress, but I am… not entirely well. Don't do that… again."

The stress in his breathing and whispered words snapped her back to herself. Twisting on her knees, she groped her way back in the direction of his voice, one hand outstretched. Her fingers collided with clothing. Lightly, quickly she ran her hands over the outline of his body, and he did nothing to stop her.

The impression she had gained from his hands held true. He was big, much bigger than she, on his knees with broad, hunched shoulders. He listed a little to one side, and she skimmed her fingers up the side of his neck to touch his face, briefly, before snatching them away again. His skin was slightly clammy.

"I didn't know," she whispered. "I was just trying to get away. I didn't mean to hurt you."

"I know you didn't," he said shortly.

"It's just—you won't tell me your name or who you are, and this unrelenting dark is driving me crazy, and I thought, what if the food was poisoned? I don't know you. I just ate it without questioning anything, and what if… what if they c-come back and break my fingers again?"

In a sudden, strong movement, he grasped one of her hands and held it tightly. Like before, everything else fell away—the chilly dampness, the darkness, and the only thing that felt real or solid was the warmth of his hard fingers pressing into hers.

"It's all right," he said. "I get it."

She gripped him back just as tightly, hanging on for dear life. "I hit you in the ribs twice. Are you all right?"

"Don't worry about it. I'm fine." His breathing steadied. "Listen to me. I am not going to tell you who I am, because ignorance is your only defense if they discover your injuries have healed and they question you."

She hung her head. "I hadn't thought of that."

He continued, "Chances are, Isabeau has thrown you in here to rot, and if nothing else happens, she'll forget about you, but you can't count on that. One day, she might want to see for herself how miserable and sorry you are. If anyone asks how your hands got healed, tell them the truth—you don't know. You fell asleep, and when you woke up, you were healed. You don't know how it happened, and you don't know who did it. That's all. Don't offer them any information. I'm assuming they know you don't have magic?"

"Yes." She should let go of him, but she couldn't seem to make her grip loosen.

"Good. Isabeau is one of the most bigoted racists you could ever meet. She equates a lack of magic to a lack of intelligence. If she finds out what happened, she'll be furious that someone defied her orders enough to heal you, but it won't occur to her that you might be able to evade her truthsense."

Now that the panic had lessened, she was able to think again. His strategy was also the only way to protect him from Isabeau's anger. What Sid didn't know, she wouldn't be able to tell anyone.

"Okay," she whispered. "I understand."

At that, his grip loosened. He would have let her go, but she held on.

"Why have you helped me?"

He sighed. "It's too dangerous to tell you anything. I know it must be very nearly impossible, given the situation you're in, but if you can, just try to trust this one thing: I mean you no harm, and I will help you as much as I can."

He seemed to have forgotten that she still held his hand, and she wasn't about to let go. Thinking back to the beginning of this whole nightmare, she said slowly, "I was kidnapped by a creature that wants to cause damage to the Light Fae."

"You talked to him?" His whisper sharpened.

"Yes. He was strange-looking, like a thin teenage boy, until you looked into his face. And he could shapeshift."

This time the man's sigh sounded heavy. "I know who he is."

"He ambushed my car, and we crashed. While the others were either hurt or unconscious, he took me," she whispered. "And when I gained consciousness again, he cried. I thought he'd been stalking me, but he said he had been stalking someone else. A man, he said, that kept going to my concerts. Since this man was interested in me, the creature took me and gave me to Isabeau. I thought he was insane. But he wasn't, was he?"

Through her grip on his hand, she could feel the tension in his body. "No. Robin is dangerous and very damaged, but I don't think he is insane."

He knew the creature by name. She swallowed past a thickness in her throat. "Are you the man he was talking about?"

"Don't ask me that question, Sidonie."

The man's use of her name, when she hadn't told it to him or to anyone else in Avalon, sent a fresh shock through her system.

She had already known the answer before she had asked it, because who else in this godforsaken demesne would care at all about what happened to her, heal her hands, bring her food, and offer comfort?

Squeezing her eyes closed, she concentrated on trying to breathe evenly, while tears slipped down her face and she held the hand of the man who was responsible for everything terrible that had happened to her.

When she could control herself enough to speak, she whispered, "So, you like my music?"

"*Like* is not the right word for it." His words came slowly, his unwillingness to answer evident. "Your music hurts, the way sunshine hurts when you've existed for a long time in darkness."

She thought of the unbearably fierce torchlight when the guard came. Even though she knew it was unlikely he could see her, she nodded and wiped her face. Okay.

Her grip loosened, and she let him go.

There was a slight rustle of clothing as he moved around. He must have stood, because when he spoke next, it was from above her head as he pressed the water bottle into her hands. "Drink as much as you can. This, along with what is in your cup, is going to have to last you all day. I'll get the grapes and bread. I doubt anyone is going to bother coming into your cell, so if you lie down on the cot, you should be able to hide them between you and the wall. If you're worried about them for any reason, you can either eat them before the guard gets here or throw them down the latrine."

He was getting ready to leave. She didn't know how she felt about him—she hadn't had any time to process the fact that he was the reason why she was in this hellhole—but the thought of him leaving her alone again brought the panic back. It beat through her veins, shook through her body in tremors, and shortened her breath.

She couldn't force herself to swallow any water until his hand came down on her shoulder and he held her again in the same kind of steady grip as before. It grounded her in a way that helped to beat back the panic. Then she upended the bottle and drank until it was empty. When she was finished, she handed the bottle back to him and hugged herself.

"I will come back, Sidonie," he said.

"You're sure you won't just leave me here?" Her voice shook as badly as the rest of her.

Because he could. He could walk away and never come back, and while it was an unbelievable miracle he had healed her hands, she was still trapped in the cold and the dark, still caught in this unending nightmare.

"I promise you, I will never just leave you here." He stepped closer until she could feel the brush of his clothing against her arm and feel his body heat. In the calm, confident way he had reassured her about everything else, he said, "It's nearly dawn, so I must go for now. In less than a half an hour your cell will lighten, and the guard will come through with food and water. You need to start throwing the food they give you down the latrine, or they'll expect to see a dead body in here eventually. After the day passes, and they have come through on their evening rounds, I will be back. I will not abandon you."

Breathing hard, she focused on soaking up his words. When he was finished, she forced herself to say, "Thank you. For everything."

She was rather proud that she had kept herself from pleading for him to stay, since he couldn't anyway, and she would not let herself sound so irrational again.

"Don't thank me." His whisper turned harsh. "It's the least I can do. See you this evening."

But what if he didn't come back? People promised things they couldn't deliver. What if he changed his mind? What if, through no fault of his own, he was detained?

The way her kidnapper, Robin, had talked, this man and Isabeau were responsible for a great many deaths. Just because he had helped her didn't mean he was a good man, or trustworthy.

Clenching her fists, she pressed them to her temples. The doubts and worries were going to drive her crazy.

There was another slight rustle of clothing, and the smallest creak of metal. The air around her changed and became cold and empty, and she knew he was gone. Carefully, she held the food he had given her.

One small loaf of bread.

Thirty-two grapes. Thirty-two.

Thirty-two.

THE PAIN FROM the new knife wound in Morgan's side was unrelenting as he eased his way down the prison tunnels. Sidonie had gotten in a few solid blows. He was glad she had so much fight in her. She was going to need it.

Despite the darkness, he could see well enough to pick out where he was going, and he knew the route like he knew the back of his hand.

Isabeau's castle had been built on a rabbit warren of natural tunnels that had been turned into a prison over a thousand years ago. Some parts had been filled in, while cells had been carved out of others, and shafts had been dug in order to provide ventilation. Without the indirect daylight from those shafts, Sidonie's cell would never lighten to gray and she would have been in perpetual darkness.

The prison guard rooms and barracks lay just above the cells. That area had several openings to above ground. He avoided it altogether and wound his way farther down, to a tunnel passageway that had been part of the area that had been originally filled in.

A very long time ago, when Morgan had begun to realize he was not going to break free of the geas, he had turned his efforts to creating his own private spaces in Avalon.

Working with earth magic to shift rock and shale, he had cleared out a few of the ancient passageways and kept them hidden with sheets of rock covering their entrances. This tunnel was only one of several secret ways he had of moving in and out of the castle.

The first time Sidonie had hit him had been an annoyance, but the second time she had struck directly on the new wound. He had felt something tear, a few of the stitches, no doubt, and wetness had seeped through the bandage.

He kept pressure on the wound, and when he lifted his palm away briefly, his skin felt sticky and wet. He would have to suture the area again before he could rest, all while avoiding detection from anyone else so Isabeau could not force him back to her side.

In the normal course of things, hiding from the Light Fae was relatively easy. They had keen eyesight and hearing, and many of them were proficient in magic, but none of them were as proficient as he was.

This time wasn't in the normal course of things. Once he'd made the decision to return to Avalon, he'd raced back as fast as he could. With the fresh silver poisoning his system, Morgan was much weaker than normal, his magic was dampened, and he hadn't had time to recover the way he'd planned.

Healing Sidonie's hands had taken everything he had and then some. To make sure he did the job properly, he'd had to use several healing potions to supplement the meager trickle of his own returning Power.

Not only that, but Isabeau's Hounds were lycan-thrope, just as he was, and they had the ability to track him by scent.

He had prepared for that eventuality by using a chemical hunter's spray developed on Earth that helped to eliminate scent. If worse came to worst, and Isabeau tried to have one of her Hounds track the person who had broken into Sidonie's cell and healed her, they wouldn't be able to glean any information.

He hoped he had brought enough of the spray to last for a while, because he couldn't think of any way to make Sidonie's situation better. While he could take her food and supplies and offer healing and whatever comfort she might accept, he couldn't release any prisoners, or aid in their escape. Isabeau had forbidden that a long time ago when she had first ensorcelled Morgan.

Thrusting aside the memories, he focused on the challenges of the present. As he eased through the narrow opening he had hidden long ago with subtle concealment spells, he looked up at the lightening sky grimly.

He hadn't expected to find Sidonie so badly injured, and he had stayed with her longer than he had meant to. The tunnel exit lay deep in the shadow of a stone buttress, but he needed to cross an open area of ground that was clearly visible in the growing morning light, all the while bleeding and drained of Power.

His other option was to hide a few yards inside the mouth of the tunnel, but the passageway was too narrow for someone of his bulk to fold his legs to sit down. He needed to get to his supplies to suture his wound again, plus he needed to eat something himself, take pain meds and antibiotics, and rest. His headlong dash back to Avalon from London had taken its toll, and he felt feverish again and as weak as a newborn kitten.

There was no other real choice. He had to dredge up Power somehow. He had such a wealth of war spells in his knapsack he could destroy the entire demesne if the geas would only let him, but the one spell he needed was the one he hadn't thought to cast into a magic item.

Digging deep, he wrenched Power out through sheer force of will and cast an aversion spell over himself. Then, as rapidly as he could, he crossed the open area. His muscles shook with the effort to hold a spell so simple a magic student could throw it, and for a moment he was tempted to let it drop. The morning was early yet, not quite dawn, and there would be few people about.

Just then, a young voice called out and another answered, and two youths dashed toward the kitchens. They might or might not notice him, but if they did, he was highly recognizable. Gritting his teeth, Morgan held onto the casting.

As he reached the stables, he knew he wasn't going to make it to his destination. Slipping inside, he let the spell go as dizziness overtook him. Reeling, he almost went down but managed to catch himself on the closest stall door.

Unsteadily, he made his way past the most spacious stalls, which held the nobles' mounts and Isabeau's own white destrier. He wanted to make it to the back of the stables where he knew there were empty stalls, but as black dots danced in front of his eyes, he changed course to slip into the stall of the gray dappled gelding he used when he was in Avalon.

A soft *whuffle* greeted him, and the gelding nosed him, looking for treats. "Sorry," he whispered. "Nothing for you today."

Catching the scent of fresh blood, the gelding pulled back and stamped its hooves uneasily. Morgan managed to latch the stall door, then the world went gray and formless, and he felt his legs buckle underneath him.

Chapter Six

THE SOUND OF rhythmic thumping and voices roused him. Isabeau's voice, calling out wordlessly.

As awareness coalesced, he realized he was lying prone in his gelding's stall. The horse had decided to ignore him and stood with his nose in a box filled with hay, as far away as he could get from Morgan.

Adrenaline kicked him into action. He had no idea how long he'd been out, but he'd been easily visible to anyone who might have glanced into the stall. Pushing himself to a sitting position, he edged back against the shadow of the stall door.

His head swam, black dots danced in front of his eyes, and the wound in his side gave a warning twinge. He pressed a hand against it and glanced down at himself. Liquid red had soaked his shirt and the hip of his pants. He had been bleeding the whole time he'd been unconscious.

The thumping increased in speed, and Isabeau cried out again. Distaste curled Morgan's lip. She was screwing someone in the stables. The man muttered something unintelligible then emitted a long, low groan. Apparently, at least one of them had achieved culmination.

Isabeau and Modred had a long-standing relationship, to which they were both unfaithful. Modred had pressed Isabeau to marry him for ages, but she refused. She would never let Modred get so close to the power of her throne. Modred was eternally ambitious, and as she had said before to Morgan more than once, he was already close enough to the throne as it was.

And so Isabeau and Modred danced around each other through the centuries, both lovers and conspirators, endlessly colluding in ventures for mutual and individual gain.

Morgan wished they would destroy each other, but as long as Isabeau kept possession of Azrael's Athame, which gave her control over Morgan and the other Hounds, Modred would never act against her. Aside from her political power, she held too much personal Power and made a deadly enemy.

Morgan had watched them destroy other friends and lovers with their dramas and jealousies. They broke people like children broke toys, carelessly throwing them away when they were ruined to reach for other, brighter playthings. This man, whoever he was, would be no different.

After the man's groan, the thumping had stopped. There was a rustle of clothing.

"When can we make the announcement?" the man

asked. "I don't want us to hide what we are to each other any longer."

Morgan recognized his voice. The other male was Valentin, a high-ranking noble from Arkadia, a Light Fae demesne whose crossover passageway was located near Mount Elbrus in Russia.

Valentin had arrived some months ago with a view to strengthening trade and ties between the two demesnes. As Arkadia's rulers were nearly as xenophobic as Isabeau and had similar views on maintaining racial purity, she had welcomed Valentin with open arms. Quite literally, it appeared.

"We must take our time, my love," Isabeau purred. "Approach matters gently, and let my court get used to your presence. Let them come to love you as I have learned to. I don't allow many emissaries from other demesnes to visit here, in the seat of my power. You are still strange to many of us."

"It's been months since I've arrived," Valentin insisted. "More than time enough for you and me to fall in love."

Valentin was another toy that would soon be broken. Not clever enough to have perceived Modred's enduring position at court, he would push either Isabeau or Modred too far, and Modred would never allow a foreign noble to supplant him.

Valentin's death would be from poison, or perhaps a fatal fall while riding—something that could be spun to the rulers in Arkadia as an accident. Either that, or he would be driven from Isabeau's court in disgrace.

"But darling, I am already dealing with so much." Isabeau's pout was evident in her voice. "Oberon's Dark Court is gaining strength. I had thought I'd blocked their access to Earth, but even as we speak, their presence in England grows. That makes my crossover passageways and borders more vulnerable than ever to this interminable war. And the captain of my Hounds is still missing."

"If one of my captains went missing, I would have him hunted down and strung up for desertion," Valentin said. But then Valentin didn't understand the true nature of the relationship between Morgan and Isabeau.

"The situation is not as simple as that," Isabeau replied impatiently. A note of injury entered her voice. "No one seems to fully understand everything I must cope with!"

As he listened, Morgan considered the precariousness of his situation. No matter what her order had been to him earlier, if she said his name—if she worded a sentence in a way that made it clear she wanted him back and he heard it—his newfound freedom would be gone, and he would have to go to her. The geas would see to that.

He had nothing he could use to stop his ears to avoid hearing her voice. If only he had a lump of beeswax, something. Clenching, he waited to hear the words that would ensure his recapture.

Valentin said, "I understand, my love! I appreciate you have so much to handle!"

"If you did truly understand, you wouldn't press me so." Isabeau wept. She was pretty when she cried. Her eyes didn't swell or redden as shining tears streamed down her cheeks. "Ruling a demesne alone can be so grueling. I swear, at times it is almost too much!"

"If there is anything I can do for you, only say so!" Valentin begged. "That's why I want to become your partner in both word and deed—in order to shoulder some of the burden you carry. Let me help you!"

It would be a cold day in hell before either Isabeau or Modred would allow that, Morgan thought cynically. Propping his elbow on an upraised knee, Morgan rubbed his tired eyes with thumb and forefinger as he listened to Isabeau manipulate the other man. Valentin was clearly pressing for an advantage, but every word the other man spoke betrayed his true intentions.

Isabeau sniffed. "You *can* help me! Only ease your insistence about when we go public with our relationship. Let me deal with what I must. When my captain is fully healed, he'll have no choice but to return to me. My borders will be strengthened, and I will gain the upper hand again in this war. Then I can give you—I can give *us*—the full attention we deserve. Just be patient with me for now!"

"Of course, I will," Valentin replied shortly. To Morgan's ears, the other man sounded truculent. "I'll be as patient as you need me to be."

Satisfaction laced Isabeau's voice as she crooned, "I knew I could count on you. Come, my love. I'm starving. Let's have lunch on the terrace overlooking the water."

"Very well."

Bit by bit, Morgan relaxed as the sound of their voices faded.

He assessed his current situation grimly. Sooner or later, sometime today a stableboy would be around to take the horses out for exercise, muck out the stalls, and give them fresh water.

Meanwhile, he was still dizzy and depleted, and it was midday. He needed to get to his safe spot and his supplies, but he couldn't. At the moment, he didn't have enough Power to throw a spell with the kind of strength it would take to cloak a man walking across an open area in broad daylight.

He would have to rest and wait for his opportunity. If a stableboy came to care for the gelding, maybe by then he could cast a spell of shadows in one corner of the stall. If not, perhaps he could spell the stableboy to forget.

Frustration nagged at him. He was going to have to wait until dusk before he could make his way to his supplies. Then he would need to eat and drink, take medication, and tend to his wound before he attempted anything else.

He was going to have to break his promise to Sidonie. There was no way he could reach her soon after the prisoners' evening meal.

Leaning back in the corner of the stall, he closed his eyes and schooled himself to patience.

SHORTLY AFTER HER mysterious healer left, Sid's cell lightened to gray and the guard came by with her morning meal. While he shoved the tray through the slot underneath the barred door, Sid took the chance to look fully around her cell.

It was as bleak as she had remembered when they had first brought her in. The plain, leather-bound cot had no blankets. The hole in the opposite corner was indeed the privy. The walls, ceiling, and floor were solid, hewn rock, all gray and brown. They reflected the fiery colors from the guard's torch.

The guard didn't remark on the fact that she no longer lay on the floor curled in a ball. Instead, he left without a word. Before the torchlight could completely fade away, she darted forward to snatch up the tray and dump the contents of the battered bowl—it looked like a watery strew with unidentifiable chunks floating in it—and the cup down the privy hole. Then she set the tray beside the door.

When the light had faded again, it took a while for her eyes to adjust to the darker gray. The sound of something small and furtive scurried nearby, and her imagination was all too happy to offer up an explanation.

It was a rat. Or plural, rats. Of course there would be rats down here. Shuddering, her thoughts went to the hidden food her benefactor had given her. She had wrapped it in her hoodie and tucked it in a corner. Retrieving it quickly, she went to sit on the cot.

The grapes would give her some much-needed moisture, and she knew she would be thirsty later, so she set those aside and ate the bread. It was as tasty as it smelled, simple, yeasty goodness. Tears pricked at the back of her eyes as she nibbled on the crust. She didn't think she had ever been so grateful for so little before.

Privilege.

It wasn't something she thought about much. In conversation and in thought, she often looked at how hard she worked (she did work extremely hard), and how much time she put into her music (countless hours). She deserved every bit of the success she had achieved.

But the truth was many other people put in countless hours developing their craft, skill, business, or passion, and they didn't achieve anything like the success she'd enjoyed. Most people didn't have the kind of support Sid had gotten from her parents, who had done everything they could to encourage her gift.

When they began to get an inkling of how gifted Sid was musically, her father had given up his faculty position at Dalhousie University in Nova Scotia to take a job at NYU. They moved from Canada just so she could attend Juilliard from an early age.

When she graduated with a master's in music from Juilliard, she'd never had to take out a student loan. She had begun her adulthood talented, highly educated, and debt free, and if that wasn't privilege, she didn't know what was.

Now the simple goodness of a well-baked loaf of bread brought tears to her eyes.

The soup, bread, and fruit weren't enough calories for a day. She would be hungry later. Forcing herself to stop eating, she set half the loaf of bread carefully with the grapes. Then she counted the strips of crosshatched leather in the cot.

This cot had eleven strips in length and thirty-five across. How irritating! It didn't match the first cot at all! She counted them again to be sure. Eleven and thirty-five. Then again. Eleven and thirty-five. Then she pulled her pebbles out of her pocket and counted them. Twenty-one. Twenty-one. Twenty-one.

Finally she forced herself to shove the pebbles back into her pocket. It was much harder to do than she had expected. The only way she could do it was by promising herself that she could count her grapes again.

Her OCD had never been so bad before. When she was at home and comfortable in New York, it was little more than an annoyance. She had to go back into her apartment after leaving to double-check all the appliances and lights were safely off. She never caught a taxi on the left side of the street, even when it was a one-way street. She always counted the light posts on each block as she walked. But it was all manageable.

Now she had the stress, the fear that never really subsided, and she had nothing to do. Nowhere to go. Nothing to see, and no one to talk to.

But she had her hands, and that gave her the will to live again.

I will not fade away into the dark, she thought. I will not.

So I must decide what I *will* do. Otherwise I'll degenerate into counting pebbles incessantly in the dark.

I will stay fit. Somehow, at some point, I'm going to get a chance to get out of here, and I'll need to be ready.

I will practice my music. I don't have any instruments to play, and I can't write down any music, but I can still compose songs in my mind.

I have my memory. I have my will.

I have my intellect and imagination.

The first thing she did every morning was exercise. Being a professional musician was strenuous work, and if she didn't look after her body, she ended up with back and neck strain. So if her running stride was approximately 1,700 steps in a mile, then in order to run three miles she needed to get in 5,100 steps before she did anything else.

(Plus she got to count something!... *AGGGHHH!* When she got free of this nightmare, she was going to need a whole lot of therapy.)

Standing, she went through a series of stretches.

Then she jogged in a circle around her cell, careful to avoid the cot, the walls, and the privy in the corner.

When she reached the right number of steps, she stopped and let herself have some of her grapes as a reward. She ate twenty-one as she fingered her twenty-one pebbles. Then she began to run through the fingering of the musical scale as she conjured up the sound of her violin in her mind.

As she did so, her thoughts drifted to her last concert. Brandon's tempo had been weak in the third number, and Derrick needed to cut back on the bass. She made mental notes of the things she had wanted to discuss with her band in Paris.

If... her thoughts faltered. *When* she got out of this hellhole, hopefully the time slippage won't have been too significant. It had taken her a lot of work to find the right backup with the right chemistry. She wanted to make sure she reached out to them as soon as she could before they found other gigs.

The momentum she built for herself crumbled.

She had eleven grapes left, along with half a small loaf of bread, and the gray, formless day was interminable. Occasionally she still heard the soft, quiet scurry of something small nearby, and the distant sound of tired sobbing never ceased. Compassion for whatever it was warred with the increasing desire to scream at it to shut up, until she felt as if her head might explode.

Finally hunger grew uncomfortable enough that she ate the last of the food and shrugged into her filthy hoodie for what comfort and warmth it gave. She had read somewhere once that the temperature underground remained a constant fifty-five degrees Fahrenheit. While that was certainly survivable, it wasn't comfortable, especially without enough calories to burn as fuel.

It seemed like forever until the bright fire of the torch began to brighten the walls of her cell as the guard brought her another inedible meal. As before, she waited until the guard strode away before taking the bowl and the cup to the privy.

This time it was a lot harder to throw the stew and water away, but she did. Afterward, she climbed onto the cot, curled into a ball, wrapped her arms around her legs, and waited. And waited.

He didn't come. He didn't come.

He didn't come.

After a long, formless time of waiting, tears welled up and spilled over. It had taken all her strength just to get through one dark day, and while she hadn't wanted to rely so desperately on him showing up, she had.

Maybe something had happened to him. Maybe this whole thing was just a cruel, sick joke.

Maybe he was Modred. Modred was on intimate terms with Isabeau—maybe he was the man her kidnapper, Robin, had referred to. When she had first met him, Modred had seemed perfectly acceptable, even charming at first, before he'd shown utter indifference to Isabeau's order and had personally seen to executing it.

At the memory of him breaking her fingers, she felt nauseous and wanted to vomit, except she refused to let go of the precious little liquid and nutrition she had in her stomach. She took deep, even breaths until the nausea passed.

Just when she thought she couldn't take any more uncertainty, despair, and paranoia, her overtaxed body decided it'd had enough, and besides, there wasn't any reason not to, so she spiraled into sleep and dreamed Modred broke all her fingers with smiling efficiency, no matter how she screamed and begged. Her thumbs, as well.

SHE WOKE ALL at once to a hard hand pressed over her mouth. Adrenaline screamed at her to move. When she would have struggled, she discovered something hard and unyielding pinned one of her arms to the cot while another hand gripped her other wrist.

"Don't hit me."

The soft growl came from overhead. Despite the darkness and the fact that she had never heard him speak in anything but a whisper, she recognized it. Recognized him.

Relief and gladness chased after the surge of adrenaline. Even as she tried to figure out just how he had pinned her, she nodded in quick response. As he slowly released her wrist, his other hand lifted from her mouth. The hard pressure that pinned her other arm to the cot lifted, and she realized he'd used the weight of one knee to immobilize her.

She bolted to a sitting position and swung her legs off the cot. The leather strips creaked as he sat beside her. Easy tears stung her eyes again. Fiercely glad he couldn't see them, she whispered, "I did as you said and threw away the food and water. Then I thought you weren't going to come."

There was a pause as he seemed to assimilate all that her sentence implied. Then he told her, "I got held up. Unfortunately, there were complications."

What complications? The last time he had been here, he hadn't been well. She laced trembling fingers together and twisted them. Whoever he was, he was virtually her only link to survival. "Are... are you all right?"

When he answered, his whisper was warmer, gentler. "I am now. I bet you're ready for some food and water."

"Oh God, yes."

Listening intently, she heard a brush of cloth, and the quiet sound of a zipper.

He pressed a flask into her hand. "First things first. Here's water."

Snatching at it, she fumbled to get the top open and drank thirstily until the flask was dry. When she finished, he took the flask from her, then grasped her fingers to guide her hand forward and down to what felt like an open canvas bag or backpack.

"Last time I was in a hurry to get here as fast as I could. This time I came better prepared," he murmured. As he talked, his hand guided her fingers to each of the bag's contents. "There's more bread and fruit—grapes, cherries, and an apple. There's also boiled eggs. They're already peeled. There's a soft cheese you might enjoy with the bread, half a roasted chicken, and a honey-and-nut pastry. I also have a few more flasks of water. You can save food for the daytime, especially since you can throw the scraps down the privy, but I can't leave a flask or the bag with you, so you should drink as much as you possibly can."

The too-easy tears slipped down her face again as she felt the largesse inside the bag. Grasping one of the eggs, she bit into it, chewed and swallowed. It was indescribably delicious.

She whispered, "I saved the grapes to eat during the day, because they carried so much moisture."

"That's smart thinking," he told her. "If you hold on to the fruit, it will help you get through the day."

"I don't know what to say, except again, thank you so much." She crammed the last of the egg into her mouth.

His light touch withdrew from her wrist. "As I said last night, don't thank me. It's the least I can do."

She started on another egg while she considered that. Maybe it was true. Maybe it was partly his fault she was here. But mostly, she thought, it was her kidnapper Robin's fault. And the fault of every Light

Fae she had met since arriving at their encampment.

"You didn't have to do anything," she pointed out. "And I would still be here, trapped in the dark, eating and drinking terrible food. I'd probably have dysentery by now. So yes… thank you."

"All right, then," he replied with a kind of grave courtesy that sent warmth running through her. "You're welcome."

She hesitated, thinking. She had things to say to him, and things to ask, but she was still hungry and didn't want to sour her only enjoyment. Finishing the second egg, she considered what to eat next.

Sweets could make one thirsty, so she should eat the honey pastry while she still had access to plenty of clean drinking water. Locating the pastry, she bit into one corner and almost moaned. It was flaky, buttery, and the top had been sprinkled with pecans. It was utterly delicious.

As she ate it, she said, "Where did you get the food? This is fresh."

"There's a night market in the city," he told her. "Certain stalls are open until midnight."

That sounded lively, intriguing. In an Other land, a market like that would be filled with exotic sights and sounds and interesting merchandise. She might want to go shopping there, if she didn't already want to burn Avalon with hellfire.

Carefully, focusing all her attention on the pastry, she finished it and sighed. "That was wonderful."

A smile entered his voice. "I have a fondness for them too."

So he liked sweets. Along with the fact that he had magical ability, it was virtually the only thing she knew about him.

She ate a chicken wing, and when she was done, she walked carefully over to the privy to toss the bones inside. Another question occurred to her. "Do they ever dig out the contents of this?" If they did, it must be beyond horrible.

"The privy? No. The hole goes to an underground river. There are grates over the river where it flows to the sea, which is why you can't shove anything like the flasks or the bag down the hole, or eventually someone will find it."

Even though he couldn't see it, she nodded, thinking. The rats probably used the underground river system to get around. She hadn't heard them since her benefactor had arrived. Perhaps he'd scared them away.

She said, "If I had the Power to shapeshift into something small, say a mouse or a rat, I could go down that hole."

"You could, if you had the stomach for it. It would have to be something small, or the grates would catch you and you would drown. But you don't have the Power to shapeshift."

"No." Now she knew a third thing about him—he knew a lot about the underground prison. She turned away from the hole and made her way back to the cot.

"Better?" he asked.

"Yes." Taking a deep breath, she braced herself to start asking the more uncomfortable questions, but he forestalled her.

"I have something else for you." The bag on the floor rustled as he rummaged in it, then he took hold of her hand and pressed something into it. Then something else.

She felt the items curiously. One was long, thin, and had bristles at one end, and the other felt like a tube. "Oh, my God," she whispered. "You brought me a toothbrush and toothpaste."

"I have a jar of lavender mixed with arrowroot that you can rub through your hair and brush out. It works like a dry shampoo. The arrowroot soaks up the oils, while the lavender adds some freshness. And there's a container of wet wipes." Even though she didn't know him, she thought she could hear a smile in his voice. "It's not the same as a shower or a bath, but at least it's something."

The tears came back, and for a moment she couldn't speak. When she did, her whisper came out thick and choked. "Now I'm beyond words."

"I know how you feel," he said gently. "A long time ago, I spent some time in one of these cells."

Her breath caught. "You did? How long were you down here?"

It was so hard to tell expression from a whisper, but his reply seemed flat and expressionless as he told her, "Over a year."

A year. She was going crazy after just a few days, and he had spent over a year down here in the dark, without extra food, water, or comfort, and he still sounded sane. She would not survive a year down here, even with his help.

Her lips trembled. "I can't imagine."

A small silence fell. Finally, still in that flat, expressionless tone, he said, "One day at a time, Sidonie. That's all either of us can do."

He had flasks, from Earth, wet wipes, and tubes of toothpaste and travel toothbrushes. That meant he had access to the crossover passageways. And he had spent over a year imprisoned, and he'd not only survived but he'd been set free again. That meant Isabeau valued him, and to some extent, despite his imprisonment, she trusted him.

Her shoulders tightened, but she was still not yet ready to start asking the tougher questions. Instead, she turned her attention to the treasures he had given her.

She asked, "And you can't see me, right?"

"I can see better than you can," he said. "I can see where you are, and your general posture. I can tell if you're standing or kneeling, but you're nothing more than a shadowy shape to me."

She considered that. Did she believe or trust him? There was something creepy at the thought of him eyeing her while she undressed, while she couldn't see him, but at this point did she really care?

He was probably telling the truth, but even if he was lying, she decided she wanted to be clean more than anything else, so she stripped off her filthy clothes and took the toiletries over to the privy.

Brushing her teeth had never felt so amazing. Rubbing the dry shampoo through her hair and brushing it out was a little odd, but she had to admit her hair felt much better afterward and the lavender scent was wonderful.

She used the wet wipes on her face and every inch of her body, only hesitating enough to ask, "Should I put these wipes down the privy?"

"No, don't do that," he said. "They won't biodegrade quickly enough. I'll take them with me when I go."

"Okay, thank you."

When she had finished and made her way back to the cot, he had one more surprise waiting for her. "I spelled your clothes," he said as he handed them to her in a folded pile. "They're as clean as I can get them without soap and water."

She buried her face in the clothes and inhaled. Before, even to her own nose, she had stank, but now they merely smelled a little dusty. "Another miracle," she murmured. "I wasn't looking forward to putting my clothes back on after getting clean."

This time the smile was back in his whisper. "I thought you might feel that way."

Beginning to shiver, she dressed quickly while he

moved about the cell, presumably to gather up the used wipes that she had left in a small pile near the privy. When he returned to the cot, she was waiting for him, sitting with her back against the wall and her arms wrapped around drawn-up knees.

It was incredible what good food, water, and cleanliness could do to strengthen one's mind and spirit. She almost regretted what she was going to do next.

As he sat beside her, she asked, "Are you Modred?"

Chapter Seven

THE AIR BECAME charged and volcanic, and as she listened to his breathing change she tensed.

But whatever she had been expecting, it wasn't what came next. Instead of either confirming or exploding in denial, he remained silent for several moments.

Then in a measured tone, he asked, "What if I was?"

She listened intently for any nuance, anything that might give her a hint of how he was reacting, but the only impression she gained from his murmured whisper was one of immense self-control. He was determined to give her no information whatsoever, yet still, despite the paranoid thoughts and questions that had plagued her throughout the day, conviction settled into her bones.

"It doesn't matter," she told him. "Because you're not him."

"How do you know?" Genuine curiosity tinged his question.

She groped for the right words. "Modred is…

charming, until he is not. He has a certain way of speaking. I don't know quite how to put it. Maybe it's ironic? It's an affectation you don't have. He has a light, almost affectionate attitude that disguises something much darker underneath. You're not nearly so light, or you haven't been with me. Modred is the one who carried out Isabeau's order. He broke my hands." A shudder ran through her. Her body would recognize Modred's touch. She knew it would. "You didn't do that to me. I would bet my life on you and him being two vastly different individuals."

Again he surprised her, as he neither confirmed nor denied what she said. Instead, he told her soberly, "Sidonie, you must stop asking these kinds of questions."

She uncurled and swiveled to face him, or at least face in the direction of where he sat beside her. "Why?"

His hand came down on one of her knees, long fingers tightening. She had gotten so used to him touching her in the dark, she didn't flinch at the contact. "Because they're not only dangerous for you. They're dangerous for me. You know too much already."

She snorted in derision. She didn't know anything. If she had bothered to take any time to read about the Elder Races demesnes before her world tour had reached Great Britain, she might have been able to puzzle out his identity. The way Robin had spoken about him indicated he was important somehow, and deadly. Her own ignorance and disinterest had trapped her in this situation as much as anything else had.

He muttered, "I wish I could take back the things we said to each other last night. If I'd not been so depleted after your healing, I would have thrown a spell of forgetfulness over you. Now it's too late. The experience has settled too firmly into your mind."

She flinched and pulled her knee away from his grasp. "Obviously I can't stop you from doing something like that, but if I ever discover you've used magic on me without my permission again, I'll do everything I can to find a way to hurt you back. Because that's what you're doing when you spell someone without their consent. You're hurting them. There's a reason why it's illegal in virtually every country on Earth. It's a rape of someone's will."

The volcanic charge was back in the air, threading the darkness with a sense of imminent danger. When he replied, his whisper was as forceful and edged as hers had been. "I know all too well what a rape of the will magic can be to those who don't consent to it. Nevertheless, if I could have done it last night, I would have, since causing you to forget might have meant saving your life. I'm trying to protect you by not telling you who I am. You have an inkling of what Isabeau might do if she's angered or crossed."

Yes, she did. Huddling away from him, she wrapped her arms around herself. After a moment, she said with dogged determination, "You said you can't help me escape. Can't, not won't."

"Sidonie," he said in warning.

She plowed on. "Does that mean you're too scared to do any more than what you've already done? You're afraid you might be punished?"

Even as she asked, the questions didn't ring true. If he was so afraid of being punished, he would never have helped her in the first place.

But she had to try to figure this out. She had to get a better understanding of what was really going on around her if she was going to have any hope of getting out of here. Besides, not knowing anything was driving her crazy.

This time when he said her name, it was through gritted teeth. "Sidonie!"

Blindly she reached out. Her fingers caught on the folds of his shirt as it pulled tight across his chest. She fisted both hands in the material.

"*Can't*, you said," she pressed. "Not *won't*. You said you were constrained. What does that mean?"

She felt the tension thrumming through his long body. "I am. Unable. To tell you."

Again, her hearing was all she had to rely on, and his voice hitched on the words in a way they never had before.

Unable. Can't. Not won't. Constrained.

Those were all his words, not hers.

And also, there had been this:

I know all too well what a rape of the will magic can be to those who don't consent to it.

She whispered, "Are you under some kind of magic compulsion?"

His hands circled her wrists in a bruising hold, but he didn't answer.

He didn't deny it either.

Her heart pounded. Licking her lips, she asked, "Are you forbidden to talk about it?"

His fingers tightened painfully. Then he seemed to realize what he was doing, because his grip relaxed. But he didn't deny it. His pulse drummed against her fingertips. His heart was pounding hard.

"And you're forbidden to help any prisoners escape," she said.

Again his hands tightened on her wrists, then loosened. Without using words, it was still unmistakably an affirmative.

She let go of his shirt and smoothed the material over his chest. "All right," she whispered. "I think I'm beginning to get it. If they find out you've been helping me, they might order you to stop. And you would have to stop, wouldn't you? You wouldn't have any choice."

"Think further," he replied softly. "If I'm ordered to hurt or kill you, I will. They must never know who helped you. Do you understand? They must never discover our connection. If you're questioned, do everything you can to keep from giving them any information. Don't lie—that would be the worst thing you could do—and you would have to tell them something, but think of ways to misdirect them. Practice those answers until they come out naturally and easily. Create your own version of truth, and *stop trying to discover who I am.*"

Her heart was hammering as hard as his. She swallowed and managed to reply, "Understood. It took me a while, but I get it now."

His chest moved under her hands as he took a deep breath. "I've got to leave. I got here late, and I've stayed as long as I can."

Her heart sank. Despite her doubts and fears, his presence was so vivid and comforting he pushed back the cold darkness while he was here. She could even feel his body warmth as they sat beside each other on the cot. The thought of him leaving again was almost unbearable.

In an attempt at lightness, she asked, "You sure you can't accidentally leave the door unlocked when you go?"

That came out a lot more taut and desperate than she had meant for it to.

He cupped the side of her head. His touch was warm and gentle. "Believe me, if I could, I would."

A tear slipped down her cheek. Biting her lip, she was grateful for the concealment of the darkness as she swiped it away. "Eh, well, had to ask."

He stroked her hair once, a light, passing caress, and then he gathered up the canvas bag at their feet and stood.

Slipping off the cot as well, she followed him to the door. When he paused, she stumbled into him. As she felt him turn to face her, she stepped forward deliberately to wrap her arms around his waist.

She whispered, "I appreciate everything you've done, so very much. I especially appreciate that you've done it despite the danger to you."

His body went rigid as she hugged him. Then, slowly, his arms came around her. As they tightened, she let her head rest against him for a moment.

She had already known he was bigger than she, but that was no surprise since most men were. Now, coming flush against him, she got a real sense of the size and breadth of his long body. He was tall and powerfully built. The chest under her cheek was broad and thick with muscle, and so were his biceps. Her head fit neatly underneath his chin.

A weight came down on her. She thought it must be his cheek.

"You're welcome, Sidonie. After the guard brings your breakfast, try to get some sleep. I'll be back as soon as I can after the evening round."

As she gave him a quick squeeze, she felt an odd thickness underneath his shirt near his waist and ran her fingers lightly over it. It felt like a bandage, as if he had taped his ribs. She thought back to how she had struck him, and his response.

He had said he wasn't well. It appeared he was

injured in some way, and she had struck him there, twice. She felt a brief remorse then shoved it aside. At the time, she had believed she was fighting in self-defense.

Stepping back, she whispered, "See you tonight. Be careful."

"Always." He slipped out the door.

As she heard a small mechanical snick when he turned the lock, she put her hands on the door.

He might be forbidden to help any prisoners escape, but that didn't mean she couldn't escape on her own. If only she had some way to block the bolt from sliding into the hole in the frame when he locked the cell door.

If she was very quick, maybe she could slip something into the hole when he was coming or leaving. A big wad of chewing gum might do it, except she didn't have any gum. All she had was the food he had left with her and the clothes she was wearing. And her shoes.

There would be seeds when she ate the cherries, but that seemed iffy. She could try shoving cherry seeds into the hole, but she would have to act very fast and they would probably fall out again.

There were also the rubber soles on her tennis shoes, but the shoes were constructed to carry her weight over almost any terrain for months, if not years. She had nothing with which to cut the rubber, and she doubted she could chew her way through a piece, even through the thinner section at the edge of her toes.

She could try knocking him out. She winced from that. It felt disloyal, especially as he had healed her and brought her food and water at some risk to himself. He was doing so much for her, and here she was contemplating an act of violence against him.

Then, deliberately, she pushed through the discomfort to really consider it. Yes, he was helping her as much as he was able. Yes, she would regret hurting him. But she needed to think of ways to save her own life, because despite his help, sooner or later, she was going to die down here in the dark if she didn't find a way out. She didn't have any doubt of that.

After pushing through the emotions, she turned analytical. Could she do it? Could she knock him out?

After her first stalker, she had taken self-defense classes at Vince's urging and discovered she liked tae kwon do. The moves were suited to her slender body structure. Because of her long habit of running, she had built up enough power to get a decent height in the leaps. She was good at the leg work and spinning kicks, and it might be the one skill she had that could be useful while she was trapped here in Avalon.

But she had only practiced tae kwon do in a studio. She'd never needed to use it in real life. She was critically hampered by her lack of sight, whereas her benefactor was tall, powerfully muscled, and could see better than she could in the dark.

Also, while he was being as kind to her as he could

with whatever constraints he was under, her kidnapper Robin had considered him deadly. Since she considered Robin deadly, that gave her serious pause.

No, trying to take down her benefactor in the dark was akin to considering how to attack an armed soldier in the wagon train... all but suicidal. If she attacked him and wasn't successful, she risked alienating virtually the only ally she had.

And even if she could manage to figure out a way to block the door lock, or knock him out and escape, what then? She couldn't see a damn thing.

He had never used a torch when he came. The light would give him away instantly. He slipped in and out, as stealthy and quiet as a thief. If she got out of her cell, she wouldn't be able to follow him when he left. She couldn't see a damn thing, and she couldn't track him by scent like some Elder Races creatures could.

She had no idea of the layout of the prison tunnels or where the guards' station was. More than likely, she would simply get herself caught again while stumbling around in the dark, and they might break her hands all over again.

Drumming her fingers on the door, she thought, no, I'm not going to be able to escape like that. And clearly, whoever he is, he won't be able to help me.

Determination hardened into a burning knot in her chest.

I'll have to find some other way to get out.

One way or another, I'm not just going to survive.

I'm going to thrive.

✧   ✧   ✧

THIS TIME AS Morgan slid out of the underground passageway, it was predawn. The open areas he had to traverse were still dark, and other than the night guard, there was a stronger likelihood no one else was awake and about.

He also had enough energy to cast a strong cloaking spell over himself, so he strode with some confidence to the small gate he had fashioned centuries ago in a remote corner of the castle wall.

Like the entrance to the tunnel that led underground, he kept the gate shrouded in subtle spells that urged the eye to travel over the area to something else more interesting.

Once he passed through the gate, it was a mile-long walk to reach the small one-room cottage hidden in a deep tangle of bramble bushes high in the hills in the unkempt area above the sprawling castle and town. Normally the walk was an easy one along a steep, narrow path, but at the moment, the wound in his side didn't make it easy to climb.

More spells of obfuscation draped the cottage like a thick layer of invisible spiderwebs. He had built the cottage himself, a very long time ago, and nobody had ever discovered it.

Isabeau knew he was a master at cloaking skills. She had commanded him to cloak the crossover passageways to Lyonesse to imprison Oberon's Dark Court and the ones to Avalon for defense. But for all that, her utter self-absorption left her curiously myopic at times.

She was cunning and unbalanced, which made her dangerous, but she also lacked a certain depth of insight for anything that might not pertain to her. She had never once considered ordering him to reveal what things he might have cloaked from her.

At least not yet.

Inside the cottage, he started a fire in the fireplace and placed a pot of water on an iron rod over the growing flames. While he waited for the water to boil, he ate.

He had saved the other half of the chicken, along with fruit, bread, and some of the soft cheese for himself. Once the empty knot in his stomach had eased, the water in the stewpot had reached the boiling point.

Wrapping a cloth around the handle, he carried it to the small table. Then he shrugged out of his shirt, unwrapped the bandages at his waist, and checked the area underneath.

The skin around the wound was a mess of puckered scar tissue that had turned livid red. Dark streaks radiated out from the sutured entry point. Fingering one of the streaks, he frowned. Usually when skin blackened around a wound, it meant the flesh had turned necrotic. At that point, the only way to help the wound heal was to debride it, or remove the dead flesh.

But he didn't sense any dying skin. He had kept the new wound scrupulously clean from the very beginning, even down to sterilizing the silver knife before the ghoul had stabbed him, and he was taking antibiotics strong enough to heal a horse.

No, this wasn't a normal bacterial infection. This had something to do with the silver in his system. The only way to heal that was to tough it out. It might take him longer to recover the second time around, but eventually his body would throw off the effects of the silver poison.

At least it would this time.

If he kept reinjuring himself and never gave his body a chance to fully heal, he would never throw off the silver poisoning. Next time he wouldn't heal as quickly or as well, and he would be slower still to recover the time after that.

His magic would be slower and slower to return. Eventually, it might never return to its full strength.

Releasing his breath in a long sigh, he faced the truth. This was only a temporary reprieve. Sooner or later, he would have to make a choice—either succumb once again to Isabeau's geas, or let the silver poisoning take him.

He had to find his way to freedom before that happened.

Getting down to business, he cleaned and dressed the wound, then bandaged his ribs again and swallowed pain pills and antibiotics. With food, water, medical care, and shelter, he'd met his needs for survival.

He had brought the books he had gathered for research. They sat in a pile on the table, waiting for his attention, but they would have to wait another day or two. Stretching out on the bed located in one corner, he let himself relax. Like the rest of the cottage, the mattress was musty and needed to be taken outside and beaten, but that too could wait.

For the first time since the ghoul had stabbed him, he could rest for an entire day. Tonight, he would slip back to the night market to get more food, and he would go to Sidonie again. He could heal and feed her, and he could even offer any comfort she might be willing to accept, but there weren't any long-term solutions for her in that either.

But if he could win enough freedom for himself from the geas, perhaps he could find a way around Isabeau's orders enough to free Sidonie too.

Sometime over the past few days, his point of focus had shifted, and it was time to acknowledge that. Instead of fighting against the urge to help her, now he wanted to. He even needed to.

When he had discovered her in the prison cell, her utter devastation had shot past all his barriers. The spirit that carried such joyous, bright creative energy had been crushed. After he had spelled her unconscious, he had sat with her broken hands in his lap and absorbed the enormity of what had happened, the wisdom in Isabeau's cruelty, the profound depth of Sidonie's pain.

He would not abandon his quest. He couldn't. But now, taking his revenge against Isabeau and Modred was no longer enough. Destroying them for the sake of all the people Isabeau and Modred had killed so long ago was no longer enough.

Now he had to fight for Sidonie's sake.

The drugs kicked in, and he closed his eyes. As the narcotics opened doorways in his mind that were better left closed, he spent the heat of the day restlessly twisting in slumber as he dreamed of people and events long past.

Kill them.

Kill them before they destroy your king and everything you love.

Kill them before they destroy Sidonie for good.

THE REFRESHING COOL of the evening air woke him.

Rising stiffly off the dusty bed, he fueled his body with food, water, and more pills. This time he only took the antibiotics. At this point, coping with the discomfort was better than enduring the narcotic-laced dreams.

Drawing more water from the well outside, he washed, dressed, doused himself with the hunter's spray to disguise his scent, and headed down to the city below to steal clean clothes for himself and enough food for both him and Sidonie.

He didn't like taking from the hardworking merchants, and he had plenty of money, but he was also
too well-known. He didn't know what orders might
have been sent down to the city, and he couldn't risk
running into any castle guards or possibly running into
Hounds.

So theft it was.

As always, the night market was crowded. Torches
and lanterns provided plenty of golden light that threw
deep shadows and was a pickpocket's delight. The
aroma of food, spices, and fragrant oils mingled with
the scents of overwarm Light Fae bodies, along with
the occasional human, ogre, Hound, and sprite.

After having lived so long as a lycanthrope, he had
gotten used to the assault such places were to his
sensitive nose and had learned how to identify and
filter through the mélange of hundreds of scents
without giving it much conscious thought.

But then he caught a hint of something that made
him pause.

That scent.

That shouldn't be here. Not down in the night
market.

Just as it had in London, he could feel the magic
that bound him shifting uneasily again as the various
orders Isabeau had given him clashed. Familiar with the
strain, he stiffened and waited to see which one would
gain supremacy.

When the geas settled again, he relaxed as his

imperative remained clear. Isabeau's last order was still the strongest. He did not have to obey any earlier orders.

He tried to follow the scent back to its source, which proved elusive. Either the source had left some time ago, or it was remarkably wily and knew how to dodge Morgan when he was on the hunt, even cloaked as he was.

After a short while, he abandoned the effort. Every moment he spent at the market was a calculated risk. Once he had gathered everything he needed, he made his way back to the cottage to pack the canvas bag, leave the clean clothes for himself, use more of the scent-masking hunter's spray, and fill the water flasks. Then he walked down to slip through the gate in the castle wall and into his tunnel.

Sidonie was waiting by the cell door when he arrived. As he picked the lock and eased inside, she rushed to him, touching his cheek, his shoulder, and the front of his shirt in rapid, agitated movements.

She told him in an explosive whisper, "I don't know how you kept yourself sane down here for a whole year. I'm going crazy!"

One corner of his mouth lifted. The feeling of pleasure as she touched him seemed incongruous with their surroundings, and inappropriate, but he had no intention of squashing it.

"I never claimed to be sane," he told her drily.

Her snort was adorable. "You're a lot more sane

right now than I am. I can't stop imagining all kinds of monsters locked up in the cells. There's something down here that won't stop sobbing, and I keep hearing rats." She turned her head as if to listen. "I think you scare them away. I never hear them when you're here."

He was the worst, most dangerous monster she could ever face down here in the dark, but he didn't tell her that.

Instead, he captured one of her hands to press her fingers against his mouth. They were long and slender, those clever, strong fingers of hers, and callused in places. He liked that, liked the evidence of how hard she worked at her craft.

As his lips touched her skin, she froze.

He froze too, listening as her breath hitched, and that was when his conscience caught up with him.

What was he doing? She was a prisoner in this ugly place, and he was her only lifeline. The balance of power between them was wildly skewed. He had no business indulging in such gestures. She would most likely feel she had no choice but accept them or risk angering him so he didn't return.

His hold loosened, and her hand slipped away.

"I survived because I didn't have any other choice," he told her, turning toward the cot. "You'll survive too, for the same reason."

Sitting, he opened the canvas bag and pulled out a flask. As she sat beside him, he nudged her hand with it. "Water first."

She didn't argue. Opening the flask, she drank until she drained it. Heaving a sigh, she capped the flask and handed it back to him. "Having the fruit during the daytime helps, but I'm not used to going so long without access to water," she said. "Especially after I exercise."

He nodded in approval. Excellent. She wasn't giving in to despair. "I exercised every day I was down here too."

"This time I got smart about it," she told him. "I slept for the first part of the day and waited until this evening to jog my five thousand, one hundred steps."

He cocked his head. "Why five thousand, one hundred steps? Why not just five thousand?"

"According to my running stride, five thousand and one hundred steps is three miles," she told him drily. "And God forbid that I do anything else, like five thousand and ninety-nine. Jogging in the evening, I had less time to wait for the water."

"Good thinking." He smiled.

Despite her musical brilliance, in many ways she was just a normal human. She was completely out of her depth here, like any normal human would be, but she was still using her mind, still thinking of ways to make the precarious situation work for her. She was stronger than she thought, and smarter than she realized.

This time, too, she was not quite as desperate for food, and she chose to clean up first. He hadn't wanted her to feel uncomfortable about undressing in front of someone she didn't know, so while he hadn't exactly lied to her—not exactly—he could see rather more in the dark than he had led her to think.

Leaning back against the cool stone wall, he enjoyed watching the play of shadow on shadow, which suggested rather than revealed her lithe, slim form. He was walking a fine line between baser instincts and his better self. If he had been able to see anything more, he would have been forced by his own conscience to either warn her or look away.

When she had finished, she sat cross-legged beside him on the cot. Then he pulled out the foods he had brought—meat and potato pies, more fruit, boiled eggs, and a plain baked potato to leave with her, and sticky pieces of maple-pecan candy.

"I haven't eaten supper yet," he told her. "I hope you don't mind if I join you."

Her voice warmed. "No, of course not."

For a while they ate in silence, and he focused on enjoying the food. There were plenty of pies to satisfy even his appetite, and they were still slightly warm from the oven. The outside crust was buttery and flaky, while inside, a filling of rich, fragrant gravy coated the meat and potatoes.

Odd, he thought. Despite the fact they were each in a terrible situation, Sidonie caught in her trap and he in his, as they sat together and shared a meal, the silence was almost companionable. Enjoyable.

He didn't have friends anymore. All his friends were long dead. Mostly now he had a smorgasbord of enemies, from those in the Light Court who looked on him in fear, to Isabeau and Modred themselves, whom he loathed with an undying passion.

Then there were the members of Oberon's Dark Court, who all hated and feared him, and with good reason, and a smattering of unfortunate people all over the world who had learned, through him, what it meant to get on Isabeau's bad side.

A couple of Isabeau's Hounds had been decent men before she had ordered him to change them as she had taken and changed Morgan. But more often than not, her Hounds had been bad men and mean fighters, and turning them into lycanthropes had exacerbated both qualities.

As their captain, Morgan often had to command through force. It was his responsibility to make sure they obeyed orders, and he'd had to put Hounds down when they refused to learn how to control their beasts. The dynamic didn't make for cozy relationships.

He had gone without for so long, he had forgotten some time ago to notice his lack of friends until this very moment. Carefully he brushed the crumbs off his fingers after finishing his last pie.

"Thank you," she whispered.

He sighed. "It's my pleasure. You don't have to thank me after every meal, Sidonie."

"You can call me Sid. Most people do."

Sid. He liked that. It was quirky. He liked her full name too. It sounded like her, feminine and elegant.

When he nudged her to take a candy, she did and popped it in her mouth. After a moment, she stirred. "You still haven't told me why you're helping me."

He didn't take a candy. Instead, he whispered levelly, "Remember what I did tell you."

She gestured impatiently. "Yes, I know. It's too dangerous for you to tell me anything. I'm not supposed to know who you are. Only I don't buy it."

He murmured, "I was just thinking how smart you were. Don't prove me wrong."

Her shadowed face lifted to his. "I'm not asking you to tell me your identity. I'm asking you for something more personal than a label or a name. I'm just asking why. Why are you helping me? Being down here has got to bring back bad memories for you. You could be anywhere else right now. Why are you here, sitting and eating with me in this awful place?"

Chapter Eight

I T WAS A fair question, but he didn't want to answer it.

The other alternative was to leave, yet he found himself reluctant to go. That would leave her alone for almost an entire day, and he hated the idea of her sitting alone in this cell. Propping his elbow on an upraised knee, he rubbed his forehead as he grappled with unruly emotions.

"You shouldn't be here," he said, very low. "You shouldn't know anything about Avalon, you shouldn't be imprisoned, and you should never have been tortured. You should never have met Modred or Isabeau, or me either, for that matter. You should be free, living a totally oblivious life. Playing your music, falling in love with someone clever, kind, and educated, sightseeing all the beauty in the world. Your music is passionate and wildly brilliant. It's some of the best I've heard in generations. Everything about you shines with bright colors, and yet look where you are right now. It is an abomination."

As he spoke her hand stole onto his knee.

At her touch, the words backed up in his throat, and it took him a moment before he could speak again, through clenched teeth. "Your presence here offends me. It goes against everything inside me to have to walk away every time I leave and to know I'm leaving you behind. To know I can't do anything to break you free from this. Robin did his work all too well."

"What did you do to him?"

The breath left him in an angry exhalation. Bitterness laced his reply. "I did everything I was ordered to do."

"Everything," she repeated blankly. Then, in the barest thread of sound, she asked, "Did you torture him?"

She asked like she was afraid to hear the answer, yet all the while her hand never moved from his knee. He forced himself to breathe evenly, although it was a heavy, audible sound.

"No," he answered. "My services were required elsewhere. But I was the one to capture him, and I would have tortured him, if I had been ordered to. If Isabeau ordered me to service her in her bed, I would obey—and never mind that the very sight of her makes me nauseated with rage."

Her fingers tightened until he could feel each separate one, digging into his skin. She breathed, "That's horrible. The thought never occurred to me."

"Thankfully, the thought has never occurred to her either." He wiped his mouth, trying to get the idea out of his mind. "Or if it has, she would never act on it. She's too bigoted. Bedding me would be akin to bestiality to her. She'd as soon have sex with one of her dogs, and while she has her own aberrant behaviors, she's not prey to that particular perversion. Also, if she tried something like that, I might have to obey, but she knows I would find a way to retaliate. The problem with a geas of control is you can never quite issue enough orders to cover every eventuality that may arise." A dark note entered his voice. "She's learned that lesson the hard way a couple of times."

She whispered, "'He who rides a tiger is afraid to dismount.'"

Curiosity stirred. "Where did you hear that?"

"It's an old Chinese proverb. Nowadays, people say somebody has grabbed a tiger by the tail as a way to describe a difficult or dangerous situation. It sounds like Isabeau has got you by the tail and doesn't dare let go." Although he knew she couldn't see him, she twisted to sit facing him. "Have you noticed something? Even though you weren't able to tell me about the compulsion, once I guessed, you've been able to talk about it."

"The geas is like that," he replied. "Sometimes I can find my way around orders to certain freedoms. I've been expressly forbidden to help prisoners escape, but that doesn't mean I can't aid them from time to time, like I am with you. I've been ordered to never tell anyone I'm acting under a geas, but you and I can discuss a fact you already know. If she had ordered me to never talk about the geas with anyone, I would be mute right now. One of her greatest flaws is her own carelessness. I hope it will be her downfall one day."

"Specifics matter," she whispered. "How you phrase things, what elements you choose to put in a spell or a bargain, or what you choose to leave out. I don't know anything else about magic, but dealing with the Djinn has taught me that much. When the first Djinn approached and wanted to bargain to attend one of my concerts, I consulted with a negotiating expert before striking a deal. I learned a lot from her."

Despite the heavy topic, he found himself smiling again. "That was smart."

"Now several Djinn owe me favors." She emitted a ghost of a laugh. "I keep them as my safety net. The funny thing is, they could have just taken physical form and bought a concert ticket like everyone else."

He chuckled silently. "I remember when a few of the Djinn bargained with me to listen to my music. Gods, I haven't thought of that in ages. It happened so long ago. One of them told me they experience music in an entirely different way when they're bodiless in their natural form. The vibration of the sound suffuses them entirely. They have a way of appreciating music that's completely alien to us. I doubt a single Djinn would consider attending a concert in an embodied form. That would be like trying to listen to music with earplugs, or appreciate a work of art while wearing a blindfold. It's simply unthinkable if you have the alternative."

He had lost himself so deeply in reverie, her surprise came like a dash of cold water to the face. She exclaimed, "You never said you were a musician! What do you play?"

His pleasure faded. "I'm not, at least not anymore. I haven't played anything in centuries."

"That would kill me." Her whisper shook. "*They* killed me when they broke my hands. I can't live without my music."

He put his hand over both of hers as she twisted them together in her lap. "You are stronger than you give yourself credit for. You have no idea what you can survive until you're pushed to find out."

Underneath his palm, her clenched hands opened, unfurling like a flower. She cupped his hand between hers, and in a gesture that shocked him to the core, she slid to his side and put her head on his shoulder. "I really can't trust you, can I?"

He let the sadness in that whisper sink in, breathing through the pain like he had breathed through every other pain he had experienced in his very long life.

He could have told her that she could trust him to do everything he could to fight the geas, to work his way around direct orders, to do for her whatever was in his power to do, and in a way, all that would have been true.

But fostering false hopes would not serve her any

good purpose. Putting an arm around her, he drew her close.

"No," he said gently. "You really can't."

WHAT ON EARTH was she doing?

Why was she cuddling up to a man who had just admitted she couldn't trust him?

A man who had alluded to the fact that he could be ordered to do monstrous things—and no doubt had done them in the past?

He could be ordered to torture her, to kill her, and he would do it. All of it.

What kind of magic had such a terrible hold over him?

"I don't know how you're still breathing." The words slipped out of her as she tried to imagine what his life must be like.

"I'm still breathing, because I was ordered to." A dark, sardonic note entered his whisper. "And I happen to be extremely hard to kill, so no one has managed that feat yet."

She sank into the horror of imagining his suicidal despair while being forbidden to act on it, a right that was so basic she had never thought to question it before. His life was literally no longer his own.

That kind of shackle could crush the music out of a man. It should have crushed all decency, moral code, and sense of compassion as well, but somehow he had managed to hold on to those things, and he acted on them, at least as much as he was able.

Nestling against him, she turned her face into his shirt. "I'm so sorry for what happened to you."

Something dropped briefly onto her forehead. Had he just kissed her?

While she felt like screaming on his behalf, he sounded perfectly composed. "Instead of being sorry, what you should be is wary."

The full import of that was beginning to settle in. It clashed with all her sensory impressions.

The heavy weight of his arm circling her shoulders was a shocking comfort. After being chilled for most of her time in this cell, he radiated heat that suffused her with a sense of well-being. She reveled in the simple, animal pleasure of feeling his muscled body against hers, the hard pillow of his shoulder underneath her cheek.

She didn't know his name, or what he looked like. She hardly knew anything about him that wasn't self-report, except that Robin thought he was terribly dangerous.

He had gone out of his way to warn her, himself, but he had also healed her. He brought food and water, and kept his word as much as he was able, and even more importantly than all that, he offered her hope and encouragement at a point when she had been so devastated she couldn't even bring herself to get up off the floor.

No matter what he had done—or had been forced to do—those were not the actions of an evil man. And while she might not be able to trust him, her life had been shattered so thoroughly she was learning to grab on to any piece of something that felt good, no matter how small or fleeting.

This moment of feeling warm with her belly full, whispering confidences to someone who didn't judge her, leaning against a strong body that seemed to welcome her presence—this moment was so good it bordered on the miraculous. She concentrated fiercely on soaking in every impression to shore up the time when she was alone and cold again.

But if she was going to have any future at all, it was also time to start laying plans.

She whispered, "Tell me more about Isabeau."

He stirred, his restless body signaling clearly the distaste he had for the subject, but he also answered. "Modern psychologists would probably call her a narcissist. Every thought she thinks, every move she makes, is all about herself. She will lie, manipulate, steal, kill, do whatever it takes to get what she wants. If you are on her good side, she's all sweetness and smiles. If you get on her bad side... Well, you know something of what can happen if you get on her bad side."

"Yeah." She rubbed her eyes. "It must be terrible to deal with her."

"I'm often away, carrying out her orders, which

provides some relief. Long ago, she embarked on a crusade to destroy another demesne with crossover passageways near Avalon's—that of Oberon and his Dark Court."

"What kind of Elder Race are they?"

"Officially they're labeled Dark Fae, which is why Oberon's court is the Dark Court as opposed to Isabeau's Light Court. But the reality is, Lyonesse is a society made of mixed races. They offend Isabeau's racist and xenophobic tendencies."

"I'm half Vietnamese," she muttered, repelled by the very concept. "So I must really get up her nose."

He tightened his arm around her shoulders. "She has no idea what a Vietnamese is. You offend her because you're a dark-haired human, and she believes the Light Fae are the superior race. And while she must hate to admit it since you're clearly of an inferior race and your looks are so different from those of the Light Fae, you're also breathtakingly beautiful, and she's always jealous of other beauties."

Well.

Well now, wasn't that something.

He thought she was breathtakingly beautiful, did he?

Sid felt her cheeks warm with pleasure and was glad for the darkness that hid her blush.

Before she could figure out how to respond, he continued, "She—*we*—drove Oberon's people out of Great Britain and imprisoned them in their own lands, or so we thought. There were only a few knights of the Dark Court left in England, until they found some way to reopen one of the passageways to reach their demesne and bring back reinforcements. All summer they've been strengthening and reinforcing their presence along the Welsh Marches in England. It's been a huge setback for Isabeau, and her moods have become more dangerous and volatile than ever."

As he talked, he wound a strand of her hair around his finger. The sensation from the small gesture rippled gently through her body. Surreptitiously she rubbed her cheek against the softness of his shirt, enjoying the feel of the thick, broad muscle underneath.

She was… she was…

She must be really messed up, because she was attracted to him.

She didn't even know what his voice sounded like, not really. The only clue she could gather was that the low, rich timbre in his whisper indicated it would be deep.

And his scent was… odd. Slightly chemical, but that might be from medicine used to treat whatever injury the bandages were needed for. Come to think of it, the only thing she could really smell was a touch of fresh air on his shirt, as if it had been hung out to dry in the sunshine, along with the lingering aroma from the meat pies they had just eaten.

What if she asked to run her fingers over his face, so she could get an idea of what he looked like? She almost asked, until she realized that knowing some details might give her clues to his identity, and she knew instinctively he would reject that possibility.

Besides, none of that was going to get her out of this cell.

Yanking her unruly thoughts back into line, she asked, "How does Modred fit into all this?"

His chest moved in a silent snort. "Modred is just like Isabeau, a complete opportunist focused on his own gain. They are in a relationship, of sorts. If you can call it relating. They're not faithful, but they pretend to be, and they often partner in mischief together."

"Modred is the one who found me shackled in the stable," she whispered, clenching her hand in his shirt at the memory. "I'd been chained with the rest of the trolls' tribute, and then they forgot about me until the next day. When he took me to the castle, I thought at first he was going to help me—feed me something, let me wash up, or take me to someone who would listen to my story so I could make a case for going home."

"It was a perfectly reasonable expectation." His voice was clipped, angry. "It's also what any decent man would have done."

She broke into a light sweat as she thought about it, and a tremor ran through her muscles. "Instead, he took me straight to Isabeau. I didn't know who she was at first, although the richness of her dress and her surroundings should have given me a clue. Looking back, there were all kinds of warning signs, but I didn't pay attention to any of them. She'd even said she'd had a bad morning, and she had a headache… but then so had I. I was dizzy with hunger, scared, and exhausted, and I'd been in a state of perpetual outrage for days. She called me ugly and bad mannered, and she fingered my hair like I was a dog or a horse. After having been kidnapped, spending several days on the road, and being treated like chattel, I lost my temper. And you know the rest."

His arm tightened around her. Cupping the nape of her neck, he pressed his lips to her forehead and held the position for a long moment before he relaxed. When he spoke, his murmur sounded pragmatic. "Modred did that on purpose."

She lifted her head. "What do you mean?"

"There were even more clues in what you told me, if you knew how to look for them. You said yourself that you were exhausted, hungry, and it sounds like you were at the end of your rope."

She sighed. "I was dirty too, and I smelled like a barnyard."

"What he did was wildly inappropriate," he told her. "One should never go into an audience with the Queen like that, unless there's some overriding reason or dire emergency. Recently I had to meet with her in just such a state, and she was quite displeased… until I reminded her I was there because of her orders, and she had left me no other choice. You said she was having a bad morning and had a headache?"

"Yes."

"Modred watches her moods with the same kind of intensity that a fisherman watches the sea. He would have known she was having a bad morning. When he took you to her, there was no way he could lose. Isabeau loves music, so if, despite everything, she took to you, he gained credit for pleasing her out of her bad mood. If things didn't go well, then he had given her someone to take her ill temper out on. It never matters to him who becomes the brunt of Isabeau's temper as long as it isn't him."

"Which was exactly what happened." Her hands curled into fists. She would give a lot for the opportunity to plant a first in Modred's handsome, smiling face.

"Yes. Isabeau might be manipulative, but she's also prey to manipulation, if you know how to handle her, and Modred has been handling her for a very long time." He shifted position and eased away from her. "I should leave."

She scowled. They had taken their time eating, but surely they hadn't talked the night away. And anyway, how could he tell what time it was down here? "If you must."

"I don't want to, but there's something I need to do while it's still dark," he whispered. When he stood, she did as well. "Here, drink as much as you can before I go."

Reluctantly, she accepted the flask and drank until she thought she would burst. When she handed it back to him, he tucked it into the canvas bag.

Following him to the cell door, she touched his shoulder. When he turned, she walked forward deliberately to hug him again.

As his arms came around her, she said haltingly, "Don't scold me for saying this, but thank you again for everything. And be careful, will you? I can tell you have a bandage around your ribs, and I worry about you when you leave."

His arms tightened. "There's nothing wrong with my ribs that won't heal. Don't worry about me. I'll be back again this evening."

With any luck, this evening she wouldn't be here to greet him, but she didn't tell him that.

Because she couldn't trust him, after all.

After he slipped away, Sid listened for the bolt sliding into place. Once the sound confirmed he was truly gone, she turned to pace around the confines of her cell, one hand outstretched and the tips of her fingers touching lightly against the wall to keep her from running into it.

Practice your truth, he had said. Practice until you believe it.

So she began to tell a story to herself.

Not a story of what had actually happened, but a story of what she wanted the truth to be. What she needed the truth to be, in order to get out of this cell and back into the sunlight. She whispered it to herself over and over again, pacing and repeating until she had it thoroughly memorized.

She had enjoyed Juilliard. While most of her time had been focused on her obsession with music, she had played with some of her electives and had taken a few acting classes. The classes helped her to find a way to bridge some of the social isolation she had grown up with.

Acting on the stage or in front of a camera was not the same as acting to save one's life, but if it was one thing she knew something about, it was how to face the pressure to perform, and how to hide her fear in front of a sometimes pitiless audience.

After she had memorized her story the way she wanted to tell it, she sat cross-legged facing one wall and ruined the zipper of her hoodie by running the metal teeth against the rock until she saw small, fleeting sparks.

Unwilling to miss a single precious flash of color, she didn't blink. Aside from the guard's torch, those sparks were the first thing she had seen in days.

The blackness in her cell started to lighten to gray. Then the reflection of a far-off fire appeared and drew closer. She listened to the squeaking wheels of the cart and the metallic clang as the guard shoved food trays into the cells of other prisoners down the hall.

Cry, she told herself. She bit the insides of her cheeks until she drew blood, and the pain became bad enough to bring tears to her eyes.

Then the guard was at her cell door, squatting to take the empty tray and shoving a full one through the slot. It was always the same guard, a dull-eyed Light Fae male with a scarred face. She had always wondered what he had done to be punished with such duty.

Jumping to her feet, she rushed to the cell door and grasped the bars as she sobbed, "Thank you! Thank you!"

Curling a lip, he sneered, "What nonsense are you spouting?"

"My hands. They're healed!" Shoving her arms through the bars, she held out her hands for his inspection while she bit her cheek harder to make tears run down her face. "Someone came to heal me while I slept. The Queen must have decided to show me mercy after all. Please give me the opportunity to thank her in some way!"

The guard paused, the dullness in his gaze sparking with surprise. Staring at her fingers while she wiggled them, he said slowly, "You think the Queen did this?"

"Well," she replied, "who else would have done it? I don't have any magic. I certainly couldn't have healed myself. If there was only some way I could repay her. I'd be so honored if she would give me another chance to play for her, but even if that isn't possible I just want the chance to apologize."

He laughed, a cynical, grating sound. "As if she would waste any more of her time on the likes of you."

"I know, I know, but... just look at my hands," she said, opening and closing them in front of his face. "Everybody knows how much she loves music. What if she wants to give me a second chance to perform?"

"You're a massive fool if you think that," the guard scoffed.

But his frowning gaze lingered on her hands for a long moment before he pushed the cart away.

After that, there was nothing to do but wait. While she could still see, she dumped the bad food down the privy hole, and after chewing her lip in thought, she dumped her good food too.

The familiar dark gray of the day settled around her. Having lost her night sight, she felt her way back to one wall where she sat cross-legged to run the zipper across the stone and watch the sparks again.

I'm getting out of here, she thought. Maybe things will get better or maybe they'll get really bad again, but one way or another, I'm leaving this particular hell behind.

While she had no ability to tell time, presently the glow of approaching torches lightened her cell again, much too soon for the supper feeding. She listened to the sounds of footsteps as they grew nearer. There were three guards, maybe four.

As they stopped just outside her cell, she wrapped her hoodie around her middle, shaking.

Here we go.

A key grated in the lock, and her cell door was

flung open. While the other guards waited outside, a powerful male strode in, grabbed her by the arm, and hauled her upright.

"On your feet," he commanded. "I have some questions I want to ask you."

It was too late to change her mind now. The pitiless audience had chosen to appear, and now she had to put on the performance of her life.

Chapter Nine

THEY TOOK HER to the same room where they had broken her fingers. Her breath shook as she looked at the grim surroundings. She had to stiffen the muscles in her legs to remain standing.

Bad things happened here. This was where they tortured people and killed them.

The guard who brought the meals was present, but he remained in the background while the powerfully built male who had dragged her out of her cell swung her around to face him.

"Who did this?" he demanded, gripping her by the wrists so he could stare at her hands, which she had clenched into fists.

"I don't know!" she exclaimed, throwing every ounce of passionate conviction she could into her voice. "I was asleep when it happened. When I woke up, my hands were completely healed."

"You were asleep when someone miraculously healed your broken hands," the male said, his tone skeptical while his eyes narrowed. "In an underground prison."

Her gaze darted around. This was a room where they questioned people as they tortured them. Someone had to have truthsense.

"Well, I couldn't have healed myself," she said flatly. "I have no magic. I can't even telepathize. You can ask *him* if you want." With a jerk of her chin, she indicated the mealtime guard. "Didn't I say thank you? I'm a musician. It's the one skill I've got that might interest her majesty. The Queen had to have ordered this, right? Who else could it have been? Like you said, it's an underground prison."

Questions weren't lies. She was banking her future on it. They just helped to support her statements as she was telling them.

When her interrogator's hard gaze lifted to the mealtime guard, he admitted, "That bit's true enough. She kept crying and carrying on, and insisting on the chance to apologize to her majesty and make it up to her."

Her interrogator released his bruising hold on her wrists. "Keep her here while I inform his lordship," he ordered the guards.

As the male strode out, Sid backed against a wooden table so she could lean against it as she massaged her wrists.

After having been in the darkness for so long, her eyesight felt weak and oversensitive. Although most of the illumination in this room came from a fire in an iron grill, everything seemed overbright, and her eyes kept tearing without her having to resort to biting her cheeks. She avoided looking at the three other guards left in the room.

His lordship. Did he mean Modred?

Well, she knew it had to get worse before it could get any better.

If it got better.

She didn't know if she would live to see another evening, and she regretted…

She regretted so many things. She was sorry she never got the chance to have breakfast with Julie in Paris. She wished she could see another sunrise. She regretted not being able to tell Vince what had happened to her, because she knew her disappearance would haunt him.

But she especially regretted not being able to look in her benefactor's eyes as she told him good-bye and thanked him one final time. She wished she'd had that eye-to-eye contact with him, just once.

The wait felt interminable, her patience stretched tight from nerves. This time the sound of approaching footsteps was rapid. The door flew open, and Modred stalked into the room.

He looked the same as he had when she had first met him, a richly dressed, handsome Light Fae male, but now there was nothing pleasant in his hard expression. Striding over, he grabbed one of her wrists and yanked up her hand to stare at it.

She had been correct. Her body knew him, and

every nerve rioted at his touch. Under his piercing gaze, she opened and closed her fingers.

He shook her hand under her nose and hissed, "Who did this?"

"I don't know!" she exclaimed. With a quick yank, she took him by surprise and pulled out of his grasp. Before he could grab her wrist again, she hid her hands defensively in her armpits, her arms wrapped around her torso in a classic defensive gesture. "I never saw who did this or heard their voice. I certainly can't see anything in that cell, and I wasn't awake when it happened." She looked at her first interrogator. "Somebody in this room has got to know I'm telling the truth."

As Modred looked at him too, her first interrogator raised his eyebrows and gave an infinitesimal shrug.

Without taking his eyes off the other man, Modred said over his shoulder, "How many Hounds do we have on the castle grounds?"

"Not many, my lord," the male said from behind him. "Most of them are on the search, on Earth. Perhaps three or four?"

"Get a couple of them down here to see if they can pick up a scent." Modred turned away. He told her first interrogator, "Bring her."

"Yes, my lord."

Oh, yay! They were taking her someplace else. Almost anyplace else would be better than this horrible room saturated with blood and pain. Except for her cell. That wouldn't be better. But from the sound of it, they had another destination in mind.

Don't get your hopes up, she told herself as her first interrogator grabbed her arm and hauled her after Modred, who strode as rapidly down the hall as he had the first time she had met him.

She would have a collection of bruises on her arms from all the manhandling. "I'm cooperating, you know," she told the Light Fae guard. "You don't have to drag me along like this. I can keep up."

He gave her a disdainful frown but released her. "See that you do," he snapped. "Or you'll end up in worse condition than you were in before."

"I'm well aware of that," she muttered through clenched teeth as she yanked her hoodie and worn T-shirt straight again. As bad as her captors were, her worst enemy was her own temper. She mustn't let any of them get to her so badly she forgot her goals, because if she let that happen, she was done for.

Modred led them up the stairs and, just like the first time, through a maze of halls. Enchanted with the dizzying array of colors, textures, sights, and scents, Sid couldn't stop staring around her. After days of sensory deprivation, the rich scenery was almost too much to take in.

He led the way past guards onto a verandah that opened to a walled garden filled with emerald green grass, flowering trees, and climbing roses. Travertine marble provided a cool, elegant floor, while columns of travertine punctuated the space.

Isabeau sat in the shade of an apple tree on the marble border of a large, round pool, throwing scraps of bread into the water while small ripples appeared as fish snatched at the food.

As before, the Queen looked strikingly beautiful, her long golden hair dressed in curls. She wore a light, sleeveless gown of pale blue silk with a plunging neckline. The material was so thin, it outlined the slender legs underneath it.

When the Queen glanced at them, her delicate brows drew together in a frown. She said in an edged voice, "Modred, I thought I told you I wanted the afternoon to myself."

"Of course you did, my love," he told her. "But trust me, you will want to hear this." Turning, he gestured at the Light Fae guard, who reached for her arm again.

But Sid saw him coming and slipped neatly away from his grasp.

Throwing herself forward, she landed on her knees in front of the Light Fae Queen, bowing so deeply her chin almost touched the manicured grass. She focused her gaze on the delicate leather slippers in front of her.

"Your majesty, I apologize from the bottom of my heart," she said. "When I first met you, I had no idea who you were. Nobody told me anything or taught me how to address you properly. Now that I *do* know, I'm embarrassed to be brought into your presence in such a state—filthy, unbathed, and in ragged clothing. This isn't an appropriate way to have an audience with a queen. If it were in my power to choose otherwise, I would have presented myself in a way that showed much more respect for your person."

With her head bowed, she could just see Modred's long legs out of the corner of her eye. As she spoke, he shifted abruptly. The air around her seemed to sharpen, as if filled with invisible knives.

You threw me under the bus the first time, she said silently to Modred. Just watch. I can throw you under a bus too.

Then Isabeau said, her tone light, measured, "Well, it appears at least someone is thinking of the correct protocol. Even if it is only the ugly brown-haired girl."

And you, Sid said to the Queen. If I could chew off your leg and beat you with it, I would. Maybe I'll get the chance one day. Now there's a goal to strive for.

"Trust me, my love. This is too urgent to wait for protocol." Modred's reply sounded edged.

"Was that true the first time you brought her to me?" Isabeau asked.

"I smelled like a barnyard," Sid murmured, ducking her head farther. "I was afraid, and I hadn't eaten properly in days. Not that it's any excuse, but it caused me to lash out. A monarch should be greeted with elegance and diplomacy. Your majesty, please forgive me."

Silence fell over the tableau, heavy with nuances

and the ripe scents of summer. Danger breathed softly along the back of Sid's neck.

Then Isabeau murmured in a guarded tone, "Perhaps I'll consider it. Now, why are you here? Modred, why is she here? Why are *you* here, when I expressly told you I wanted to be alone?"

"Show her, ugly brown-haired girl," Modred said.

Holding up her hands, Sid turned them over and opened and closed her fingers. The silence grew heavier, like the press of a knife to her jugular.

"What is this?" Isabeau asked.

She couldn't answer with anything but questions. "Isn't it mercy?" she asked. "Didn't you order this, yourself? The moment when I awoke to discover my hands were healed was indescribable. Your majesty, I'm so glad to get the chance to apologize."

As she waited, her pulse pounded in her ears. Isabeau said nothing for so long, she plummeted into certainty. They were going to kill her and be done with it. A flash of heat washed over her body, followed by a wave of nausea.

Then she jettisoned past terror to realize Isabeau's extended silence meant she must be telepathizing with someone. Perhaps Modred. Perhaps Sid's interrogator. Isabeau would be demanding an explanation from her people and getting their versions of the truth.

Sid knew she had convinced the interrogator she knew nothing, but she had no idea what Modred believed.

Tightening every muscle in her torso, she willed the nausea away and waited.

With a rustle of silk, Isabeau left her seat. Long, bejeweled fingers curled around one of Sid's hands, turning it first one way then the other.

"Look at that," Isabeau murmured. "They are perfectly restored, aren't they?"

Did the Queen believe she knew nothing? Was she going to claim credit for the healing? Sid didn't dare look up. She hadn't been given permission to do so.

"I'm grateful from the bottom of my heart," she said, again pouring all the conviction of that truth into her voice.

Isabeau ordered, "Look at me."

Lifting her head, Sid looked into the Queen's intent, narrowed gaze.

Watching her closely, Isabeau asked, "Now will you play music for me, ugly brown-haired girl?"

And there it was, the chance to take her money shot. Her opportunity to deliver the closing statement, to seal the deal.

Filling her mind with the memory of the unending bleakness in her underground cell, Sid said with perfect, heartfelt honesty, "Your majesty, there is nothing I want more in this world than to play the very best music I can for you."

A smile broke over Isabeau's lovely face, like the deadly blooming of a poisonous flower.

"Excellent," the Queen said, releasing her hand and

standing. "Luckily for you, my music master Olwen is away for a fortnight, so I suppose I might as well give you one more chance. But you will not play anything while you're like that. Your smell is too offensive. The next time I see you, I want you bathed and in proper attire. You may come to me this evening."

The wave of relief that hit was so strong, Sid saw black spots dance in front of her eyes. Swaying, she murmured, "I apologize, your majesty, but—"

An edge entered Isabeau's voice. "But—*what*—*now?*"

She simply didn't have it in her to act servile any longer. Sitting back on her heels, Sid looked up at the Queen and said bluntly, "If you want me to play something for you tonight, I will do my very best, and all the passion of my heart will be in it. But if you give me at least until tomorrow, the music will be much, much better. My hands might be healed, but I've lost the conditioning in my fingers, and I haven't played anything since before the injury." Thinking back over everything her benefactor had said about Isabeau, she added, "You wouldn't race a horse directly after it was hurt, would you? The horse couldn't possibly win, and you would just injure it again."

Comparing herself to an animal must have hit the right chord, because the irritation in Isabeau's expression faded somewhat. "I suppose you have a point."

Watching her carefully, Sid added, "Trust me, it will be worth the wait."

"Oh, very well." Isabeau raised one perfect blond eyebrow. "You have three days. I will expect something spectacular from you then, and if it isn't, what was healed can be rebroken, and there's always your cell waiting for you down below. Now, I'm done with this." She snapped her fingers, and a plain-featured, elegantly dressed woman appeared. "Kallah, see this creature gets everything she needs and bring her to me on the evening of the third day."

"Of course, your majesty," Kallah murmured.

As Isabeau paused to glance at Sid one last time, a gleam entered her eyes. She added, "And cut off that dark hair. It offends me."

Just when Sid thought she couldn't be outraged or shocked any further, something else happened. Rage raced through her like a flash fire. As it passed, it left her shaking.

There was no reason whatsoever for Isabeau to have ordered her hair cut. It was a mean, petty cruelty, and a display of absolute power.

Gazing unblinkingly into the Queen's eyes, she said mentally, *After I play my heart out for you, I will find a way to destroy you. I don't know when, and I certainly don't know how. But I buried my mom and dad when they died in a plane crash. I graduated top of my class with a master's in music from one of the most demanding and competitive schools in the world. I'm a successful musician, business woman, and multimillionaire, and if I could find a way to do all that, I can* find a way to do this too.

The thought made her happy. She gave Isabeau a small, wry smile of acquiescence and bowed her head, while Kallah said, "As you wish. Come along, human."

With every appearance of meekness, Sid did as she was told, and as she followed the Light Fae woman back indoors, she got the unsettling impression of the castle swallowing her whole.

Kallah led her through the immense maze, past the kitchens to an area where both the halls and rooms were rough, plain stone. She stopped at a small room at the end of a hallway. The Light Fae woman said, "These are the servants' quarters, and this will be your room for the time being. Did you memorize the way we took to get here?"

"I think so," Sid replied as she took in the details of the room.

There weren't many. It was furnished with a narrow bed, a simple table with some kind of lamp, and what looked like a plain wardrobe. There was a small window as well, with a wooden shutter.

But the bed had a real mattress, the lamp itself was a miracle, and *the window.*

There would be light and fresh air. She felt the impulse to cry from sheer relief but reined it in. She refused to show any weakness to the composed, elegant woman who stood watching her so closely.

"Good," Kallah said. "I don't want to have to show you the way again. Follow me."

She led Sid to the servants' bathrooms and left her to wash. The rooms were clearly communal, with large pools and spouts of continually running water, so Sid did so quickly, dipping into a wooden bowl filled with soft, unscented soap to scrub her body, face, and hair.

She rinsed in cold water that poured out of one spout. It was icy cold and she was soon shivering, but she was in no mood to complain. She was truly clean for the first time since she could remember. Having nothing else, she used her dirty hoodie to dry off. She had just pulled on her jeans, T-shirt, and shoes when Kallah appeared again, carrying a thick pile of what looked like folded laundry.

She followed Kallah back to her room, and Kallah set her load on the bed. A pair of scissors lay on the top of the pile. "Here is bedding, a drying cloth for future baths, and clothes. You have two outfits, a dress, and a tunic and trousers. Look after these things and keep them clean. It's easy to do, since the fabric has been spelled. All you need to do is rinse them."

She raised her eyebrows, intrigued. "Does that include the blanket?"

"Yes. The water will run off the fabric and rinse away any dirt. If you ruin your blanket or your clothes, you'll have to account for your things to the laundry mistress. She doesn't take kindly to people who make unnecessary work for her, do you understand? And I won't take it kindly if people come to me to complain about you."

"I understand," Sid told her.

Kallah assessed her with a cautious gaze. "Good. Now as soon as you change out of those horrible clothes, I'll cut your hair. Then I'll show you to the music hall so you can get started."

Setting her jaw, Sid did as she was told. Both her new outfits were a nondescript brown, so she chose the dress and the leather slippers. She wasn't quite sure how such a plain dress could be so ugly, but she couldn't care less what it looked like. It was clean, and while the slippers were used, they fit well enough to stay on her feet.

When she folded up her dirty Earth outfit, surreptitiously she slipped her hand into her jeans pocket and scooped out her twenty-one pebbles. As she transferred them to the pocket of her dress, Kallah held her hands out. "Give me those clothes."

This time it was Sid who gave her a narrow-eyed glance. "Why?"

Kallah's nostrils curled in disgust. "They're disgusting. I'm going to have them burned."

Rage flashed through Sid's body again. Filthy as they were, the jeans, T-shirt, shoes, and underwear were the only things she had in this place that were truly her own.

She wanted to lash out so badly it left her shaking again, but now was not the time to show a rebellious streak. She had barely gotten herself out of prison.

When she felt she could speak calmly, she dropped

the pile of clothes in one corner of the room while she suggested, "Why don't you leave that to me? I can take care of it later. The sooner you cut my hair and show me to some musical instruments, the sooner I can start practicing, and you can get on with your regular duties."

There was a brief hesitation while Kallah thought that over. Then the Light Fae woman shrugged and picked up the scissors. "Very well. Sit down."

As Sid perched on the corner of the bed, Kallah cut off her shoulder-length hair.

She'd already had her moment of outrage. Now she felt unmoved as she watched the long, silken black strands fall to the floor. Isabeau had meant the order as an assault on her autonomy, but Sid wasn't going to let her have the victory. What happened to her hair was the least important thing about all this. It would grow back soon enough if she wanted it to.

Kallah didn't spare an extra inch but snipped the hair as close to her scalp as she could. When she was finished, Sid ran her fingers through the short length. She'd worn her hair short before, and remembered how much she had liked the sensation as it lay against the curve of her scalp. Shorter haircuts highlighted her best features, making her eyes seem larger while accentuating her cheekbones, the shape of her mouth, and her neck.

As she looked up, she caught Kallah staring at her with an odd expression. Sid didn't know the other woman, but if she had to guess, Kallah looked troubled, almost pitying.

"What is it?" Sid asked. "Aren't you done?"

"I don't think her majesty will be quite as pleased with this new look as she thinks she will," Kallah murmured.

Oh, for crying out loud.

"Why not?" Sid demanded. "She said she wanted it gone, and you followed her orders to the letter. You barely left anything for me to run my fingers through."

Kallah's expression closed. "Never mind. Yes, I am done. You will clean this up later when you burn your clothes. Most of the castle is cleaned with magic, but the servants' rooms are their own responsibility."

The castle was cleaned by *magic*? But they couldn't manage to share any of that with the servants?

Exasperated, Sid said, "Fine."

Standing, she shook her dress to rid herself of the last of the loose hair and brushed off the back of her neck. When she was finished, Kallah led her back to the richer part of the castle.

"Remember this route, human," Kallah said. "For the next few days, you will either be in the music hall or in your room. You will take your meals in the servants' quarters. I do not expect to hear reports of you going anywhere else, do you hear? You have been granted leave from prison to do this one thing. Don't waste the opportunity."

"I understand," she muttered grimly. She hadn't

won her way out of that prison cell yet. She had only won the chance to try to stay out of prison. "Believe me, I have no intention of doing anything but getting ready for my next audience with the Queen."

"As you should."

Kallah stopped at tall double doors made of rich, polished wood. Opening one door, she stood back to let Sid step inside.

Stepping into the music hall, Sid's curious gaze ran over the room. Horror blindsided her, followed by a flash of panic.

The door settled into place behind her. Kallah hadn't bothered to step inside the room. Instead, Sid could hear the rapid click of footsteps fading down the hall as the Light Fae woman left her to her fate.

The richness of the music hall revealed just how much music meant to the Queen. The space was large and beautiful, decorated with paintings, intricate tapestries, and bookshelves, and what looked like crystal globes attached to the walls in iron sconces.

Tall windows let in copious amounts of light, and there was comfortable furniture grouped around a large fireplace—couches and chairs, and a table strewn with parchment paper, inkwells, and pens. There was a variety of musical instruments set on wooden stands— tall, stately floor harps, lap harps and lyres, flutes, dulcimers, and lutes.

Sid's primary instrument was the violin. That was her performance instrument, her area of expertise, the one she knew she could always pick up and create a soaring crescendo of music. She was also quite comfortable playing a viola, a cello, a guitar, and she did a lot of her composing on a piano.

Her confidence had been built on a lifetime of study, practice, testing, and performance. It had been built from a very early age, when her mother had forced her to practice, whether she wanted to or not, and had stood over her to make sure it happened. Then she had discovered she loved music and practiced of her own accord, while her parents showered her with praise and encouragement.

It had never occurred to her to question her own proficiency, or what kinds of music the Light Fae Queen might prefer, because she had an entire library of music living in her head.

Aside from her own burgeoning body of original work, she knew whole concertos by Bach, Brahms, Saint-Saëns, Vivaldi, Mendelssohn, Tchaikovsky, Beethoven, Paganini, and Mozart by heart. She also knew pop and jazz, and could make her violin weep when she played the blues.

But she had never once played any of the instruments sitting in Isabeau's music hall.

Moving like a sleepwalker, she went to one of the couches, sat, and put her face in her hands as she breathed, "I am so fucked."

✧   ✧   ✧

AFTER RETURNING TO the cottage to drop off the supplies, Morgan went on the hunt to find the source of the scent that by all rights shouldn't have been at the night market and yet had been.

He knew that meant the scent would be elsewhere as well, its source delving into places it shouldn't be, snooping and spying. Causing dangerous mischief without regard to consequences. Hurting innocent people.

He ignored the moon's passage across the heavens and the approaching dawn. His sole focus was on catching his prey.

He caught the scent again two miles outside the city. The source had hidden its trail with a lavish array of cloaking spells and spells of aversion, but Morgan was the better sorcerer. He shredded those spells like they were so much tissue paper.

Finally he came upon a cold camp hidden in a dense thicket of trees and overgrown foliage. No fire ring or woodsmoke gave the location away. It was how Morgan would camp if he wanted to keep his presence a secret.

The camp appeared to be empty, but his sharp, in-human gaze caught the subtle, stealthy slither of a snake slipping away in the underbrush.

Gathering himself into a lunge, he caught the snake by its tail. Hissing, it whipped around and would have bitten him, except he grabbed it by the throat. The snake's body heaved and bucked in his hands, and changed, and suddenly he clutched a lion by the throat. It roared in his face and thrust its powerful body forward for the kill.

Twisting his whole body in a way that made the wound in his side flare with fresh fire, Morgan lifted the lion bodily in the air and slammed it on the ground. Magic flared, a quick, desperate spell of corrosion. Morgan jerked his head back and rapped out a dissipation spell, while the lion melted away underneath his hands, and in its place, he held an alligator with a long, wicked snout filled with razor teeth.

The alligator twisted to snap at his legs. With another whole-body twist, he flipped onto its back, wrapped an arm around its neck, and locked it in place with his other arm. As he began to squeeze, he gasped out a null spell.

Silence fell over the scene, punctuated by the alligator scrabbling at the earth, mouth gaping, while both bodies strained. "Give in before I snap your neck," Morgan growled. "I'll do it."

As he spoke, he felt the null spell dissipate. Before his adversary could attack again with more spells, Morgan spun quick threads of Power around him, binding his adversary's magic to himself.

Suddenly the alligator's body collapsed and melted away, and in its place, Morgan held a slim, wiry body roughly the size of a teenage human boy's, only this was no human teenager. It was something older and much more dangerous.

Letting out a wail filled with equal parts rage and despair, it gave up the struggle. Once again, Morgan had captured Robin the puck.

Chapter Ten

PANTING, MORGAN RELAXED his hold, rolled off the puck's back, and came stiffly to his feet. Fresh wetness seeped into the bandages covering the wound in his side. He'd broken it open again. He pressed the heel of one hand against it.

At this rate, he would never heal, and actually, he was okay with that. The longer he could go between stabbings, the longer he could stave off that final, inevitable choice, and the more time he might have to find a way to break free from Isabeau.

As his weight lifted, Robin curled into a ball, both fisted hands pressed against his head in impotent rage. With his magic bound, the puck was no physical match for Morgan. Morgan was faster and stronger. If the puck tried to run, Morgan would only catch him again.

He asked hoarsely, "What are you doing here? Are you suicidal? You do know the Queen has ordered me to find you and bring you back to her."

Robin lifted his feral face. The glow from the waning moon lit his gaze as he hissed, "And you always do what your mistress wants, just like the dog you have become."

The insult rolled off Morgan's shoulders. He'd heard much worse. He considered binding the puck physically but was suddenly so fed up, he didn't bother.

"Give me one good reason why I shouldn't kill you and be done with it," he snapped.

Robin's thin, feral expression shifted. Suddenly he looked lost. "I can't," the puck keened. "I can't give you one good reason. She'll bind me with the burning rope again and make me do things I don't want to do."

In a burst of exasperation, Morgan bent down, grabbed the puck by his jacket, and hauled him to his feet. He roared, "*Why her?*"

"Tell me the Queen doesn't want to kill my Sophie." Robin's face clenched. "Tell me that one thing, sorcerer, and make me believe it."

A heartbeat went by, then another. Morgan could feel his pulse thudding in his clenched fists. "You know I can't tell you that."

Bitterness laced the puck's voice. "And you would do it, wouldn't you?"

"If she gives me a direct order to do so, yes, I will."

"Yet you still wonder why I have done what I have done?" A touch of sly cunning flashed in Robin's moonlit gaze. "The musician makes you want to disobey, doesn't she? She may be the only thing that can. Isabeau will hurt her and hurt her, the way she hurt me, unless you stop it. Her fate is your choice, sorcerer."

"You fool!" he spat. The impulse to violence took over, and he shook Robin. "You have no idea what you've done. You have no clue what is really going on."

The puck laughed. "No? I know enough. Once, you were a kingmaker, and what a king he was. He was your best, brightest work, the most brilliant star in the night sky."

Morgan went somewhere inside that was darker than the underground prison, undershot with red. He spat out, "You're not fit to say his name."

"Neither are you, anymore," Robin said simply. "Now you're just Morgan le Fae. A man without a real home or conscience, a man known only for his association with a people who are not his own. Why did you turn against him the way you did?"

"I never did," he whispered.

The ache of that never lessened, never went away. Over the centuries, he had grown to live around the ache. That was all.

"But you must have. You abandoned him. He went to war, and he lost, and you did nothing to stop it or save him. What did she offer you that meant that much? How did you stop caring for a boy you raised to be both man and monarch, a boy you raised as if he were your own son?"

"I never stopped caring." His throat closed as the geas tightened around it. After a moment, he said, "And if you could ask me that, you still know nothing. As unhinged as you are, your ignorance is the deadliest thing about you. Do you know what Isabeau did to Sidonie? She broke all her fingers and threw her in the dungeon."

"I know." As Morgan stared, Robin lifted one thin shoulder and said wryly, "I make a most excellent rat."

Fury torched through him, as coruscating as a nuclear blast. He snarled, "You knew—you went down into the dungeon and saw her, and—and *you still did nothing?*"

"I didn't have to do anything," Robin told him. "You did it. Just as you'll have to be the one to defy your Queen if you want her freed. I intend it to force a wedge between you and Isabeau that is so deep it will finally drive you two apart."

The geas pulled tighter. For a moment, it cut off Morgan's breath.

We are all spellbound, he thought. Sidonie can't leave Avalon on her own, and I can't help her escape. And I hold Robin captive again, while Isabeau holds me.

When he was able to speak again, he said, "Isabeau ordered me to recapture you and bring you to her. Luckily for you, another of her orders takes precedence. I will set you free, if you—"

If you help her escape.

They were five simple words, but the geas clamped down, and he couldn't say them.

"Fuck it," he finally managed to say in a strangled whisper. He loosened his hold on Robin's jacket. More than enough had been done to the puck. If he had a choice—and right now, he did—he wouldn't add to that. Besides, if Robin was free, he might relent and choose to help Sidonie of his own accord. "Someone else is going to have to capture and kill you. Robin, I'm sorry for what happened to you, but what you did to Sidonie was ugly. It was wrong. You are so wrong about almost everything."

The puck straightened his jacket while he stared at Morgan uncertainly. "Am I? Then prove it to me. Change. If you want Sidonie freed, then free her. Break with your Queen and become a better man again. You were... Do you even realize how many legends have been told about you? How the truth has been twisted by the winds of time?"

Morgan rubbed his eyes. He said, "Get out of here before I change my mind. And, puck?" Robin had already begun to slip out of the clearing. As he paused to look over his shoulder, Morgan told him, "Next time I might not be so lenient. If you know what is good for you, you will leave Avalon and never return."

Robin's mouth twisted. "Those might be the wisest words you've spoken this evening. But, sorcerer, I never know what is good for me."

Before Morgan could say anything else, the puck vanished into the underbrush. There was a brief rustle, then all he heard was the wind blowing through the trees.

All that effort he had expended to track Robin

down. Ultimately it had been a waste of energy, when he could have been going through the texts he had gathered and reading about Azrael's Athame.

Slowly, he made his way back to his hidden cottage, where he went through the mechanics of survival again. Food. Water. Cleansing the blasted wound again. The fact that it couldn't heal—that he couldn't let it heal— was some kind of goddamn metaphor he didn't want to inspect too closely.

When he finally laid down on his dusty bed, he managed to fall into a light, uneasy sleep, rousing only when the sun dropped low in the sky.

Then he went through the mechanics of survival again. Using the hunter's spray. Stealing at the night market. Gathering fresh, clean water for the flasks. This time he stole silver earrings and cherry pies. Given how she had responded to the other sweets, he was almost certain Sidonie would enjoy cherry pies.

As he slipped into his secret tunnel, a whispered spell brought faint illumination to the fingertips of one hand. He didn't want a light so bright it ruined his night vision. He made his way to the end of the tunnel, where he had used earth magic to drape a thin sheet of rock over the entrance to hide it from discovery.

Placing one palm over the rock, he gently shifted it to one side and stepped into the prison tunnel that lay on the other side. Dousing his faint light, he made his way quickly to Sidonie's cell.

As he drew close, he paused. There were too many

scents in the tunnel, many more than there had been the last time. Something had happened. Silently, he moved forward to the cell door, listening intently.

His keen hearing picked up the soft sounds of breathing inside, from too many people. There were four, maybe five individuals in the cell, all but unmoving, except for the slight rustle of cloth and the quiet scrape of a boot against the stone floor.

Realization was like another knife thrust to the gut.

Sidonie was gone. The prison guard knew that he—or someone—had been there, and had set a trap.

Fury roared through him, born in large part from fear. Before he had fully formed a conscious intention to do so, he was springing forward. The battle with Robin had cost him, so he had to dig deep for the strength to cast a stun spell into the cell that would be strong enough to lay out several warriors. It flashed with white brilliance, highlighting the five guards inside.

They toppled to the floor. Quickly, he unlocked the cell and stalked inside. Setting aside his pack, he chose the nearest guard at random, put his palm to the other man's forehead and, with another spell, forced him awake.

As the man came to with a muffled groan, Morgan pinned him and hissed in his ear, "What happened to the woman?"

"The w-woman?" the guard stammered.

He was the victim of two competing spells, both stunned and awake, but Morgan had no patience for the other man's confusion. He snarled, "The prisoner from this cell. *Is she dead?*"

"No… no, not dead. I don't know what happened to her… but I heard she might be back in a few days."

Christos. The relief at hearing Sidonie was still alive was staggering.

The gods only knew what Isabeau had done to her, but where there was life, there was hope.

Whispering the spell that would erase the guard's memory, Morgan straightened. Should he squander his waning energy on finding out what the other guards might know? One of them, Hoel, was a sergeant. Hoel would be in charge of the team.

He might know something, but each time Morgan talked to one of them he ran the risk of hearing them say something that might trigger the geas and force him back to Isabeau. They knew someone had gotten into Sidonie's prison cell and healed her, and the choices were limited.

Robin could have done it, and, of course, Morgan himself. But to the best of their knowledge, they had to believe both Robin and Morgan were on Earth.

Robin had escaped Isabeau's leash near the Welsh Marches earlier in the summer, and it was the height of insanity to consider that the puck might be so rash as to choose to return to Avalon of his own accord.

None of them would believe such a thing. Hell, Morgan himself wouldn't have believed it if he hadn't tracked Robin down and seen it for himself.

And Morgan had been injured and sloppy when he had left Avalon directly after Isabeau's orders. He had put the guards to sleep at the crossover passageway and had left a clear trail. When he had returned a few days ago, he had covered his tracks much better.

So they couldn't know for sure who had healed Sidonie. If they had truly believed it had been either Robin or Morgan, there would have been several of Isabeau's most Powerful magic users waiting down here, perhaps even Modred himself. And Morgan had left no trace of his scent, plus he had kept the tunnel opening covered with the sheet of rock.

Sidonie wouldn't be able to tell them anything. To the best of their knowledge, they had a locked-room mystery on their hands—but the weakest part of the mystery was Sidonie. Isabeau wouldn't like an unsolved mystery in her basement. So she had set a trap to see what she might catch.

And she would keep Sidonie close, so that she could question her again at her leisure.

Certainty solidified underneath him. Sidonie was still somewhere close by, in the castle.

Morgan had to solve their locked-room mystery for them, so they would have no reason to question Sidonie again at length.

Stepping over bodies, he reached Hoel and threw the spell that would wake him. With a snap of his fingers, he called light back to his hand. As Hoel shifted and groaned, Morgan pressed a hand over the

202 ✧ THEA HARRISON

other man's mouth.

"Wake up," Morgan said. "Look at me."

The sergeant blinked dazedly at him. Awareness widened his eyes.

When Morgan was sure Hoel had recognized him, he said in a voice laced with Power, "You will not speak unless it is in answer to a direct question. Is that clear?"

Hoel nodded.

Pulling his hand away, Morgan asked, "Where did you take the prisoner?"

"The Queen has given her leave to prepare for an audition while we hunt for—while we investigate who might have healed her." Sweat broke out on Hoel's forehead. "My lord, I-I-I'm supposed to tell you…"

Morgan clapped his hand over Hoel's mouth again. He snapped, "I ordered you not to speak unless it was in answer to a direct question."

Orders that had been laced with Power were difficult to disobey. Hoel must have a compelling reason for fighting Morgan's directive, and Morgan had a feeling it might have something to do with Isabeau wanting him back whether he was healed or not.

Should he bother to try asking Hoel any more questions? Was it worth the risk?

After a moment, he decided it wasn't. If Sidonie wasn't dead, he could find her.

It was time to give the guards another story to take to the Queen, one that had just enough plausibility to set her suspicions to rest.

Looking into Hoel's eyes, he said, "Don't fight me. If you fight me hard enough, it might break your mind. Relax, sergeant. Relax every muscle in your body, and relax your mind. Relax your thoughts. Let them float away. There's nothing urgent you need to do, and there's nothing to worry about. All is well. There's only the truth that you're about to discover."

As he spoke, he dug deep into the other man's mind until he was sure he had a strong hold. Instinctively Hoel struggled against the control, at least at first, but the stun spell Morgan had originally thrown worked in his favor, and Hoel quickly lost the battle.

"A friendly water sprite had heard Sidonie's cries of pain," he whispered to the sergeant. "She traveled up the privy hole to see what was the matter. When she found Sidonie broken, she sent her to sleep and healed her hands. While you were waiting here in the cell, the sprite returned to check on her handiwork. She would have fled and cast a spell of sleep over the other guards, but you convinced her to stay and talk to you— at least for a few minutes. Remember, she asked after Sidonie, and was angry and concerned that she was missing from the cell. Water sprites don't let go easily when they become attached."

"A water sprite," Hoel murmured, relaxing into the story. "That would explain it."

"It explains everything," Morgan told him, still working his magic on the man's memories. "The lack of scent, the lack of any other evidence of an intruder in the tunnels. You've looked everywhere down here, and you know for a certainty there is no other way out, or in."

"There truly isn't." Hoel shook his head, smiling. "We checked every inch of the tunnels, and every nook and cranny in the cells. She was beautiful, the water sprite, wasn't she?"

Now Hoel's mind was working with him to spin the tale. "She was extraordinary," Morgan murmured. "Delicate and shimmering, and appearing to be made completely from water. She fit easily through the privy hole—after all, she's a water elemental and can shrink or grow according to the space she's in. You already know how water sprites populate this area of the river, and the shores of the sea beyond. They may be shy of the Light Fae, but they're still there."

Hoel sighed. "I've always wanted to see one."

"She's going to leave in a few minutes, and when she does, you're going to rouse your men. You now have a story the Queen wants to hear." Morgan touched his forefinger to Hoel's forehead. "But for now, you're going to immerse yourself in the experience of talking with the sprite."

"Aye, she's a tricky one, coming up the privy hole like that," Hoel said with a grin. "Who'd have ever thought it? A disgusting way to travel, if you ask me... but she's made of water, so she could just shrug off the waste."

"That's right," Morgan told him as he pulled out the flasks of water from his bag and emptied them around the privy hole. "Nothing sticks to her as long as she flows. Watch for her now.... Look, she likes you."

With those words, he walked out of the cell, locked the door, and made his way back to his tunnel. After he had stepped inside, he shifted the sheet of rock back into place.

The events of the past day and night had skated much too close to disaster for his liking. Robin was loose to propagate whatever mischief that came into his head, and Morgan had depleted what precious magic strength he had begun to accumulate as he healed.

But at least he'd had a chance to spin a tale of how Sidonie had been healed, and it should hold up under scrutiny. Plus it was still night, still the best time for him to move about, and he didn't know where Sidonie might be kept.

Angling his jaw out, he headed down the tunnel. And he still had work to do.

SID SPENT THE rest of her day exploring the sounds each of the instruments could produce, and mechanically, she went through hand and finger exercises to help bring back the conditioning in her hands. Since she had started the exercises in the prison cell, at least she had a head start, but those exercises weren't as effective as playing against the tension of a stringed instrument.

Not that her efforts would get her anywhere. Even if she taught herself how to play one of them—and she could—there was no way she could be prepared in enough time to play for the Queen.

The instrument she felt the most affinity for was the lute. It was similar to a guitar, so she thought she should be able to play it well enough to perform informally in a couple of weeks.

Not in three days' time. Not for a woman who had a sophisticated palate, a demonstrated lack of tolerance, and very little reason to forgive any errors.

Finally she sat down at the table and put the lute to one side. She hadn't bothered to go to the kitchens to find food. She felt too disheartened to eat.

She recollected all too vividly the sounds her fingers had made as Modred snapped each one, followed by the blinding shock of pain and despair.

She had hoped she would escape the darkness of that awful cell, but it turned out she had brought the cell with her. Every bleak detail lurked inside, waiting for a moment of weakness so the memories could flood through her mind.

Exhaustion weighed her down. Earlier in the evening, she had lit a fire, more for the comfort and light than the warmth, and the flames were dying, throwing the music hall into deep shadow. Intending to only rest her eyes for a little while, she lay her head on crossed arms and plummeted into sleep.

Something roused her, some slight sound of movement and change in the air. A large, broad hand came down between her shoulder blades.

"Sidonie."

Some part of her knew his touch, even before she recognized his whisper.

Her benefactor. The magic man.

She jerked upright and stared at the broad, tall silhouette of the man standing beside her.

The flames in the hearth had died down completely, but a pale, indistinct glow came through the wall windows from a moon obscured by heavy clouds. The fugitive glimmer gave a rough outline of the room's furniture and touched on the back of her benefactor's head and shoulders.

"You found me," she said stupidly, her voice still blurred from sleep. "I wish I'd been able to leave you a note."

Something changed. The air grew heavier and sultry, as if in a storm before a lightning strike. The hand he had put at her back pressed down, and through that touch she felt the tension that ran through him.

Then the hard, pressing weight left her back. Lightly, he stroked his fingers over her head. "What happened to your hair?"

The whispered question sounded calm, even gentle, but suddenly she knew it was a lie. He was toweringly furious. She shrugged impatiently. "It doesn't matter."

That light, fleeting touch passed along the bare

nape of her neck. The sensation of callused fingers caused a shiver to run down her spine. "It matters to me."

"Isabeau ordered it to be cut off." Pushing back from the table, she stood. "It was vindictive and childish, and the least important thing that happened today." Eyes wide, she studied the outline of his head, his shadowed features, but she could only gain impressions.

His hair was short, or at least shorter rather than long, and it appeared to be brown, or even darker, maybe even as black as hers. If he had darker hair, that would mean he wasn't Light Fae. While she couldn't make out any definition of his features, he seemed to have a strong bone structure that would be in keeping with his tall, broad-shouldered height.

She still couldn't see enough to identify him if she were to see him in daylight. She wasn't even sure about the hair color. Maybe his hair was really blond, just darkened by shadows. If the moon would only come out from behind the clouds, she could get a good look at him.

"Don't dismiss what happened as quickly as that," he replied. That gentle touch stroked along her throat to her chin, and he tilted her face up. "Isabeau was trying to take away your beauty, and she failed. You're quite striking with short hair. She won't be pleased."

She let loose an explosive sigh. "That doesn't matter either. I fucked up. In fact, I fucked up so badly there's no fixing it. Nothing else matters aside from that."

He tilted his head sharply. "What do you mean? What happened?"

The events of the day crushed down on her, the unending stress, the fear, and she felt her face crumple. Suddenly remembering that his eyesight was sharper at night than hers, she bowed her head and dug the heels of her hands into dry, tired eyes.

"I did it all," she gritted. "I told my version of truth and padded it with supposition and questions, and I got past the prison interrogator, past Modred, and I even survived a second meeting with the Queen. I won a second shot at playing for her, and she gave me three days to prepare." Her voice broke. "It never occurred to me that I might not know how to play anything here. I play five instruments really well. *Really well.* Not one of those instruments is here in this hall."

He took in a deep, audible breath, then let it out slowly. Grasping her by the shoulders, he pulled her into his arms. "Okay," he murmured. "We will figure this out."

"There's nothing to figure out," she said into his chest. "I can't magically learn how to play a new instrument well enough to satisfy a music aficionado in the next... Today is over. It's two days now, not three. She's going to throw me back in prison, and next time I won't have a nifty story I can tap-dance around to get somebody's attention."

"Don't be too sure about that," he told her. "It's going to be all right, Sidonie. Just trust me and relax for a minute while I think."

To go from such intense isolation and stress to someone actually caring enough to put his arms around her was an almost impossible emotional journey to encompass. Her breath shook in her throat as she fought to regain her composure.

He rubbed her back until gradually, muscle by muscle, she eased into the shelter of his long, hard body and slipped her arms around his waist. He was still wearing the bandage around his ribs, she discovered.

"I'm not supposed to trust you," she whispered.

"Well, there's that," he replied dryly. "Let's reframe that for now, shall we? For the time being—for tonight—you can trust me. Isabeau still doesn't know I've helped you, so she hasn't issued any countermanding orders."

The solid weight of his arms around her felt too good. She couldn't rely on it, and she shouldn't enjoy it as much as she did.

But she did enjoy it, intensely. Comfort stole into her in like a thief and made itself at home. Burying her face into his chest, she said, "So I didn't create any problems for you when I broke out of jail?"

He put his face in her short hair. She felt him smile. "You've been nothing but problems from the moment I found out you existed."

"That sounds unfortunate," she muttered, partly

chagrined but mostly just grateful that what happened to her mattered to him in some way. The loneliness she had felt since being kidnapped was stronger than she'd realized.

One of his hands came up to cover the nape of her neck. "It was not a good moment when I discovered your presence in the cell had been replaced by five guards."

Her head jerked up. "Oh, no."

"Oh, yes." Cupping her face, he rubbed his thumbs along the plump curve of her lower lip. He added, as if to himself, "I shouldn't be telling you this. You're still learning too much about me."

She grabbed his wrists. "You can't stop now. What happened? They didn't attack you, did they?"

"Never mind. It gave me a chance to spin a story for how you got healed. It was a bit of a stretch, but they don't have any other explanation—or any evidence—for what really happened."

But her mind had gone down a different track. She said slowly, "You know I'm going to figure out who you are, don't you? That is, if I live past the next two days. The whole reason you kept hidden from me was so I couldn't tell anyone about you, or what you've done for me."

"We're not out of the woods yet," he said softly. "You could still be questioned. Isabeau has kept you close for that very reason. If she does have you questioned, and she forces the truth out of you, right now the only thing you can tell her is an unknown man helped you."

Her fingers tightened on his wrists. "I know she has you imprisoned in a spell," she said tautly. "How many people does she control this way?"

Chapter Eleven

"ENOUGH ABOUT THAT." His hold loosened. "I have a present for you, if you would use it."

"What?" That had come so far out of left field, she floundered a moment. "I—thank you. What is it?"

He reached into his pocket. "It's a pair of earrings. Are your ears pierced?"

"Yes…" She blinked at him in confusion. How on earth could it be relevant for him to give her a pair of earrings right now?

Taking one of her hands, he dropped them into her palm. She fingered them, frowning. Small and still warm from being in his pocket, they felt like they were simple ball studs with round metal backs.

As she explored them with her fingers, he told her, "They're very humble and plain, I'm afraid. They're made with silver and they're quite small. They look like something a servant might wear, but I've spelled them with telepathy."

"Telepathy earrings…," she breathed.

She didn't know about Avalon, but on Earth there was a booming industry for magic items. Quite a few magic users used items to expand or enhance their abilities, and many deadhead humans liked exploring and using magic items. Telepathy earrings were one of the most common and affordable commodities on the market.

Curious, Sid had bought a pair and tried them once, but she found the sensation of hearing someone else's voice in her head so uncomfortable she never wore them.

"I don't like not being able to talk with you telepathically," he said. "There are sharp ears in this castle. We're fine for now. Most of the castle is asleep, and at the moment, there's no one near this room. But there may come a time when we need to talk while someone else is close by. Would you consider wearing them?"

She turned them over in her hands. "I didn't do so well with the earrings the first time I tried them. Telepathy felt too strange and intrusive, but at the time it didn't matter if I got used to them or not. I'm certainly willing to try them again, but won't somebody notice?"

The smile came back into his voice. She loved it when she heard him smile. It warmed his deep whisper. "Trust me, the spell I infused in those earrings is so subtle and insignificant no one will notice it at all. Telepathy is something even the youngest Light Fae child can do, and besides, there are flares of magic all over that fill the senses. Magic is imbedded in artwork, in weapons, sometimes utensils, the witchlights—those globes fastened to the walls—and most of the nobles are wearing much more Powerful items of jewelry. Many, including Isabeau, are wearing multiple pieces at once."

"What do the witchlights do?" Her gaze slid sideways to eye the nearest one curiously.

"They're simple illumination spells. You can activate them with a touch." He paused. "Or at least, those with a spark of magic can activate them. But don't worry, most rooms also have a few candles too."

She sighed. "Normally I don't care about being magicless, but the way you describe things makes me realize just how much I'm not seeing in the world around me."

He cupped her head with both hands. "You're full of your own kind of magic, and it's much more rare and beautiful than all the other spells around you. They are commonplace. You are unique."

She flushed all over at hearing his words, her body warming with pleasure. "Thank you," she whispered. "If you think we can get away with it, I'd be glad to try the earrings."

"Excellent." He paused. "Have they searched you or shown any interest in what you might be carrying?"

She snorted. "Not at all. They probably scanned me for dangerous magic, and I just didn't know it. But I still have the worry stones I picked up on the caravan trip. Nobody's checked what I have in my pockets or even asked me what my name is. The indifference has been staggering. If I'd had an inflated ego, it would have been trampled to death days ago." She thought for a moment. "The one person who might notice is the woman who cut my hair. Her name is Kallah. She's Isabeau's... what do the Light Fae call it? Lady-in-waiting?"

"They're called court ladies here," he told her. "Kallah is smart and observant. You'll want to be careful about wearing the earrings around her when she has the leisure to notice you, at least until you have some plausible explanation for having acquired them. Other than that, I think you'll be okay. Everyone knows you don't have magic."

"Okay. Let's try them!" Eager to know what his telepathic voice sounded like, she pulled the small metal back off one of the posts and poked along her skin until she felt it slide into the piercing in her lobe. Quickly, she fastened the back and slipped on the other earring.

"Got it?" he asked.

She nodded. "Got it."

"Good. Let me know when you're ready."

Why did she suddenly feel so nervous? Clasping her hands together, she told him, "Ready. I think."

He settled both hands on her shoulders. Then a deep, rich voice sounded in her head. *Hello, Sidonie.*

Gasping, she gripped his forearms and her legs wobbled.

His fingers tightened. *Are you all right?*

She gasped again, while the world seemed to spin around her. "Yes," she breathed. "Your voice in my head... it's so *intimate*. How can you stand to do this all the time with just anybody?"

A soft laugh escaped him. *That's a perspective I've never considered before*, he told her. *It makes sense now that you've said it, but when children use telepathy from a very early age, it becomes just another way of talking.*

As she listened to him, she had to clap both hands over her mouth to stifle the incoherent sound of glee that escaped. Listening to his telepathic voice sent shivers down her back. *She loved it.* Loved!

After a hesitation, he asked, *Is it okay?*

Should she confess how delighted she was, or that she never wanted him to stop talking to her? She would listen to him say anything. He could read the phone book to her, and she would love it.

Unsteadily, she told him, "It's great. It's just a huge adjustment. The last time I tried telepathy earrings, I couldn't get the shop assistant out of my head fast enough, but you're different. I... I trust you." Even though she had said it softly, the last three words seemed to echo in the music hall. He had gone silent and tense. Listening to the implications in what she had just said, she added lamely, "At least, for tonight, I do."

He released the breath she had sensed him holding. *Good. Now, you try talking to me. Just reach out, like you would if you looked across the room and tried to catch my gaze.*

She thought that through for a moment. Then she

shouted, *HELLO? ARE YOU THERE?*

He recoiled as if she'd slapped him. Then he burst out laughing. The sound was so foreign to anything thus far that they had shared together, she stared.

Why, yes. His telepathic voice sounded strangled. *I am indeed right here, and you just made a hell of a noise. Try to tone it down next time.*

Sorry, she said loudly, scowling from the intensity of concentration. *Is this better?*

He laughed harder. *There's no need to strain, or shout, and for God's sake, don't make faces like that! In fact, you can whisper telepathically, and I would hear you perfectly fine.*

Her scowl deepened, but she didn't really mind him laughing at her. It sounded good and healthy, almost as if they were enjoying themselves as they carried on a normal conversation about normal things.

God, she wished they could have a normal conversation about normal things. Whatever *normal* might mean to him. She was sure any conversation she had with him would be as exotic as the ones they'd already shared. She just wanted to talk with him and be easy together without having everything feeling fraught with impending doom. The brief moment of levity made her aware just how starved she was for more.

Heaving a gusty sigh, she whispered, *How's this?*

Still intense, but much better, he told her. *We can practice as much as you like.*

"That would be good," she said aloud, quietly. "I need to be sure I don't look like a grimacing fool when

I telepathize, but how do I know I'm going to reach *you* instead of someone else?"

He switched to speaking aloud too. "That's easier than you might think. If you focus on me, you will contact me. If you focus on someone else—for example, Kallah, Modred, Isabeau, a guard, or one of the dogs—you would contact them. But of course, the dogs don't have telepathy, so you wouldn't get a response back."

"Oh, of course," she echoed with a touch of sarcasm, when in fact she didn't know any such thing. As far as she knew, every dog in Avalon could have been a telepathic, talking dog.

"Just remember, the earrings have a range of about twice the size of this music hall," he told her. "More like the size of the castle great hall. If you can't contact me, I'm not in range. We can practice as much as you like until you're completely comfortable with it."

"Maybe later. I'm getting a headache," she murmured as she glanced at the lute on the table. Her earlier glee evaporated, leaving her feeling dull and afraid. "The earrings are wonderful, and I'm glad you thought of them, but they're not going to solve my immediate problem."

That whole impending-doom thing had to go and rear its ugly head again.

"No, they're not, are they?" He strode over to the table and fingered the lute. "But I think I know what will."

She hated not knowing what to call him. It was bugging her more and more as time passed. She even hated it more than not being able to see what he looked like. She had grown accustomed to the play of shadows across his face, attuned to the nuances and shifts in emotion in his body language and in his quietly murmured words.

As odd as it sounded, she had even grown accustomed to touching him and being touched. She had more than grown accustomed. She looked forward to it. She... yearned for it. His touch brought comfort and reassurance at a time when she badly needed both.

Every time his fingers brushed her skin, it was like sunlight and fresh, sparkling water to a dying plant. She needed food to survive, but when he touched her, it nourished her in ways that nothing else ever had.

By comparison, not knowing his name was growing to feel like sand in a shallow cut. It was abrasive and wrong. And assigning an arbitrary name to him didn't help.

Fred. John. Thomas. They were all empty syllables that carried no meaning.

Magic Man. At least *that* had meaning.

"Okay, Magic Man," she said as she walked over to his side. "What's next?"

MAGIC MAN.

When he heard the nickname she had given him, he

smiled.

She had been traumatized in a way that few people ever endured. She was still in danger, afraid, and vulnerable to the malignant forces all around her, and yet here she walked toward him, ready to hear what he had to say.

Bravery wasn't facing something you knew you could vanquish, he thought. Bravery was facing the impossible and saying, what's next?

"I know a spell," he told her.

She chuckled quietly and touched his shoulder in a quick, affectionate gesture. "Of course you do. What is it?"

"It's actually a battle spell," he replied. "You can transfer your skills to another person for a battle. The effects are temporary, and the spell is draining for both people, so it isn't something anyone would cast lightly. In battle, using it tends to be an act of desperation, in an all-or-nothing kind of scenario, because if you're in a situation where you need to cast it, it's unlikely either participant will survive anyway. The times I've seen it used were when warriors were battling for the greater good. One badly wounded soldier cast the spell to transfer his abilities to a younger man. They both died that day, but they were able to guard a narrow pass long enough for reinforcements to arrive, which saved their settlement from an invading force."

She wrapped her arms around her middle, and he sensed her shiver. "Sounds grim."

Putting an arm around her, he drew her against his side. "It is, rather. But here's the thing—I've played both the lute and the harp before. Once, I played them quite well. But that was quite a long time ago."

As she tilted back her head, he caught a shadowed glimpse of her sparkling, elegant eyes. "Just how old are you?"

"Very old," he replied. "I stopped aging when I was thirty-seven. That was when Isabeau trapped me with the geas."

Leaning against him, she turned her face into his shoulder and sighed. "I daydream about tearing her face off."

That was so unexpectedly bloodthirsty, he coughed out a laugh. "As do I," he told her. Obeying an impulse he didn't want to examine too closely, he pressed his lips to her forehead and said against her soft, creamy skin, "As do I."

Whenever she came close, he wanted to touch her, stroke her face, cradle her slender body against his, rest his cheek on top of her head. Touching her had awakened a hunger he hadn't felt in centuries, or perhaps ever.

In his human life, he had been self-contained and autonomous, driven by his intellectual passions, the pursuit of magic, and the brilliant realization of political ambitions. Sex had been enjoyable but not something he had obsessed over, and he hadn't needed the kind of physical demonstrations of affection that so many other people seemed to need from their lovers.

This compulsion to touch Sidonie was completely foreign to him. He didn't understand why he had grown to need it or why it had to be her that he touched.

But it did have to be her. He wasn't interested in seeking or offering comfort to anyone else.

Frowning, he loosened his hold on her shoulders. "The only way to know if the spell will work is to try it. Which instrument do you want to focus on?"

She blew out a sigh. "It should be the lute. I'll have the best chance to learn and play that quickly—or at least quicker than the other instruments. I'd enjoy exploring the harp, but that will take more time."

He liked and respected the confidence with which she spoke about her musical ability as she assessed the challenges in front of her and what she could do to meet them. When it came to music, she knew herself very well. Right now, her attitude was akin to that of a master swordsman surveying a battlefield.

Reaching around her, he picked up the lute. "Come with me."

She followed him as he walked over to one end of the couch and sat. Snagging a footstool, he dragged it over to position it between his knees. "Have a seat here and put your back to me."

"Okay." She settled on the footstool, facing away from him.

He leaned forward and reached around her waist to

put the lute in her lap. "I think you're right," he said in her ear. "A lot of what you already know from playing the guitar will be applicable to the lute, so it was a good choice. But there's a lot that's different as well."

A subtle shiver ran over her, all but undetectable. She leaned back against him. "For one thing, a guitar has six strings, and this one has fifteen."

"This is a Renaissance lute. Baroque lutes have even more strings. You won't use a nail to play it either. You'll use your fingers to pluck at the strings, or maybe for some songs use double-plucking. On the fretboard, you can also move the frets—they're not fixed in place."

"Fascinating," she murmured. "I didn't notice that."

"Plus you hold it differently than you would a guitar." Putting his arms around her, he positioned the lute against her chest and adjusted her arms and hands. "Like this."

"Got it," she said, somewhat breathlessly. "What about my right hand?"

"Feel for your position by touching the soundboard with your little finger, and tuck your thumb in, which is the opposite of how you'd play a guitar." He ran his fingers along her hand, readjusting as necessary. "More like that."

"Ah. That is very different."

The sense of her leaning back against his chest was messing with his concentration. Her slim, lithe body felt like a perfect fit in his arms. Huskily, he told her, "Put your hand over mine, so you can feel how mine feels in the correct position."

Readily, she complied, lifting her hand away. As he positioned his hand over the strings, she laid hers lightly over the top, her sensitive, clever fingers fitting themselves along the backs of his.

He played a simple melody slowly, allowing her to feel how his hand moved along the strings as he plucked and double-plucked at them. "Do you see?"

"Yes." Her reply sounded husky. She cleared her throat. "It's a completely different technique than what I'm used to."

"You're not going to develop a solid technique in two days," he murmured. "I can imagine that will be frustrating, especially since your violin playing is so flawless and transcendent. But all we need to do is to get you to produce something that sounds enjoyable to someone who doesn't know how to play the lute herself. Perfecting your technique can come later."

"I'm not used to the neck being so short," she complained. "The only way to get comfortable with it is by practicing, and the only way to practice enough is over time."

"True," he replied. "But that's where the battle spell should help. It should give you a feeling like an epiphany as the ability to play infuses your mind and body. It won't last, and you'll be drained afterward, but if Isabeau wants you to play in the evening, you should be able to go to bed shortly after you finish."

"That's if your spell works," Sidonie said darkly. "You said you weren't even sure you remembered how to play."

"The memories are there," he said. "I just have to access them. Besides, the only way we'll know is if we try. Are you ready?"

Her shoulders tensed. "Yes. Will it hurt?"

"What, the spell itself?" Having been immersed in magic his entire life, he tended to forget how very little she knew of magic, spells, and Power. "No, not at all. It should feel exhilarating, like a surge of adrenaline."

"Okay, good." She relaxed again.

In order to cast the spell, he had to think back and immerse himself in the memory of playing. Aside from this night, he wasn't sure when the last time was that he'd picked up a lute, let alone played one.

Thankfully the spell didn't have to be based on the last time. It could be based on an earlier memory.

When he cast back far enough, a memory surfaced.

It had been a hot afternoon, and much of the court had been relaxing by the cool of a deep river. There had been food and wine, and people had napped, read, and talked while Morgan had leaned with his back against the trunk of a willow tree, looked out at the silver sparkles on the sunlit water, and let his mind wander lazily as he plucked the notes of one of his favorite songs.

He'd been happy then, at peace and relaxed. While

there had certainly been challenges to face, he'd had absolute confidence they would overcome them. They'd still had so much to build in their thriving, young kingdom....

He didn't realize that he had tensed, and his breathing had shortened, until Sidonie leaned her head back against his shoulder and tilted her face to him.

She asked, "What's wrong?"

The breath from her words touched his cheek in small, warm puffs. He had to force a swallow before he could reply in a bare thread of sound. "This is difficult for me."

She leaned her cheek against his and asked sympathetically, "Is the spell that difficult to cast?"

He had taken pains to make sure she had no idea who he was, but still a small snort escaped him. "No," he said. "It's not the spell. It's the memories. I was... happy then."

Immediately, she pushed the lute away, arched, and twisted. As she came to face him, she put her arms around his neck and hugged him.

"If this is difficult for you, then we won't do it," she told him. "I'll think of something else. Maybe I can throw myself down a flight of stairs or something. If I have an accident, she can't expect me to play so soon, can she?"

Both warmed by her concern and alarmed at the direction of her thoughts, he dropped the lute on a nearby cushion and pulled her closer. "Don't be ridiculous. You are not going to injure yourself just because I don't like looking back. The past is done, and there's nothing I can do to change it. What is happening right now is the most important thing—now and what can be done for the future. And we can do something about that."

"I don't like the thought of you being in pain," she persisted stubbornly. "You have done so much to help me, when the truth is you don't owe me anything."

"For God's sake, Sidonie," he said, exasperated as he cupped the back of her head. "Now is not the time to start refusing my help. Otherwise, you run the risk of undoing everything I've done for you already. Now stop arguing about this, and let me get back to casting that spell."

Her body felt tight with tension. She told him, "And I don't like the fact that after everything you've done for me, I still don't know your name. You call me by name all the time, and I can't do the same with you."

His arms tightened. "We're not having that conversation again."

"I don't see why not. You should at least promise to tell me who you are after we know Isabeau has accepted whatever cockamamie story you cooked up to explain how I got healed in an underground prison."

"Are you always so stubborn and single-minded?" he demanded.

Even as they argued, he realized he didn't want her

to know who he was. He didn't want her to look at him with the same kind of fear that he saw in other people's faces when they looked at him.

The man who played music by a river was as dead as the others in his memory. He had become someone much harder, more cruel, and ruthless. The shadows gave him a sort of anonymity, a certain distance from the man he had become, and he was not in a hurry to give that up.

When she laughed, she sounded genuinely amused. "*Stubborn* and *single-minded* are my middle names. I also have a growing problem with OCD, and you know why? Because I can't let go of things, and I can't relax. I never give up on anything, ever."

He could believe that. All those qualities had gotten her where she was. She was tenacious, strong-willed, exasperating. Talented.

Adorable.

With her face tilted up to his, the subtle edge of moonlight touched along the edge of one high cheek-bone, the tilted edge of one eye, and those beautiful, enticing lips. Obeying an impulse he couldn't put into words, he lowered his head and covered her mouth with his.

As his lips touched hers, he felt her quick intake of breath. Then he lost himself in the shock of rare pleasure as he kissed that full, sensual mouth.

A shudder ran through her, then her arms tightened, and she kissed him back.

She kissed him back.

Her mouth moved under his, lips parting to allow him access. A rush of euphoria hit him, clean, sharp, and all-encompassing. He bent her back and lost himself in voracious pleasure, spearing her with his tongue as he ravished her luscious, plump mouth.

She made a tiny sound. It was both throaty and surprised at once, and it went straight to his cock. As he grew erect, he came back to himself with a jolt.

When was the last time he had felt such sexual tension, such sensual pleasure?

He couldn't remember.

But he did remember how inappropriate this was. He had no business kissing her. He had no business touching her or thinking about her in this way. She was trapped and in danger, and his life literally was not his own.

She wasn't the only one who couldn't trust him. He couldn't trust himself.

It was nearly impossible to pull away from her giving responsiveness. Breathing hard, he lifted his head and said hoarsely, "Forgive me. I shouldn't have done that."

With a soft growl, she sank her fingers in his hair and raised herself up so that she could kiss him back. This time she was the aggressor, and as she darted her tongue into his mouth, his erection tightened to the point of pain. Each of her fingers sent tingling sensations across his scalp, while her lips shifted and moved over his in an irresistible siren's call.

For long moments, he lost himself in her. As he ran one hand down the side of her torso, she arched herself up to his touch like a cat asking to be stroked. He wanted—needed—to tear off her clothes and lose himself in the voluptuous heat of her slender, muscular body.

But in a distant corner of his mind, unease began to jangle. It grew louder quickly.

They had gone from one impulsive kiss to a level of raw, urgent need that was unbalanced and dangerous. If only he could remember why it was so dangerous…

He dragged his mouth away from hers. It was much harder to do the second time around, and both of them were breathing raggedly.

For long moments, they each held tense. He couldn't force his fingers to relax and let go of her.

He wanted to never let go of her.

That last thought was like a bucket of cold water hitting him in the face.

If there was anyone in the entire world who shouldn't be thinking thoughts like that, it was him.

As his hands loosened, she gave a little ghost of a laugh. In a shaken whisper, she said, "That escalated fast."

"Too fast," he gritted. "I had no business kissing you like that."

"Well, I didn't exactly object, did I?" she pointed out. She slid her fingers out of his hair with a slow sensuousness that heated his blood.

Catching one of her hands, he kissed it. "No," he agreed against her fingers. "You didn't. And I didn't want to stop. But this isn't going to get you through your audience with Isabeau. That's what we need to focus on right now."

Straightening on the footstool, she took a deep breath and squared her shoulders. "Of course it is," she agreed in a flat, dull voice.

Had he hurt her feelings? He rubbed his face then decided to let it go, because even if he had, it didn't matter.

Reaching for the lute, he thrust it into her hands. "Time to find out if that spell will actually work," he told her.

Cradling the lute against her chest, she asked, "And if it doesn't?"

If it didn't, he had no idea what to try next.

Infusing his voice with a confidence he didn't feel, he said, "We'll cross that bridge when we come to it."

Chapter Twelve

SID KNEW SHE was still embroiled in a fight to stay out of prison. A fight to save her life. She knew she had no business necking like a teenager with a man she knew so little about.

But kissing him had been the best thing that had happened to her in a long time. The absolute very best thing.

And as she looked back over her work-driven life, she realized she didn't just mean the very best thing from the time she'd been kidnapped. Kissing him had been the best thing to happen in a really, *really* long time.

She had dated a total of four men somewhat seriously in her life, and she had shared intimacy with two of them. That wasn't exactly a memorable dating score, but as she had a difficult time being social anyway, she had never gotten too worked up over it.

She was pretty, and she knew it. She also knew most men who were initially attracted to her because of her looks were put off by the intense laser focus she had on her career. And Magic Man was right—she *was* stubborn and single-minded.

She was ambitious too, and all that meant she wasn't exactly good wife or baby-making material. She had never really understood when other women talked about their biological clocks ticking. She wasn't convinced she had a biological clock.

Neither one of her previous lovers had made her catch fire the way Magic Man did. It didn't matter what he said, or even what her own mind insisted. Her body trusted him. When he touched her, she relaxed. When he'd stroked down her torso, pleasure had followed in a languid wash of fire.

And she had discovered it didn't matter what he might look like to the eye. He was handsome to her fingertips, and his body felt strong and powerful when he came flush against her. He was easy to talk to, to confide in, and he had a kind of confidence in his own abilities, both magical and otherwise, that was incredibly sexy. He had a strong, sure touch, while his hands were gentle and sensitive. And he was not only experienced, he was intelligent—possibly even much more intelligent than she.

Other than the fact that Isabeau had a magical hold over him that he didn't consent to, she didn't know anything about what he did, or what his job was. She didn't know his name. She didn't know what he looked like, or who his friends were, what places he liked to frequent, what his hobbies were… or even if he had any hobbies.

Under normal circumstances, she would have never considered letting him kiss her, or kissing him back. But currently she was embroiled in a situation that was anything but normal. Normal didn't apply to her life anymore.

Right now all she wanted to do was neck in the dark with a man she didn't know, and when he put on the brakes—*and rightfully so*—then all she wanted to do was sulk. She was tired of thinking in crisis mode, tired of living with stress.

Her body craved pleasure and it instinctively knew he could give it to her. Her soul craved comfort, and it was unbelievably comforting to touch him, and to have him touch her. Her mind just wanted to switch off.

But no, they had to focus on keeping her whole and unbroken, and keeping her ass out of prison.

Bah!

Magic Man didn't pull her back against his chest again, although she really kind of wanted him to.

Maybe more than *kind of* wanted.

Maybe really, *really* wanted.

He was probably thinking so clearly about what they should be doing because he... hadn't been as affected by their kiss as she had been. *(BAH!)*

Instead of pulling her into his arms, he put one broad hand at the back of her neck, and the other hand at her forehead. Then he began to whisper.

When she tried to focus on his words, they wouldn't stick in her head. Instead, it felt like they fell against her skin like heated rain… and then the words soaked into her.

Pressure built up, like the sense of an impending storm, or the feeling she got just before she stepped out onto a stage. She felt itchy and restless, like she needed to move.

Unable to sit still, she shifted underneath his hands, muttering, "Is it supposed to be this uncomfortable?"

He didn't respond. Instead, his steady, intense whisper continued until he bit it off at the end. As he finished, he removed his hands, and tapped her forehead firmly with two fingers.

And *snap*.

She felt the epiphany.

Of course that was how you played the lute. Of *course*.

Snatching it up, she plucked through the strings, adjusted the frets, and then began to play. She got it. She knew how to play it perfectly well, and the knowledge came easily to her.

She didn't know any of the songs that he must have known all that long ago. Instead, she played her own music, adapting her songs to the fifteen-stringed lute as she went, humming with happiness that she had an instrument, any instrument to play again, adding riffs, two-plucking with style.

The shadowed music hall turned luminous with harmonic sound. It ran through her like fiery gold, and it didn't matter what was going on around her or what might come in the future. Everything was right with the world. Everything was more than right....

She lost track of time, and that didn't matter either until, a formless while later, the epiphany ran out of her, like a tide pulling away from the shore.

Her fingers stumbled on the strings. Tiredness swallowed her whole. Unsteadily, she muttered, "Oh, wow. That was just amazing. If you could bottle that, you'd have addicts waiting in line down the street."

"That was a combination of my spell and your talent." His whisper sounded rough with exhaustion. "Those addicts would never be able to play like you just did."

"But how are you going to get the spell to me?" She chewed her lip as she worried over the problem. "I don't think I'm overdramatizing when I say my life depends on this."

"I swear I will figure it out. Somehow I will get it to you." The iron determination in his voice soothed her anxiety. "Sidonie, it was a hell of a day before I got to you, and I can't be found here. I need to leave before I crash."

"Of course," she said, swaying where she sat on the footstool. "Same here. I'm wiped out."

His hand came down heavily onto her shoulder as he stood. He dug into the pack he had left by the table and pressed something into her hands. "Here, eat this before you sleep, or you'll regret it tomorrow."

Her fingers were throbbing. She hadn't been lying

when she had said she'd lost the conditioning in her hands, and she didn't have calluses built up from playing the lute.

She made her stiff, aching hands curl around what he had given her. "Okay, thank you."

Before she managed to finish the three-word sentence, a fresh current of air circulated the large room and she knew he was gone.

Forcing herself to stay upright through an act of willpower, she sniffed what he had given her. It was a pie of some sort. As she bit into it, the sweet, tart taste of cherries filled her mouth, balanced by the sugary goodness of the crust. It was delicious.

Suddenly aware that she had not eaten since the night before, she didn't stop eating until she had finished the whole thing.

Then, feeling a bit steadier, she tapped her fingers on the table while she thought. How could she possibly explain how she came to have earrings, if she were asked?

Carefully removing them, she slipped them into the pocket of her ugly brown dress as she whispered, "Sometimes I wear my earrings, and sometimes I carry them in my pocket."

Would that be true enough to pass Kallah's truthsense? How the hell should she know, when she'd never felt truthsense in her life.

She took the earrings out and put them on the table. Now they're not in my pocket.

Then she put them back in her pocket. Now they are.

In my pocket. Out. In. Out again.

Could she have finally found a use for her OCD tendencies?

Fixing the earrings in her ears, she told herself, "Now I'm wearing them. Because sometimes I wear my earrings, and sometimes I carry them in my pocket."

That had to be enough. She was too tired to do anything more. Staggering over to the couch, she curled up at one end. Cast adrift, her mind wandered toward sleep.

Magic Man's lips had been firm, warm, and hungry. Thinking of how he had kissed her made her tired body pulse with remembered heat. His skin had been hot, and the muscles in his arms taut with tension. His hair had felt thick, clean, and silken when she had run her fingers through it.

And his ears had been round, not pointed.

Opening her eyes, she stared up at the shadowed ceiling as she realized.

Magic Man wasn't Light Fae.

"WHAT ARE YOU doing?!"

Kallah's sharp voice penetrated the thick blanket of sleep that wrapped around Sid. Struggling to sit up, she blinked at the bright morning light streaming through the tall windows. She felt headachy and dull, as if she were hungover.

The Light Fae woman stood stiff with outrage over her reclining figure. Kallah was dressed impeccably in a simple, well-cut, rose-colored gown, her blond hair pinned at the nape of her neck.

Closing one eye, Sid squinted up at Kallah. "Did I misunderstand something? I practiced last night until I was too tired to go back to the servants' quarters," she said in a rusty voice. "You did say I could be either here or there, right?"

Her stiff posture unbending somewhat, Kallah frowned at her. "Cook said you hadn't shown up for meals, and both your dirty clothes and the pile of your hair were still in your room. You can't simply nap in the music hall whenever you feel like it!"

Swinging her legs off the couch, Sid looked down at her sore hands. Her fingers were reddened, and there were blood blisters on the tips. She had played for a long time last night under the influence of Magic Man's spell. She rubbed the tips of her fingers gently over the balls of her thumbs. There was just no part of this that was going to go easy, was there?

"Understood," she sighed. "I'll try not to practice quite so late tonight."

"What is that?" Kallah asked abruptly. When she glanced up in inquiry, the other woman nodded at her hands. "Those red marks."

"Those are blood blisters from practicing," Sid told her. "They'll pop and be painful for a while, but eventually I'll build up calluses there."

Kallah's frown deepened. "I forgot that humans don't heal as quickly as the Light Fae do. You would still play like that?"

Sid thrust to her feet and said grimly, "I'll do everything I have to in order to play well for her majesty tomorrow evening. I'll do anything I possibly can to keep from going back into that prison. I'll play while my fingers bleed if I must. Have you ever been down there?"

Kallah hesitated, then replied quietly, "No."

"Trust me, you don't ever want to go." Sid met her gaze. "Not ever."

Kallah studied her for a long moment, her lips pressed tightly together. Finally she ordered, "Come with me."

Oh, great. This day was getting off to a terrific start. What fresh hell was in store for her now?

Angling her jaw out, she followed Kallah, who led her through the castle to a place Sid had never seen before. Curiosity overcame her bad temper as she stared around a large, clean room filled with a variety of jars and pots. Different herbal scents vied for supremacy. Menthol and eucalyptus and other scents she couldn't identify.

An older Light Fae woman stepped into the room from another doorway. "Yes, Kallah? What can I do for you?"

"Myrrah, can you heal this human's hands? She's damaged herself." Kallah made a short gesture at Sid.

"Show her."

Eyebrows raised, Sid complied, holding them out for the strange woman's inspection.

"Of course I can heal those," Myrrah said. When she smiled at Sid, laugh lines creased at the corners of her eyes. "They're a minor injury, but they must be irritating and painful."

"Yes, I've had blisters before," Sid replied.

Myrrah told her, "A simple spell will take care of the problem. What's your name, love?"

"Sid," she replied, unsure of what had startled her more—Kallah's brusque act of kindness, or Myrrah's friendly demeanor. Still, she didn't give them her full name. She didn't want to allow the Light Fae to have any more of her than they had already taken. She also couldn't resist adding pointedly, "I can't believe somebody finally asked what my name was, after... I've lost track of how many days I've been here."

Kallah's mouth acquired a sour tilt, while Myrrah took in a gentle breath and simply released it again with a wry smile. Covering Sid's hands with both of hers, she said a quick spell of healing.

Tingling ran through Sid's arms, and when Myrrah lifted her hands away, the blood blisters had completely disappeared. Where they had been, a new, thin layer of callus covered the tips of her fingers in exactly all the right places for playing the lute.

"This is wonderful," Sid told the healer. "If it hadn't been for you, it would have taken me days to get to this point."

"I can give you salve that will soften that thickened skin, if you like."

"I appreciate the offer, but no." Rubbing her fingers together, she smiled. "I need them just the way they are."

"I understand. If you change your mind, you are always welcome to find your way back to me."

"Thank you," Sid told her sincerely. She looked past the healer to meet Kallah's gaze. "Both of you."

"You're welcome," Myrrah replied. "Now, I'm needed back in the infirmary. You can see yourself out."

"Yes, of course," Kallah said. As the healer left them alone, she regarded Sid for a moment. "Well now…er, Sid. What an odd name that is."

"Yours is just as odd to me," Sid told her.

"I imagine so," Kallah murmured. She tapped her foot. Then she seemed to come to some decision as her attention refocused, and she said, "Very well. You will do as you were told and clean your room. After that, you will eat something for breakfast. I don't want to hear of you going back to the music hall until you've looked after your own needs and refreshed yourself properly. And for the gods' sake, don't fall asleep in the hall again! It is totally inappropriate to use the music hall as your bedroom! You have been given leave to practice there for the time being, nothing more."

Sid just looked at her for a moment. She said, "You

can't let your own act of kindness go without a lecture, can you?" Then, when color suffused Kallah's face, she relented with a small laugh. "Never mind. I appreciate what you did, and I'll follow every single one of your orders. I'll clean my room, eat, and use the music hall only for practicing from here on out."

"See that you do," Kallah snapped. "The servants' quarters are down that way, to your right. Now, you've taken enough of my valuable time this morning. I don't want to hear from you, or about you, again today. Is that clear?"

Working for Isabeau as her court lady must be a particular kind of unending hell, Sid thought as she listened to Kallah's scolding. Sure, there might be a certain amount of respect to the job title, but holy God, having to deal with that crazy bitch day in and day out… year in and year out…

Gently, she replied, "It's quite clear. Thank you again, Kallah."

Briefly, Kallah met her gaze, and she gave Sid a short nod. Then she pivoted on one heel and strode away.

"Because saying, 'you're welcome' is such a dangerous, difficult thing to do around here in these parts," Sid whispered to herself.

She had forgotten to take into account the Light Fae's keen sense of hearing. Down the hall, Kallah spun around to glare at her.

Barking out a laugh, Sid held up a hand. "Sorry,"

she choked out. "Have a good day."

Kallah glared harder. "You're welcome," she snapped. Then she whirled around and stalked down the hall until she was out of sight.

Oh lord, Sid thought. This place is so awful, it makes things that are not quite so hellish stand out. Teasing Kallah had been the funniest thing that had happened in days. Weeks.

Rubbing her face, she went in search of her room. Once there, she cleaned up the pile of hair on the floor, made her bed with the blanket, and tucked her tennis shoes into the plain wardrobe.

Then she regarded her dirty outfit from Earth. Somehow the clothes didn't seem as important as they had the day before. The important things were in her pocket—her twenty-one worry stones and her telepathy earrings.

If... *when* she made it back to Earth, she had an entire walk-in closet filled with all kinds of clothes and every type of shoe imaginable. She didn't need this outfit. Still, she couldn't quite bring herself to burn it.

With a sigh, she pulled out her clean tunic and trousers from the wardrobe, gathered up the dirty jeans and hoodie, and took her drying cloth to the bathrooms. After spending a strenuous amount of time washing her clothes in the tubs of warm water, she wrung them out as best as she could and then washed herself quickly.

Again she lucked out and didn't run into anyone

else while she worked. It must be the wrong time of day to have much traffic in the bathrooms. She was glad for the privacy and made a note to avoid mornings and evenings whenever possible.

On the shelves that held the soft, unscented soap, there were stacks of sticks with stiff bristles at one end set beside jars of mint-scented powder that seemed, when she cautiously tasted it, to be like bicarbonate of soda.

After inspecting both items, she concluded the sticks must be some type of toothbrush. Taking one, she used it with a small amount of the minty powder she shook into one palm and scrubbed her teeth.

The last thing she did was wash the dress she'd been wearing. That went much easier than washing her Earth clothes had. Kallah had been true to her word. After she had dunked the dress into the water several times, she held it up, and the water ran off the material. Within a few moments, the dress was clean again, and almost completely dry.

By the time she had finished her toilette, she was chilled and starving. Heading back to her room, she hung up the wet clothes and draped the drying cloth over the wardrobe door. The clothes would dry more quickly if she could put them out in the sun, but she didn't know where she could hang out laundry, and she hadn't been given leave to step outside.

It was clear her behavior was being monitored, and she didn't want to run the risk of another scolding. She and Kallah might have had a less than acrimonious interaction, but she didn't confuse that with believing they had built a true rapport, and she didn't want to strain the Light Fae woman's patience any more than she already had, especially since Kallah had the ear of the Queen.

Once she had finished her personal chores, she went in search of the kitchens. They emitted a blast of heat, noise, and energy, and were easy to find. Several people worked on different dishes at once while an intense man barked orders.

Sid had slipped in and out of hotels through the kitchens several times in the past in order to avoid overzealous fans and the press, and as she looked around with interest, she thought this kitchen was not unlike those hotels. They had to feed a lot of people every day.

The intense man caught sight of her, left what he was doing and strode over. "Yes?" he snapped. "What do you want?"

"I missed breakfast," Sid told him. "I hope it wouldn't be too much trouble to get something simple, like maybe a slice of bread and butter?"

He pointed at her. "You miss a meal, it's on you. I create court meals every single day, and I see the servants get fed as well. I don't have time for anyone who shows up here looking for a snack."

Sid narrowed her eyes. Clearly, there was a pecking order to this castle, and she was tired of being the one who got pecked on.

"I understand," she said in a soft, even tone. "I have been rehearsing so intensely to play for the Queen I haven't been able to make mealtimes yet. Perhaps you will make an exception just this once. If I don't have the energy to practice properly, I'm sure her majesty won't be pleased at the result or be very forgiving of the reason why."

By the slight widening of his eyes, she knew she had scored a hit. "Very well," he said stiffly. "I will make an exception in your case."

"I appreciate that." She smiled.

The Queen's love for music must be well-known. Perhaps there was leverage to be gained from that. It might not win Sid her freedom, but she could make her life a great deal more comfortable until she could find a way to go home. And there was nothing wrong with doing whatever she could to make her life better in the meantime.

The intense man stalked away. She watched him pluck a small, round golden loaf of bread from a pile set on a large platter. Then he went over to a steaming pot that hung suspended over a fire in the giant fireplace.

His back was to her, so she couldn't see what he did then. When he returned, he thrust the loaf into her hands, and handed her a plain metal spoon. An appetizing fragrance rose from the loaf. As she inspected it, she saw that he had cut away the top, scooped out the middle of the loaf, and filled it with a thick, meaty stew.

It was so much more than what she had hoped for, she stared at it. "This is amazing," she told him. "And it smells delicious."

She must have said the right thing, because his stiffness relaxed. While he did not quite smile at her, he gave her a short nod in acknowledgment of the compliment.

"Be sure to let her majesty know how honored I am to support her love of the arts," he said. "And you may have as much food as you require whenever you like. Be sure to ask for me."

If only Sid could reach such an accord with everybody so easily. She nodded in return. "I will," she replied. "I'll be sure to ask for you by name."

"I am Triddick. And you?"

"Sid."

His expression filled with curiosity. "When do you play for her majesty?"

"Soon," she told him. "Tomorrow evening."

"She has exacting tastes," he told her, not without a good amount of pride, since that reflected on him. "You must be quite nervous."

"I was yesterday," she replied with a smile. "Now I'm looking forward to it."

Arching one eyebrow, he studied her with that intense, narrow stare. "With her music master, Olwen, away visiting his family, you have a rare opportunity. Good luck to you, young lady."

"Thank you," she said. Indicating the loaf, she added, "And thanks for breakfast."

He inclined his head in reply. As she turned away, she almost bumped into a man who had come up behind her.

Looking up, she was about to apologize, when she froze, staring.

The man was obviously human, or at least human-like, with dark hair, a weathered, cynical face, and wolfish eyes. He had a powerful build and wore leather armor, along with a knife and a sword.

As he ran his gaze down her figure, cold interest glittered in his eyes. "Well, well," he said. "What delicious tidbit do we have here?"

From behind her, Triddick snapped, "She is not for the likes of you, Warrick."

"I'll be the judge of what should be for the likes of me," the man named Warrick replied in a soft growl while he showed hard, white teeth in a semblance of a smile. "What's your name, precious? And where can I find you?"

As she listened to the exchange between the two men, her stomach tightened. Heart hammering, she searched Warrick's cold gaze for any hint that he might be her Magic Man. He seemed to be the right size and build, although she didn't think she could know for sure unless she put her hands on him.

But the thought of touching him, or allowing him to touch her, made her recoil. His gaze was so predatory. This couldn't be the man who had healed her, who had talked with her so compassionately and offered her help from a well of his own painful memories.

This couldn't be the man who had run his hands so gently down her body as he kissed her so passionately…. Could it?

If she'd been wearing the telepathy earrings, she could have asked him. But she had kept them, along with her stones, safely tucked into her pocket. Maybe they worked when they came in contact with her skin?

As she started to slip a hand into her pocket to find out, Triddick snapped, "She's the Queen's new musician, and you *will* leave her alone! Now, this is my domain, and you are not welcome here. Be off with you!"

Warrick's interest in her shifted to a much more chilling expression. Setting one hand on the hilt of his knife, he said softly to Triddick, "One of these days you'll snap at me one too many times, old man. And I promise you won't like what happens next."

The activity in the kitchen had stilled. Sid noted that all eyes were on them.

"Wow," she said to Warrick, loud enough for everyone to hear. "How mad do you think the Queen would get if you messed with her food?"

He didn't like that, she saw as his eyes narrowed and the expression in them flared, quick and hot. But he said nothing more. Instead, after a slow, cold look around the room, he turned on one heel and left.

Watching him leave, she muttered to Triddick, "What an asshole."

But what if that had all been an act? Warrick was literally the only other person she had seen so far who wasn't Light Fae.

Triddick focused his attention onto her. "Warrick is one of the Queen's Hounds, and he's very dangerous," he told her in a quiet voice meant for her ears alone. "He would never dare to act in such a way if Morgan were here. You'll stay away from him, if you know what's good for you."

Very dangerous, *hmm*? With a sinking heart, she realized that would fit with everything Robin had said to her. She didn't want it to, but it did fit.

And who was this Morgan guy?

Just as she was about to ask Triddick, he strode away, snapping orders to his kitchen staff, and their brief moment of accord was over.

Maybe Kallah would answer some of her questions if Sid could catch her in the right mood. Or better yet, perhaps Myrrah.

Or maybe she should just keep her mouth shut, eat her food, and get back to the music hall. She mustn't forget all these people had lived here for a long time before she showed up. They would have alliances, grudges, and motivations she couldn't possibly know anything about.

She also mustn't forget they were all still watching

her.

More than a little rattled, she carried her meal to the music hall. On the route, she had to dodge several servants dressed in brown clothes. One stood still, eyes closed, while a whirlwind like a small tornado moved systematically back and forth over the hall floor.

As Sid stared, dirt was sucked into the whirlwind, and she remembered what Kallah had said about the castle getting cleaned by magic. Even the house cleaners had a generous amount of magic.

After watching for a few moments, she slipped past the worker and hurried on to the music hall. After she ate, she got back to work.

She hadn't slept enough. She still felt draggy and hungover, but years of discipline had taught her a long time ago how to keep going.

Besides, she could sleep when she was dead.

Chapter Thirteen

MORGAN SLEPT DEEPLY until late the next morning, and when he woke, he knew he had turned a corner. Despite the fact that fighting with Robin had torn open his wound again, he felt stronger and steadier, and even though he had spent himself utterly the day before, he felt more of his magic had returned as he'd slept.

He had been in a desperate scramble ever since he had heard of Sid's kidnapping. Now, for the first time, he felt like he had enough energy to start digging through the books he had brought with him. Eager to get started, he rose to wash and eat a quick breakfast, and then he settled at the table in front of the books.

He had stolen from the Bodleian Library a wide sweep of anything that might bear useful information, so he was prepared to run into dead ends and irrelevancies.

Still it was disheartening to spend hours poring through the books, reading esoteric passages about the Deus Machinae, or God Machines. The Deus Machinae were legendary items of massive Power that legend said the seven gods of the Elder Races had cast into the world to ensure their will continued to be enacted throughout time. Yet nothing he read tied those legends to Azrael's Athame.

In fact, he found no reference to Death's Knife in any of the passages he read. Personally, he had never heard of the Knife before the night Isabeau had stabbed him. That single act had irrevocably transformed his life and changed the course of history at once. Since that time, he had studied it carefully, albeit at a distance, for the many years he had watched it dangle from Isabeau's waist.

It was an item of tremendous Power and age, so theoretically it could be one of the God Machines. If it was, it would be indestructible.

If it wasn't one of the Machines, there might be some hope of breaking it. But he couldn't learn how to do that until he learned more of the Knife's provenance and origin.

He needed to travel to the Louvre while he still had the freedom to do so, to consult the Elven book. But he didn't dare leave Sidonie while her fate was so precarious. Perhaps he could slip away after her audience with the Queen, although he scowled to consider that.

He hated the thought of leaving her, period. She didn't know her way here at court, and she was vulnerable to the vipers that had manipulated their way to positions of power.

One step at a time. One obstacle at a time.

For now, the next step was getting through tomorrow evening.

Restless after a day of physical inactivity, that evening he prowled around the neighboring hills to see if he could catch the scent of the puck, but either Robin had decided to go back to Earth or after their confrontation he had grown stealthier, and Morgan didn't find any hint of his presence.

Distrustful of such a clear and open lack of evidence, Morgan returned to his cottage, where he tended to his wound and rewrapped it and doused himself with more of the hunter's spray.

This time when he slipped down to the night market, the need was not so urgent to steal food. Sidonie would be fed, at least until tomorrow evening, and he wasn't hungry.

This time he was interested in information.

Cloaking himself tightly as always, he threaded his way like a ghost through the crowded streets and the lantern-lit stalls. At Gardin the cloth merchant's stall, he heard Sidonie's name and paused, his attention sharpening.

"I heard this human named Sid found her way to court to petition the Queen for an audience," Gardin told the noblewoman who fingered a length of damask silk as she listened.

Morgan knew the noblewoman, Freya, who was a notorious gossip. Freya leaned close, her eyes avid.

"The music master will not be pleased when he returns to discover his hall has been invaded by a human upstart," she told Gardin.

The cloth merchant shrugged. "Eh, Olwen has nothing to worry about. No human musician, no matter how ambitious, can possibly hope to supplant a master Light Fae musician who has been working at perfecting his craft for centuries."

"True," Freya agreed. "If this woman is hoping to find a position at court, I'm sure she will be sorely disappointed."

Morgan suppressed a derisive snort. Sidonie's talent was light-years beyond Olwen's. Once they overcame the hurdle of tomorrow evening's audience, if she wanted, she could ascend rapidly in favor to become a true power at court in her own right.

Not that she would care about any of that. She only wanted to return to her rightful life.

"I'll wager you she'll be sent packing before tomorrow evening is out," Gardin declared.

Freya laughed. "I'm sure you're right."

The pair knew nothing. The only thing of note in the conversation was that news of Sidonie's presence and her upcoming audience with Isabeau had reached town. Morgan moved on.

Rounding a corner, he stopped dead. Not six feet away, three Hounds had gathered in front of Zacharias's stall. Zacharias sold pints of dark, yeasty beer, fried meats, boiled eggs, and fish and potatoes.

The three men sat at a rough plank, eating and drinking.

Warrick, Johan, and Harrow. They would have led the hunt for Morgan, back to Earth. If they had returned to Avalon, that meant the other Hounds would be returning as well, and that meant sneaking around the castle and town just became a lot harder.

He was also running low on the hunter's spray. Whether he decided to travel to the Louvre or not, he needed to make a quick trip to Earth for more. With the Hounds returning, he needed the spray now more than ever.

Morgan tightened his cloaking spell until it lay against his skin like a heavy, hot layer of rubber, blocking everything else out, even the slightest breeze. He wanted very badly to step forward to eavesdrop on the other men's conversation. But if anyone might say in passing the words that could activate his geas, it was those three.

And he didn't dare hire someone else to eavesdrop for him. Not knowing the triggers to avoid, they would simply repeat what the other men said, and he would still be trapped. Simmering with frustration, he backed away and left the night market altogether.

It was time to move on and see how Sidonie had fared with her day.

On his way out, he stopped by the honey merchant to steal a piece of honeycomb. After he sucked the sweetness of the honey out of the comb, he would have wax he could use to stop his ears.

He stopped just long enough to suck on the honeycomb, savoring the rich, golden sweetness as he chewed the wax until it was soft and pliable enough he could mold it into earplugs. Then he made his way through the castle.

It was harder this time. Before, he had stolen through in the middle of the night. Now, it was earlier in the evening, all the witchlights were aglow, and more people were awake and about. Also he had to concentrate on using his magical senses to avoid detection, not his hearing.

Finally he reached the doors of the music hall, only to discover the hall was dark and empty. Sidonie wasn't there.

Growling under his breath, he went on the hunt to find her. Her scent was clear and easy to follow. It led back to the servants' quarters. That area was much darker than the rest of the castle, as most of the sensible, hardworking servants were already in bed.

One room had candlelight glowing from the crack at the bottom of the door. Candlelight, not the cooler glow of a witchlight.

The area outside that room also smelled like Sidonie. Pausing outside the door, he said telepathically, *I'm here. Douse your candle.*

For a moment, he wasn't sure if he had made a telepathic connection, and he pulled the wax from his ears so he could hear what was happening on the other side of the door.

Then, cautiously, she asked, *What if I don't want to?*

Frustrated again, he rubbed his face. Part of him wanted to shove through that door and take her into his arms, but the other part held back. *We've already talked about this more than once. You know it's not safe.*

Not safe for whom? she asked. Her telepathic voice sounded tense. *Me or you?*

The tension could have been due to her discomfort at the new use of telepathy, but he thought he had grown to know her better than that. He replied quietly, *Not safe for either of us. What's wrong?*

I'm no longer comfortable with our arrangement, she whispered.

Why? he demanded. Had she discovered who he was? The urge to storm through that door was getting stronger. *What's happened?*

Are you Warrick? she asked.

The question hit from out of the blue, and it made him recoil. *Gods, no!* he exclaimed violently. *Why would you ask such a thing?!*

Do you swear you're telling the truth? She probably had no idea how telepathic speech mimicked verbal speech. Doubtless she was unaware of just how shakily she had asked that question.

But Morgan heard it, and furious concern roared through him. What had that bastard done to her? In a soft, evenly controlled voice, he said, *If Warrick has done anything to hurt or frighten you, I swear I will cut out his heart and feed it to him.*

On second thought, that probably hadn't sounded as reassuring as he would have wished. Pressing one fist against the wooden door, he willed her to believe him.

A shadow passed in front of the candlelight shining underneath the door, and there was a soft, muffled sound, close by.

She said, more calmly, *He didn't do anything to me. He was boorish and suggestive, and he wears weapons. It's not a good combination. He also threatened Triddick, who stood up for me and backed him off.*

Morgan was going to kill Warrick. He didn't know how, and he didn't know when, but it would be soon. He had always known Warrick had a rough edge, but he'd always been able to keep the other man in check before. Now that Morgan was supposedly gone from Avalon, Warrick's true colors were emerging.

Quietly, he asked, *Why on earth would you think I was Warrick? Have I done anything boorish or suggestive to you?*

No! she exclaimed. Then, more calmly, *No, of course you haven't. You're… you've been amazing. I literally don't believe I would still be alive, if it weren't for you, and you didn't stop with just saving my life. You keep helping me. I've grown to rely upon you. But you are the one who keeps warning me not to trust you, and I know you're not Light Fae. Warrick is the first man who isn't Light Fae that I've seen since I've gotten here. And when I thought about how I know so few facts about you, I got a little freaked out.*

He absorbed all that in silence. Finally he said, *You*

know I can't promise what might be done under the geas, but I will never hurt you. I—the man—will never hurt you. I will never push past any barrier you erect, or coerce you into doing something you do not want to do. I will always support, respect, and defend you.

How chivalrous, she whispered.

Well… yes. His lips pulled into a wry smile.

Your well-being matters to me, he said. *The music your spirit creates… it matters to me. If you want to talk to me through a closed door, and if you want to keep your candle lit so you aren't in the dark, I am not going to do anything to change that. And if you tell me to go away and leave you alone, I will go. Just… for your sake, we should arrange to meet tomorrow, so I can cast the battle spell on you before you play for the Queen.*

On the other side of the door, he heard a quiet thump, as if she had banged her forehead against the panel. She said, *Thank you for saying all that. I believe you. Hang on.*

A moment passed, and then the light went out in her room. None of the servants' rooms had locks on the doors, but he made no move to open hers. Clenching his fists, he made himself wait, until *she* opened the door.

When she did, he strode forward and snatched at her. At the same moment, she leaped at him, throwing her arms around his neck, and something raw and angry eased inside, and he was so tired of thinking about what he should or shouldn't do, he threw all of it out of his head, lifted her off her feet, and kissed her.

Raising her face, she met him halfway. Their lips collided, not gently. A muffled laugh escaped her, then she parted her lips, and he delved inside as deeply as he could go.

Kissing her was a euphoric experience. The softness of her wet mouth, the eagerness with which she kissed him back, the velvet sensation of her tongue sliding across his.

His conscience made one last effort. Lifting his head a little, he whispered against her mouth, "We shouldn't be doing this."

"Shut up and get inside so we can close the door," she whispered back.

Quickly, he complied and shoved the door gently with one foot so that it settled into place. He glanced around. The walls of the servants' rooms were made of thick stone, but someone could still eavesdrop at either the window or the door. With a flick of his fingers, he cast a dampening spell in the room so that all the sound inside the room was muffled.

"I spelled the room," he told her. "We can talk freely. Nobody outside will be able to hear anything."

"Okay, good to know. Wait a minute." In the faint illumination of the moonlight shining into her small window, he watched her tilt her head. She asked, "Why didn't you throw that kind of spell when you came to visit me in prison? But instead you said, oh no, we needed to whisper."

"We do need to whisper without the dampening

spell," he snapped. "Either that or use telepathy. I've been dealing an injury, and after I healed you that first night, I had no magic left. Besides, I didn't want you to be able to recognize my voice. But I let that one out of the bag when I gave you the telepathic earrings."

She threw up her hands in exasperation. "What on earth are you talking about now? Remember, I know almost nothing about magic items."

"A person's telepathic voice sounds like their physical voice," he told her. "As soon as you heard me telepathize, you've been able to identify me by my voice. But since you'd gotten yourself out of prison, I thought we needed to be able to communicate any way we could, so I made the earrings. And right now it doesn't matter if we whisper or not. It just matters that we not be overheard—but there'll be plenty of times I can't throw the dampening spell."

Heaving an aggrieved sigh, she said, "Okay, I'll bite. Why not?"

"Because it would never go unnoticed in a crowd. Dampening spells are cast over areas, not over people, and as soon as someone walks into a dampened area they know it." Resentment boiled over. He accused, "I can't believe you thought I might be Warrick."

"Oh, I get it now," she remarked, dark humor lacing her voice. "You really spelled the room so we could argue."

"Can you blame me?" he snapped.

"Fine—go ahead and be mad at me. But I didn't

know what to believe!" she exclaimed. "You're so insistent on not telling me any details about yourself.... Or at least as few details as possible. Even just now, you only told me about telepathic voices sounding like physical voices because you had to."

He clenched his jaw at the accusation, but he didn't say anything because she was right.

She continued, more softly, "Sometimes it's really hard to trust that. If we were in any kind of normal situation back home in New York, I wouldn't have exchanged two sentences with you. I probably would have called 911 at the first sign of any of this cloak-and-dagger stuff."

"I know," he muttered. "This is far outside anything you've ever had to deal with before, and I don't blame you for having doubts. And I was the one who told you that you needed to be wary of me."

"Yes," she murmured. She smoothed her hands across his chest. "Yet despite that, and despite the fact that you keep hoarding information about yourself, I still ended up trusting you anyway."

And despite the fact that he tried to hoard information about himself, snippets still kept escaping, a little here, a little there. Some things, like the telepathy, were pieces she didn't know how to put together yet, but she was bright, curious, and tenacious, and she was right. Sooner or later, all the pieces would come together and she would figure out who he was, but he was determined to delay that moment as long as possible.

When she did discover his identity, he thought it very likely she would not want to have anything more to do with him. And even if, by some miracle, she did, they would still need to keep their relationship a secret.

Isabeau must never connect them together or realize how much Sidonie had come to mean to him. If she ever discovered that, her hold over him would be complete. All she would have to do is threaten to have Sidonie tortured or killed, and Morgan would do whatever she wanted without resistance.

And he could never find ways to retaliate against Isabeau as long as she held Sidonie captive. He would lose the last corner of his soul that he had fought so hard to keep.

Her hands slid down to his waist, and she traced the edge of his bandages, murmuring, "How is your injury?"

"It's getting better," he said. "It's healing well."

"Good."

As soothing as Sidonie's touch was, he still couldn't let their argument go. He said accusingly, "But Warrick!"

She laughed softly, but it didn't sound amused. "Believe me, the thought didn't sit well with me either."

He had to feed his own addiction. He touched her neck lightly, and rubbed her cheek with the ball of one thumb. Her skin felt softer than a rose petal. Suddenly, he wanted to lick her all over, wanted it so badly his whole body went taut.

To distract himself from the temptation, he asked, "How did you discover I wasn't Light Fae? What did I do to give myself away?"

"It was when we kissed last night." Slipping her arms around his waist, she leaned against him and rested her head on his chest. "I ran my fingers through your hair, remember?"

"I do." The memory heated his blood.

"It was only after you left that I realized your ears weren't pointed," she told him, her voice muffled against his shirt. "You couldn't be Light Fae."

Not yet able to smile at her cleverness, he pressed his lips to her forehead. "And your busy mind did the rest."

"Of course. I told you, I can't let go of things. And then I ran into Warrick." She shuddered. "I didn't want to think you and he might be the same man, but I also didn't know any differently."

His arms tightened. "Okay, fair enough," he said. "For your information, there are several men around the castle and in town who look human but aren't, and more should be arriving over the next few weeks. Take care around them, because they're all dangerous."

"Oh, great."

He could just imagine her expression accompanying that. Biting back a smile, he added, "There are also a few humans scattered throughout the town. They're the last surviving descendants of what had once been a thriving human kingdom in Avalon. There are a few other Races as well, so the population isn't purely Light Fae. You just haven't seen evidence of the others yet."

She stirred in his arms. "What happened to the human kingdom?"

"Isabeau and Modred happened," he replied curtly. "They killed the rulers, and either destroyed or drove off most of the population. Many of them fled to Great Britain. Isabeau has always been single-minded in consolidating her power base. Some years before, she had driven away her twin sister, along with anyone who supported her, and once the humans had been conquered, she claimed all Avalon as her own."

"Does she have any redeeming qualities whatsoever?" Sid demanded.

A quiet snort escaped him. "I'm the wrong person to ask," he said dryly. After a moment's thought, he added, "I suppose there may be one thing. She doesn't tolerate rape, especially in wartime—at least, she doesn't tolerate physical rape. Clearly, she has no issue with using magical coercion. But physical rape is a capital offense, and soldiers who are found guilty of it are beheaded."

Sid shook her head. "She may not tolerate rape, but she still embraces torture and, apparently, genocide too. She also has no problem with keeping people in captivity, coercing them to do her bidding, and throwing them in prison whenever she gets a stick up her ass. I'm feeling no compulsion to rush to be her friend."

"Nor I, but let's not waste any more time talking about her." Loosening his hold, he clasped one of her hands and led her to the narrow bed, where he sat and leaned his back against the wall. "We're able to get so little time together as it is."

"I agree." She readily climbed onto the bed too and curled against his side.

Pulling her close, he buried his nose in her short, clean hair. There were no perfumes to clog up his sinuses when he inhaled, just her pure, feminine scent.

The fact that she came so readily to his arms was a towering miracle. Sharing this one moment of peace was a rarity so fragile and precious it was almost indescribable.

It was too bad he had to shatter it.

Bracing himself inwardly, he said, "I have some news. I should have told you about it yesterday, but there has been a lot to deal with, and the most important thing was for us to find a way for you to play for Isabeau tomorrow."

And the truth was, he hadn't wanted to tell her. It was another piece of himself that he had to let go. But the stakes were too high for him to keep silent.

Her head lifted from his shoulder. "What is it?"

"Robin is here in Avalon," he replied. He felt the shock of his words ripple through her body. "Or at least he was here yesterday, and I do not believe his sense of self-preservation is strong enough to have made him go home between now and then."

The ripples quaking through her slender frame intensified. Tightening his hold, he willed for the shaking to ease. While he had known the news was significant, he hadn't realized the deep level of distress it would cause her. Upon reflection, he should have.

She whispered as if to herself, "'Hell is empty, and all the devils are here.'"

He recognized the quote from *The Tempest*. Then he thought of all the devils she'd had the misfortune to encounter—Robin, Isabeau, Modred, the guards in the prison below, the Light Fae commander who had refused to let her go and who had, instead, brought her to Avalon.

And not least among the devils, if she could but know it, was himself.

"Unfortunately," he said as gently as he knew how, "it would appear so."

✧   ✧   ✧

SID TREMBLED AS fever-bright memories raced through her mind.

Jogging through Regent's Park in the morning fog.

Standing frozen in the wings of the stage, convinced her stalker was in the concert audience, watching her.

The immense, black horse, rearing in the car's windshield, fire flying from its hooves, and the groaning scream of the metal as the car flipped.

Being dragged away from the wreck, and racing

over the ground, tied to the back of the horse. Robin binding her hand and foot, healing her, gagging her.

Sobbing over her as if his heart had broken. *The motherfucker.*

Her lips had gone numb. She had to lick them before she would whisper, "Did you talk to him?"

"Yes," he said, which shook her further. "It was more of a confrontation, rather than a rational conversation. I chose not to kill him when I had the chance, and I hope I don't regret that." He sighed. "Robin doesn't understand anything, not the real reasons for things that have happened, or what I'm truly capable of—for good or for ill. I tried to ask him to take you back to Earth, but the geas wouldn't let me say the words."

As she listened to him, her shivering eased. She said, more calmly, "You mean, he doesn't know about the geas, which means you can't talk about it with him."

"Yes, there's that." Pulling his arm from her shoulders, he twisted and lay down, and put his head in her lap, laying one forearm across his eyes. "And also, remember, I can't help prisoners escape. You may not be in the cell down below, but both I and the geas know fully well you're still a prisoner here.

"Yeah," she whispered. "I am."

"He was treated very badly here for a long time," he said. "I'd be surprised if he would risk sneaking into the castle, but I'm surprised he had it in him to come back to Avalon at all. Just be careful. He said he makes an excellent rat, but he could just as easily become a cat, a sparrow, or one of the castle dogs."

Or a troll.

"I'm glad you warned me." Absently, she stroked his hair. "I'll be on the lookout."

Because I have things I want to say to that sneaky shit, she thought.

I have things I want to say very badly, indeed.

Chapter Fourteen

MAGIC MAN CAPTURED one of her hands and brought it to his mouth. She actually kind of loved how he did that. It seemed so old-fashioned and courtly.

Curling her fingers along his lean cheek, she felt the short stubble along the strong, clean line of his jaw. He must have shaved some time earlier that day. What an intimate thing to sense about someone she didn't know.

But that statement was ringing less true the more she repeated it.

She *did* know him. She didn't know certain details, but she knew the ring of sincerity in his voice when he promised to support, respect, and defend her.

She knew the private hell he was living. She knew he had an innate decency and sensitivity. He appreciated music, he mourned deeply for something in his past, and he was stronger than she could ever hope to be.

"So honey," he said with a smile in his voice. "Tell me about your day."

She tilted her head as she considered how to

answer that. "You know, for being caught in a bigoted, racist, sadistic kind of hell, today wasn't quite as nightmarishly awful as the past couple of weeks have been. You said the battle spell would fade away completely, but when I went to the music hall to practice, I remembered quite a bit of how to play the lute. On my own, I still wouldn't be ready to perform tomorrow night, but there's more there than I thought there would be. I'm encouraged."

"That's because you're an accomplished musician already in your own right," he told her. His voice was pure pleasure to listen to, deep, warm, and steady. "Your skills are adapting."

"Thank you." She sighed. "I miss my Vuillaume something awful though."

"Your violin?"

She didn't know why she was surprised he knew what a Vuillaume was. "Yeah."

"I'm so sorry about that," he murmured as he played with her fingers.

"I just have to believe that I'll either see it again, or have another beautiful violin I love just as much," she said huskily. Then, eager to change the subject, she asked, "How was your day?"

"It was not quite as hectic as my recent days have been," he replied wryly. "I was able to get back to researching the geas."

"Oh?" She perked up. "How did that go?"

"It went nowhere. But I have a lot more to read."

He hesitated, then added, "There's the possibility I might need to make a trip to Earth soon."

"What? No!" The words burst out of her before she could stop them. Then she caught herself. How selfish she sounded. Biting her lip, she added reluctantly, "I mean I suppose if you have to go, you have to."

"I don't want to leave you alone, not here, not in this place," he told her. "But there's a book in the Louvre I should consult about the geas, and I need a few other essentials from Earth if I'm going to keep sneaking around here without getting caught. The Queen's Hounds have highly sensitive noses, and the only way I can disguise my scent is by using a scent-blocking spray sold on Earth. I'm running low on my supply."

Agh! Near to tears, she realized just how much she had grown to rely on him. The thought of facing the daily challenges in Avalon without him was almost crippling. "I understand."

He gripped her hand so tightly it neared the point of pain. She felt the strength in his hand and the tension running through his long body.

"Sidonie," he said deeply. "I *really* don't want to go. I'll try not to, but I may not have a choice."

He had done so much for her, all while coping with his own injury, and here she was being a needy whiner. Swallowing hard, she injected strength into her voice. "It will be okay. I promise. But I'll miss you."

I'll miss you so terribly. She clamped down on the

words and didn't say them.

He was silent for a long moment. Then he whispered, "Lie down with me."

I would love to.

Her internal reaction had been so thunderously loud, for a moment, she didn't know if she had said it aloud, if she had telepathized it, or if she had managed to keep it private. He didn't react, so she must have kept it to herself.

Slowly, she eased down beside him, and he opened his arms to draw her closer. The bed was narrow enough, and he was so big she had to mold her body close to his in order for them both to fit. As she settled against him carefully to avoid jostling his injury, he let out a long sigh and guided her head onto his shoulder.

She slipped one leg over his, so the bowl of her pelvis fit closely next to his hip. The heavy weight of his muscled arms provided a sense of shelter and an anchoring that she couldn't remember ever experiencing before.

All his warnings had trickled out of her mind. He had become her single point of safety, warmth, and security. Resting against him felt like she had come home for the first time in her life. She could not imagine how they could continue as they were, yet at the same time, she could not imagine not having him in her life.

Tucking one hand underneath the nape of his neck, she turned her face into his shirt. The comfort of lying beside him was staggering. She felt tension she'd had no idea she was carrying melt away, until her muscles felt loose and relaxed.

"God, this feels good," he murmured.

Unable to verbalize the overwhelming strength of her emotions, she simply nodded. As she shifted to settle more comfortably against him, she felt again the bulk of bandage underneath his shirt.

Resting one hand lightly on it, she asked, "What happened here? I don't think you ever told me."

He turned his head so that his mouth rested on her forehead. "It's a knife wound."

"What?!" She jerked up her head. Despite her own growing acquaintance with violence over the past few weeks, she still hadn't become accustomed to it. "That's terrible. What happened?"

Chuckling slightly, he stroked the back of her head. "It's okay. It's self-inflicted. Sort of. I paid someone in London to stab me. Originally it was an arrow wound."

Blinking several times, she muttered, "I-I just don't know what to say."

"It all goes back to the geas. I was wounded in battle earlier this summer." His stroking hand wandered down to the tense spot between her shoulder blades. Gently, he massaged the area. "Isabeau was furious at the outcome, and she said she didn't want to see me again until I was fully healed. The nature of the geas is such that I could take that literally. I disappeared before she could realize what she'd done and issue another order contradicting it. I couldn't let the wound from the arrow heal completely. While I can't harm myself, the geas didn't stop me when I hired someone to stab me."

He had been badly injured for weeks, yet he had still returned to Avalon to help her. Overcome, for a moment she wasn't able to say anything. When she could, she whispered huskily, "I don't like the idea of you being in so much pain."

He touched her lips with his fingertips, in a feather-light caress. "This is the most freedom I've known in centuries," he said. "I'm reveling in it. But in order to stay free, I can't hear someone tell me if Isabeau has changed her mind and wants me back. Do you understand? Be very careful what you say to me of what you may overhear."

What a deadly situation, when even words became as dangerous as weapons. She captured his wandering hand and gripped it tightly.

"I'll be careful," she promised. "I swear it."

"I know you will, now that you know what's at stake." He squeezed her fingers.

"I'm surprised you told me about it." A touch of wryness entered her voice. "It's more information about you."

"You needed to know. If I don't find some way to break free of the geas, I'll need to return to Isabeau in a few weeks, unless…"

"Unless, what?" she pressed, when he hesitated.

"Unless I can talk you into stabbing me next," he said.

Hollow dismay spread through her middle. It had, unfortunately, become a familiar emotion. How would it feel to press a knife into someone she had grown to care for so deeply?

Someone she... loved? It was no use telling herself it would help keep him free, because trying to imagine the visceral reality of it turned her stomach.

"I-I don't know if I could do it," she whispered. "I've never hurt anyone in my life, not even in a good cause."

"I understand," he told her gently. "But, Sidonie, you may be the only one I trust enough to do it. Someone else could try to hurt me worse than necessary, or even try to kill me."

He trusted her? That should give her a warm and fuzzy feeling, except for the reason they were discussing it in the first place.

As she tried to imagine someone else stabbing him, a horrified protectiveness surged up so strongly she said, "If you need it, I'll do it. I don't want you going to someone else for something so dangerous."

She hadn't realized he had tensed until he relaxed again. "Thank you." He kissed her forehead. "I know that couldn't have been easy for you. Maybe I won't need it. I've still got a couple of weeks of healing left. I'm hoping to have made headway on learning more about the geas by then."

"God, I hope so," she said fervently. The closer she drew to him emotionally, the more terrible his entrapment felt. "How did she trap you in the first place?"

"She struck me with a Powerful magic item. She calls it Azrael's Athame, or sometimes Death's Knife. It's a knife she wears on a gold chain around her waist. I don't know where she got it, or where it's from, but when she struck me with it, it transformed me into ... well, into the creature I am now. Once, I was human like you."

Creature, he said. And she had noted his hesitation.

He didn't want to tell her what he was. That meant it was important, either another important piece of information that could help her identify him, or ...

Or it was something so terrible, he didn't want to share it.

But, what *creature* could be so terrible?

Pushing away, she sat up. What was he? Before, he was just a man with extraordinary magical abilities. Now, she didn't know what lay beside her in the dark.

Was she really going to push him on this? Was she ready to know whatever it was he didn't want to tell her?

Steadily, she said, "I think you'd better tell me all of it."

He flattened a hand at the small of her back. "I don't want to."

Warmth from his palm spread through her muscles. Even now, his touch gave her a solid sense of comfort.

"I know you don't, but I think you'd better anyway."

The bed creaked as he sat too. "I'm a lycanthrope, Sidonie. I'm one of the Queen's Hounds."

Lycanthrope. She mulled it over. Where had she heard that word before? She had read about it recently, in one of the London daily newspapers.

Tilting her head at the large shadow of the man beside her, she asked, "You're a werewolf?"

"Yes, or at least a certain type of one." His reply was calm, which somehow made the outlandish words easier to hear. "The Hounds don't lose control when there's a full moon, and when we change, we retain our intelligence. We have vastly expanded lifespans, and we don't go into a mindless frenzy. And we can telepathize. I think that might have something to do with the fact that we're made from the Athame—or at least I was made from the Athame. When she orders me to, I make the others."

Without his body radiating heat against hers, the world felt cold and less vital. Shivering, she wrapped her arms around herself. "You make other lycanthropes. The other Hounds."

"Yes."

She heard the stress in her breathing and tried to correct it. "You make them by … how? Do you bite them?"

"When I'm in my lycanthrope form, yes," he said again. His hand withdrew from her back.

Then it clicked. That was what she had read—the

article in the newspaper had focused on treating lycanthropy the disease. A peculiarly British problem, there were other lycanthrope clans scattered throughout the world, but most of the population lived in the UK.

Like vampirism, lycanthropy was incurable. Unlike vampirism, if a person who had been bitten got treatment quickly enough, they didn't have to turn.

She rubbed her face. "We've kissed?"

Rather deeply. Erotically, even.

She didn't want to feel betrayal. She *believed* he would not do anything to hurt her. But still, she needed to hear the words.

"Kissing or having sex isn't an issue, as long as there isn't any bloodplay," he said gently. "Childbirth is risky. Conception isn't a problem, but often the mother passes on the disease to her baby anyway if she gives birth naturally. Most lycanthropes who want to be mothers choose in vitro fertilization and a surrogate. I would never expose you to this disease. Lycanthropy is only passed to humans through a blood wound. If you had to stab me, I would insist you wear protective gear so there was no chance of you risking infection. But make no mistake about this, Sidonie. I am a monster, not a man."

No. *No.*

She had already started shaking her head before those last words had fully sunk in. "Don't denigrate yourself like that," she said. "The two things are not mutually exclusive. You might be a lycanthrope, but you are also a man."

After a moment, he said softly, "Many people don't see us that way."

"*I* see you that way."

Reaching out, she took his hand and sat cradling it in her lap. A fine, almost undetectable tremor was running through him. This was hard for him. She stroked his fingers as they sat quietly. The silence gave them both a chance to recover from what he had told her.

"Thank you for telling me," she murmured. "I'm glad you did. Now, is this it? Is this the worst of what you've got to tell me?"

"No."

"Are you going to tell me about it now?"

"No."

He said it so calmly. How could he say that so calmly?

She wasn't calm, at least not inside. She was rattled again, and she worked hard to hide it.

She had fully expected him to say *yes*. Because what could be worse than telling someone you were a werewolf? Everything else should have gone downhill at that point.

What could be *that bad*?

"You know we're fucked if Isabeau chooses to interrogate me again," she said in a conversational tone. Look at me! she thought. I sound so calm and rational.

Those acting classes really paid off!

"I know," he said. "I've told you enough that she can identify me from what you know."

She gripped his fingers hard. So, the reason why he wasn't telling her the rest wasn't because of Isabeau. It was because of her. It was something else he didn't want her to know. Could it possibly have something to do with why Robin was so afraid of him?

"Just when I was coping with the idea that I'd necked with a werewolf," she muttered. "Just when I was beginning to flirt with the idea of possibly … *possibly* inviting sex with a werewolf. I'm trying to imagine how I would tell this story to my best friend. I think it would go something like this: See, I've never seen him in daylight. He's just this werewolf guy, I don't know his name. Damn, he's got some really heavy-duty layers. And do you know what she would say? She would say, Run, Sid. Run very fast and far."

Beside her, he had stiffened. Very quietly, he said, "Sex?"

Emphatically, she took his hand and deposited it in his lap. "I appreciate you, and I care about you— probably too much for my own good. I have a huge amount of sympathy for your situation, and I will gratefully take your help with one more battle spell tomorrow evening. But other than that, either show me your face and tell me your name, or get the fuck out of my room."

He laughed under his breath. It sounded angry.

"You don't pull any punches when you get going, do you?"

"No, I don't." Wanting to get some distance, she slid to sit at the head of the bed, as far from him as she could get.

He was going to leave. She knew it. His secrets mattered too much to him. It made her heart hurt.

Then the room flared to golden light as the candle's wick burst into flame. She stared at it for a split second. The flame burned unnaturally high, a good foot in length.

Out of the corner of her eye, she saw the tall, broad-shouldered man beside her rise off the bed. He came around to go down on one knee in front of her, and braced his hands on the bed on either side of her thighs.

She stared, eyes wide, hungrily soaking in every detail about him.

He was deeply tanned, and he had chestnut-colored hair, a strong-boned, intelligent face, and brilliant hazel eyes. Slight lines fanned out from the corners of his eyes and bracketed his unsmiling mouth.

He looked like he was thirty-seven. There was no sign of his advanced age, except, perhaps, for the bottomless, disciplined composure in those brilliant eyes.

Her gaze flitted everywhere at once, noticing other details, like taking an instant snapshot of the moment. He wore a plain black shirt and trousers, the sleeves rolled up past muscled forearms sprinkled with the same dark chestnut hair. Although the cut of the cloth was simple and sturdy, rather than stylish, it emphasized the lean, muscular power of his body.

He was *gorgeous.*

"My name is Morgan," he told her in his deep, pleasant voice. "I'm called Morgan le Fae, and it's not meant as a compliment. I abandoned my king and let his courtiers be killed, and caused his kingdom to fall. I'm known as a traitor and a murderer, and I'm an instant pariah in virtually any demesne I choose to enter."

Tears sprang to her eyes as she listened. Impulsively, she placed both her hands over his mouth. "Stop."

But he didn't stop. Instead, he switched to telepathy, and as his steady hazel gaze met hers, he told her in the same pleasant, even voice, *There is no such thing as normal in my life. I am eternally at the Queen's beck and call—I kill for her, I lie for her, I assassinate heads of state and destroy governments.*

Stop, she pleaded, stroking his face.

Gently, he folded his hands around hers and kissed each one. *If she wants a land scorched, I will do it and seed it with poison so nothing else will grow. If she wants me to sleep at the foot of her bed, to guard her through the night while she dallies with her lovers, I will do it. When she orders me to create more Hounds, I hunt down experienced soldiers to attack. Once they're transformed, I force them to obey her orders. I built her an army of monsters and command it. If you become the Queen's enemy, I am your worst nightmare. If she tells me to do a thing, I will not stop, ever, until it is done.*

All said in that same steady voice, with that same steady, self-contained gaze, and she realized he believed he was utterly, eternally alone.

He hadn't wanted to tell her who he was because he didn't want to lose her. And now he clearly believed he had.

"Please, for the love of God, stop," she said in a gentle voice. Reaching out, she slid off the bed to kneel on the floor in front of him, put her arms around him, and hug him as tightly as she could.

He was holding himself so rigidly she was afraid he might shatter. That massive composure was coming at a cost, and now her heart hurt for an entirely different reason. Blindly, she rubbed her cheek against his, stroked his hair with both hands. Stop, please stop.

Then his rigidity broke with a suddenness so sharp it was almost audible. He clenched around her, bowing his shoulders as he held her with his entire body. She could feel each one of his fingers pressing along her back and at the nape of her neck.

"You are my friend," she said softly in his ear. "You are the best friend I have in this wretched place."

He put his face in her neck, which muffled his voice. "I'm your only friend in this wretched place."

"True," she acknowledged. His heartbeat hammered against her breasts. "Even so, I trust, respect, and rely on you."

"Oh, Sidonie," he said.

She insisted, "On *you*, the man, not the geas. I know *you* will never hurt me. I know *you* will support, respect, and defend me, and *you* will never coerce me, and never try to push past any barriers I may erect." She pulled back just enough so she could look deeply into his eyes as she said, "And I am so glad I get the chance to tell that to you face-to-face, Morgan."

As she watched, a flood of emotion tightened his face. Huskily, he said, "Your music might be transcendent, but I'm not so sure about your smarts."

Widening her eyes, she gave him a wry smile as she gestured around the bleak little room. "I know, right? Who else could get herself in such a pickle? I mean, look at these clothes!"

Reluctant laughter flashed across his handsome face. Then, almost as quickly, it vanished, to be replaced by an expression of such vulnerable heat her eyes sparked with wetness.

"Morgan," she whispered, to savor the taste of his name in her mouth. "Morgan."

Shadows grew in the room as the unnatural candle flame died down to its normal size, the intense, burning gold replaced with a soft, gentle glow.

Giving her a slow, coaxing smile that turned the heat in the room up by a thousand degrees, he stroked her lips with the balls of his thumbs as he murmured, "Can we get back to talking about possibly inviting that werewolf for sex?"

She was wearing clothes, but they were no barrier to the deep, rich sound of his voice as it caressed her skin. A shiver ran down her back.

She couldn't stop staring at him. So this was what he looked like.

This was the man who had healed her, held her, empathized with her pain, driven away the cold and the loneliness. This man with the sun-bronzed skin, strong features, and intelligent eyes had shown her nothing but kindness.

This magic man, this Morgan.

As she paused, he laughed a little. It was a warm, accepting sound. "Too soon?" he asked as a wry, self-deprecating smile twisted his lips.

"Not at all." She pulled his head down and kissed him.

Immediately, his firm, well-shaped lips molded to hers. Slanting his head, he tilted her back and kissed her with such raw animal hunger, it sent shock jolting through her body.

Coaxing her lips apart, he speared her with his tongue, over and over, while his breathing deepened and turned ragged. Digging her fingers into his shoulders, she held on as she kissed him back.

He was in her mouth. Inside her, in the most intimate imitation of the sexual act.

She felt so much need, too much for her body to take. It ran through her in deep tremors.

Lifting his head, he whispered against her wet,

throbbing lips, "Too much?"

Wasn't that sweet. Considerate, even.

But oh, hell no.

She gasped, "Not enough."

It was as if she had opened a floodgate. If she had thought he had been intense before, it was nothing compared to the hurricane of male aggression that came at her now. He ate at her ravenously, while with one restless hand he cupped her breast then gripped her by the thigh to pull her flush against him so she felt the hard, thickening length of his cock against her pelvis.

She couldn't touch him enough, and she needed to get closer. Squirming against him, she tried to unbutton his shirt, but she was hampered by her own actions. Growling with frustration, she yanked at the cloth.

Scooping her up, he laid her on the bed, then paused only long enough to tear his shirt off.

Oh, dear God, just look at him. He was tanned everywhere, his chest covered with a light sprinkle of hair that narrowed down to a strip that arrowed into his pants. In contrast, the bandage winding around the lower part of his ribs was very white.

The black shirt had hidden the real breadth of his chest and shoulders, and every muscle was cut. He had scars too, scattered across his torso. In the dark, she had never really gotten a clear idea of how he moved with such distinct fluidity.

His shape might be human, but he moved like a

dangerous animal.

The outline of his erection was clearly visible against the confines of his trousers.

She wanted to lick that narrow sprinkle of hair on his long, muscled abdomen so badly.

Suddenly, she was burning up. Sitting, she pulled her tunic over her head. Her sports bra from Earth was still damp and hanging in the wardrobe, but she was built slightly enough she hadn't bothered to try to figure out what might pass for a bra in Avalon. The ugly clothes Kallah had given her were made of a cloth that was thick enough her nipples weren't visible, and that was all that had mattered to her.

As her head came free of her tunic, she found that he had frozen with one knee on the edge of the bed. He stared at her.

She glanced down at herself. She was an A-cup, but at least her nipples were perky.

"Not exactly a wealth of curvature," she said dryly.

Tenderness softened the hunger that had etched his face. He touched one of her breasts, stroking gently along the underside, then caressing the jut of her nipple so lightly it felt like a passing breeze along her skin.

He said deeply, "Sidonie, you're the most beautiful thing I've ever seen."

Her lips parted as she drank that in, and she didn't need to have truthsense as she looked up into his face. She could see the sincerity in his gaze. Suddenly, she felt more beautiful than she ever had before.

It made her feel different in ways she didn't fully comprehend. Bolder, more confident.

She had always been confident about her music, fueled by the sheer relentlessness of unending practice, testing, and feedback.

But this new feeling had nothing to do with her music. It had everything to do with believing she was a desirable woman in the eyes of her lover.

When his hands moved to the fastening of his trousers, she took hold of his wrists and said huskily, "Here, let me help you with that."

His torso flexed as he sucked in a breath, and then he let his hands fall to his sides.

Rising to her knees, she undid the fastening. He wasn't wearing anything underneath, and as she pulled the opening wide, his large erection spilled into her hands.

He was perfect in every way. His cock was thick, the sides corded with veins, the mushroom head broad. As her fingers curled gently around him, discovering the velvety heat, his breathing deepened again. She glanced up.

His gaze had fired with so much passion and emotion, she could not quite believe this was the same self-contained man who had listed all his crimes with such relentless composure. Her eyes prickled with tears.

In a move she had never made before with either of her previous lovers, yet one that felt entirely right, she bent her head just enough to lay his cock against her cheek in a heartfelt gesture of affection.

Whispering her name, he stroked her hair, her temple, the delicate skin at the side of her neck.

The next step seemed as simple and natural as breathing. Pressing a quick kiss to his shaft, she opened her mouth and took him in.

Chapter Fifteen

WHEN MORGAN FELT Sidonie's mouth close over him, the breath left his lungs. A few minutes ago, he had been convinced she would repudiate him.

To go from that to this raw, frank sensuality was shocking, exhilarating.

He stared as the complex muscles in her mouth tightened on him. His entire personal experience with her had been through touch, scent, and the sound of her voice. He had only ever seen her when she was onstage, or in digital images on his phone.

He had known her bone structure would be as slender and graceful as her hands and wrists, but seeing the wings of her shoulder blades, the long curve of her neck, and the champagne-glass shape of her beautiful breasts was quite a different thing from imagining them. Her nipples were a deep, rosy pink and jutted from the round, creamy mounds of flesh. He longed to take them in his mouth, to stroke and tease them.

She licked at him gently. The velvet glide of her tongue over the sensitive skin at the head of his cock made him stiffen further.

"Stop," he said huskily, stroking her cheek.

Immediately, she pulled back, her elegant eyes darkening. "What's wrong?" she asked, the tip of her tongue licking at her lower lip.

She was stunning. He touched one high, delicately molded cheekbone then pushed her back as he came over her. Uncertainly, she complied, stretching out on the bed. It felt incredible to settle on top of her, to feel her body adjust in position to bear his weight.

He propped himself on his elbows and cupped her head in both hands as he stared into her searching gaze. "I'm supposed to pleasure you first," he whispered. "Not the other way around."

A quiet smile widened her lips. Her smile was as beautiful as the rest of her was. As she stroked both hands down the long curve of his back, she whispered in reply, "I don't think there's any particular way this is supposed to go."

"Then humor me," he murmured, returning her smile.

Her eyes widened. Her expression held same kind of hungry fascination that he felt for her, as if she couldn't get enough of the sight of him.

Bending his head, he kissed her, long and deeply. With a nearly inaudible murmur of pleasure, she ran her fingers across the breadth of his shoulders as she kissed him back.

The pleasure from their tongues colliding, their lips molding and remolding to each other, was so extreme it ignited something ravenous in him. Losing control, he ate at her like she was the only feast he had ever been offered, and that was a truth that hit deep in his bones.

He had been starved for ages. Ages.

Her slender, strong arms tightened around him. Lifting one leg, she wrapped it around his waist as she kissed him back.

He needed her mouth. But he needed the rest of her just as much. This feeling was exceptional, terrible. Pulling away from the kiss, he ran his shaking lips along her petal-soft skin, down her slender neck, across the graceful flare of her collarbones. She tasted clean and feminine. He *loved* her skin.

As he kissed his way down to her breasts, her breathing turned ragged. Nipping at her gently, licking and stroking the succulent curves, he pulled first one nipple into his mouth to suckle, then the other.

While he worked on her, she grew restless. Her body heated as the delicious, intoxicating scent of sexual arousal perfumed her skin. Twisting underneath him, digging her fingers into the muscles of his biceps, she tried to rise, but gently, pressing the palm of one hand on her collarbone, he urged her to lie back down.

With a frustrated whimper, she complied. A dark rosy flush had washed over her cheeks. Marks stood out against her pale skin from the gentle things he had done to her. He fingered one mark as he contemplated it, his cock pulsing with need.

"I want to taste you too," she said. "Lick and kiss

you. Bite… I want to bite you."

Goddamn, he wanted it too.

A growl escaped him. Coming into a crouch over her, he slipped one hand underneath her neck and lifted her up to him. *"Do it."*

Her expression was nearly indescribable, both a surrender and a sharpening of intent. As erotic need rose to take over, it was like watching her fall into a bottomless pool. She bared her teeth and reached for him.

He caught just a glimpse of it—both elegant and savage at once. Then she nuzzled her face into his neck, and her teeth fastened on the tendon that ran to his shoulder. With steady, deliberate pressure, her jaws tightened. As he felt the tiny pain, he hissed with pleasure and his cock jerked in response. When she would have pulled back, he pressed her back.

"Harder," he urged.

Her response was immediate. She bit down harder, then sucked at the bite, and he almost spilled himself over her stomach. Withdrawing, she whispered, "I've never done that before. I-I made a mark."

"*Good*," he growled.

This time when he kissed her, the gentleness had vaporized into hot, aggressive need. Kissing him back, she cupped his erection in both hands and pumped him. Her strong, eager fingers almost did him in. Gasping, he pulled away from her touch.

"Seriously, give that back to me," she complained.

He muttered in her ear, "I'm too close, and I don't want to come yet."

"Oh, fine!" Exasperated, she flopped back down on the bed, throwing her arms over her head. "You can do whatever you want to me, but I can't do anything I want to you, is that it?"

He grinned at the sight of her laid out underneath him like a banquet. He had grown used to the nuances of emotion in her voice, and he could tell she wasn't really annoyed. "You don't want me to come yet either."

Her expression turned needy. "No," she agreed throatily. "I don't. Not yet."

The brief levity died away, replaced by a need that had become painfully urgent. He tugged at the waistband of her trousers, and willingly, she raised her hips so that he could pull them off along with her underpants.

The sight of her nude body brought such strong emotion welling up, for a moment he was unable to speak or move. She was beautiful everywhere, her legs lean with muscle. A small tuft of dark, silken hair curled along the juncture between her thighs. He gripped one of her legs, just above the knee.

As she watched him, her expression changed. Placing a gentle hand to his cheek, she whispered, "Are we okay?"

"We're better than okay." His voice came out deep and husky. "We've gotten lost in the realm of 'I don't

know what I did to get so lucky.'" Sliding down the
bed, he buried his face in that small, soft tuft of hair.

"I feel the same way." Her fingers stroked through
his hair. "I think maybe we should have a quick talk.
You mentioned the possibility of lycanthropes dealing
with pregnancy, so I wanted to let you know, I have an
IUD. I don't like taking the pill, and I don't trust
condoms—although sure, condoms are good for safe
sex…"

As she rambled on a bit breathlessly, he lifted his
head to smile at her. As elegant and as talented as she
was, she was still a little nerdy, kind of shy but still
determined to say what was on her mind. He could tell,
without her saying so, that she had thought this one
through, and she was determined to hit all the important points.

Ducking his head, he kissed along the edge of her
pelvic bone. "I can prevent pregnancy too," he told
her. "It's a simple spell."

"Naturally, it's a spell," she said. Humor laced her
unsteady voice.

"Naturally." He pressed his lips to the juncture at
the top of one thigh. A fine, subtle tremor shook in the
muscles of her leg. "And as I haven't had sex since…
maybe we'd better not get into how long it's been since
I've had sex as there's no need to keep emphasizing our
age difference. But I'm clean, and I'm respectful."

"Of course, you are," she whispered.

"I can also tell from you bringing up the topic that

you've been careful with yourself as well. And now I want you to part your legs for me." He stroked his fingers along the outer edge of her sex, teasing lightly at the sensitive, delicate flesh.

Her breath shuddered. Then she obeyed and exposed the most intimate part of her. The trust in that gesture shot straight to his chest more accurately than any arrow could. As he gazed down at the fluted petals of her private flesh, he thought of how much he had dreaded seeing fear of him in her expression.

Stroking one finger along the seam of her entrance, he said almost inaudibly, "Thank you."

Her hand skimmed over him, touching his hair, his shoulder, his chest, as she whispered back to him. "Thank you."

The urgent hunger built up again. He couldn't wait to take her in his mouth. Going down, he parted her petals to expose the small pearl of her clitoris. As he licked, nibbled, and tugged gently at her sex, her body flexed in instant response.

She began to shake everywhere. Closing his eyes, he focused all his attention on learning what pleased her. As he explored every part of her, the wetness of her arousal slicked his fingers and his mouth.

She tasted like love, like pleasure, like all the finer things he had grown to believe he didn't deserve and would never experience again.

Lifting herself up to his mouth, she gasped, "That feels so amazing, I can't even describe it. But—but—"

What is it, love? he asked telepathically.

Her shaking fingers stroked his temple. "I-I'm not very good at climaxing with others," she confessed. "I can climax by myself just fine, but… well, I've only had two other lovers, so, you know, I haven't had a l-lot of practice…"

Only two other lovers?

A storm of reaction swept through him, both triumph and possessiveness. The fools lost her, and if he had anything to say about it, nobody else would ever get the chance to be with her again.

He murmured in her head, *Shame on them.*

"What?" She sounded confused.

I said shame on them. They had a unique treasure, and they didn't know how to take care of it. He nuzzled her then pressed kisses along her inner thighs. *Just relax, my love. I'll take you there.*

"That would—that would be amazing." Her voice trembled. "But if it doesn't happen, I want just to tell you it's okay. This feels so good. You feel so good."

You're beautiful, he told her. *Every part of you is so lovely, your voice, your scent, your passion, your music, your strength, and your femininity. Relax, Sidonie, you're safe with me. You taste like heaven, and I could happily stay here like this all night. We have all the time in the world. Shh, don't strain for it, just relax.*

It was a lie.

They didn't have all the time in the world. In the back of his mind, where the lycanthrope virus lived, he could feel the moon traveling across the night sky, and he raged internally at the knowledge that he would have to leave her again before daybreak when he never wanted to leave her again. Not ever.

But his soft-spoken, telepathic words did what he wanted them to do. He could feel her relax as he talked to her, and as the tension flowed away, she opened herself further to him.

While he flicked at her clitoris with his tongue, he slipped two fingers inside her. She was tight, so tight, her inner muscles gripped his fingers, and he wanted nothing more than to plunge his aching cock into her lush, wet heat.

For now, he satisfied himself with fucking her gently with his fingers while he worked her. Gradually he increased his rhythm, until her breath came in sobs.

"I can—feel it's there, but I can't quite reach it," she gasped.

Don't try so hard, my love, he said gently, making love to her mind while he stepped up the pressure and he fucked her more deeply. *In fact, don't try at all. Ease up, and let me bring it to you. I want you so badly, it hurts. I feel thick as an oak tree. When you took me in and sucked on me, you shocked me so much I almost came in your mouth. All I can think about is planting myself so deep inside you, I never come out again.*

"Oh, God," she said on a note of complete amazement.

Her torso arched off the bed.

He could feel her climax start deep inside. She flushed all over, and tears spilled out of the corners of her eyes. It rippled outward in waves, and the raw, inarticulate sounds she made as she came were the most beautiful music he'd ever heard.

It set a fire burning in him, but he held himself back, watching her intently while he kept up the relentless pace. He said, *Again, my life. Let's go there again.*

"You've got to be kidding." She wiped at her face. She looked broken open. "It's a miracle I went there once."

I believe in miracles. At least he did for this one night. As the ripples eased, he sucked at her hard.

Her eyes flew wide. With a strangled shriek, she came off the bed again, and there it was, her second climax. Gods, she was lovely.

He wanted to watch her climax all night, but his own hunger was a savage goad so that abruptly he knew he couldn't hold back any longer.

Rising up, he said between clenched teeth, "I need to get inside you. Now."

Her face flared with eagerness. "Yes."

She took hold of him and guided his cock into place, stroking him back and forth, until his head was slick with her arousal. The sensation was excruciating. Gritting his teeth, he endured it so she would be ready for his entrance.

Then she seated him at her opening, and he pushed into her. Rocking almost all the way out, he pushed back in again, this time a little farther. She was so tight, so hot. He watched her closely as pleasure illuminated her expression.

"You feel incredible," he told her. His voice had gone guttural.

"So do you," she breathed. Then, suddenly, she looked deep into his eyes, and the instant snap of connection between them was so strong he felt as if she pulled his soul halfway out of his body. Raking her nails down his back, she hissed, "Stop being so damn careful."

And that was it. It was like she unzipped him. The civilized veneer fell away, and what came leaping out was primal, wholly ungoverned.

He thrust in all the way in one long, brutal move, and she ignited. His fire fanned hers again, and she met each of his long, hard strokes eagerly, lifting to him as he hammered down while she clenched down on him as tight as a fist.

She felt like wet silk and molten fire. He couldn't get in far enough, hard enough. Plunging into her with his cock, he delved into her mouth with a punishingly hard kiss, and she took all of it, all of him, goading him on when he would have eased up, until he lost all vestige of control and rutted on her in a frenzy.

Gripping her by the thighs, he pushed her open wider so he could get deeper. He thought she climaxed again, but he wasn't sure. Her hands roamed every-where, and her mouth—that beautifully formed, soft, demure-looking mouth—whispered filthy things in his ear.

Where did she learn to talk like that? Angling his head, he stared at her, and she gave him a smile filled with such fierce joy, it was like she shoved him off a cliff.

He fell... he fell into her as inexorably as Icarus, who had flown too close to the sun. The climax he plunged into was a completely involuntary thing, beyond his control.

As he spurted into her tight, hot passage, he twisted up and back with the intensity of it. Vaguely, he was aware of her hands spread flat across his chest, helping to support his weight.

Sex had never been a transformative experience for him, until now.

Making love had never been transcendent.

Until now.

Now he finally understood why a queen might betray her husband for a knight who forsook his vows. Why Helen of Troy had been seduced by Paris and left everything in her life behind to follow him.

Why love could become a driving compulsion stronger than honor or death.

And as his climax slowed and he came back down to her again, covering her completely as he lost himself in the sensual extravagance of her lips, he realized he had come to a final point of completion in this dangerous journey he and Sidonie shared.

His heart still thundering in his chest, he pressed his lips to her forehead, and thought, I will do anything I have to do in order to keep you.

Anything.

✧   ✧   ✧

THEY MADE LOVE two more times.

Obsessively.

Unable to stop, or relax. Unable to unclench.

Morgan's body. The ripple of muscles in his long limbs, the sensation on her skin as she rubbed her face in the hair on his chest. His face, that deep voice, the wisdom with which he seduced her, those brilliant, brilliant eyes.

It wasn't comfortable, this roaring need for him. It wasn't balanced. It hurt. She felt like she had plunged into a crisis of some kind. Reality had altered and had ignited her with invisible flame.

At one point, he held her by the throat while he took her from behind, and *she loved it so much.* It was so far beyond anything she would have once considered acceptable she didn't know who she was anymore.

Finally exhaustion flattened her onto the narrow bed. "I need more," she whimpered. "But I can't."

His voice had gone hoarse. He held her tightly, muscles locked. "So do I, but we've run out of time. It's almost dawn."

The thought of separating from him was like someone slicing at her with a knife. She buried her face against his chest. "No."

"You have to find a way to come back to your room before your audience with Isabeau," he told her as his breathing evened. "Don't let anyone keep you from doing it. I'll figure out a way to get the battle spell here to you."

Lifting her head, she searched his face anxiously. His handsome features had already become so familiar to her—she could see the man she had come to know in the darkness shining out in every one of his expressions and gestures.

It all fit in seamless harmony together, like a lock and a key. How she had ever entertained the idea that he could have been Warrick was beyond her.

"How?" she asked. "It's harder for you to move around in daylight."

"I don't know." He stroked her short hair. "But I'll figure it out. I'll work on that today. The main thing you will need to do is not trigger the spell before you're ready to play, because when it activates it will be unstoppable. You don't want to squander it beforehand, but you also don't want to trigger it in front of anybody in case they sense it. Once it settles into your skin, you should be all right, and you'll know when that happens. You'll feel it."

Remembering the flood of epiphany from the last time, she nodded. Her stomach tightened as she thought of what was to come.

But she wouldn't let him see how afraid she was of

all the many things that could go wrong. She had been selfish enough earlier when he had mentioned the possibility of leaving for a while. She wouldn't do that to him again, not when he was already doing everything he could for her.

"It's going to be all right," she said, pushing conviction into her voice. "I've been performing since I was four years old."

He tilted his head. "Really?"

"Really." She smiled at him. "This will be just another performance."

A performance that her life depended on. Neither one of them said it.

He shifted position so that he could lean his forehead on hers and stare deeply into her eyes. She had never felt so connected to another person before. She touched his mouth and ran her fingers along the lean line of his jaw.

"I'll try to be in telepathic range when you play," he told her. "But I might not manage it."

"I understand." Throwing her arms around his neck, she held him as tightly as she could. "Oh, Morgan, I…"

I love you. I need you. My body aches all over, yet I still want you so badly I can hardly breathe.

She didn't think she could say any of it and still make her arms loosen enough to let him go. Biting her lips, she pulled back. When he looked at her inquiringly, she gave him a twisted smile and shook her head.

She told him, "You'd better go."

With a muttered curse, he rolled off the bed, scooped up his clothes, and dressed in short, violent movements. As he fastened his trousers, he said, "The hunter's spray I was wearing wore off quite some time ago. I have more in my bag, but you can't let anybody in this room until you've had a chance to freshen it with some other kind of scent. Go to the chatelaine Preja and tell her you want to clean your room. Preja is a good woman. Ask her for some of the soap scented with lemon, and cedar chips for the wardrobe to keep moths out of your clothes. Both the cedar and the lemon are strong fragrances."

"I will, first thing," she promised. She glanced at the bed. It was time to test what Kallah said about the fabric being spelled. "I need to wash the blanket too."

Slipping on his boots, Morgan dug in his bag and pulled out a bottle. After spraying himself thoroughly, especially down his legs and his boots, he tucked away the bottle, then pulled her upright to kiss her. "I would help you if I could."

She touched his jaw. "You're helping me more than enough already."

He glanced again at the window, where the darkness was beginning to lighten, and his face set. "I need to go."

She fisted her hands in his shirt. "Be careful."

While his expression had turned grim, his eyes warmed. "And you as well."

He kissed her one more time, a quick, burning caress of the lips that made her body pulse. In one swift movement, he pulled away and slipped out of her door.

The sense of his presence lingered in the room for a few moments. Then she felt the chill of the early morning on her skin and shivered.

I hate everything and everyone, she thought savagely. If fact, I'm going to live for the opportunity to rip off somebody's head today.

As tired as she was, the thought of the danger to Morgan—to both of them—if she didn't clear her room of his scent fueled her with adrenaline. She scooped up the blanket, the clothes she had worn, and the clean dress, and headed for the wash rooms.

This time, early as it was, she wasn't so lucky about privacy. Several of the castle servants were using the rooms, both men and women. Self-conscious and wary, she collected the soap she needed and found a tub where she could work, but while she could sense the others casting curious glances at her, they left her alone.

As before, she washed everything else first. The clothes and the blanket were remarkably easy. After she plunged them into the water, she scrubbed them with the soap to be safe, and when she lifted them out, almost all the water ran off them, leaving them slightly damp. They would be dry before the day was over.

Then she washed herself, dressed and brushed her teeth. When she was sure she had thoroughly cleaned everything, she gathered everything up and headed back to her room.

As she stepped out of the wash room, she discovered Warrick standing with another man at the intersection of two hallways nearby. Another pulse of adrenaline hit, making her heart pound and her hands shake.

Ducking her head, she headed for her room. The last thing she needed was a confrontation with Warrick. She wanted to bite somebody's head off, but in his case, she might be biting off more than she could chew.

But he clearly didn't have mischief on his mind that morning. Instead, as she passed by, she heard him mutter to the other man, "I swear by the gods, I caught a hint of Morgan's scent."

"But he hasn't been seen, or scented, anywhere since we know he left Avalon," the other man said. He carried a pile of clothes under one arm and looked as if he were headed to the wash rooms.

Sid's stride hitched. When she thought of how close she had come to them being able to scent Morgan on her body and clothes, her heart jumped to her throat. A few feet down the hall, she paused and bent, pretending to adjust the heel of her shoe.

Surreptitiously, she glanced behind her, but neither man paid any attention to her. She wasn't a threat, and she wasn't important—she was just another servant moving about, doing her chores.

"I'm not crazy," Warrick snapped. "I know what I smelled."

"I believe you," the other man replied with a shrug. "But Morgan has also wandered this castle for centuries. Like so many others, his scent must be imbedded in the stones. To be sure, we need to do another circuit around the castle and the town. That's going to be the only real test of accuracy. He couldn't have left a fresh scent in here without leaving one out there, right?"

A shiver went down her spine as she listened. Morgan had been alive—had been a slave—for centuries? She could hardly fathom what it must be like to live for so long. What he had witnessed and experienced.

"I don't want to wait to gather the other Hounds together," Warrick told the other man. "You and I should head out right away."

As the two men strode down the other hallway, Sid slowly straightened. Fear tightened her stomach. If they had chosen to go down the hallway that led to her room, they might have scented Morgan had been in there.

If only there was some way she could warn Morgan... but there wasn't. She had to trust he was smarter and wilier than the other Hounds and he could remain hidden from their searching.

In the meantime, she needed to get the cleaning supplies from the chatelaine and thoroughly clean her room.

By the time she had finished, her room was filled with the robust scents of cedar and lemon. To be on the safe side, she mopped down the hallway in both directions. Working quickly was as decent a workout as a three-mile jog.

After she put away the cleaning supplies, she went begging for a breakfast she could take with her to the music hall. Triddick gave her a strip of bread that had been wrapped around cheese and meat and then baked. Her empty stomach rumbled at the appetizing scent.

"Thank you." She gave him a smile.

He nodded to her. "I hear your audience will be held in the great hall. I look forward to your performance."

Really? Why had he heard that before she had? Angling her jaw out, she felt ready to bite someone's head off again, but it wasn't fair to take out her bad temper on him. Pivoting on her heel, she strode to the music hall.

Once the door closed behind her, the privacy of the long, empty room was like a soothing balm, and her angry energy faded. She had come to think of this hall as "hers," and she would miss giving up the private sanctuary when Isabeau's music master returned.

Sitting at the table, she ate part of her breakfast to ease the empty ache in her middle. Then she shoved the rest to one side and buried her head in her hands.

Her body ached all over with remembered pleasure. She thought of the things she and Morgan had done to each other throughout the heated night, and need pulsed through her again.

This obsession with him was the height of insanity.

But she had never been successful at controlling her obsessions...

Tiredness hit, and she slumped. She longed to curl up on the couch to take a nap, but today, of all days, was going to be unpredictable. Kallah or someone else might come in at any time to announce she would be playing in the great hall.

She could never afford to forget her behavior was being watched.

That feeling of being watched—it was in her bones, a prickle at the nape of her neck...

A sudden conviction struck. Suddenly, she was sure someone was watching her, even though she was supposedly alone.

There was no magic to it, just good old human intuition.

Pushing to her feet, she turned in a circle and studied the seemingly empty room. The huge, intricate tapestries did not reveal any bulge. Instead, they lay flat against the walls, just as they should.

The bookcases stood flush against the wall, so no one could hide behind those. The stands holding the instruments were artistically crafted, but not solid pieces. Rather, they were constructions made with strips of carved wood, almost like an artist's easel. There was the furniture arranged near the fireplace, the couches and the chairs, but as she walked slowly toward the area, the shadows behind the furniture appeared empty.

There was no other place she could see for a body of any size to hide.

But what if it was a body that was not of any substantial size?

Not one of the castle dogs. They were too big.

But a rat, for instance, could hide very well in a room such as this. Or a cat.

He might not even be in this room, but somewhere close by. Reaching for the mental image of her kidnapper, with that thin, strange face, she said telepathically, *Robin?*

She felt nothing, no sense of whether she had connected to someone or was talking to dead air.

Then one of the dark shadows behind the couch detached from the others. It was a black cat, and it stalked toward her with smooth, sinuous grace. Between one step and the next, it transformed into a thin, upright figure.

The figure almost looked like a human teenage boy. Almost... except for those wild, ancient eyes.

Robin said, "Hello, Sidonie."

Chapter Sixteen

A SUDDEN BLAST of fury hit her like a tornado. The maelstrom whited out all caution or common sense, and it impelled her to leap forward. She had the sensation of leaving her body.

"You!" she snarled.

She slapped him so hard his head jerked back. Then she slapped him again.

And again.

The next thing she knew, she was pummeling him with both fists and feet, while tears of rage ran down her cheeks.

He made no move to stop her or to try to protect himself. Raining him with blows, she drove him backward until his shoulders hit the edge of a bookcase. Bracing himself against it, he stood stoically under her onslaught.

"She broke my hands, you son of a bitch!"

He did not look surprised. He merely nodded and tilted his chin up, turning into her punch. "She cut out my tongue, once. It took years to grow back."

That statement cut through her mindless rage. She

hesitated a moment too long, absorbing the strangeness and barbarity of it. When she reached again for her former fury, the firestorm had already subsided into glowing coals. Not gone, not by any means, but not out of control either.

When he made as if to straighten from his leaning stance, she shoved him again and said between her teeth, "I hate you so passionately."

His strange gaze met hers steadily. "I deserve every ounce of it."

"I can't believe you have the audacity to look me in the eyes, let alone creep around the castle. Morgan thought not even you would be that crazy." She glanced over her shoulder at the closed doors. "Why are you here?!"

"I've come to bear witness to the consequences of my handiwork," he told her. "Evil deeds should never go unpunished."

Whose evil deeds was he talking about, Isabeau's? Or his?

Bitterly, she told him, "You can never make amends for the pain and the fear you put me through."

"I'm not here to try, although I will gladly take every blow you need to hurl," he told her gently. "Some actions are unforgiveable. And before you ask, no, I will not take you home again."

"You fool, I don't want to go home," she hissed. Surprise flared in his feral gaze. He had not expected that. "But I do want to set the record straight, and when I do, you'd better try to do something sensible to help fix things, or I swear to God, someday I will find a way to burn you to ashes."

"I see the passion of which you speak," he whispered.

Glancing at the doors again, she said rapidly, "I have no idea how much time we might have, so I'm going to cut to the chase. Morgan is bound by a geas. Everything you wanted to have happen when you kidnapped me *can't happen*."

Those words were the first blow she had struck that caused him to look shocked. He breathed, "What are you talking about?"

"You thought you would try to drive a wedge between two people who partnered together in crimes." A resurgence of rage made her punch him in the chest. She said between clenched teeth, "Well, it's not going to happen! Morgan is as much a prisoner as you were—as I am right now! He was never going to tell you about it. The geas prevents him from telling people. The only way I know is because I guessed from certain things he said. Once I knew about the compulsion, the geas loosened its hold and we were able to talk about it."

"Could that have been true all this time?" he muttered to himself as his gaze clouded, dark with doubt and memory. "I saw them fight like they hated each other, but lovers play at those games. *She* plays at those games. The pretty smiles and the deadly rages... both are carefully constructed acts. Behind all the sound and fury, she watches with unceasing care for any opportunity to mold fate to her advantage. And never forget Modred. He is the willing sword to her hand."

"Don't worry, I'll never forget Modred," she said, breathing hard. "Not after what he did to me. But right now, we're not talking about him or Isabeau. We're talking about *you*. There's only one way for you to get what you want. And you still want it, don't you... to break the tie that binds Morgan and Isabeau together?"

His gaze snapped back into focus. "I want that more than my conscience or my soul."

Searching his gaze, strange though it was, she saw nothing but sincerity.

"All right," she said. "Isabeau wears a knife on a gold chain around her waist. It's called Azrael's Athame, or maybe Death's Knife. Have you heard of it?"

"No." He frowned. "I remember that old knife in its scabbard. It shines with darkness."

"Who is Azrael?"

He raised his eyebrows, looking surprised again, apparently at her ignorance. "Azrael is Lord Death, one of the seven gods of the Elder Races. Sometimes they're also called Primal Powers. There's also Taliesin, the god of the Dance, who is first among the gods because dance is change, and the universe is constantly in motion. Then there's Inanna, goddess of Love; Nadir, goddess of the depths or the Oracle; Will, god of the Gift; Camael, goddess of the Hearth; and Hyperion, the god of Law." He paused, taking in her growing impatience, then added almost chidingly, "Unlike the gods from other religions, the seven Primal Powers are very real and active in the world."

"You sure about that?" she asked cynically. She was not in the mood for any detour of proselytizing.

"Oh, I am quite sure," Robin said in a soft voice that was, nevertheless, unshakable in its conviction. "I have heard Lord Death's horn sounding the call for his Wild Hunt, and the baying of his hounds on a wind-swept night. It's never wise to be away from shelter when Azrael rides at the death of the year. That is a sound I will never forget, although..." He frowned. "I have not heard the Wild Hunt in many years now."

His words caused a shiver to trickle down her back. "Well, Morgan said the knife Isabeau wears is a very old, Powerful magic item." Driven by a sense of urgency, she talked faster. Their luck couldn't possibly hold for too much longer. "Apparently, she struck him with it, and she not only bound him somehow with the geas, but it turned him into a kind of lycanthrope. He's the one who creates her other lycanthropes." Pausing, she added slowly, "He called them Hounds too. It's not that common of a word in the United States, so it stood out to me."

Robin's eyes narrowed. "Hounds created by Death's Knife," he murmured. "I would like to get to the bottom of the truth behind that tale."

"So do it," she hissed. "The only way to break Morgan and Isabeau apart is to free him from the geas. He's trying to do it himself, but he keeps getting pulled away from his research to save my useless ass *because of you*! But he can't help to free me, because he's been forbidden to help prisoners escape. And he's running out of time."

"How so?" Robin asked quickly.

Voices sounded outside the doors. One of them was Kallah. Robin's form shimmered and transformed into a black cat again.

Picking up the cat, Sid switched to telepathy. *I can't tell you right now. You're just going to have to trust me. For God's sake, go find him and see what you can do to help! I'm not leaving Avalon without him.* Lifting the cat up, she stared into its wide green gaze. *You and I—we're never going to be friends, and apparently, you can survive just fine without my forgiveness. But I will forgive you anyway, if you help set Morgan free.*

Because without her kidnapping, she would never have met her Magic Man. She would never have experienced the night they had just shared. She would never have gazed into his eyes as he moved so deeply, so gently inside her, or experienced the profound emotion with which he held her.

Everything she had endured to reach this point had suddenly become worth it, all the pain, the terror, and the uncertainty.

Just as Robin had not struggled against her blows,

the cat hung limp in her grasp, not struggling against her hold.

His telepathic voice sounded oddly gentle as he said, *That is no small thing you offer, Sidonie Martel.*

I know, she replied curtly.

As she strode toward the doors, carrying the cat, one of them opened, and Kallah walked in, carrying an outfit over one arm. Kallah raised one eyebrow as Sid dropped the cat outside the room.

Sid watched the cat race down the hall, a sleek black streak of speed. When it had disappeared around a corner, she shut the door, turned to face Kallah, and said, "I have no idea how that got in here."

"Cats are everywhere," Kallah said indifferently. "They keep the castle free of mice and rats."

"Pity they can't do the same for the underground prison," Sid said, ending each word with a delicate bite. When Kallah frowned at her, she shrugged. She couldn't care less what the other woman thought.

"I have news for you," Kallah said as she walked over to the table.

Sid followed. "Let me guess, this evening I'll be playing in the great hall."

Kallah paused. "Yes, how did you hear?"

"Triddick told me this morning, when I went to beg some breakfast from him. I don't know how he heard of it."

"I must say, you're taking the news quite calmly." Kallah gave her a quick, keen glance.

Sid compressed her lips into a tight smile. The casual contempt buried in Kallah's assumptions was like having her skin rubbed with sandpaper. As Sid had performed regularly in front of thousands of people in almost every type of venue imaginable, she hadn't given the great hall a second thought.

However, she *was* going to have a serious struggle with not being able to practice three times in the great hall before the performance.

She managed to bite back the snarl that wanted to come out. Instead, she said blandly, "I'm not concerned about where I will be playing. The only person's opinion that really matters is her majesty's."

Kallah's voice turned wry. "True enough. I also wanted to warn you. It's possible you play well enough that you might rouse one or two of the harmonics set in the hall."

Sid's eyes narrowed. "What does that mean?"

"There are spells in silver glyphs set throughout the hall that respond to music. Lights and colors may appear. True masters can evoke images. If any colors appear, you mustn't be startled into faltering."

So the Light Fae had their version of a light show. She managed not to roll her eyes. "Got it."

Kallah's expression turned curious. "You and Triddick have struck up an acquaintance?"

Sid watched her lay the outfit over the top of the table. "I've been too busy to keep to the meal times, and he's been good enough to accommodate me."

"I am somewhat surprised," Kallah remarked as she pulled folds of the garment straight. It was a dress. "He can be temperamental."

"We came to an understanding. He wishes for the Queen to know he supports her love of the arts in any way he can."

"I will be sure to pass that on." Kallah let go of the fabric and straightened. "This dress is for you to wear tonight. Your other two outfits won't do."

Angling her head, Sid inspected the dress. It was brown, which was seriously unfortunate. She had never been a big fan of plain brown. But despite the color, it was a much richer, finer outfit than her regular brown dress, made of velvet with black decorative stitching at the wrists and the hem.

"Okay," she said.

Kallah turned to face her, eyes narrowed. "Is there anything you want to ask me about this evening?"

She shook her head and shrugged, then thought better of her surly attitude. "Actually, I do. How am I supposed to behave when I get to the hall?"

"You should eat a light supper before the evening starts," Kallah instructed. "You will be expected to play while others eat their supper, so you won't be given food, although you may have as much drink as you wish. You will get a few short breaks. Other than that, it's difficult to plan ahead. If her majesty doesn't care for your music, the evening will be brief for you."

If this was a movie, Sid thought, that would be a

cue for an ominous swell of music. "Understood," she bit out.

Kallah looked mildly taken aback. She continued, "If her majesty does enjoy your music, you should expect to play for a couple of hours, so be sure to come to the hall well rested. I will send a page to collect you when it is time."

"Fine." She bit back a sigh. All the impending doom was working on her last nerve. "I'll go back to my room this afternoon. Anything else?"

"No, I believe that should cover everything." Kallah paused, and her eyes narrowed. She murmured, "I don't remember you wearing earrings when I cut your hair."

"Oh, for God's sake," Sid snapped. "What else do you people want to take from me? Sometimes I wear my earrings, and sometimes I put them in my pocket. Why, do you want them?"

If nothing else, she thought, this place has taught me one thing. I have learned how to lie like a champion while telling the absolute truth.

The other woman drew back in affront. "Of course not," she snapped back. "Now, if that will be all, I need to return to my own duties."

"See you in the great hall," Sid said shortly.

The other woman turned to go. When Kallah turned back the irritation had faded from her plain features. In a sober voice, she said, "I know you must be feeling an extraordinary amount of stress right now.

Good luck tonight. I hope you do well."

The starch left Sid's spine, and she made an effort to soften her own voice in reply. "I appreciate that, Kallah. Thank you."

✧   ✧   ✧

AFTER LEAVING, MORGAN returned to his cottage, ate mechanically, and tended to his healing wound.

It looked better than it had last time. The black streaks shooting out like jagged thunderbolts had faded somewhat, and the wound itself had closed over solidly. It felt better too. Now it was a dull, irritating ache as opposed to a burning spike of pain. Nothing he and Sidonie had done in the night had broken it open again.

He guessed he had two weeks at most before the geas forced him to return to Isabeau. He needed to take another wound before then.

After dealing with necessities, he began work on solving the problem of how to get the battle spell to Sidonie.

As much as he railed against the conclusion he had come to, trying to cast the spell in person was not the best choice. If he cast the spell, it would begin to work immediately, and Sidonie needed to be able to control when it was activated. He would have to set the spell into an item and then figure out how to get the item to her.

The other challenge was, while he was certainly

proficient in magic and not without a capacious bag of tricks, the thought of trying to move about in the daytime was daunting. There were areas of the castle where he could move around much more freely, hidden nooks and private spaces that had been forgotten by everyone centuries ago, except for him.

But the well-trafficked area around Sidonie's room was not one of those spaces. Also several other Hounds and courtiers were proficient in magic, including Isabeau and Modred, and Morgan didn't have the puck's ability to change shape at will.

So delivering the battle spell in person was not the best option. The risk of discovery was too great.

Perhaps Myrrah might help. She was kind-hearted and a talented healer, and one of the few people Morgan trusted, at least somewhat. She wouldn't like not knowing why he wanted to get a magic item to Sidonie, yet she might do it if he asked her.

But he didn't like the uncertainty in that either. What if Myrrah felt too uneasy with the request? Then he would have not only exposed his presence, but he would also have exposed his link to Sidonie.

No, Sidonie needed the battle spell for a certainty. That mattered more than anything, even keeping his presence a secret. He would voluntarily go back into active service with Isabeau before he would risk Sidonie going into her performance tonight without the help she needed.

Setting aside the problem for now, he got to work.

First, he took a length of cloth and infused it with the same spell of concealment he had placed on the velvet pouch that carried his deadly array of weapon spells.

When he had finished, he opened the small wooden box that held his supply of unspelled jewels and picked through them thoughtfully. The battle spell was a major one, so it needed a high-quality jewel to house it. None of the semiprecious stones would do.

Finally he chose a small, perfect diamond. Setting it on the table, he began the process of casting the spell into the stone. Casting a major spell was one complex process. Setting the spell into an item was a second process that was just as complex.

Added to that, he needed to infuse this particular spell with a thorough impression of the right skills to pass on to Sidonie. Normally the battle spell was cast in the heat of the moment, and the transfer of skills was both broader and immediately apparent, based on the focus on need by the one casting the spell.

Casting this spell was different. He was not in the heat of the moment, and he had to build a meticulous mental image of the lute, along with his memories of playing it. By the time he sat back to contemplate his handiwork, he was drained, and the sun had risen high in the sky and had begun to heat the cottage.

It was a good, solid casting, the spell tightly woven into the structure of the jewel itself, but he was no closer to figuring out how to get it to Sidonie safely in a way that didn't risk his own freedom too.

Frustrated, he rubbed his face, then went to open the cottage windows to let in some fresh air. As he did so, the sound of voices caused his hackles to rise.

Even though the speakers were some distance away, he recognized them. It was Warrick and Harrow.

While he was confident the concealments he had woven over the cottage would hold, he still needed to find out what they were doing out here, so close to his hiding place. He wrapped the diamond in its concealment cloth and tucked it into his pocket, along with the lump of beeswax.

Then he grabbed his weapons, doused himself with hunter's spray again, cast a strong cloaking spell around himself, and slipped out of the cottage to stalk after the two men as their voices faded away.

Locating Warrick and Harrow was easy since they made no effort to be stealthy. Carefully, he followed as they walked along the path that led to an area of high ground. The place they were headed to was an excellent lookout point, as it offered the most complete view of the castle, the town around it, and the harbor where the fishing and sailing boats were docked.

Once there, the men paused. Weighing the relative risk of overhearing something he didn't want to hear versus the need to know what they were up to, Morgan eased closer until he could catch snatches of their conversation on the wind. He fingered pieces of the beeswax, molding them into earplugs even as he listened.

"I agree with you," Harrow said. "The scent was fresh, especially in the stables…"

Realization struck.

The stables, where Morgan had lain unconscious and bleeding for quite some time. He had forgotten to do anything to disguise or get rid of his scent after he had recovered enough to get back to the cottage. Angry at his own oversight, he swore under his breath.

Warrick replied, "So if he came back from Earth like we think he did… any number of places where he could be staying… Also I want to know why the bastard sneaked back into Avalon after sneaking out in the first place…."

"Seems pretty clear…" Harrow said. Doesn't want to be found?"

"Yeah, looks like… go back and tell the others…"

As Morgan took in the gist of their conversation, he faced facts grimly.

The game had changed.

Now that Warrick and Harrow had grown suspicious he might be in Avalon, plugging his ears with beeswax wouldn't do much to protect him. If just one of them thought to try to reach out to him telepathically to made contact—and if they told him Isabeau wanted him to return whether he was injured or not—he would be forced to obey.

Tensing, he ran through his capacious repertoire of spells to see what might be useful in blocking telepathy. The obvious one would be a null spell. For it to last for any length of time, he would have to cast it into yet another item and wear it. It would protect him from telepathy, but it would hamper his abilities severely too.

As he stalked the other two Hounds, Morgan's mind switched over to cold, ruthless logic. It sounded like Warrick and Harrow hadn't told anybody else yet. Did he have it in him to kill them, even though they presented no immediate physical danger?

But the danger they did represent was very real. If they took their suspicions back to the other Hounds, and to the Queen, the search for him in the immediate area would intensify.

It hadn't happened yet, but now that they were suspicious he could be within range somewhere, sometime very soon, someone would get the bright idea to start calling for him telepathically.

If he got trapped again, he would be sent away from Avalon to continue his attack against the Dark Court.

Sent away from Sidonie.

And maybe she would solidify her position at court that very evening, but if for some reason Isabeau stayed adamantly turned against her, Sidonie could continue to be in danger, and Morgan would not be able to do anything to help.

He watched as, in the distance, the two men walked farther up the path and paused at the highest point to look out across the land. Now they were too far away for him to overhear their conversation. Harrow pointed west, and Warrick shook his head.

All it would take was one massive push of air. With a quick spell, he could throw a blow like a battering ram and both men would go flying over the cliff. They might not die from the fall, but they would be severely injured enough he could reach them to finish the job before they recovered.

Warrick was a brute, and Morgan would feel nothing but relief at his death, but Harrow was a decent enough man.

At war with himself, he tensed.

There was a small rustle in the underbrush beside him. Robin remarked in a quiet voice, "It's a fine day for a little murder, don't you think?"

Morgan's heart kicked. Robin always did have a knack for seeing through his best concealment spells. Whirling, he grabbed the puck by the throat and slammed him to the ground. Robin did nothing to try to stop him.

Morgan hissed, "Are you fucking crazy? I should have killed you before, when I had the chance!"

Robin met his gaze. For the first time in a very long time, Morgan saw a sober kind of sanity in the puck's eyes.

"It would be most unfortunate if you chose to carry through on that threat, sorcerer, since I've come to offer help," Robin told him. "For the first time in history, a member of the Dark Court is choosing to offer his services to one of the Light."

"What nonsense are you spouting now?" Morgan snapped, his fingers tightening.

Robin's face darkened from the increased pressure, but he still showed no signs of struggle. He whispered, "I had a most illuminating conversation with Sidonie."

Instantly, Morgan relaxed his hold. A quick glance up at the lookout point told him the other two men had disappeared from sight. He had not only lost his chance to kill them, but he had lost track of where they were.

"Come on." Hauling Robin upright, he dragged the puck back to the concealment of his cottage. Once there, he shoved the puck inside and followed, slamming the door behind him. As Robin turned to face him, he snarled, "Start explaining."

"I was spying on her," Robin said simply as he adjusted his clothes. "I have this compulsion to witness the damage I've wrought. Somehow she sensed me watching. Instead of denying my presence and remaining silent, I chose to reveal myself. She was… violently furious, as you may imagine."

"If you did anything more to hurt her…," he growled, feeling his face change.

Robin's eyes widened, and he threw up his hands. "Peace, sorcerer! Your lady is fine! I took every one of her blows, because I deserved them, and when she calmed down enough to talk, she told me of the geas you're under."

Morgan hesitated, breathing hard, and his features

eased back into their normal shape. Warily, he asked, "So what now, Robin?"

"Sidonie was right," Robin breathed, staring at him. "Now I know the geas exists, I can see it lying over you, like fate's shadow. Before, I always thought it was the shade of your dark arts. Now my reasons for her kidnapping no longer exist, but she made it clear she doesn't want my help to go home. She said she won't leave Avalon without you."

Morgan hadn't seen that coming. He spun away to hide whatever might be showing in his expression.

After everything she had been through—everything she might still go through—she refused to leave him. A mixture of feelings swelled in his chest, closing his throat.

When he could speak again, his voice was roughened. "We need to talk some sense into her. You need to get her back to Earth."

"While I appreciate her brave declaration and your unfounded belief in my abilities, I can only act stealthily on my own behalf," Robin said wryly. "I cannot change another creature into a mouse, or a squirrel. Although I might wish with all my heart things were different, I don't have the capability of slipping her past the passageway guards."

At that, Morgan swore, viciously. "You've been nothing but a curse."

"Yes. I cannot undo what I have done, but I *can* do everything in my power to aid her and help break you free from that which binds you." Robin paused. "If you'll let me. I'll understand if you will not. But, sorcerer, think carefully before you repudiate my offer. You don't have many options, and with the right motivation I can be a powerful ally."

Powerful, but chaotic. Lowering his eyelids, Morgan studied Robin intently, trying to decide if accepting his offer of help was worth the added danger and aggravation. If there had been a hint of insincerity or duplicity in the puck, Morgan would have killed him right then and there. Instead, he saw nothing but an earnest desire to help.

Am I really going to gamble everything on the word of my enemy? he wondered.

But the puck was his best choice. As a nature sprite, when Robin was a cat, he smelled like a cat. When he was another creature, he smelled like that creature. There was nobody better to slip around the castle, and the puck's audacity proved it.

Morgan dug into his pocket and pulled out the diamond wrapped in its cloth of concealment. "Sidonie needs this before her performance," he told Robin. "She doesn't know how to play any of the musical instruments here well enough to perform."

Robin's expression changed to one of surprised dismay. "None of them?"

"No. Her expertise lies in other instruments… the violin, the guitar, and I don't know what else. She said she can play five instruments well enough to perform with them, but none are collected in the music hall. The closest instrument is the lute. She's been picking it up incredibly quickly, but not in enough time for tonight's performance."

"How can she survive the night?" Robin's expression looked troubled.

"With this battle spell." Morgan held up the cloth-wrapped diamond. "I've amended it to transfer my experience of playing the lute to her. It will last long enough to get her through tonight. She needs this spell, and you need to get it to her." His voice roughened. "No excuses, puck, and there's no room for failure."

As Robin held out his hand for the jewel, his gaze darkened with sincerity. "I will see she gets it," he promised. "I swear it on my life."

Yes, he would. Morgan would see to it.

He said harshly, "I've shown you more mercy than you deserve, and right now, I'm showing you more trust than you've earned. If you don't get this to her, I will pull your lungs out with my claws and watch every moment of your struggle to breathe until you die. I swear *that* on my life."

Soberly, Robin accepted the jewel. "I believe you."

"Tell her the spell will be triggered by her touch, so she shouldn't unwrap the jewel until she's ready for it." He took a deep breath, his mind already leaping to the next obstacle. "And tell her there's a hiding place in the rafters above the great hall. I will do my very best to be there for her performance."

In fact, he would make damn sure he was there. If Robin failed to deliver the diamond, he needed to have a backup plan. He didn't have time to create another magic item of such complexity, so he would have to get within enough proximity to cast the battle spell himself, despite the increased danger of being discovered.

"I will pass along your message." Robin slipped the jewel into his pocket then hesitated. "About the geas that binds you... I remember very well the knife Isabeau wears on a chain at her waist. Sidonie said it's called Azrael's Athame, or sometimes Death's Knife?"

Morgan raised an eyebrow. "Yes, that's what Isabeau has called it. I've wondered if it might be one of the Deus Machinae, so I've been searching for references in various texts to try to find ways of breaking or dissolving the geas, but I haven't had any luck yet. Why, do you know of it?"

"No, but when we were talking earlier, I realized I hadn't heard Lord Azrael and his hounds on his Wild Hunt for a very long time. A very long time indeed. Perhaps even as long as you have been ensorcelled." Robin tilted his head, and the feral gleam was back in his eyes. "I've listened for sounds of the Wild Hunt, you see. I thrill to hear it, even as I hide safely indoors."

Morgan narrowed his gaze. "Just how old are you?"

"Old, sorcerer," he said. "As old as you are, you are but a child to me."

Before he could ask the puck any more questions, Robin slipped out the door and was gone.

As the door settled into place behind him, Morgan thought, we've cast our dice, Robin, Sidonie, and me.

Now all we can do is watch them tumble and land where they may.

Chapter Seventeen

MORGAN HAD ONE more casting he needed to do that day, a simpler one that should go much faster than the creation of the battle spell. Tired though he was, he sat down with his tools to see it got done.

Once the null spell had been set into an uncut sapphire, he wrapped it carefully in a plain piece of cloth. Like the battle spell he had crafted for Sidonie, the null spell would activate when it came in contact with skin, so he didn't want to touch it unless he absolutely had to.

Then, finally, he let himself relax on the dusty bed to nap until the light changed and the cottage cooled in the early evening.

Coming to instant, full alertness, Morgan straightened off the bed. Remembering he had entrusted the jewel that would save Sidonie from prison to *Robin*, of all creatures, made adrenaline surge until his muscles tightened and he felt ready for battle.

There was only one way to get to the place he had described to Robin, in the rafters that soared over the great hall, and that was by climbing one of the buttresses outside to reach the top of the windows. Long ago, Morgan had broken one of those windows and covered the break with a small spell of illusion.

The challenge would be to reach the buttress and climb it without being detected. Once he had reached the rafters, the shadows would hide him from the people down below.

He finished his second-to-last bottle of the hunter's spray as he prepared for the journey. The sun was setting when he stepped out of the cottage. As he strode toward the castle, a slim black cat bounded up the path to him. The cat's form shimmered and changed, and suddenly it was Robin who jogged up the path.

Morgan stopped, and as Robin joined him, he rapped out, "Well?"

"All went very well," Robin told him. "I slipped through the kitchens carrying the jewel in my mouth, and when I reached her door, I scratched until she opened it to let me in." The puck's gaze gleamed. For all the danger in the situation, he looked like he was enjoying himself. "She was most surprised when I spat out a diamond."

"She didn't touch it, did she?" Morgan demanded. "You told her how to activate it?"

"Indeed," Robin said. "And indeed. She was calm, sorcerer, and relieved to hear you were safe. She looked ready. She also has a plan for when to activate the spell. A nervous musician may take a few moments of privacy to ready herself just before a performance, perhaps even make a trip to the privy."

Relief eased the knot of tension between his shoulders. "Good. You did well."

"You do not need to sound quite so surprised." Robin fell into step beside him. "I am capable of good deeds as well as ill."

"You have a long way to go to make up for what you did." He shot the puck a hard look. "Don't get too complacent."

Robin's face tightened. "Understood." After a moment, he asked, "Have you thought any further about the Athame?"

"That's all I think about," Morgan replied shortly. "That, and how to help Sidonie." And how to stay free as long as possible. "Why, have you?"

"Yes, I have had a thought or two. I don't believe it is one of the Deus Machinae. It has been too stationary for too long. The Machinae are active manifestations of the gods' will. They were meant to tumble through the world. When they come into someone's possession, and they're prevented from that movement, they create more and more havoc around them until the person who holds them undergoes some kind of crisis and releases them back into the world. I don't witness that kind of dynamic in Isabeau's life."

Frustration clawed at Morgan. If the puck was right, all the research he had been doing would have been for nothing. So much precious time had been wasted. "So you believe the Athame is something else."

Robin glanced at him, feral eyes gleaming. "If Occam's razor is to be believed, the simplest explanation is usually the best. In that case, Isabeau herself may have given you the answer, and the blade is quite literally Azrael's Athame—Lord Death's Knife."

Morgan tilted his head, thinking that through. "When I first met her, she mentioned Azrael and his Wild Hunt. She said, 'When Lord Azrael rides, nobody on this earth is ready.'"

"She was correct," Robin whispered.

"At the time, I hadn't paid much attention to it, but that moment keeps coming back to me in my dreams." Morgan rubbed the back of his neck. He was getting a headache where his skull connected to his spine, deep in his hindbrain where the most primitives urges dwell.

Where the lycanthropy virus lived.

"Perhaps your soul knows more than your mind has allowed. Azrael's Athame helped to create you, and Sidonie said you create the other Hounds." Robin frowned. "But you and the other Hounds are different from the lycanthropy plague that was loosed in England hundreds of years ago."

Coming to a halt, Morgan turned to face Robin. "I've thought for some time that that strain of the virus has spread from the bites of the other Hounds. I create Hounds only when Isabeau orders. What happens when those Hounds attack others who survive?"

"They are a weakened form of what you are. They

do not have the same strength or control that you do. They suffer bouts of frenzy as they lose themselves during a full moon, and they live the normal span of a human's life." Robin's gaze met his. "You and the other Hounds let loose that bloodcurdling sound when you lunge to the attack, so like the baying I've heard on those distant past winter nights. What if you are, indeed, Death's Hounds, and as long as Isabeau has possession of Azrael's Athame, she controls the Wild Hunt?"

NOT LONG AFTER that unsettling conversation, Morgan knelt on the massive rafter high over the great hall, while Robin crouched beside him. The puck wrapped both thin arms around his legs while his eyes gleamed with interest.

It was a good vantage point from which to watch what happened down below. Morgan got a clear view of the high table, where Isabeau, Modred, the visiting nobleman Valentin, and other notables sat.

He could also see the musician's alcove where Sidonie would be seated. The alcove was located on a mezzanine above the ground floor near the high table but still far below where he and Robin were perched. Various personages from town clustered around the other tables, prominent merchants and officials, along with other courtiers, Hounds, and those from the castle household who were elevated above the class of servant.

While Morgan had been careful to use the hunter's spray to hide his scent on the journey to the castle, he knew he was perched too high for the Hounds below to catch his scent. He doubted anyone at the evening's gathering would think to try to telepathize to him here, of all places, but to be safe, he pressed one finger to the sapphire in his pocket to keep the null spell activated, while he plugged his ears with beeswax. He was determined no stray comment would entrap him.

When servants began to carry out huge platters of food and jugs of wine and beer, the alcove curtains parted and Sidonie stepped out. Behind her, in the shadows, Kallah handed her the lute. She nodded to the other woman, and Kallah let the curtain fall into place.

A hush fell over the people below as they turned to gaze up at this new entertainment. Morgan caught sight of Freya in the crowd. Her expression was avid.

He turned his attention back to Sidonie, who looked magnificent and composed. The brown dress she wore should have been drab, but instead the rich cloth made her skin look creamy. The golden glow of the torches highlighted the curve of her cheekbones, those long, elegant eyes, and her short, black hair hugged the sleek, graceful curve of her skull.

Morgan's jaw tightened as he stared at her. Even dressed as plainly as she was, she looked too spectacular, and it was too late for him to give her all the advice he longed to say.

Don't play too well. Don't show your real genius. Isabeau doesn't like other stars that shine more brightly than she.

As Sidonie bowed to the head table, he glanced at Isabeau. She lounged in her chair, looking bored. Beside her, Modred studied Sidonie with narrowed eyes, while Valentin sat forward with an arrested expression.

The conversation in the hall resumed. Isabeau gestured at Sidonie with one hand, and Morgan removed his earplugs. Taking Isabeau's gesture as her cue, Sidonie began to play.

He had not thought to give her advice until it was too late, and Sidonie did nothing to hide her talent.

The conversation below faltered to a halt again as she played....

What was she playing? He didn't recognize any of the songs.

Suddenly Robin clapped both hands over his mouth. When Morgan glanced at him, the puck appeared to be shaking with laughter.

Taking his hand away from the null spell, he demanded telepathically, *What?*

I believe she just played a song called "Mrs. Robinson," Robin told him, eyes dancing with glee. *Oh, and that one—I forget what that one is called. "You're Vain"? Maybe "You're Very Vain." No, it's "You're So Vain." She just played a song about vanity to the Queen, who will never know it.*

Morgan sucked in a breath. Sidonie was playing

adaptations of pop music, one right after the other, with unmistakably beautiful prowess.

He tried to recognize the songs she played, and he thought he knew a few of the tunes—while he had lost interest in music before he'd attended her concert, he hadn't been living under a rock—but he only knew one thing for certain.

He couldn't hold back a grin as he told Robin, *She's not playing any of her own music.*

She wasn't giving them anything of herself. Instead, she put on the performance that had been commanded of her, without offering one iota more.

The music was brilliant, of course. He didn't think she had it in her to be anything less than brilliant. But it was the most flawless, professionally executed *fuck you* he'd ever witnessed, all delivered to her xenophobic audience with a perfectly composed expression and a slight, unshakable Madonna-like smile.

After the first few strains, the harmonics in the hall activated. At first, streams of pure color flowed over the open space above the audience. Then, after a few songs, the colors entwined, blended, and vast, transparent images began to appear, sweeping across the hall.

Haunting and evocative, the images hinted at stories not quite told, and adventures in exotic places. Lovers entwined in a kiss, then broke apart in anger. A herd of wild horses ran along a shore. A foreign city sat golden upon a hill, and a wild storm crashed across a desert. Morgan had never seen the harmonics respond with such rich, vibrant complexity before.

And they loved it. Loved it. Isabeau's music master, Olwen, had talent, along with a great many years of polish, but he didn't have the same fire of genius that Sidonie had.

At one end of the hall, someone began to pass around the performer's hat, a long-held tradition for the audience to show appreciation. People threw coins into the hat, sometimes flowers, silken handkerchiefs, gold rings.

Sidonie's hat filled quickly, evidence of her resounding success. As Morgan glanced at it, he saw that she would have enough from this evening's performance to support herself in style for a few months. She could rent a house in town and hire servants, if she so wished... and if Isabeau let her.

Oh, that song. Robin sighed with pleasure. *I think it's by the Garfinkels, or someone like that. "Scarborough Fair"—I like that one. That's an adaptation of a very old song. She's amazing.*

Yes, she is, Morgan agreed.

"Musician, stop." Isabeau's order rang out.

Sidonie froze without changing expression. She looked perfect and almost as lifeless as a mannequin. The images died and silence filled the great hall, while alarm and dismay flashed across the faces of the people throughout the hall.

Modred angled his head, rubbing one thumb along the edge of his lips while his quick, assessing gaze took in the scene. On the other side of Isabeau, Valentin appeared transfixed. Lips parted, he never looked away from Sidonie.

Isabeau leaned forward, her expression alive with more delight than Morgan could remember seeing in quite a very long time.

"That last song," the Queen said. "Play that one again."

Smoothly, Sidonie began playing "Scarborough Fair" again. Relief and pleasure rippled over the audience, and a smattering of applause broke out. The knot of tension that had driven Morgan through the past three days eased.

She had done it.

She had successfully appeared for her audience with the Queen, and the Queen was quite pleased.

SUPPER HAD FINISHED for the diners below, and Sidonie had just begun to reach the dregs of the battle spell.

Like the first time, the tide of epiphany began to withdraw, but this time she could feel something was different. She had played the lute long enough now that she felt confident in her plucking technique, and the position felt familiar, even comfortable.

Still, her energy waned to such an extent she was starting to get worried when, finally, the curtains behind her parted, and Kallah whispered, "Make this your last song."

Relief coursed through her. Without glancing back, she gave a slight nod and smoothly brought the song to an end. While she played the final notes, she looked around at the images from the harmonics. As if the magic understood it was the end, a gossamer, panoramic sunset over the ocean filled the hall, the colors deepening into night.

After she finished, a smattering of polite applause sounded throughout the great hall.

It sounded anemic, almost begrudging, nothing like the normal wild enthusiasm of her concerts.

Blinking, she tried to absorb the feedback. What had she done wrong?

Sure, she had played pop songs, but nobody here would have known what those songs were... and she had played them as well as she possibly could. That, together with Morgan's spell, should have made things okay, and the magical imagery had been great. Had she misjudged her audience that badly?

The last of the adrenaline from the battle spell left and the crash hit. The shaking started deep inside, and with an effort, she stiffened her legs to remain standing.

Kallah pulled back the curtain and beckoned her with a bright smile. "Her majesty would like to speak with you now."

"Of course," she said. Dread dragged at her feet. As she followed Kallah down a narrow flight of stairs, she asked tightly, "How bad is it?"

"What do you mean?" Kallah looked over her shoulder. Whatever she saw in Sid's expression made her stop and turn completely around, looking up as Sid hovered on a step above her. Gently, Kallah told her, "You were utterly, shockingly wonderful. I can't remember when I last heard music as sublime as yours. Some of the songs brought tears to my eyes, and I've never seen the harmonics respond to a musician as they did to you. Everybody loved it—the queen loved it. Your life has gone through a profound change, Sid. You have become quite the sensation here, now."

Her shaking worsened, and she had to wipe her eyes before she could speak again. Thickly, she muttered, "There was so little applause I thought it hadn't gone well."

Kallah touched her hand in a quick, impulsive gesture. "You couldn't be further from the truth. It's considered bad manners to overwhelm the hall with unseemly signs of enthusiasm. The real show of appreciation is waiting for you down below. Your performer's hat is overflowing.... I can't remember when I've seen a hat so full."

"I have no idea what that means." Sid would just be glad if she didn't get her fingers broken again.

Kallah gave her another smile. Her demeanor toward Sid seemed to have warmed significantly, as if she had been waiting for her to prove herself. "Come and see. I think you'll be very pleased."

Only then did Sid remember she could try to telepathize with Morgan. She hadn't used the telepathy earrings enough for them to become commonplace. Reaching for him mentally, she asked, *Are you there?*

Immediately, Morgan's rich, warm voice filled her mind, and it was such a balm to her abraded nerves she had to grasp at the banister to keep her knees from buckling. *I am. You did beautifully, Sidonie. Now, hang on. You're almost there. You've got a bit more you need to get through, and then you can rest.*

Her breathing roughened, and her eyes prickled, but she was not about to face that walking, talking piranha with tears in her eyes. Pushing the emotion aside, she squared her shoulders and followed Kallah to a room that was much smaller than the great hall, more intimate, with plush, comfortable furnishings arranged into a sitting area.

Isabeau lounged on one couch, her feet tucked under her. Two men kept her company. One was Modred, who stood leaning against one corner of a fireplace, and the other was a Light Fae male Sid had never met before, who sat in a nearby chair.

The unknown male was speaking. "Quite a stunning performance, especially given her inferior breeding."

"Indeed," Modred said.

Sid's gaze skidded over Modred. She could not look at him without remembering the smile he had given her down in that ugly, pain-filled room when he took away her reason for living.

But instead of squandering her fast-waning energy obsessing over past events, she turned her attention to the only person of relevance in the room.

When Isabeau saw her, she set aside her wine goblet, rose, and walked toward Sid with both hands outstretched. Sid drew back in instinctive alarm, but then she saw Isabeau's warm smile.

When she gets what she wants, she's all warm, pretty smiles...

"Musician! What is your name, again? Sid? Tonight was lovely, simply lovely. I had no idea you would bring such sublime music and beauty into my life!" Isabeau grasped her hands, gaze wide with delight. "Where did you get such an amazing gift? That one song especially shot such arrows into my heart!"

I wish I could shoot arrows at you with my music, Sid thought. Now, that would be a skill worth developing.

Aloud, she murmured vaguely, "Where does anyone get their talent for things?"

Isabeau squeezed her fingers. Her touch made Sid's skin crawl. "Exactly!" Isabeau exclaimed as she turned to face the two men. "Talents are given by the gods. Who knows where they might land, or for what reason? Heaven can be housed even in a vessel such as she."

Suddenly Sid struggled with an entirely inappropriate desire to laugh. She thought, Just when I think I'm all out of fuck yous, somehow, I manage to find inspiration for yet another one.

I might be done playing music, but my performance isn't over yet.

Rallying, she returned the Queen's squeeze. "Your majesty, I can't begin to tell you how much it means to me that you enjoyed tonight's music."

"Why, you're trembling!" Isabeau exclaimed. "I hear performing can take some musicians that way. It is the artist's temperament. Do have some wine... you have earned it, my dear."

"No, thank you. It's good of you to offer, but if I drink wine right now I will fall over." The fixed stare from the unknown Light Fae male was beginning to grate on her, and Modred's relaxed presence compounded the feeling.

What could she do to make this nightmare end? She swayed, and caught herself up.

She had forgotten Kallah, who murmured in a tactful voice from behind her, "Your majesty, perhaps it would be a good idea to keep this visit short. Sid wanted to honor you, and she has been working night and day to prepare for this evening. Not only that, but she went through several challenging days before then."

Isabeau's expression cooled at the oblique reference to Sid's time in prison, but she adjusted smoothly enough.

In a brisker tone, she replied, "Kallah is quite right. It must have been exhausting today, preparing to perform in front of the entire court. Well, musician, you pleased me tonight. You pleased me very much, and I look forward to hearing more of your beautiful music. Your performer's hat is over here, on the table. I wanted to give it to you personally."

Sid looked where Isabeau pointed, and her eyes widened. On a side table, a velvet hat sat. It was overflowing with flowers, coins, jewelry, and bright scraps of silk. "Are you saying that's mine?"

The queen laughed. "But of course! My court loved you, and this is how they show it. You may also ask one thing of me as well. Choose carefully. A boon from me is no small thing."

Sid drew in a breath as she tried to cope with the unexpected largesse.

As she hesitated, Isabeau watched her closely. She added, "And before you think to ask for it, no, you may not have your freedom." She softened the statement with a quick, pretty smile. "I could never bear to give up such a treasure, now that I have found you."

"But you can give me the freedom of the town and the surrounding land, can't you?" Sid asked. "Fresh air and new sights are good muses. After all, it's not as though I can escape from Avalon, anyway."

An expression of comfortable contempt slid over Isabeau's face. "No," the queen agreed. "It's not as though you can. Very well, you have earned it. You may have the freedom of the castle, the town, and the surrounding land, up to two hours' walk away. But, come—that was too easy. Lengthening your leash was nothing. You must ask a boon for something worthwhile, otherwise I might feel insulted."

Only Isabeau could make a gift sound like a threat. Sid was suddenly so exhausted, she could barely see straight. All she wanted to do was sleep, while this psycho tyrant prattled on about her boon like it was some kind of real goddamn gift.

How long would she have to live like this? The realization that she might spend years trapped in Avalon caused her to clench her hands. How could she survive here for so long?

"I want you to get me a violin, and a guitar," she said suddenly. "As beautiful as a lute is, it isn't my instrument of choice."

Isabeau's expression went blank with surprise. "Not your instrument of choice?"

"I play the violin much better," Sid told her. "The guitar too."

Isabeau's lips parted. She breathed, "Better than how you played this evening?" Turning to Kallah, she ordered, "We must get these instruments at once! Make sure they are of the finest quality!"

"Of course," Kallah murmured. "I will see to it first thing in the morning."

"I also want a week to myself," Sid said roughly. "I want to sleep when I feel like it, eat whatever I want, and feel sunshine on my face."

And during all that time, she thought mentally, I don't want to worry if I'm going to be killed or tortured, or feel like I need to brace myself to face some fresh hell. I want a week off, and I want all of you to leave me the fuck alone.

The light in Isabeau's expression soured again, and she tilted her mouth as if she had tasted something she didn't like. Tapping her foot, she considered Sid.

"To go an entire week without your sublime music is too much to ask," the Queen said finally. "But I will give you this much. For one hour each day, you will play for me at a time of my choosing. I will not command you to perform in public. The hour will be for my own private enjoyment. Other than that hour each day, you may have the rest of the week to yourself."

Behind her, Kallah touched Sid's back quickly.

Taking the silent prompt, Sid bowed to Isabeau. "Thank you, your majesty. I'm most grateful for the respite."

Isabeau waved a hand at her. "Now, go before you fall over and I need to order someone to carry you out. You've turned such a pasty white, it really is quite alarming."

As she spoke, the unknown Light Fae male walked over to the performance hat. Working a ring off one of his fingers, he dropped it into the hat. Then he scooped it up and carried it to Sid, who gathered it into her arms. She hadn't expected it to be as heavy as it was.

"Here is your very well-earned reward, musician," he said as he gave her a look that seemed filled with some kind of significance. "I look forward to enjoying more of your talents soon. Isabeau, you must invite me for some of those private sessions."

"We'll see, Valentin." Isabeau gave the man a blade-sharp look underneath a pretty, catlike smile. "I can get very jealous of my pleasures, and I don't like to share."

Suddenly desperate to leave, Sid had to keep herself from running for the door. As she turned away, the look she gave to Kallah must have shown her desperation, for Kallah put a hand at her back and urged her out quickly.

As Kallah walked her back to the servants' quarters, Sid struggled with absorbing her change in fortune. "So I can leave the castle now," she said hoarsely. "I can simply walk out whenever I wish?"

"As soon as I pass the Queen's instructions to the castle guards, yes, you may," Kallah replied. "I will do so this evening after I say good night. Just make sure you leave word of where you are going, so the guard knows how to find you. But it will take some days for us to acquire a violin and a guitar."

"That makes sense." Outside her room, she turned to face Kallah. "I'll get the dress back to you clean."

Kallah smiled. "No need. It is yours now. You can use it for future performances. Rest well, Sid. You earned it."

As Kallah walked away, Sid fumbled at the knob to open her door. Once inside, she shoved it shut with one foot and set the hat and its contents on the bed. As she picked up the tinderbox, her candle flared to light.

Her heart leaped with gladness, and she whirled with an eager smile.

The black cat lay curled at one end of her bed. It gave a great yawn, showing sharp, white teeth, green eyes gleaming.

Disappointment dragged at her tired limbs. She had wanted it so very much to be Morgan.

She said flatly, "You."

Yes, Robin said telepathically. *Me.*

Chapter Eighteen

"I DON'T KNOW what you want, but you're going to have to get out," Sid told the puck. "I'm not staying."

Speak telepathically, Robin warned. *The ears in this place are very sharp.*

Sid struggled with the unfamiliar fastenings of the dress and shimmied out of it. Then she grabbed her tunic and trousers.

As she changed, she said, *Isabeau gave me a longer leash. I can go up to two hours' walk away from the castle, and I don't care how tired I am right now—I'm not going to spend one more night here. If I have to, I'll sleep outside on the bare ground or in an alley.*

That is most excellent news, but there's no need to put yourself in such discomfort, Robin said. *Go into town to one of the inns. The Seafarer's Rose is not a ten-minute walk from here. They have good food, fresh linens, and you have plenty of money.*

As if to emphasize his point, the cat batted lazily at the performance hat.

She hesitated, torn. The inn sounded wonderful, but the thought of trying to figure out where it was in her exhausted state sounded daunting. *Is it easy to find?*

Not only is it easy to find, but the cat will keep you company on your walk, Robin assured her. *As long as you are able to put one foot in front of the other, we will get there easily.*

Then we'd better get going, because I don't know how much longer I can stay upright. Laying out her two dresses and her outfit from Earth, she set the performance hat in the middle and rolled the clothes around it. Tucking the bundle under one arm, she blew out the candle and walked out. *I don't even know how to get out of here.*

I will tell you. The cat trotted at her heels, tail up.

She followed the puck's telepathic directions, plowing forward through sheer determination. She shouldn't feel so disappointed Morgan wasn't waiting in her room. It was unrealistic to have hoped for him anyway. The castle hadn't settled for the night, the witchlights glowed everywhere, and many people still wandered the halls.

Several smiled at her and called out congratulations, and one or two made as if to approach her, but she nodded to them with a set smile and kept moving.

Mindful of Kallah's instruction, she left word with the guard that she would be staying at the inn. The exhilaration of stepping out of the castle and into the open air lent fuel to her steps. The route to the inn was filled with cobblestone streets and spacious buildings with arched doorways. In the distance, light spilled out of a street that intersected theirs.

She asked, *What is that light from?*

The night market is still open, Robin told her. *It is not midnight, yet. The inn is at the end of the street. Ask for their best room. It has a balcony with a view of the sea. I leave you here.*

As much as she still resented and hated what he had done to her, his presence had oddly become something of a comfort. Frowning, she looked around for the cat, but he was already gone.

She had meant to ask him to let Morgan know where she had gone. Feeling alone, cranky, and unreasonably abandoned, she made her way down the street to the large inn. Pushing her way inside, she discovered the taproom was busy and full of heat and noise. The smells of food, beer, and woodsmoke washed over her.

Most of the patrons were Light Fae, but there were a few monstrous creatures she couldn't identify, along with slender, ethereal creatures with pointed chins, and possibly some humans, although she wasn't sure about that. Several turned to look at her as she paused, then her gaze went unfocused and the crowd disappeared in a blur.

One Light Fae woman stood out. As she hurried toward Sid, she wiped her hands on a cloth. Beaming, she said, "Welcome, musician! I'm Leisha, one of the owners. We're honored to have you here. What can I do for you?"

"I would like your best room," Sid said. "The one with the sea view and the balcony. Is it available?"

"It is, indeed, and it is yours now."

The innkeeper led the way upstairs. The room was spacious and well-appointed, with a bathing alcove behind a carved screen. As Sid set her bundle down on the large bed, Leisha lit the stacked logs in the fireplace and went to balcony doors to throw them open wide. Picking through the unfamiliar coins in her hat, Sid paid her for a week and ordered a breakfast tray for the morning.

By the time the innkeeper took her leave, the heat from the fireplace had begun to spread throughout the room, mingling with the freshness of the sea air. Closing her eyes and breathing deeply, Sid came to a dead stop. She didn't think she could say one more word to anyone, not even to save her life.

Staggering to the bed, she pulled off her clothes and crawled underneath the covers, and she fell deeply asleep the moment her head hit one of the soft, clean-scented pillows.

"SIDONIE."

Someone cupped her bare shoulder and stroked the short hair back from her forehead.

She was tired, so tired, but she fought to surface out of her deep sleep because she knew that whisper.

She knew those hands. She would know them anywhere.

Dragging heavy eyelids open, she tried to focus on the large, powerful figure bending over her. The fire still crackled in the fireplace, and it was dark outside.

She couldn't have been asleep that long.

Looking up into Morgan's shadowed face, she raised her arms. Sitting on the edge of the bed, he gathered her up, and she buried her face in his neck. Huskily, she whispered against his skin, "How did you get in here?"

"The inn backs against a series of buildings built very close together. As soon as Robin told me where you were, I knew how to get here. I came over the rooftops." He cupped the back of her head, holding her tightly.

Needing to feel his skin against hers, she plucked at his shirt. "I can't keep my eyes open. Take off your clothes and come to bed."

Easing back, he gave her a swift kiss and stood to strip. Lying back against the pillows, she watched him through slitted eyes. She might not be able to open her eyes fully, but she also couldn't stop watching him.

He was muscular all over, tanned, and beautifully formed, and his strong, corded legs were sprinkled with chestnut hair. He took everything off except the bandage that wrapped around his lower ribs. His large penis stood half-erect over tight, round testicles, but he did not appear to notice. His expression was sober, contemplative.

One arm flexing, he pulled back the covers, and when he slid in beside her, the sensation of his nude body coming against hers was so much what she had been yearning for, she lost her breath on a shaken sigh.

Lying back against the pillows, he pulled her to him, and she went readily, curling around his body like a limpet, drawing one leg over his while he guided her head to his shoulder. His body relaxed, and breathing deeply, he nestled his face in her hair.

She pushed more tightly against him, greedily drinking in every detail—the tickle of crisp chest hair against her cheek, the feeling of warmth as his body heated the bed, the stroke of his fingers as he cupped her biceps, the length of his erection resting against her thigh.

"I had to come," he murmured. "I couldn't stay away. I wanted to come to your room in the castle."

"I'm so glad you didn't. It wouldn't have been safe." She pressed kisses to his pectoral muscles and nuzzled him.

"Waiting to find out how your meeting with Isabeau went was agonizing." His words stirred the hair at her temple. "But since you were able to come into town, apparently, it went well."

"Well enough, I guess. I tried to get a week to myself, but she insisted I play for her an hour each day." She sighed. "I also asked for her to get me a violin and a guitar. I guess those will be arriving in the next few days."

"Robin said you have leave to go up to two hours' walk away." He laced his fingers through hers.

"I can't tell you what a relief it is." She closed her eyes. "Or what a relief this is. Tell me you're going to stay the night."

"Just try to stop me." He pressed his lips against her temple and whispered, "It's okay to relax for now. Go to sleep."

Despite knowing everything she knew about the continuing precariousness of their situation, in that moment, what stole over her was an almost indescribable sense of comfort and safety. She knew better, but she let herself believe in it anyway.

When sleep came again, it was not gentle. Instead, it hit hard and fast. She plummeted into a black pool. Then something happened. He shifted, or she did, and the oddity of sleeping with another person brought her back up.

Before she had fully surfaced, she knew she was sleeping with *him*, and this time hunger drove her all the way to wakefulness. It was not quite dawn outside, but the sky had lightened from full darkness. The fire had long since died down, and the room was cool with the fresh seaside breeze.

She didn't want to wake him. He needed the rest as much as she did, but something roused him too. Maybe it was the change in her breathing or the tension in her muscles.

Angling his head, he looked down at her, saw her eyes were open, and with a soft growl, he rose and settled her fully onto her back. As he did so, she reached for him, and his head plummeted down to her. His hard, searching lips took hers, and he kissed her with the same kind of ravenous need that pulsed in her body.

She arched up to him, kissing him with all her strength while she threaded her fingers through his hair. He pushed one knee between her legs, the hard length of his cock lying against her hip.

Readily, she opened for him, and he settled himself at the bowl of her pelvis, kissing her as he cupped her breast. Running his callused thumb back and forth over the tip, he teased at her nipple until it felt unbearably sensitized.

This desire she felt for him thrummed through her body like the pulsing heartbeat of a beast. It made her feel unhinged. She needed him inside her more than she needed the pleasure of foreplay.

Grasping his erection, she urged him to her, muttering against his mouth, "I can't wait. I don't want to wait."

"You're not ready." His voice had gone guttural, and he was breathing hard, as if he had been running for a long time.

"I don't care." She ran her fingers down his length greedily.

He hesitated only for a moment. She could feel it when he gave in. A sharpening of intent changed his body. Gently, he stroked the fluted petals of her private flesh, then delved into her, drawing out evidence of her arousal, heightening her need, until she pushed his hand away and brought the broad, thick head of his cock to her entrance.

"Come inside me now," she whispered.

He pushed in. She was already aching and swollen from their lovemaking the night before, and as he entered her, he felt bigger than ever. He tilted his head back, teeth gritted. She thought his taut expression was the most beautiful thing she'd ever seen. It sharpened the bold lines of his face, which were darkened with a sensual flush.

Touching his mouth with the fingers of both hands, she whispered, "I'm so glad I'm not alone with this feeling."

His brilliant hazel gaze focused on her. "You're not alone," he said against her fingers as he pushed farther in. "You've set me on fire."

"I'm obsessed," she whispered back. "My skin hurts when it's not touching yours."

Rocking, he thrust farther until he was in to the root. Only then did something like relief pass over his expression. Kissing along the side of her neck, he began to move inside.

"I can't get enough of you," he said against her neck. "When I walk away from you, I feel like I've cut myself off from breathing."

Yes. Yes, it was like that.

Everything else in the world fell away as he moved over her, and eagerly, she reached up to meet his thrusts, impaling herself on him over and over again. The heat began to rise, along with the pleasure. As he fucked her, he braced up on one elbow, watching her so intently, it felt as if she was the only thing in the world that mattered.

His gaze tracked every shift in her expression, the catch of her breath, the way her mouth trembled. She had never felt so exposed nor so protected at once. Gradually he picked up the rhythm, and she tightened her hold on him, holding him with her arms while she cradled him with her legs, and the pressure built and built to such a spike she couldn't bear it a moment longer.

Then he reached between them to stroke her, and the pressure shattered into fiery pieces. She cried out hoarsely, muffling the noise against the back of her hand. As he watched her climax, he lost control. Thrusting hard in quick, savage movements, he peaked. She felt his cock pulsing inside her.

Tears slipped out the corners of her eyes and soaked into the hair at her temples. Touching one, he kissed her forehead, and she was truly at a loss for how something so carnal could be so emotionally profound at the same time.

She had once thought sex was a game, something to be role-played and compartmentalized from the rest of her life. She'd had no idea. No idea. Now she knew she had never made love before in her life.

She had played at passions, like trying on different outfits, but she had only ever known one true passion, the one for her music.

Until now.

This passion she felt for him was like a crucible, forging her into something new.

This love she felt for him…

There was no surviving some loves. No matter what happened to the love affair, whether it flourished or failed, those loves struck mortal blows one carried for the rest of one's life.

This love she felt for him.

This love was like that.

ONCE HE HAD reached Sidonie's room and was able to hold her in his arms, Morgan had finally been able to relax. He couldn't remember the last time he had slept so deeply or awakened with such urgency.

After making love, he was still inside her when he fell asleep again, while her arms were still twined around his neck. When he stirred next, it was well past dawn. As he shifted position, his cock slipped out.

Rousing briefly, Sidonie murmured in disappointment. As she curled on her side, he spooned her from behind and pulled her back against his chest. Time was running out, he knew, and there were things that needed to be done, but they were both exhausted. The delicate skin underneath Sidonie's eyes looked bruised with dark purple shadows.

Everything else would have to wait a few more hours. Burying his nose against the back of her neck, he slept again.

A knock on the door woke them next. Rolling over, he grabbed the sword he had brought with him. Sidonie rolled over with him and took hold of his arm.

She met his gaze and shook her head while she raised her voice to ask, "What is it?"

"I've got your breakfast tray, mum." It was a boy's cheerful voice. Morgan's grip on the sword hilt relaxed. "It's nice and hot."

Sidonie cuddled against his back and nuzzled his shoulder, calling out, "Thank you! Just leave it on the floor, and I'll get it."

"Yes'm."

Morgan listened to the boy's quick footsteps fade away. Leaning back against the pillows, he watched with pleasure as Sidonie slipped out of bed. She was perfectly built all over. As she bent to scoop up her tunic from the floor, the graceful curve of her spine caught at him. He couldn't look away from the perfection of her fluid movement until she had pulled the tunic over her head and the fabric had settled over her torso.

Padding to the door, she unlocked it and brought the breakfast tray in. Pausing to lock the door again, carefully, she carried the tray to the bed. There was sausage, egg, and potatoes, hot tea, and a flaky, buttery biscuit.

She climbed back under the covers and they shared the food. He paused between taking bites to press kisses at the back of her neck, which made her murmur with pleasure as she cuddled against his side.

A small thump sounded out on the balcony, and a black cat strolled into the room. Once it had passed within the sheer curtains, it changed into Robin.

"It's about time you both woke up," the puck said. "I was beginning to think I might have to walk on your heads."

Sidonie heaved a sigh and leaned back against Morgan. She murmured, "I suppose it was too much to hope the peace would last."

"No, it wasn't. We could have taken a day before facing everything else. Just one damn day." He slipped an arm around her waist as he eyed the view out the balcony doors. Even in daylight, he couldn't fault the puck's choice of rooms. The inn was built high enough none of the windows from neighboring buildings provided line of sight. The only way Morgan could be spotted was if he stepped onto the balcony without a cloaking spell. "What do you want, Robin?"

"Have you told her yet?" With no apparent sense of shame or discretion, Robin sat at the food of the bed and swiped the last of the biscuit from the breakfast tray.

"I haven't had time." Pouring the last of the tea into the single cup, he handed it to Sidonie, who cupped it in both hands.

"Oh, you had time." The puck's eyes gleamed. "You just had other priorities."

"Our priorities are none of your business," Sidonie snapped. She looked adorable when she was cranky. Her short black hair stood in tufts like a bird's feathers. Scowling, she buried her nose in the cup.

Robin did not appear as charmed by Sidonie as Morgan was. "No, they're not," the puck snapped back. "Unless they interfere with what we all need to see done."

"What is he talking about?" Sidonie twisted to face him. "What haven't you told me."

Morgan sighed. "Robin thinks Isabeau's Hounds might actually be from Azrael's Wild Hunt."

Her expression went blank. "Okay. I'm sure that's not comfortable."

"I've told you this already, human. You have no real knowledge of the gods, their Powers and aspects, and how they move through this world," Robin said, giving her an irritated glance. "Lord Azrael leads the Wild Hunt at the death of each year, or at least he did. The more I have considered this, the more I have grown convinced he has not called the Wild Hunt for a very long time, perhaps even as long as Isabeau has been in possession of his knife."

"You were imprisoned for a long time," Morgan told him. "Maybe you missed it."

"It's possible." Robin acknowledged as he ate the morsel of biscuit in quick, clean bites. "But I think my explanation rings truer. There were also a great many years I was not imprisoned, and I still did not sense the

Wild Hunt."

"What does this hunt do, and why does it matter?" Sidonie asked.

Robin looked exasperated, so Morgan answered. "Some believe the hunt is to chase unclean spirits from the earthly realms. Others believe Azrael is hunting down souls that have escaped his domain. Still other tales make mention of random prey, such as a lost maiden, or unwary travelers. From what I understand, no one knows for sure."

Closing her eyes and hunching her shoulders, Sidonie sipped her tea. She said, "So what?" Robin's thin face sparked with ire, but before he could say anything, she opened her eyes and looked at him. "I mean that as a serious question. So what? Half what you've said is supposition, and the other half sounds like folktales. What is the useful bit? Give me the condensed version."

Morgan told Robin, "She doesn't know about the Deus Machinae." As Sidonie twisted to look up at him inquiringly, he explained, "There are seven indestructible God Machines active in the world, put here by the seven gods. For a while, I thought the knife might be one of those. Robin thinks otherwise."

"Which is *good* news," Robin said. "Just not easy news. If it is literally Lord Death's Knife, it's still an item of immense Power that was created by a god. But if it isn't one of the Machines, perhaps it can be destroyed. And also, unlike the Deus Machinae...

wouldn't Lord Azrael want his knife back?"

Morgan felt the shiver that ran through Sidonie. She whispered, "But he's a god. If he wants his knife back, why wouldn't he just take it?"

Morgan pressed a kiss to her temple. "Perhaps because he's not the only god. Will is also one of the seven Primal Powers. He's the god of the Gift, which can mean anything from individual gifts, or gifts of the spirit like your talent for music, to acts of sacrifice and philanthropy. He's also the guardian of free will, which is one of the linchpins in the universe. The gods must respect we all have free will to act as we choose. Azrael might not be able to take back the knife if Isabeau doesn't want to give it to him."

"So...," Sidonie said slowly as she looked back and forth between the two males. Her gaze settled on Morgan. "We have free will too. Our choices are to try to break the knife—which you can't do."

"No, I can't," he said.

"Or," she continued, "we try to take the knife— which you can't do."

He replied, again, "No. The freedoms I have to act must be oblique ones as I find ways to work around the geas. I can't do anything to act directly against Isabeau."

"You might not be able to," she said, tapping a thumbnail against her bottom teeth. "But I can."

Chapter Nineteen

B EFORE MORGAN HAD a chance to react to that, Robin said, "And I can too. We can achieve more when we act together."

"Gods help us," Morgan muttered. With the puck on their side, they might not need any enemies.

Robin told him, "What you can do, sorcerer, is find a way to summon Lord Azrael. Perhaps we can enlist his aid. After all, we too can act of our own free will— or at least, two of us can."

It was an audacious suggestion. In all his years as a sorcerer, Morgan had never attempted to communicate with one of the gods. He rubbed his mouth as he considered it. Would the geas allow it, or would the action be too direct?

He needed to check the texts back at the cottage to see if any of them offered a ritual for contacting the gods. Reading did not activate the geas. If the texts didn't contain anything useful, he would either need to look elsewhere or construct the summoning himself. At that thought, he could feel the geas's coils shifting uneasily and knew he was skating very close to the edge.

Both Sidonie and Robin were watching him for his reaction.

"I don't know if I can," he said. "But I'll work on it. My biggest concern right now is I've only got one bottle of hunter's spray left. Either I need to curtail my movements drastically until we find a solution to this problem, or I need to slip back to Earth to get more."

"How big are the bottles?" Robin asked.

In answer, Morgan reached for his bag of supplies, pulled out the bottle, and showed it to the puck. Robin scratched his spiky hair with both thin hands as he considered it.

Finally he said, "I can't smuggle something as large as a human across the crossover passageways, but I might be able to hide a few bottles of that in one of the cargo caravans. Unfortunately, the caravans aren't very frequent."

Straightening her spine, Sidonie exclaimed, "Kallah is going to arrange this morning for the acquisition of a violin and a guitar for me! There'll be some kind of caravan coming from one of the passageways this week! But... I guess that might not call for a caravan. Someone could bring those instruments on the back of a horse."

Morgan raised his eyebrows. "Do they know that?"

Her startled gaze flashed to his. "No. They have no idea how big a violin or a guitar is."

"So they'll arrange for a caravan." He frowned.

He didn't like relying on Robin to perform such an important task. If the puck didn't make it back with more hunter's spray, Morgan would need to become housebound, or eventually he would be caught and he would have to go back to Isabeau.

But the thought of leaving Sidonie alone to deal with life here while he traveled back to Earth was intolerable.

"What's wrong?" Sidonie touched the back of his hand.

There wasn't any real choice. Realizing he had paused too long, he added briskly, "Nothing. They'll want to make the caravan as efficient as possible, so they'll be sure to transport anything else they might have stored at the encampment until the next trip. It might not be a very big caravan, but there will be one. The time slippage from Avalon to Earth is not significant, so with travel and enough time on the other side to acquire the instruments, the caravan should return in four days, maybe five."

The puck grinned. "That's more than enough time. I just need to get the bottles across the passageway, so I'll tuck the package in with other things. Once everything has been transported to Avalon, I can steal them back and bring them the rest of the way, myself."

A shadow passed over Sidonie's expression. She asked, "Will you do me a favor as well, Robin?"

"If it is within my power to do so, yes," he replied. "I owe you that much."

"I want you to mail a letter for me." Her jaw tightened. "I have friends who are worried about me, and a business that has ground to a standstill. They need to know I'm alive and to hang on until they hear from me again."

Robin's gaze dropped from hers. Softly, he said, "Of course. As long as it's small, I can get a message back to Earth."

"Thank you." Taking a deep breath, she turned back to Morgan. "So Robin has his task, and you have yours. What am I supposed to do?"

"Nothing," Morgan cupped her face in both hands. "You do nothing. You play for the Queen when she asks you to, and you listen to every conversation you can. When it comes to the Athame, she has always been extremely careful in my presence—she always wears it around me, even if she has nothing else on, and while she has reminisced enough that I know she had the Athame for a while before she trapped me, she has only referenced it in passing. So there's always the possibility she might let something slip around you. But that's all, Sidonie. You don't put yourself at risk *for any reason*. Do you hear me?"

She scowled, but said, "I'll be careful, and I won't do anything that puts me at risk. I promise."

He relaxed. "That's our plan, then. We stay in a holding pattern for the next few days, until Robin returns. Sidonie plays for the Queen when she asks for it, and I'll limit my movements and see what I can do about researching a summoning spell." At the flash of anxiety in Sidonie's expression, he added, "If I'm careful and go across the rooftops in town, this last bottle should be enough for me to get back and forth from the cottage to this room. We won't be separated for all that time."

Relaxing somewhat, she gave him a twisted smile. "Okay. But what about your scent here in my room?"

"Tell the proprietress you'll take the room indefinitely, and there'll be no reason for the Hounds to come up here," he told her. "I have plenty of money if you need more. Sometimes they do come to the taproom to drink and eat, so you'll need to be on your guard when you go downstairs. Whenever you leave, make sure you wash thoroughly and always wear a clean outfit, and you should carry the sheets down yourself to be laundered. I believe there's a back staircase for the servants, so you wouldn't have to run into anyone from the taproom."

She nodded. "I can do that. I don't usually wear perfume, but perhaps I can buy some rose water or an essential oil. I need more clothes and some stationery so I can write my letter."

Taking one hand, he rubbed her fingers as he thought. "It's a shame Isabeau couldn't give you some time to yourself. It's going to be hard on us both if I have to cast a battle spell on you every day."

"I don't think you need to." Her fingers tightened over his. "When I was playing last night, I felt the ability to play the lute solidify again. When the spell wore off, I was exhausted but I didn't feel like I had lost it."

"Are you sure?" He frowned.

"Don't worry," she told him reassuringly. She leaned her forehead against his shoulder. "I might be out of my depth here in Avalon in virtually every other subject, but this is the one thing I do know something about."

"Okay." Angling his head, he rested his cheek on top of hers. "I'll trust you."

Robin stood. "I will return midafternoon for your letter. That should give you time to go to the market and get what you need. In the meantime, good luck to both of you." He added to Morgan, "Find that summoning spell."

Morgan didn't tell them about the geas shifting uneasily. No need to worry them unless it became necessary. Instead, he said, "I'll do my best."

Without anything further, Robin melted into the cat again. It blinked at them at the foot of the bed, then trotted to the balcony and disappeared.

Sidonie dug the heel of her hand into her eyes. "I can never really relax when he's around. I can't forget what happened."

"Nor should you." He thought perhaps the puck regretted what he had done, but that did not lessen Robin's accountability.

A sharp rap sounded on the door. Sidonie looked

at him quickly as she called out, "Yes?"

A deep male voice said, "Castle guard, ma'am. The Queen requests your presence at your earliest convenience."

Alarm flashed over her expression. Jumping off the bed, she ran to the door. Without opening it, she exclaimed, "I don't have any clean clothes!"

"You don't... have any clothes?" The guard sounded taken aback.

"Last night I gave them to Leisha, the inn owner, to have laundered, and I haven't gotten them back yet. I don't have that many outfits!" Turning, she rolled her eyes at Morgan and said telepathically, *I can't put off going shopping.*

"Ma'am, I will check on your laundry," the guard said.

She raised her voice again. "If they're not ready, ask Leisha if she has an outfit I can borrow!"

"Yes, ma'am." The sound of his footsteps faded.

While Sidonie talked with the guard, Morgan left the bed and dressed quickly. When she turned around to face him again, disappointment darkened her gaze.

Striding over, he kissed that soft, pouting mouth. She hooked an arm around his neck, kissing him back. The fire he felt for her was always present. At the touch of her body pressed against his, it burned hot and fierce.

With an immense act of will, he dragged his lips away. Taking care in case the guard was closer than he thought, he said telepathically, *This is good news. Your hour will go quickly, and then you'll have the rest of the day.*

She grasped the front of his shirt in both hands. *When will you be back?*

Tonight, after sunset. Her bottom lip looked plump and still wet from their kiss. He rubbed it with a forefinger while his unruly cock stiffened. He added in a whisper, *And I'll stay all night, if you'll have me.*

She looked drugged, her elegant eyes dilated. *God, yes.*

Be careful. Don't trust anything or anyone, especially her. Don't believe anything she promises you. She lies more easily than breathing.

Don't worry, I won't.

But he did worry. The thought of Sidonie walking back into the castle was like watching her voluntarily step into a pit of snakes. With a final, scorching kiss and a nearly inaudible, frustrated growl, he tore himself away from her. Scooping up his sword and bag, he cloaked himself and slipped out onto the balcony.

Another knock sounded on her door, and he paused outside, listening.

"Yes?" Sidonie asked.

A familiar woman's voice sounded on the other side. It was Leisha herself. "Musician, I apologize profusely, but your clothes have not had a chance to dry. I did not realize there was some urgency to your laundry, but when you told me last night that bundle was all you had, I should have."

"Oh, great." Sidonie thunked against the door.

"I *do* have a few spare outfits that patrons have left behind…. I think one or two of these dresses might work? They're not new, but they're decent, clean, and well cared for."

"Let's see them." Sidonie unlocked the door. "You, guard. Wait for me downstairs."

"Yes, ma'am."

As Leisha stepped into the room with an armful of clothes, Morgan relaxed. Finding nothing further to keep him, he scaled the side of the wall to the roof.

He had almost the full day ahead of him, and he needed to use every minute of it to see if he could discover a way to summon a god.

He had a sense of time trickling away, important time he could never get back. With every moment he healed, he became stronger—and grew closer to the next wound, which would weaken him critically again.

Also his movements had become even more hampered now, and if the puck failed to bring back more of the hunter's spray, Morgan didn't have a backup plan.

And there were too many pieces at play in the game that were unpredictable.

Isabeau. Robin. The geas. Even Sidonie had managed to surprise him more than once.

And never, ever, did Morgan forget Modred.

✧   ✧   ✧

OF THE FOUR dresses Leisha brought, only one fit well

enough Sid could get by wearing it for an hour or two. It was a dull gold with yellow embroidered flowers, and given how short it was, the dress had probably been a Light Fae girl's dress. When Sid told Leisha she would take the room for the foreseeable future, the innkeeper insisted she keep the dress as a gift.

After she left, Sid tore off the dress, hung it on a nearby hook, and raced to the bathing alcove. It was too late to worry about getting Morgan's scent on the new dress. Hopefully she hadn't worn it long enough for it to matter.

In the alcove, she discovered a pleasant surprise. There was a soft soap in a dish that smelled like patchouli. The bathing tub was small, and the water from the tap was cold. She had to either sit with her knees up or stand to sluice off.

However long she might end up trapped in Avalon, she would never get used to washing in cold water. She scrubbed thoroughly, washed her hair twice, and after haphazardly drying off, she dressed. When she had finger combed her hair as best she could, she pocketed her twenty-one worry stones.

Then she considered her small pile of coins and jewelry. She also had forgotten to give Morgan the diamond that had held his battle spell. What did people do here to keep their valuables safe? Should she wrap it up and take it with her, or should she hide it?

Surely an experienced thief would know all the hiding places better than she would.

She didn't have time to dither over it. She tied the coins and jewels into a silk handkerchief someone had dropped into her performance hat and stuffed it into the pocket of her dress. Then she left, taking care to lock the door behind her.

And unlock it. And lock it again.

And again. And again. *Agh!*

Running down the stairs, she joined the waiting guard, who led the short way back to the castle and the waiting Queen.

They stopped by the music hall so she could collect the lute, and then the guard led her to the private garden with the travertine pillars and the fishpond.

Kallah met them at the doors. When she saw Sidonie, she exclaimed softly, "Where have you been?"

"I had to bathe, and I had nothing to wear!" Sidonie exclaimed back. "My clothes are being laundered. I need to go to the market to buy more."

Kallah glanced down her figure. Her eyes widened with an expression of dismay, but she said grimly, "Well, it's too late to do anything to rectify that now. When you buy more clothes, be sure not to choose anything quite so appealing."

Right, Sid had forgotten. Wear only ugly clothes around the Queen. How old was Isabeau, several centuries going on seven?

Biting it back, she asked, "What do I do?"

"Slip over there, around the rosebushes." Kallah pointed across the garden. "I've set out a wooden stool for you. Play soothing songs, don't say anything, and don't stop until I come for you. Understood?"

"Yes." Sid started forward.

Kallah put a hand on her arm to stop her. "And Sid—don't breathe a word to anyone about anything you might see or hear." Kallah looked hard into her gaze, mouth set. "Not a word. You've experienced what can happen when her majesty takes offense, but you've not witnessed anything like what could happen if she considers herself betrayed."

Sid's heart leaped at the possibility of overhearing something they might be able to use. Dropping her gaze to hide her reaction, she muttered, "I understand."

"Good."

As soon as Kallah released her, she started forward. Around the outcropping of rosebushes, there was a small, private grassy area with a stool. Beyond that, there were more rosebushes. Through the bushes, she could see the outline of a low divan with pillows strewn over it.

It looked like the perfect spot for a private assignation, and for a moment, instinctively, she strained to make sense of what she was seeing on the other side of the rosebushes. Then the movement became clear, and she realized that was exactly what she was seeing. Two bodies lay entwined on the divan. Isabeau and a man. Loops of gold and white pearls threaded Isabeau's hair. It was the only thing she was wearing.

Fierce heat washed over Sid's face. Turning her

back to the scene, she sat on the stool and began to play, striving hard to ignore the sounds behind her.

But try as she might, she couldn't miss some details. The man wasn't Modred; she was sure of that. He might be the male in the private sitting room from the night before, the one who had slipped a ring into her performance hat.

And Isabeau made love with the abandonment and lack of shame of a cat, crying out, sometimes swearing. Once her lover swore too, with such vicious surprise, Sid had to bite both lips to keep an unexpected bubble of laughter from popping out. She was pretty sure laughing at the Queen's sex life was not a good career move.

Somehow she held it together until Kallah came across the garden and motioned to her, and her time was up for the day.

Escaping the confines of the castle felt as freeing as it had the first time. Instead of heading back to her room right away, she wandered down the street until she found the market.

There she bought a large canvas bag to carry her purchases in, and she spent a couple of hours picking out enough outfits so she would always have something clean to wear when she left her room, making sure to buy plainer clothes that were either black or some other dark color.

She also bought a smaller leather purse to carry essentials in, some toiletries, a comb, more scented soaps and a small vial of rose water, along with a pen, an inkwell, and ten sheets of parchment paper. Her final purchase was food and wine for that evening.

The sense of freedom she felt was so intoxicating she dawdled on the way back to the inn, enjoying the sights of the harbor and sea. Optimism came on the heels of her improved condition. They were going to find a way to break Morgan free of Isabeau's control. She was certain of it.

Back in her room, she opened the balcony doors to the fresh breeze and took her pen, ink, and paper to the table outside to craft a letter to Vincent and Julie. It was harder to do than she had expected, and Robin had warned her the message needed to be a small one. After considering and discarding several ideas, she kept the note very short and wrote it as small as she could.

> *Don't give up hope. I'm alive and okay.*
>
> *I've been kidnapped. I'm no longer on Earth, but I'm working to find a way to get back home.*
>
> *Be careful what you do. My captors could retaliate at what they see as aggression. I'll be in touch again as soon as I can.*
>
> *Love, Sid*

After reading and rereading the note, she sighed and folded it as small as she could get it. The note covered all the relevant points and would have to do. When Robin came, she gave it to him.

He didn't linger. They had said everything of

importance earlier. Instead, he tucked the note into his pocket, shapeshifted, and the cat slipped away.

Morgan had said it would be four days, or maybe five, for the caravan to return. She realized she'd forgotten to ask Robin to bring back news. Oh well, there was nothing she could do to rectify that now.

For the first time in weeks, she had the rest of the day to herself. She was relatively safe for the moment, the sun shining, and the water in the distance sparkled a gorgeous aquamarine blue. For a while, she sat on the balcony, basking in the sun and letting the warmth heal the cold shadows of injury that lingered deep in the corners of her mind, then she moved into the room to nap the rest of the day away, until the sun set and Morgan came.

THAT SET THE pattern of the next several days.

Sid returned to the castle to play when the Queen commanded. Aside from that, she spent her days sleeping, sunbathing on the balcony, and taking forays out of town to jog her three miles a day.

The good food, fresh air, and exercise brought back a sense of robustness she hadn't realized she had lost. They were good days, certainly good enough for someone who had lost control over her own destiny, and far better than she had once feared she would ever see again.

But they weren't what brought her fully alive.

The nights were.

She was just biding her time, waiting with barely controlled patience for the moment when Morgan pushed through the sheer curtains. When he appeared, she ignited, a candle bursting into flame, and they collided together with such intensity she wondered that the whole of Avalon didn't feel it.

She lived for those nights, for the touch of his body against hers. For the times he took her and took her, driving her out of her mind with burning pleasure.

The peaks with him were so high at times they frightened her. She felt sometimes as if she were clawing her way directly into the sun. They worked each other to exhaustion, then dozed long enough to rally again, and each night Morgan lingered until the dawn broke over the rooftops. Then he left her, reluctantly, with lingering kisses.

They talked too, desultorily, about their days. She related all the small details of her hours playing with the Queen, the times Isabeau spent by herself reading, or the afternoons she shared with her court ladies. Sid always took note of the knife Isabeau wore on the gold chain at her hips. The only time it had been absent, at least that Sid saw, had been when Isabeau had made love in the garden with the unknown Light Fae male.

When Sid asked Morgan about his research, he pulled a frustrated face. "I haven't found anything useful yet in the texts," he told her. "And when I try to construct a summoning spell, my mind slips away from the task. I can't hold on to it. My intent is too clear, and the action too direct. The geas won't let me complete it, and I haven't found a way to work around it."

The tension in his body when he talked revealed the depth of his anger at the invisible cage. Stroking his back, she let the subject go and didn't ask again. He would tell her whenever he had a breakthrough.

They never talked about the future, or at least, not in detail. Afterward, Sid would wonder why. For her part, she was afraid they might jinx things.

What if they broke free yet found, after everything they had gone through, they didn't suit each other? She didn't think she could bear it.

Or what if they never broke free?

Also perhaps the geas wouldn't let Morgan speak too much of building a life without it. The full extent of its binding on him was still a mystery.

Then early one afternoon, she received the summons from the guard. After readying herself, she walked back to the castle and collected the lute. The guard led her to the private garden, where Kallah waited by the doors.

She waved Sid on, her expression pinched. "I'll come get you when your hour is over."

Sid nodded. They had developed a routine. Making her way to the small semi-enclosed area with the stool, she took her seat. This too had become quickly familiar.

But this time was not like the others.

This time Isabeau lay weeping on the divan, her

dark green dress looking unusually stark against the brightness of the nearby flowers. A man reclined with her, his back to Sidonie. At first, she couldn't tell who he was.

Turning so she could look over the garden, yet still keep sight of the divan in the corner of her eye, she began to play a soft lullaby, the delicate strains gently permeating the air. All the while, she listened as intently as she could.

"I can't tell you enough how horrible it is," Isabeau sobbed. "Nobody truly understands what I go through. I never sleep, never. He's always there if I sink too deep, walking through my dreams. Whispering things to me—There's that damn girl. It's about time she showed up."

With a start, Sid realized Isabeau was talking about her. She angled her head away and kept her gaze lowered, not willing to risk even the slightest chance of meeting anyone's eyes on the other side of the roses.

"You should not have let her leave the castle if you wanted her so closely at your beck and call," Modred said. The sound of his voice sent an icy shiver down Sid's spine. "Darling, are you quite sure it is he, and not simply a bad dream?"

"No, it's him." Isabeau's voice shook. "Sometimes I dream I'm in this huge hall, with black and white marble floors and bloodred roses. It's so silent there. Nothing moves. There's not even any wind. Then I hear his footsteps approaching, and... just the sound of those steady, quiet steps fills me with such horrible dread I want to scream and scream."

"Yes, you've told me about this dream before," Modred murmured. "Has it changed? Have you seen his face?"

At least that was what Sid thought he murmured. He spoke too quietly for her to be sure. She switched songs, and began playing "Scarborough Fair."

"No, not in that dream. I just hear him coming for me. In other dreams, I see his face. I don't ever re-member what he looks like, but I do know I have seen him. He has the most piercing green eyes, and… and when he speaks, it's in a gentle voice that is somehow so much worse than anyone else's scream." In a sudden movement, Isabeau sat and turned to grip Modred by the shoulders as she cried, "It's unnatural! *We're not supposed to have anything to do with him! Mortal creatures are his prey—not us! WE'RE SUPPOSED TO LIVE FOREVER!*"

Could Isabeau be talking about Azrael? Sid almost forgot herself and stopped playing. Catching herself up, she switched songs.

"Isabeau," Modred said sharply. "Calm yourself! You've been having these dreams for ages, and nothing has changed. They haven't harmed you. There's been no catastrophe. You are perfectly, beautifully, whole as always."

"But I'm so tired," she wept. "Nobody understands how tired I am. He wants it back, and he never lets up, yet I can't give it to him. If I give it back, Morgan may be freed—and the first person he will want to kill is me."

"And me," Modred muttered. "I killed his king, after all."

"That was battle. People die all the time in battle. But me... I've held him captive for centuries, and I've made him do things he found revolting. Oh, I wish I had never found it! And I can't hide it in the crystal caverns again, not while I hold Morgan with the geas. I've got to keep it close, and it's so cold, yet it burns at the same time. I feel like a poker is pressed into my side. I wish I had never heard the Hunt passing or had never gone to look—and I wish I'd never found it lying in that frozen field!"

"How many times do I have to say this?" Modred said, impatience creeping into his words. "Give it to me. Let me carry it for you, just for a short while, and we can find out once and for all if the knife is causing your dreams. Maybe then you can get some rest and recover your equilibrium."

Sid caught movement out of the corner of her eye as Isabeau pulled away from him. "I appreciate your willingness to sacrifice for me." Her voice had turned cool and edged. Dangerous. "Dearest Modred, always so selfless. But no, just like the crown, this is my burden to carry."

He sighed sharply. "I'm going to get Myrrah to make a poppy drink for you. I know you don't like it, but it's the only thing that will calm you down when you're like this. Maybe then you can take a nap."

"What would I do without you to look after me?" Isabeau said softly.

"I don't know. Turn to Valentin, perhaps?" Now Modred's voice had turned cold and edged.

There was a small silence. Drawing away, Isabeau told him, "You know he doesn't mean anything to me. He's not like you. You and I, we've been together from the very beginning of my rule."

"And I will continue to stand by you. Of course, I will." Modred's voice changed. "But watch him, Izzy. Valentin has not shown you his true face. The chambermaids have hesitated to say anything, because you're so taken with him, but more than one of them has gone to Myrrah to be treated for bruises and other injuries."

"You would vilify anybody I have developed an affection for." Isabeau's voice thickened. "My headache is back, and now it is worse than ever. Get out, Modred. Leave me alone!"

"As you wish. You know how to find me. I'll send Myrrah with the poppy drink."

Modred thrust to his feet and stalked out of the garden, never once looking in Sid's direction.

But then, she was so very insignificant. She had no Power, no connections. She fulfilled a function, no more.

Once he had left, Isabeau flung herself flat on the divan and began to weep again. Tuning out the noise,

Sid played the lute on autopilot as she turned over the pieces of information she had gleaned.

It seemed the puck was right, after all. Isabeau had found the knife one night after the Wild Hunt had passed, and Azrael wanted his property back.

But how did this help them?

At least it solidified their understanding of the problem, yet what could they do about it? Morgan's constraints wore on him more every day, and if Robin had known a spell for summoning the god of Death, he would have told them so already.

She wasn't entirely clear on why they needed a spell to begin with. Mere magicless mortals didn't cast summoning spells when they wanted to communicate with their gods. Instead, they prayed and hoped their god would take the time to hear them, and answer.

Surely now, if there ever was such a time, a god might be motivated to listen.

The thought was frightening. Sid wasn't a praying kind of person—she had been raised in a secular household, and she lived a secular life—so she wasn't quite sure how one was supposed to talk to a god.

Perhaps it was something like telepathy.

Fixing on the images Isabeau had described to Modred, Sid reached out and said telepathically, *Lord Azrael, I'm not much for religion, and I'm only a Powerless human, but I hope you will take a moment to listen anyway. We are trying to find a way to get your knife from Isabeau and to free Morgan from his bondage. From what I've heard, I believe you want your knife back too. Please help us help you. I ask this of my own free will.*

As she spoke, a shadow seemed to pass over the sun, and everything in the garden appeared cooler, darkened. For a moment, there was no sound anywhere, not even the sound of a breeze. Sid glanced up. The sky was a cloudless, clear blue.

Had Lord Death listened to her awkward prayer, and answered? A shudder ran through her, as if someone had walked on her grave.

Then Kallah strode across the garden toward her and beckoned, and Sid's hour came to a close.

Grateful as always to have the time behind her, she hurried to the music hall to deposit the lute on its stand. As she turned away, a shadow fell in the doorway, and a man walked in.

It was the Light Fae male from the night of her great hall performance, the one with Isabeau and Modred in the sitting room who had given her a gold ring.

"Musician." He greeted her with a smile as he strolled toward her. "I wondered where you had gone after that stunning show of artistry in the great hall."

Was this Valentin? The man about whom the chambermaids had hesitated to say anything?

With a wary smile, she slipped to one side so that she put the table between them. "I'm not staying in the castle."

"No?" he replied as he came closer. His body was

loose and relaxed. "This is the first time I've seen you without the lute in your hands. Always before, you've been playing for her majesty." He gave her a gleaming smile. "I especially liked your music in the garden. I thought of you when I climaxed inside her. It made me come harder than I have in a long time. Did you like what you saw?"

Revolted shock slapped her. For a moment, she stared, at a loss for words. No one had ever said anything like that to her in her life.

Then fury hit. Curling her hands into claws, she hissed, "Stay the fuck away from me, or I will hurt you."

"Oh, pretty musician." He laughed. "I would truly love to see you try."

Balancing on the balls of her feet, she watched and waited until he rounded the corner of the table. Then she sprinted for the doorway with all the speed she could kick out. The Light Fae were fast, but so was she, and she had been running all her adult life.

"You know I can find you," he called after her, still laughing. "And I will."

She hit the doorframe at full speed, her wrists taking the brunt of it. Using the impact, she sprang out into the hall. Once free of the room, she spun around to face the door. When he didn't appear right away, she fled down the hall.

The memory of his laughter followed her, like a disaster building momentum, all the way back to the inn.

Chapter Twenty

WHEN SHE REACHED her room, she felt like she had been running for miles. Her breathing coming short and fast, she slammed the door and locked it.

Unlocked it. Locked it.

Unlocked. Locked.

She had her own invisible compulsion that held her prisoner, her own geas that tightened its constraints upon her behavior. Finally she rested both shaking hands on the panels while she tried to think.

Her stay in Avalon had been only lacking that one thing, the threat of sexual assault, to made the nightmare complete.

Her mother had told her once, long ago, when people show you who they are, believe them. The monster had shown her who he was, and Sid did believe him.

You know I can find you, he had said. And he was right. He could. Several people, including the castle guard, knew where she was staying. An offhand conversation, a few carefully worded questions, and he would know exactly where to come.

I could run, she thought, turning to lean back against the door as she looked around the room. I could just head out of town, ignore the two hours' walk limit, and keep going.

But then he could have me tracked down to a place where there weren't any witnesses. And if I tell Morgan, he'll kill him. There's no question in my mind. He'll kill him, and that might expose him, and he could lose what little freedom he has fought so hard to gain.

I could move to another inn.

But even as she considered that, she knew that wasn't a solution either. Valentin could find her wherever she went.

Suddenly, her mind switched gears.

She thought, I could go back to the castle. Approach Kallah in confidence and tell her what happened. Maybe Kallah would let me stay in her room. Surely not even Valentin would dare to attack Kallah, not when she was so close to Isabeau.

But if I did that, I would always be looking over my shoulder. I would always be strategizing how to avoid dark corners or find ways to keep from being alone, and I can't keep that up indefinitely. Sooner or later, I'll find myself in a vulnerable position.

Or...

I could kill him.

When that thought occurred to her, it clicked home, like the key turning in the lock. She let the thought settle to see if it held true or vanished in a train of logic, while she stared out at the sparkling sea.

It held true.

Quickly, she sprang into action. She stripped off the bedsheets and carried them down the servants' staircase. Down below, she threw the sheets in with the pile to be washed in the morning.

Then she got a bucket and soap from one of the servants, and went back to her room to scrub every available surface she could. She finished by washing the floorboards on her hands and knees.

It was early evening, and the sun was beginning to dip down toward the sea, when she finally poured the last of the soapy water down the drain in the alcove. Setting the bucket by the door, she dressed in a black tunic, trousers, and butter-soft boots.

Pulling out her pen, ink, and paper, she wrote, *Go back. I can't see you tonight.*

Because if she saw Morgan, he would want to know what was wrong. And if she weakened and told him, he would want to do something about it. She knew her Magic Man well enough to know that much.

Pinning the note to the balcony table with an unlit lamp, she closed and locked the balcony doors. Then, pausing for a few minutes, she took off her telepathy earrings and slipped them into her pocket. Settling the strap of her leather purse across her torso, messenger-style, she left her room, locked it, and headed down the stairs.

The taproom was filled with the dinner crowd. Light Fae and humans, some of them probably Hounds, along with a few of the creatures she had discovered were ogres, and a few sprites who were drawn to the conviviality like bees to honey.

Across the room, Leisha was serving dinner to several men. She saw Sid and gave her a nod and a smile as she approached. "Headed back to the castle?"

"I thought I would check out the night market," Sid told her. "I heard there are metal smiths at the other end."

"There are." Leisha eyed her curiously. "Looking for anything in particular?"

A good, sharp knife would do. She didn't think she should attempt anything like a short sword. Like a gun purchased by someone who didn't know how to use it, a short sword would be more a danger to her than to anyone else, if someone knowledgeable were able to take it away.

Tae kwon do was an unarmed sport. She could try striking to immobilize and then hopefully finish the job with the knife.

Listen to her, plotting someone's murder. When Leisha's expression changed, she realized she had gone silent for too long.

Moving closer, Leisha lowered her voice. "Are you all right, love?"

Leisha lowering her voice was a courtesy, nothing more. Sid knew there were many sharp Light Fae ears that could still hear every word that was spoken.

Oh, screw it. She was tired of being so damn careful all the time. She couldn't win her way through this fucked-up situation by being careful, and there was no place for her to hide.

She replied, "You know, no, I'm not. Someone threatened me today, and I want to buy a knife to protect myself."

There was a nearly indefinable change in the people around them, a sharpening of focus. Coldly, Sid watched a few of the guard set down their forks. Witnesses before the fact should be useful.

Dismay darkened Leisha's features. "Dear goddess, I hope it didn't happen here!"

"No," Sid said, glancing around the taproom. "Your inn must be one of the safest places in town. But I have to leave here sometimes and go to the castle or go buy supplies in town. I can't barricade myself in your inn."

Leisha grabbed her hand. She whispered, "Go to the Queen. Tell her what happened. She's your patron. She'll protect you."

Sid almost pitied Leisha's naïveté. Either that, or she envied it. Isabeau might not tolerate rape in most cases, but she had already shown who she was too, earlier, when Modred had tried to warn her.

Sid forced a smile. "I can do that. This is your busy time of day. Go back to your customers." As Leisha lingered with a frown, she added, "Don't worry about me."

"The night market is well lit and perfectly safe," Leisha said finally. "Just don't wander down to the docks."

"Thank you."

Sid made good her escape. Quickly she made her way to the night market and threaded through the growing crowds, searching for the metal smiths. She found them clustered at the other end of the market.

Perusing their stalls, she looked through the array of weaponry. There was everything imaginable on sale—swords, maces, pike axes, throwing stars… now that would be handy to learn… bows and arrows, and knives. Plenty of knives, and in all sizes and shapes, housed in a variety of scabbards.

The vendor of one stall watched her for a few minutes, then approached with a smile. "Is there anything in particular you're looking for?"

"I don't want something too big," she told him. She held up a small knife in a square piece of worked leather. "What's this?"

"It's for your arm. Look." He helped to wrap the leather around her forearm, threading a leather thong through loops and tightening until the knife fit snugly along the inside muscle.

"Oh, I like that." She held up her arm to study it. Her tunic had long sleeves. When she shook the sleeve down over the scabbard, the knife was completely hidden from sight. The hilt lay downward, close to her wrist.

Reaching for it with her other hand, she drew it. Sheathed it again. Drew it, and sheathed it. There was a satisfying *snick* when the knife hit home in the scabbard. It was well constructed, so the knife wouldn't slip out by accident.

The vendor grinned. "Smooth as butter, eh?"

"It is." She drew the knife again. "My only question is, should I buy one or two?"

He took her seriously, as he should. "Are you good at knife work with both hands? Because otherwise, there's no point in wasting your money. Those are good blades, and they'll cost you."

She narrowed her eyes as she considered. She didn't have any knife work with either hand, but she was predominantly left-handed with most things. "I'll stick with just one."

"Aye, that's a smart choice. You can always come back for another if you change your mind."

"I will, thank you. How much is it?"

He quoted a price that made her swallow, but the handiwork was of clear quality, and with some haggling, she got him to go down a little in price. Paying him depleted her stash by quite a bit.

If she survived for very long, she was going to have to play for money again, soon.

If she survived. If she were attacked, and if she told the truth after she killed him.

If, if, if.

Had this all come about because of her prayer to Lord Azrael?

Maybe. Maybe she would never know. Maybe they had skirted along the edge of calamity for so long, something like this was inevitable. All she really knew for certain was that she had gone through enough, and she wasn't going to be a victim any longer. Not if she had anything to say about it.

As she turned away from the vendor, she wore her new purchase. Now where should she go?

The answer to that question, when it came to her, seemed inevitable. She should go back to the music hall, of course.

She walked up the road to the castle. At the gate, the guard glanced at her indifferently. She recognized him from previous trips. He asked, "Back twice in one day?"

"I need to practice," she told him.

He waved her through, and she made her way to the music hall.

The evening wasn't late enough for the inhabitants of the castle to have settled for the night. She passed clusters of people, some of whom smiled and nodded to her, while others studied her curiously.

Back in the large, familiar room, she left the doors open, lit a fire in the fireplace, and also lit several candles in nearby candelabras. Picking the lute up from its cradle, she plucked at the strings and adjusted the frets until she was satisfied with the tuning.

Would he come? Did he dare?

If he did, and she killed him, it was going to look premeditated. There was no hiding the knife she had strapped to one arm, or taking back what she had said in the inn.

So be it. This was now the pair of dice she had to throw.

Settling on the footstool, she began to play, easily, gently, the kind of songs one might choose to play for practice, if one needed to practice. Angling her head, she listened for sounds outside the door.

She heard people pausing to listen, comment to each other, and then move on. Nobody stepped inside the hall to disrupt her at her music. That was okay. She wasn't in any hurry.

Then there was a single pair of footsteps that stopped outside the doors. They didn't move on.

Like the afternoon, a shadow passed over her again, and the light from the fireplace and the candles dimmed. A dark, gentle voice whispered, *He will be faster than you, and stronger. Be ready.*

She caught her breath. Now she knew for a certainty Lord Azrael had heard and responded to her prayer.

She had set her telepathy earrings aside, so that Morgan couldn't distract her from her purpose if he found her. Still, she reached out to the dark voice, whispering back, *I'll be ready.*

The darkness settled around her like a cloak of shadows. It was a hell of a thing to know a god had taken the time to notice you. Her fingers shook, and she had to concentrate fiercely to steady her playing.

Valentin walked into the room, and unhurriedly, he closed and locked the doors behind him. Taking in deep, steady breaths, she told him, "You're not welcome here."

"I am welcome wherever I choose to go in this place," Valentin responded. "You speak above your station, musician."

Strolling toward her, he looked the epitome of Light Fae entitlement, confident, arrogant, and relaxed.

Anticipatory.

Her muscles tightened. He was not the only one who was anticipating the encounter. She murmured, "If you don't leave now, this will turn out badly for you."

"So much cockiness for a human," he said, circling around her. "How could you possibly think this might go badly for me? I am stronger, faster, and far older than you. I am trained and experienced."

After a moment's hesitation, she gritted her teeth and set the lute aside. While not her instrument of choice, it was still far too beautiful to allow it to be ruined. Standing, she turned to face him.

"So you rape," she said. "You are a rapist. You believe you have the right to take anything and anyone you want. To force your will on them. To make them do your bidding. To deny them their own free will."

He smiled. The light from the fireplace glittered in his eyes. "You protest too much, my dear," he told her.

"This doesn't have to be an unpleasant encounter. I believe you will enjoy this far more if you simply let yourself go."

She tilted her head as she studied him. "You know, I think you're right. Come take me if you can."

"You are a true delight." He laughed. "And, oh yes, I can."

When he walked toward her, she strode forward to meet him.

MORGAN WAS GLAD to leave another frustrating day behind as he climbed over the rooftops to Sidonie's room. That afternoon he had finished going through the last of the texts. There hadn't been anything useful to use in summoning Azrael, and he continued to fail to create a summoning spell himself.

He had tried various tricks, but nothing worked. He couldn't even successfully create a general summoning spell for any god. The geas had clamped down, disrupting his thought patterns and hampering his Power.

Despite their best-laid plans, he might have to go to Earth after all to search for a spell. Isabeau could have something useful in her personal collection, but she had never allowed him to see her books on magic, and she'd expressly forbidden him from accessing the library. Maybe when Robin returned, he could sneak in to look at the titles to see if she might have something they could use.

Sliding down the iron pipe attached to the inn's gutter, Morgan leaped over the balcony railing. The rising moon was only half-full, but the pale square of the note pinned to the balcony table was immediately apparent. He didn't have to glance inside to know the room was empty. He could sense it from where he stood.

Striding over to the table, he snatched up the note.

Go back. I can't see you tonight.

Wrongness curled around him like the smoke from a burning building.

Sidonie didn't write that Isabeau had asked for her hour of music late in the day. She didn't ask him to wait for her. Instead, she told him to leave. Why hadn't she asked him to wait?

The balcony doors were closed and locked. Looking in the room, he saw the sheets had been stripped from the bed, and a cleaning bucket sat on the floor by the door.

She had washed the room clean of his scent. She hadn't asked for him to wait, because she wasn't expecting to come back.

Placing the flat of his hand against the balcony door, he tilted his head as if to listen to whatever may have happened inside that would have made her leave.

It wasn't something Morgan had done. He would swear to it. If he had done something, Sidonie would think through the issue, then talk to him about it, carefully hitting all the important points. Besides, when he had left her early that morning, she had been sleepy, relaxed, and affectionate.

No, something had happened during the day, yet she'd had enough freedom to clean the room and leave the note. She'd felt secure enough to write the note, and confident enough that he would find it, but she still hadn't offered any explanation. Why?

Because she didn't want him to know what she was going to do.

His hand tightened to a fist as he pressed it against the door.

She didn't want him to know, because what she was doing was dangerous. She would have told him virtually anything else. She would have told him if it was something they could do together.

She would have told him if it was something Morgan could have fixed, but there were two things constraining him—the geas and his dwindling supply of hunter's spray.

And anything related to those two constraints led back to the castle.

He didn't have to waste time tracking her. He didn't know why, but he knew where she'd gone.

If he followed her, he would be using the last of his hunter's spray to avoid detection. She could have warned him to go home for that reason alone. But as he glanced back into the room, at how carefully she had left everything, the sense of wrongness washed over him again, and he knew that wasn't true. Again, it was something she could have told him.

And going back to his cottage wasn't an option, not even if he lost the last of his freedom that night.

Digging into his supply bag for the spray, he used the rest of the bottle to douse himself thoroughly, then he slipped his lump of beeswax into his pocket. Afterward, he threw the bag high onto the roof, settled his sword scabbard between his shoulders, cast a cloaking spell, and climbed down to the street.

Setting off for the castle at a sprint, he thought through possibilities.

Where would she be? Not the servants' quarters. If Isabeau had simply ordered her to return to the castle, Sidonie would have told him that too.

He would start with the music hall and work his way through the castle from there.

Layering a spell of aversion over the cloaking, he slipped like a shadow past the guard at the gate and through the castle halls. A feeling of urgency drove him forward. Even though he had brought the beeswax, he didn't use it.

Instead, he listened keenly to everything around him. The snatches of conversation he caught from courtiers as they passed by seemed untroubled. Warrick and Johan lingered near the great hall, flirting with two of the court ladies. Their demeanor was relaxed as well. Whatever had compelled Sidonie to act the way she had, it was a private matter.

As he drew near the double doors of the music hall,

he heard a loud thump from inside the room. Springing at the door, he found it locked. A quick spell unlocked it. As he slipped inside, he saw Valentin backhand Sidonie.

She reeled from the blow, but instead of crumpling, she used the momentum of the movement to spin around, jump, and land a flying kick to his jaw. It was a spectacular move, full of elegance and speed.

Valentin's head snapped back, and he staggered.

Breathing hard, she hesitated.

It was a rookie mistake, that hesitation. Morgan would have drilled that out of anyone on his training field. As Valentin recovered, he grabbed Sidonie by the throat.

Baring his teeth, he snarled, "It would have gone so much better for you if you had just submitted."

By then, Morgan had already begun his lunge across the room. His focus narrowed down to one thing—the hand Valentin had around Sidonie's pale throat.

He was fast, so much faster than either Valentin or Sidonie, yet he was still too far away when he saw her reach into her sleeve and draw out a knife.

She slashed Valentin across the jugular.

Eyes bulging, he let go of her and grabbed at his own throat with both hands, vainly attempting to stop the bright crimson arterial spray.

Morgan reached Sidonie's side as Valentin sank to his knees. She stared at Valentin, her face ashen. When

Morgan grabbed her by the shoulders, she started wildly and bit back a shriek.

Dropping his cloak and aversion spells, he snapped, "What happened?"

Her gaze clung to the dying man. Her eyes were dilated, and her lips looked bloodless. Droplets of Valentin's blood stood out against her white skin. "He threatened to rape me. He's been at the chambermaids. And I wasn't going to be raped."

"You should have come to me!" he hissed. Fury boiled over. If Valentin wasn't already dying, Morgan would have gutted him.

Her gaze snapped to his face. She hissed back, "You shouldn't be here! I told you to go back to the cottage!"

He barked out an angry laugh. "That was never going to happen, Sidonie!"

"I was trying to save you from getting involved!" she snapped. She was shaking visibly. "You're too close to exposure as it is!"

She was the one who had been threatened, yet she had tried to protect him. The blood pounded in Morgan's temples. He held so much rage in his body, he didn't think his skin could contain it.

Grabbing Valentin's head, he gave it a sharp, vicious twist, breaking his neck. Then he let the body fall. As Sidonie stared at him, he said, "I killed him, not you. Remember that. Now, give me your knife and get out of here."

She stammered, "I-I have his blood on me. Morgan—whatever you're trying to do, it's not going to work."

Then a new voice entered the tableau.

From behind Morgan, Warrick said, "What the fuck, Morgan. You and the musician know each other?"

Morgan grabbed the knife out of Sidonie's hand and cast a death spell on it.

As he whirled, Warrick added, "The Queen wants to see you right away. Now that you've killed Valentin, that should be a hell of a reunion."

Morgan had already flung the knife, but it was too late.

Even as the blade buried itself in Warrick's throat, the geas flared to life and he was caught.

Chapter Twenty-One

WHEN MORGAN WENT to Isabeau, she wouldn't see him at first.

Instead, she ordered him to wait in the great hall. He stood in stony silence, arms crossed, and watched as the castle guard ignited the witchlights and brought in first Valentin's body, then Warrick's.

The last to arrive was Modred, who escorted Sidonie. He held her with one hand gripping her biceps. Locked in the privacy of his mind, Morgan watched the two. He wanted nothing more in the entire world than the chance to gut Modred and cut off the hand that touched her.

Modred looked ironic, as he so often did when events turned unpredictable. Sidonie's expression was set, jaw tight. Where Valentin had struck her, the side of her face had begun to turn purple with bruises.

When Modred paused on the other side of the bodies, Sidonie looked at his hand on her arm, then up at him. In a tone both weary and scathing at once, she asked, "Where do you think I could possibly go?"

Modred's jaw flexed. With a curt tilt of his jaw, he

acknowledged her point and lifted his hand away.

Then Isabeau stalked into the hall. She wore a black dress without any other adornment other than the knife on the gold chain at her waist. She had pulled her hair back into a plain knot, and her face was lined with grief. It looked so real, so poignant.

Her gaze fell onto the bodies and flared with fresh emotion. Flying to Morgan, she slapped him as she shrieked, "What did you do?!"

Out of the corner of his eye, he watched Sidonie shift suddenly, but he couldn't look at her. Instead, he kept his expression stony as he answered, "I found Valentin attacking this woman, and I killed him. Warrick must have interrupted the scene."

"He wouldn't have done that!" she cried hoarsely. "He loved me!"

"You know I told just you the truth," Morgan said, his voice hard. "You can hear it in my words. He attacked her. I killed him. End of story. You don't tolerate rape in your kingdom."

She whirled to face Sidonie. *"You!"* Her voice was filled with loathing. "You did something to provoke him, didn't you? How could he possibly have wanted *you?!"*

Eyes widening in outrage, Sidonie exclaimed, "What could I have done to encourage that kind of crime? *He wanted to rape me.* He talked about it. He really liked the idea, and he looked forward to doing it."

Modred spoke up unexpectedly. "Remember, Izzy.

I did try to warn you, but you wouldn't listen. He has hurt other women in the castle. All you have to do is ask Myrrah and the chambermaids."

Pressing both clenched fists to her forehead, Isabeau screamed wordlessly.

Modred went to her and clasped her by the shoulders. When she looked up at him, he said gently, "Hard as it is for you to accept, my love, Valentin's crimes and death are the least interesting thing about all this."

That was when Morgan knew they weren't going to get away with it. Isabeau was overwrought, and when she got in that state she grew sloppy and overlooked details. But Modred never did. Modred was always thinking things through.

Wiping her face with both hands, Isabeau asked, "What are you talking about?"

"Ask him." Modred nodded to Morgan. "Ask him why he showed up just in time to kill Valentin, after having been gone all these weeks. Ask him where he has been, and what he has been doing. Ask him to describe exactly how Warrick died, and why. Ask him to show you his wound, if that was really what kept him away for so long, and if he still has it, ask him why he hasn't healed. And then order him to tell you the complete truth with no innuendoes, misdirection, ambiguity, or statements of supposition."

Morgan couldn't keep from glancing at Sidonie. Horror hollowed out her eyes. She opened her mouth. The gods only knew what she meant to say.

He forestalled her by saying in a harsh voice, "I killed Valentin. There is no ambiguity to that."

"I hear you speak the truth, no question, and yet there is ambiguity laid out on the floor in front of us." Modred knelt by the body and tilted his head back and forth. "His neck is broken," he said matter-of-factly. "Oh, but look—his jugular has also been cut. How doubly unfortunate for him, and how unusually inefficient of you, Morgan. Your killings tend to be much more straightforward."

Isabeau angled out her jaw as she turned in a circle, looking at each piece of the scene.

"What is going on here?" she hissed. Her eyes were sharper, more clearly focused. Modred had brought her back on point.

Striding over to Morgan, she tore open his shirt and yanked off his bandages. The site of the wound, with the dark thick scab turning to scar and the black lines radiating outward, made her pause.

Behind her, Sidonie's eyes widened with horrified compassion. He had never let her see what lay underneath the bandages.

And all the while Modred took everything in with a sharp gaze that missed nothing. His attention snagged on Sidonie's expression and lingered.

Every muscle in Morgan's body tightened, straining with the need to kill Modred, to switch off that bright, unrelenting mind forever. His Power built while the geas held him locked in place. His body heated, and sweat trickled down his spine.

"Start asking him, Izzy," Modred urged, rubbing the edge of his mouth as his gaze remained on Sidonie. "Let's see what he has to say. Be sure to make him tell the complete truth. I feel certain the tale must be fascinating."

"Do as he said," Isabeau snapped at Morgan. "Tell me what you've done since I last ordered you away. Don't lie. Don't prevaricate, and don't try to misdirect me. Tell me everything."

Everything.

Everything would reveal how he had healed Sidonie when she had been held in prison, and how Sidonie had worked with him and Robin to break him free of the geas so they could escape.

If he told Isabeau everything, Isabeau would kill her. Morgan's life held some value for Isabeau, but as much as she liked Sidonie's music, Sidonie wasn't indispensable.

Finally he came to the end of a very long and lonely road. There was no further turn to take, and no way to go back.

The tale that told everything came down to just one thing.

I fell in love, he thought, and smiled. It was a miracle, and despite everything he had been through, he felt blessed with having been given such a fortune.

As he remained silent, Isabeau's face distorted with rage. Flying at him, she hit him over and over. "Tell me! Tell me what you've done!"

He grew hotter, his Power grinding against the geas, and blood thundered in his ears.

Gritting his teeth, he said, "No."

"You have to!" she shouted, hitting and slapping his face, his chest. "You have to tell me!"

He barely felt the blows. The pressure built in his chest. It felt like a heart attack, radiating out his left arm, while the geas pounded in his brain. As it forced his mouth open, his Power rose to meet it, and he stopped the flood of words from flowing.

"No," he gasped.

Dimly he was aware of Sidonie shouting. At some point Modred had grabbed her again, and she struggled against his hold. "Stop it—you're killing him!"

He had fought before against the geas, many times, and lost. This time he couldn't afford to lose. The geas tried to wrench the words out, and he clenched down harder. Desperately, as he reached for anything he could pull strength from, he connected to the earth magic.

Digging deep, he drew hard on it. Something shifted down below, and with a great, yawning noise the floor in the great hall cracked.

"You have to do what I say. I command you." Isabeau's face had purpled, and blood vessels burst in the corners of her eyes from the force of her scream. *Otherwise what has been the point of this whole bloody nightmare! I'll make you tell me!"*

He was blinded to almost everything from the forces tearing him apart, except for Isabeau.

With a wrenching cry, she dragged Azrael's Athame from the scabbard and then fell to her knees, as if she had tried to lift an unimaginable weight. Hunching over, she dragged herself to her feet.

Tears spilled over. He couldn't breathe. His chest was being crushed from within.

Still he managed to whisper, "No."

His final act would be one of his own free will.

"Then what use are you anymore?" she cried.

Baring her teeth from the effort, Isabeau thrust the knife into his heart.

✧   ✧   ✧

THE BLACK BLADE hit home.

There was no mistaking it for anything but a mortal blow. Morgan's expression changed; it was obvious he knew it too. Isabeau froze, staring at what she'd done.

Sidonie heard herself scream as if from a long distance away. She felt like her heart was being cut out of her chest.

Then Morgan's face sharped with such ferocity, he no longer looked human. Grasping Isabeau's hands as she gripped the hilt, he bared his teeth and roared at her. Light shone out from the entry wound in his chest, and a blast of boiling heat blew out across the room. Struggling against his grip, Isabeau shrieked in agony.

Gradually the light and heat faded. As they

dimmed, all expression faded from Morgan's features, until he almost looked peaceful. He fell in a sprawl.

Still howling, Isabeau stumbled back, holding up her shaking hands. They were withered and blackened like claws.

Modred abandoned his grip on Sidonie and raced to the Queen. Scooping her into his arms, he ran from the hall.

Sid barely noticed. All her attention was on Morgan.

He lay so still. She knew he was dead.

Despite that, she ran to him, fell to her knees, and clawed at the knife protruding from his chest. It was wrong, *so wrong*, and she had to get it out of his body. Someone was sobbing. Wait, that was still her.

As she pulled out the knife, everything around her shifted and darkened. It was the heaviest thing she had ever held, both icy and burning at once.

The hall darkened further, and she looked up.

She still knelt over Morgan's body, but they were no longer in the great hall of the castle in Avalon.

They were in another hall altogether. It seemed to go on forever. The floor was made of black and white marble, and there were rows of black marble pillars. Between the pillars, tall black marble stands held huge vases of onyx filled with bloodred roses.

Sidonie's breath scraped in her raw throat. It was the only sound she heard. Utter silence filled the hall. There wasn't even the sound of a breeze.

Then she heard quiet, measured footsteps approaching.

A tall, straight figure walked into view. He wore plain, elegant clothes, and his eyes were green like summer leaves.

His face. She saw his face.

His face was the answer to a question she didn't know how to ask.

He knelt beside her and held out one hand. She didn't even think of trying to keep the blade as her own and offered it to him immediately. When he took it from her, the relief was immense.

"I will have to make a new scabbard for it," Lord Death said as he turned the knife over in his hands. His voice was as gentle as before.

Sidonie sank her fists into the edges of Morgan's shirt, tears spilling over. She had never known such pain. It was tearing her apart.

She whispered, "Give him back."

Azrael raised an eyebrow. "But this is the answer to your prayer. Morgan is now free from bondage. The first blow the Queen struck was irreversible—death was the only way to release him."

"I don't care." The words scraped in her throat. "You're a god. You can find a way. Give him back to me. Please, I'm begging you."

Azrael's expression turned indifferent. He stood and, from his tall height above her, said, "I've heard begging before, countless times. The echoes go back through history. Some beg for death, others beg for more life."

The tears wouldn't stop falling. Wiping at them, she stood. "Then take me. He was a slave for so long. Let him live in peace for a while and take me."

"I have heard bargaining too, and I will have you soon enough." Death turned to walk away.

She was losing him. Desperation drove her to speak faster. "You'll have my death," she called after him. "I'm offering you my life."

Azrael paused for an infinitesimal moment, head turned to one side, the line of his jaw sharp as a scythe.

In that infinitesimal moment, her mind raced at supersonic speed as she desperately scrambled to think of something else to offer him, something that would make him stay.

But she didn't really have anything. She was no-body of importance, and she had no Power of her own. Her connections were all mortal.

All she'd had ever had was her music.

"I'll play for you," she said. Stepping over Morgan's body, she walked toward Death. "Let me play for you. Please. You have your knife back because of me. Give me this one thing: if I am able to move you in any way with my music, you will give him back to me. If my music doesn't touch you, then you've lost nothing but a few moments of time. And what is a few moments of time to a god?"

Azrael still stood with his back to her, head tilted as

he listened. His lean cheek creased as he smiled.

"Very well, musician," he said. Turning, he flung ravens at her. At a midway point in their flight, they turned into a violin and bow, tumbling end over end. Heart leaping, she tried to catch them, and they flew into her hands. "Play for me. Show me what you are made of."

Shaking, she clasped the instrument to her. What could she play that could move the god of Death? She had fought with everything she had just for the chance to play, but now that it was presented to her, she felt hollow, small, and inadequate.

Mortal. She felt mortal.

Closing her eyes, she fit the violin under her chin, and set the bow to the strings. Faith had never been as blind as this.

The first thing that came to mind was the sound of her fingers breaking. Her life, as she knew it, dying. The shock and the pain of it, and the utter devastation.

They've killed me, she thought.

So she played it.

Next came the memory of warm, strong hands reaching for hers in the darkness. The unknown clasping her fingers, healing her, lending her strength and reassurance. It was the only thing in the world when she had nothing. It had been her lifeline.

And she played it.

Then came trust, the tentative unfurling, when she believed against all evidence that the person who came to her in the darkness would help her in any way he could. The impossibly intense adventure of his arm, sliding around her shoulders. The miracle of warmth when she had known nothing but coldness.

That first kiss, oh, the surprise of it! The agonizing uncertainty... was it all right to allow this? How could it feel so incredibly good?

Could she possibly kiss him again?

Oh, when could she kiss him again?

The burning that took hold, the incandescent light that shone despite all the shadows stacked around them. The unbearable, delicious hunger that was the sweetest pain... that she would give anything, anything, if only she could feel it again...

Always before, when she had played, she'd had the awareness of the violin and the bow as instruments in her craft. Her music had been self-conscious, aware.

Now, as she played, she went somewhere she had never gone before. She lost awareness of the violin altogether.

She became the music.

She was the story, the vibration.

She became the story of love, the notes written in kisses and caresses on her skin. She felt the symphony, the swelling highs in the lifts, and the terrible lows in the falls, and hope was the cruelest note of all, the devastation that came afterward, utterly intolerable.

She poured it all out, all the emotion, the experience, the exquisite delight along with the terror. There was no hiding any of it from a god anyway. The only other being she had been so naked with was Morgan, and he was gone.

Gone, while the love she felt for him had become the very breath of life to her.

Give him back to me, she begged with her music.

Give him back.

When the last note speared through the air, she had nothing left to give. Lowering the violin, she stared pleadingly at the back of the one who held her future in his hands, whatever that future might be.

When he turned, there were tears on his cheeks.

Death whispered, "I knew a love like that, once."

Her lips formed the words she no longer had the energy to say. Give him back.

Azrael strode to her, and she braced herself to bear the onslaught of his proximity.

Tilting her chin up with long fingers, he said, "You have moved me, musician. You've won your wager. But as I told you, the first blow Morgan took with my blade was irreversible, and Isabeau cast a spell with that blow that cannot be undone. Only death releases him from the geas."

Despair crushed down, bending her spine.

Before she could crumple, he added, "The only way I can give him more time on this Earth is if someone else holds the handle of his chain, so you must claim it. But you must give me your life in return. Your life, not your death, which I already own. That is the only bargain I am willing to make. Do you have the courage to take it?"

She swayed as she tried to absorb the enormity of what Death offered. Morgan would never be free of the geas. If there was one thing she could do that he would never be able to accept, it was this.

She whispered, "He'll never forgive me."

"You did not ask for forgiveness," Azrael said. "He'll have life, which is what you begged for."

"Dealing with you is going to be the death of me," she breathed.

His answering smile was a blade. "Of course."

Two tears slipped out of the corners of her eyes. "What do you want me to do for you?"

"You will control Morgan's geas, but he will remain as leader of my pack," Azrael told her. His green gaze gleamed with fierce light. "At the end of each year he and the other Hounds will join me on my Hunt. I always claim what is mine. Together we will chase down any souls who have sought to cheat Death. At this year's end, we will have plenty of prey, as it has been quite some time since I've sounded the Hunt. As for the rest of the year, he may live it as he chooses. And as for you... you will be Death's musician. Your music will be mine. Whenever you find yourself alone, and you remember what has happened, play for me. And wherever you are, I will hear you."

"Yes," she said. "I'll do it."

His smile widened. "A sacrifice made of your free

will, with the gift of life made in return. My brother god will be pleased. Now I will offer one more gift, if you have the will to take it. You may become one of my Hounds, if you wish. The Hounds born of my blade are subject to no other leader. The sorcerer will command his pack, but you would be sovereign in your own right and may walk your own solitary path, wherever the muse may lead you. It will give you longer to wander this Earth you care so much about, and you will be faster, stronger, and immune to human disease. Perhaps most importantly, you will no longer be Powerless in a Powerful world. But be very sure of your answer, Sidonie Martel. Remember, the first blow from my blade is irreversible."

"I'm sure. I'll take it."

She closed her eyes, so she wouldn't have to see the strike coming.

A thin, sharp pain pierced her heart. The pain grew into a gigantic wave of agony that reformed her flesh and bones. She would have screamed if she could, but she had no breath. After an eternity, it began to fade, until at last she could see and think again.

Panting, she looked around. She was no longer in the black and white hall. Instead, she was back in the great hall, on her hands and knees.

Morgan lay nearby. He still looked peaceful, but that would change soon enough. The shreds of his shirt lay to either side of his torso. There was a silver scar where Isabeau had stabbed him, and another one where his other wound had healed completely.

All the smells and sounds were a cacophony in her head. In the distance, she heard shouts and people engaged in urgent movement. From the snatches of what she heard, she gathered the foundation of the castle had cracked, and the Queen had suffered a terrible injury. The court was evacuating to the summer palace, wherever that was.

Reeling from the deluge of information, she clapped her hands over her ears. Becoming a lycanthrope would take some getting used to.

On the cracked floor beside her lay an open violin case. The ebony violin she had played for Death rested inside, along with the bow. The golden strings gleamed in the torchlight. Of all the instruments that were famous works of art, this one was the most exquisite she had ever seen.

And of all the instruments in the world, there would never be a more expensive one she could acquire. She had paid for it with an endless lifetime of service.

Carefully, as she closed the lid and latched it, she thought, I was broken, and broken again, until I became someone else.

Chapter Twenty-Two

MORGAN STIRRED.

Instantly abandoning the violin, she leaped to his side. The boundless power in her muscles flowed effortlessly. That would take some getting used to as well.

Leaning over him, she stroked the hair back from his face, watching ravenously for every small shift in movement, every telltale sign of life.

His dark lashes lifted, and his eyes were cloudy with confusion. The Power his body contained… it almost made her reel. He carried a massive inferno of magic, and she had never been able to sense it before now. She had known he was skilled, but she had never suspected anything like this.

Frowning as his gaze fixed on her, he reached for the area of his chest where Isabeau had stabbed him.

"Yes," she whispered, laying her hand to his cheek. "It happened."

"I don't understand." His voice was gravelly, as if he had just awakened from a deep sleep. "I… died."

"Yes," she said again.

Leaning down, she nuzzled him. The last of the hunter's spray had worn off, and his warm, masculine scent was intoxicating. This moment they shared was so fleeting. She concentrated on soaking up everything so she could remember.

When she pressed her lips to his, he kissed her, touching lightly at the skin beside her mouth, just as he always did when he awakened first thing in the morning.

Then he drew back sharply, nostrils flaring. As he stared at her in incredulity, she sat back on her heels. Letting him go felt like another kind of death.

"What happened?" he demanded, springing up to crouch before her. "You're a lycanthrope!"

This time she didn't bother to repeat an affirmative. The evidence of what she had become was clearly before him.

Whirling, he stared around the empty great hall. The two bodies sprawled on the cracked and ruined floor were their only witnesses. His breathing roughened. "I could have sworn I hurt Isabeau too badly for her to strike at you too."

"You did," she told him. Standing, she walked over to the violin case and slung it over her shoulder. "You also broke the castle's foundation. The court is evacuating. Isabeau didn't do this to me. Azrael did."

At that, he spun to face her. "You spoke to... you *saw* Lord Azrael?"

"First I prayed to him. I told him we wanted to

help him get his knife back, and I asked him to free you." This was too hard to say face-to-face, when he was staring at her like that. Turning, she walked away at random, traversing the great hall aimlessly. "Then I heard him speaking to me, and... everything happened the way it happened. But Isabeau had cast the geas on you using Azrael's knife, and the first blow from his blade is irreversible, so the only way to free you from the geas was through death. I didn't know that when I asked for your freedom. By the time I learned, it was too late. You were already dead."

"You're saying I'm still under the geas." A hollowness entered his voice, along with an edge of urgency. He followed her in pursuit across the hall. "And Isabeau didn't die."

"As far as I know, she didn't." She couldn't run from what she had to say any longer. Turning, she dug the heels of both hands into her eyes as she said from the back of her throat, "I was so selfish. I've never done anything so selfish in my life. But you were dead, and I couldn't bear it. So I begged and pleaded, and I offered Azrael a wager. I asked him to let me play for him, and he did. And then he gave you back."

"He gave me back to a life of slavery?" Morgan snarled. Hard hands clamped on her shoulders. "You should have left me dead!"

Dropping her hands from her eyes, she exclaimed, "I know!"

He whispered, "This nightmare will never end. I'll

never be free of Isabeau. How could you do such a thing?"

"You're no longer under a geas to obey Isabeau." She had to force the words out. It was more difficult than anything she had ever said. Bearing the burden of what she had done was heavier than carrying Azrael's knife. "Azrael gave control of the geas to me."

Horror and betrayal etched his features. He stared at her as if he had never seen her before. "You're saying I'm *your* slave now?"

Her face was wet. She whispered, "It was the only way I could get you back."

"You don't have me back!" he roared. "You took something that wasn't supposed to be yours!"

The words echoed off the walls of the hall like bullets, each one striking at her where she was most vulnerable, underneath her skin.

He pivoted on his heel and stalked away.

She called after him, "Stop!"

Watching his powerful figure freeze broke what was left of her heart.

Walking to him, she came around to face him. Now the betrayal in his expression had turned to loathing.

Just as she had known it would.

She forced herself to concentrate on what she needed to do. Specifics matter. How you phrase things, what elements you choose to put in a spell or a bargain, or what you choose to leave out.

"Listen to me," she said. "This is the last time you

will ever have to see me." Well, except for the Wild Hunt, but that was another issue entirely. "This is *very last time* you will ever have to hear me speak. Every order Isabeau ever gave you means nothing now. I order you to live a completely free and autonomous life. I order you to obey no one else's commands, unless you wish it. I order you to go find joy wherever you may, with whomever you may—to find love, if you like, with someone clever, kind, and educated while you sightsee all the beauty in the world. I order you to follow your heart and your best impulses. I order you to rediscover what it is like to live a life of your own choosing. I order the geas to rest forever and never compel you to do anything again. These words I speak are paramount. Nothing I can possibly say at any point for the rest of my life will ever override the orders I give you right now. Anything else that may fall out of my mouth will be simple conversation, and will signify nothing."

A muscle bunched in his jaw. He said through gritted teeth, "Are you finished?"

Wiping her face, she thought through what she had just said. It was as good as she could make it. "Yes."

Stepping around her, he strode to one of the doorways. She turned to watch him go. As he neared it, he began to run. Clearly, he couldn't get away fast enough.

Well, neither could she.

She left the great hall. Everything was in chaos. Servants were carting out treasures and artwork as fast as they could work. Kallah was nowhere to be seen. Presumably she was helping tend to Isabeau. Thankfully, Sid didn't see Modred either, or anyone she wanted to say good-bye to. No one paused to talk to her. She was, after all, nobody of any importance to them.

Leaving the castle, she walked the crowded road that led out of town. Then she climbed the long, rolling hills to reach the vantage point where the caravan had once stopped and she had gotten her first glimpse of the castle.

Turning, she looked back one last time. How picturesque and romantic it all looked in the moonlight. As she looked over the scene, one of the main turrets tilted and collapsed with a rolling noise like thunder.

Sighing, she turned away. It was time to try out her new form. For the first time, she reached for the shapeshift, and when she had changed, she found the strap on the violin case fit perfectly around her neck. Azrael had planned well.

She began to run down the road. From various things she had overheard, several crossover passageways ran between Avalon and Earth, but she only knew of one. And this time she knew how to sense it.

She ran through the night and into the morning, reveling in the tirelessness of her lycanthrope body. When she came to the edge of the river where the caravan had once camped, she paused to take a long drink from the cool running water.

There, for the first time, she saw the reflection of

what she had become, the monstrous visage, the wicked long teeth, and the powerful, hunched shoulders. It shocked her into changing back into her human form. Wrapping her arms around herself, she sobbed for everything she had lost.

Her humanity.

Morgan.

When she had finished, she wiped off her face and drank more water. Then she pulled out of her pocket the small handkerchief-tied bundle that contained the diminished contents from her performance hat.

Opening it, she fingered through the last of the coins and jewelry. Picking out the small, perfect diamond she had forgotten to give back to Morgan, she threw the rest into the river. She wrapped the diamond in the handkerchief, tucked it into the violin case, changed back into the lycanthrope and started to run again.

She could sense the magic of the crossover passageway as she drew closer, and she was confident none of the guards stationed there would know what had happened. There hadn't been time for anyone back at the castle to send word. As she loped into the clearing, where she had once been held overnight, a guard strolled unhurriedly out of a nearby building.

As he walked to stand in front of the entrance to the passageway, she picked up speed. Drawing closer, she bared her teeth and growled telepathically, *Get out of my way.*

Fear flashed across his face. He hesitated only for a moment, but she was a Hound. For all he knew, she was acting on the Queen's orders. He stepped aside quickly.

She bounded into the passageway and loped along the magical path. The forest around her changed, and then she burst out the other side, into England. The guards on the other end were as clueless as the first. They watched her race through the encampment and did nothing to try to stop her.

She didn't pause from her breakneck speed until she had put a few miles between her and the passageway. Then she slowed to a stop and changed back into her human form. She might be free from Avalon at last, but she also had no idea where she was.

In any case, there was no need for further strain. Walking along the shadowed forest until she cooled down, she reached for one of the Djinn she had bargained with, calling out telepathically, *Jamael?*

Enough time passed that she began to wonder if calling him would work. As far as the Djinn knew, she had no telepathy, and Jamael would not know what her telepathic voice sounded like.

Then a swirling tornado of energy appeared. It coalesced into the form of a tall, elegantly spare male, with nut-brown skin and darker chestnut hair flecked with gray at the temples. Jamael was a first-generation Djinn, and the Power in his shining, diamond-like eyes rocked her back a step.

His usual smile of greeting was missing. Gazing at her gravely, Jamael said, "You have been sorely missed, Sidonie. I see you have also undergone a great change."

She tightened her jaw. She had done her crying back on the riverbank. "I have. How long have I been missing?"

"Two months," he told her gently.

She flinched at the news. Morgan had said the time slippage wasn't much, and from his perspective, she supposed he was right, but two months was still a shock. Rubbing at dry, tired eyes, she muttered, "It could have been worse."

Jamael replied, "Yet clearly, whatever happened, it still could have been so much better."

His compassion touched areas that felt raw from unhealed wounds. Pressing her lips together, she straightened her spine. "I want to call in that favor you owe me."

"I'm honored to be of service." He bowed. "What can I do for you?"

As much as she had longed to go home to New York, she wasn't ready to. She needed a halfway house, somewhere she could come to terms with everything that had happened.

"I need somewhere to go," she said. "Somewhere wild and windswept, with a lot of room to run. Somewhere I can just be for a while, where I can recover from—" She cut that sentence off without finishing it. "And I need a cell phone, so I can call my people. Also,

I-I don't have any money with me. Jamael, I don't know how to condense what I need into one favor. Should I call on the other Djinn who owe me favors too?"

At that, he strode to her with hands outstretched. "My dear Sidonie, be at ease. Do not concern yourself with counting favors and managing obligations. You may use my favor to acquire everything you need. I will gladly help out of pleasure in knowing you are still alive and we have not lost your beautiful music."

The Djinn were not usually known for such generosity. After everything, the relief in hearing his offer was staggering. Taking hold of his hands, she let Jamael sweep her away.

WHEN MORGAN LEFT Sidonie in the great hall, the sense of betrayal burned like acid in his belly. The orders she gave him might have been well-intentioned, but they meant nothing—she only had to change her mind and rescind those original orders, and she would have him back on a leash again.

But at least he was free from Isabeau and her orders. That one thing impelled him forward.

Servants and guards raced through the castle, pulling priceless tapestries from the walls and carrying out furniture. Morgan caught sight of Harrow and strode to catch him by the shoulder.

The other Hound turned swiftly. "Morgan! I heard

you were dead!"

"I'm not," he said. "And the Hounds no longer work for the Queen. Find Johan, gather the others together, and go to Earth. I want you to wait for me at our encampment outside Shrewsbury. I have some business to take care of, then I'll join you."

His expression filling with curiosity, Harrow said, "Yes, sir."

Harrow was one of the decent Hounds. He had once been an officer in the British army, and Morgan had always felt bad for forcing the transformation on him.

Morgan added telepathically, *Don't say a word to the others, but when I get there, we're going to cull the ranks. Isabeau no longer controls what we do, and we're going to live the way we're meant to. The way we want.*

Harrow's eyes shone with sudden wetness. *Do you mean I might be able to go home to my family?*

Morgan tightened his fingers on Harrow's shoulder. *I mean exactly that, but we need to clean up our mess first. I'm not going to loose Hounds on the world who'll be a danger to others. I hope you'll help me.*

Gladly, sir!

He watched Harrow race off. Then, cloaking himself to avoid unwanted attention, he went to the stables, which were half-evacuated already. His gelding had not yet been taken. The horse was restless and uneasy in his stall, but he came readily enough to Morgan's familiar voice and touch.

Saddling him, Morgan rode to his cottage to collect his velvet bag of weapon spells. Nothing in the supply bag he had left on the roof of the inn mattered anymore, but the spelled jewels were too deadly to leave behind. Besides, they would come in handy.

Then he left both castle and town behind.

Riding through the rest of the night, he didn't stop until midmorning, when he reached a valley thick with long grasses and overgrown with wildflowers. As the wind blew from the west, it caused the grass to ripple like waves on a sea.

Hobbling the gelding so it could rest and graze, he walked through the valley for the first time in centuries.

There were the ruins of a great castle that had once sat facing the morning sun. There had once been a large, thriving metropolis too, but now the only things left were the foundations of stone walls covered in moss and lichen and whispers of long-ago enchantments.

He spent the afternoon in the ruins, listening to the ghosts of magic while the lonely wind played with his hair. Some of the spells had been his. He remembered the banners and pageantry of a prosperous long-ago kingdom that had been built on principles of rule of law, justice, chivalry, bravery in battle, generosity in victory, and courtesy to women. It had been a good, fine dream, and he'd been proud to be a part of it.

He had not been there for its ending, although he should have been. He should have died along with the others, fighting for their kingdom and their homes, but he had been held captive somewhere else and forbidden to return.

Only when the sun began to drop toward the horizon did Morgan rouse himself to leave. Collecting his gelding, he rode to his next destination, the placid, silvery bowl of a shining lake surrounded by a peaceful forest. Dismounting, he walked to the edge of the shore and knelt on one knee. The most ancient Powers of the world were due such courtesies.

The surface of the lake remained untroubled and serene, but the air around him acquired a listening attitude.

He had come as a supplicant, so he bowed his head. He said, "I would seek justice in his name. Will you let me borrow it for a short while, my lady? For his sake?"

Silence greeted his request for so long, he almost gave up and left. Then, as the gloaming twilight stole over the scene, a graceful, powerful woman's arm rose out of the darkening water.

In her hand, she held a long sword sheathed in a scabbard worked with jewels and incantations.

Morgan's heart rose to his throat. He stood as the woman's arm flexed and threw the sword. It sailed end over end to him.

Plucking it out of the air, he bowed to the Lady of the Lake, and promised, "Thank you, my lady. I will return it very soon."

The arm sank down below the water's surface, and after the ripples died down, the surface was smooth and as placid as before.

Morgan watched and waited until the last of the ripples had died down, paying due tribute to the Lady of the Lake. When he turned away, his purpose settled like a dark mantle across his shoulders. Fastening the belt of the scabbard around his waist, he mounted his horse.

Revenge and justice.

It had taken far too long, but now he would have them both.

THE SUMMER PALACE of the Light Fae Queen was a lighter, more elegant affair than her castle, a place meant for dalliances, art and music festivals held along the seashore, and evening regattas with golden witch-lights on sailboats shining on midnight blue water.

The city surrounding the palace was larger than the town by the castle. Morgan left the gelding in a safe location, in a nearby clearing by a stream. Then he strode to the city gates.

They were closed and barred. Frightened faces looked out of the peepholes on either side. The captain of the watch called out to him. "We heard rumors you may have survived the calamity that befell the castle, my lord."

Calamity was as good a word as any, he supposed.

He pointed at the gates. "Open them."

"I-I have orders to k-keep them closed at all costs," the captain stammered. "Please forgive me, my lord!"

The captain's name was Bruin, Morgan knew. He had a wife and a child.

Morgan told him softly, "Run. Spread the word. Tell everyone to run while they can. I will not leave a single stone standing in this place. It's more warning than any of you gave my people, and more mercy. Eventually you might rebuild again, but on this day, I will kill anybody who opposes me. Go."

The captain hesitated, then his face disappeared from the peephole, and a moment later, the guards threw both gates wide open, abandoned their post, and ran.

Morgan strode down the main street into the city. Reaching deep for the earth magic, he caused the ground to shake. Terrified people raced past him, clutching babies, children, and random household goods. Buildings began to collapse around him.

When he reached the outside steps of the palace, more guards appeared.

These were higher in seniority than the guards at the gate, and a few were proficient magic users. Looking doomed, they threw spells at him—fiery morningstars and other offensive spells.

But Morgan wore his hate like a carapace, and he had forged it with magic. Their spells sizzled harmlessly against his shield. Conserving his personal energy, he used his array of weaponized jewels in return, throwing them in swift succession.

Spells of blindness hit the palace guard, along with death curses, flesh corrosion, morningstars, charms of confusion, and incantations of havoc that made them fight each other, until they were soon overcome.

Catching sight of a palace captain, Morgan cast a whip of magic around the other man's throat and forced him to his knees. He asked, "Where is she?"

The man's eyes bulged as he clawed uselessly at his own throat. "My lord, I don't know. I swear it."

"Oh, let him go," Modred said from the top of the palace steps. "You were never one to take your anger out on battle fodder, anyway."

Morgan looked up. Modred descended the steps at a leisurely pace. He wore his ensorcelled battle armor that shone bright silver in the sun. He looked heroic, handsome, and he held his drawn sword relaxed at his side.

Morgan's entire focus narrowed. He had waited centuries, hoping he might get the chance for this one moment.

Releasing his hold on the palace captain's throat, he told the man, "I will give you the same chance I gave the others. Go tell the palace servants and guard to run while they can."

Coughing, the captain scrambled to his feet and raced up the stairs past Modred, who never bothered to watch him go.

As Modred reached the bottom of the steps,

Morgan turned to face him. "Where is she?"

"Gone to a hiding place you know nothing about," Modred replied. "She used you like a tool, but she never trusted you. She always knew better than that. She left me behind just in case."

"Foolish of you not to go with her." Morgan began to circle around the other man, leisurely stalking his prey.

"Well, what can you do." Modred looked ironic, while he turned to keep facing Morgan. "When we heard rumors circulating that people had seen you leave the castle alive, neither of us believed it. She was, after all, the one who had stuck the knife in your heart, and I had watched her do it. The Hounds had deserted, but that was no surprise, since you weren't around to keep them in control. So here we are. It's been a long road getting here, hasn't it?"

"You killed my boy." The raw words burned Morgan's mouth. "My good, kind, just king."

"Of course I did, you fool," Modred said. "What else did you expect? For Isabeau to truly solidify her hold on her new kingdom, she had to eradicate the humans who lived here in Avalon. As short-lived as you were, you multiplied like vermin. Besides, he wasn't good enough to vanquish me. I was the better swordsman."

"You're not better than me." Morgan drew the sword from its scabbard.

Modred's gaze fixed on the blade and widened. He

whispered, "Now, that's a sight I had not expected to see again in my life."

"No?" He strode forward. "Come take a closer look. I promise you, it will be the last thing you see."

Modred sprang to meet him, raising his sword to parry Morgan's attack, and the clash of blades rang out over the empty square. The Light Fae noble was fast and lethally efficient.

With every blow Modred struck, and every maneuver, Morgan imagined him using the same tactics in that final battle centuries ago, the flawless footwork, the elegant pivot.

Morgan had watched him closely ever since and had learned it all.

When Modred effortlessly switched the sword from his right hand to the left, Morgan was ready and smoothly adapted to the change. With a quick lunge, Modred sought to drive him back, and he accommodated the attack, deflecting while he retreated.

Two things he had learned—how to hate, and how to wait. He didn't have to rush to completion, or extend himself needlessly.

Instead, he let the other male work, until gradually, the sweat stood out on Modred's forehead and he began to tire, and Morgan could see in the other man's gaze that Modred was beginning to realize he had been playing with him all along.

"Gods damn you." Modred's handsome lips pulled into a snarl. He exploded in a furious attack, raining a rapid series of blows on Morgan's guard. "Don't fucking dance around. *Fight me!*"

Now it was Morgan's turn to give him an ironic smile. "As you wish."

He drove forward, smashing with the force of a sledgehammer at Modred's defense. His attack had nothing to do with technique, elegance, or footwork. It was pure, murderous intent.

At long last, Modred faltered. His back foot slipped, the one bearing his weight, and when he staggered, Morgan found the slip in his guard and slid his sword through it.

While both men wore magical protections, Modred's ensorcelled armor could not withstand a direct blow from the sword Morgan carried.

The tip of Morgan's blade sliced through the metal like it was mere leather. He felt the sword grate against the bone of a rib, and then it went all the way through. Morgan stepped closer, pushing it farther in until the hilt grated against armor, and he stood face-to-face with Modred, looking into his eyes as the crisis in his body began to take over.

"When you struck him down, did you really believe you weren't going to be mine?" Morgan whispered, watching unblinkingly as Modred's gaze began to darken. "Did you relax over the years? Did you think I might have given in or broken? I never did. You killed my boy. I watched you every day. I resent every breath you've taken, begrudge you every meal you've eaten, every smile, every laugh. I wish I could kill you twice."

A ghost of a laugh left Modred's pale lips, along with a gush of crimson blood. He gasped, "Once will be quite sufficient."

Modred's knees buckled, and as he went down, Morgan pulled the sword out, making the rest of it go quicker. When Modred's eyelids closed for the last time, Morgan laid his hand over the dead man's face. It was the only area of his body unprotected by the armor.

Whispering a firespell, he released it quickly and stood over Modred's body until it had burned to ash.

Finally it was done. Breathing evenly and flexing his shoulders back, Morgan sheathed the sword as he dug deeper and reached harder for more Earth magic.

He had never let his Power flow in such an ungoverned flood before. It poured out of him, as relentless as a tidal wave.

He didn't rein it in again until the summer palace had broken apart completely and the very last of the ruins had slid into the foaming, turbulent sea.

Chapter Twenty-Three

JAMAEL TOOK SID to Scarborough in North Yorkshire, of all places.

When she found out the name of the English town, she had to cough out a laugh. Life could sure have a dark sense of humor at times.

With remarkable efficiency, Jamael consulted the local tourist office and found a furnished farmhouse to rent located outside town, an easy walk from the coastline.

With four bedrooms, the house was rather too large for one person, and the massive kitchen hadn't been updated since the 1960s. It also wasn't much to look at. Built of stone and brick, it sat squarely on its patch of land and looked like it had weathered many years and would see many more.

But it had fireplaces in almost every room, and from the end of the long, narrow drive, one could see the ruins of Scarborough Castle sitting high on a rocky promontory, standing sentinel over the sea.

"I'm curious," she asked as Jamael unlocked the door and they walked inside for the first time. "Why did you choose Scarborough of all places?"

"The town lies at the border of the North York Moors National Park," the Djinn told her. "You said you wanted somewhere wild and windswept. The North York Moors is one of the largest wildernesses left in the United Kingdom." He gave her a keen glance that seemed to see everything. "You will have privacy here, and plenty of room to run."

The tension between her shoulder blades began to ease. "That sounds so good."

"I will bring you groceries, a car, and a phone," Jamael said. "Do you need anything else?"

I need Morgan to forgive me.

Suddenly, she was so exhausted it took a conscious effort to remain upright. "No. What you're doing is more than enough."

The Djinn was as good as his word. Within an hour, someone drove a car up to the farmhouse. Sid wasn't familiar with European cars, but she thought it might be a Peugeot. Soon after, a wealth of groceries arrived, everything from prepared meals to pantry staples, fresh foods, and even wine.

God, to simply relax and enjoy a glass of wine. She no longer knew what that felt like.

The Djinn weren't known for their kindness, yet Jamael had proved the exception. When he pressed a smartphone into her hands, she said, "I don't know what to say except thank you. I don't know when I'll hold a concert again, but when I do, you will always be more than welcome."

"Just be well. That will be thanks enough." Jamael smiled. "Can I do anything else for you?"

"No. What you've already done is amazing."

He bowed. "Don't hesitate to call me again, should you think of anything."

"I won't."

She watched as he dissipated in a maelstrom of energy.

When he left, she dragged linens and blankets out of a cupboard and made the bed in the largest bedroom. Then she crawled into it and slept straight for almost thirty hours. After waking, she ate one of the prepared meals, a chicken curry dinner, took a short walk, then slept another fourteen hours.

Except for Jamael, nobody knows where I am, she thought, reveling in the peace and silence in the farmhouse.

She didn't turn on the television or the radio. Instead, over the next few days, she took longer and longer walks. One night she took her new violin with her. When she reached an open place where she could look out over the land meeting the sea, she remembered the black and white hall and her pact with Lord Azrael, and she played all the wild grief in her heart for an audience of one.

On the third day, she thought she might be able to make a phone call but backed away from that almost immediately. Had Robin managed to get her message to any of them?

Sitting at the kitchen table, she stared at the phone. Instead of calling, she punched in Vince's phone number, which was one of the ones she had memorized, and sent him a text.

This is Sid. I'm just outside Scarborough, and I'm okay.

Okay being a relative term, of course.

Almost immediately, her phone rang, and she winced from the strident noise. But everyone on Earth had endured two months of uncertainty, and it wasn't fair to avoid talking to them just because the phone seemed strange, and her emotions felt raw enough already.

So propping her forehead on the heel of one hand, she answered and began to let her old life back in.

"I'm different," she warned Vince. It was easier to talk to him. He could deal with what happened privately and not break down on her like Julie would. "It was bad, I'm not human any longer, and I'm dealing with a lot of emotions. I can't stand it if any of you fuss at me right now. Got it?"

"Got it," he said, keeping his voice quiet. Easy. "It's all going to be okay. Just tell me where you're at. Let me be your guard dog. Nobody will get to you again without going through me first."

At his words, a silent, unamused chuckle shook through her. She almost told him, Vince, I could guard you now.

But she didn't. Instead, she said, "Okay."

She told him where she was staying, and he drove up to the farmhouse within a matter of hours. Vince had set up a temporary office in London from which to direct the search for her, and Robin had, in fact, delivered her message to him.

After they talked, she felt ready to talk to others. Two days later, Julie and Rikki came, along with Vince's wife, Terri, and it turned out the farmhouse wasn't too big after all. They had all been wounded by what had happened, and not just emotionally, although Sid knew they each cared about her.

But Vince had not been home to the States since the car wreck. After recovering from his injuries, he had spent all his time spearheading the search. Sid was the biggest client at Julie's boutique PR firm, and for two months, Rikki, her manager, had been living in limbo. They all needed to take a breath and figure out how to move on.

At first, careful though everybody was, the air felt raw and charged with too much emotion. Sid escaped a lot, changing into her lycanthrope form to run for miles over the vast moorland of the park.

As she said to them, her need to run away wasn't personal. She was dealing with both PTSD and the sensory overload from the lycanthropy virus.

Gradually, they all adjusted. Patience and steadiness were the house rules, until she could finally unbend enough to hug Julie. From there, things got better.

Not terrific. Not even okay. Nothing soothed the

gaping hole in her chest where she mourned how things had ended with Morgan. But still, better.

Within a few days, they had sketched into place a rough game plan for how to proceed. Julie crafted statements for the press on Sid's return and recovery without going into detail about what had actually happened.

There were some legalities that would need to be taken care of. The British authorities wanted information about how the kidnapping occurred, but Vince would field as much of that as he could over the next week as the news broke. Then Sid's contract with his security firm would be terminated until the next concert tour, whenever that might be, and he could finally return home for good.

As for the rest of the current tour, it would be cancelled, not postponed, and the remaining ticketholders' money refunded. Sid didn't know when she would be ready to perform in public again. She needed to get used to the stimulus of being in large crowds before she crossed that bridge, and she didn't know how long that would take.

"It will happen someday," Sid said to Rikki's worried expression. "But definitely not until next year, which is apparently only four and a half months away anyway."

To Rikki's credit, her response was instant and sincere. "You get to be who you are. You get to play when you want, for whom you want, and when you want.

You've been going ninety miles an hour for several years anyway. We'll just throttle back until you're ready to go again. I promise you, none of this is going to be a problem, Sid."

After the third day, her houseguests began to leave. Terri left for the States, and Vince went back to London to finalize things before heading home. Julie was the last to let go.

"I hate to leave you stuck here in the middle of nowhere!" she exclaimed.

Sid smiled. "In the middle of nowhere is exactly where I want to be. I'll be home in a month or so. Maybe two."

Julie sniffed. "If you're going to stay that long, I'm coming back again in a few weeks."

"That would be fine. But just you. Not any of the others."

Julie studied her face. "What are you going to do here all by yourself?"

"I'm going to relish having time off. I'm going to read books I've been meaning to read for years, and watch TV. I might even go sightseeing."

And somehow I need to figure out a way to live without Morgan, because there's no point in trying to go forward with anything else until I can do that.

But she didn't say it. She hadn't told any of them what had happened in Avalon, and after a couple of gentle attempts, they had wisely given up asking, at least for the time being.

Finally Julie left as well, and welcome silence settled back in the farmhouse.

By the end of the second week, Sid was beginning to sleep better. She was no longer succumbing to the long bouts of exhaustion, and her appetite had evened out. She thought she might possibly try a trip into town.

After all, she had coped with a houseful of guests. She didn't have to stay long. Planning her first excursion carefully with the help of the new laptop Julie had brought for her, she decided she would check out a bookstore. She wanted some books to read, and there was a local Waterstones, or she could go to The Book Emporium.

If there were too many people, or she got overwhelmed by sensory input, she could just leave. No big deal, right?

The next day, she headed into town, driving carefully since everything was on the wrong side—the gearshift, the steering wheel, the road. By the time she had pulled into a car park, she was feeling rather proud of herself.

Studying the map on her smartphone, she walked down the street. The bookstore should be two blocks forward, then to her right. It was a sunny, late summer day, and there were lots of people on the sidewalks, many of them looking like tourists, but the scents and the sounds were not too overwhelming, at least not yet.

Then, up ahead, a tall figure rounded the corner at

a leisurely stroll.

It was Morgan.

He wore a long, tailored jacket of expensive-looking black leather, a white dress shirt, and plain, dark gray slacks. The inferno of magic she had sensed in him after she had just become a lycanthrope was gone. Or cloaked. After sensing what burned inside him, she didn't doubt for a moment he could cloak what he was.

His brilliant hazel gaze fixed on her, and he walked toward her. To her starved eyes, he looked more vital, more compelling than ever, his strong, bold features calm, even contemplative. The tanned skin around his eyes carried laugh lines she had barely gotten the chance to enjoy. The stern cut of his mouth was relaxed.

He looked for all the world like a handsome, charismatic man might look on holiday.

Panic ran over her, shrieking like a freight train. Whirling, she sprinted in the opposite direction.

Her hearing was sharp enough now that she could hear him swearing from a block away. As she glanced over her shoulder, she saw him running after her in pursuit.

She pelted down the sidewalk. She couldn't move fast or far enough away from him, and between one stride and the next, she changed into a lycanthrope. Exclamations sounded all around, and someone shouted in alarm.

From one moment to the next, something shimmered and changed. She could *feel* the magic, like she had never felt it before in her life. She was running in some kind of bubble, and while several people pointed back to where she had been, nobody looked directly at where she was.

Had he thrown a cloaking spell around her?

It didn't matter. Tossing out all speculation, she lowered her head and ran for all she was worth.

And he followed.

He followed her out of town, and along the road that led into the North York Moors National Park. He followed her when she plunged into the park and ran across the wild, open space. The magic bubble encasing her dissipated. Glancing back again, she saw that he had changed into his lycanthrope form as well.

She couldn't outrun him. If he chose to, he could keep pace with her forever.

Sidonie, will you stop? he said telepathically. *We need to talk.*

No. No. The panic locked up her mind.

Changing course in a giant circle, she raced back to her farmhouse. Once there, she shapeshifted quickly back into her human form. With shaking hands, she dug into her pocket for the key, let herself in, and slammed and locked the door.

Backing away until her shoulder blades hit the nearby wall, she sank to the floor.

Her lycanthrope senses were such that she knew

the moment when his footsteps sounded outside. Something *thunked* against the door. His hand, perhaps, or even his head.

She also heard him say quietly to himself, "What the hell."

✧ ✧ ✧

AS MORGAN WATCHED the ruins of the summer palace slide into the sea, he wondered, where did one go after an age has ended?

What was one to do with the rest of one's life when one actually had a choice?

At what point did one stop seeking justice and vengeance, and began, instead, to seek out his own life?

Was it enough, now that he had killed Modred? Could he stop looking back, and begin to look forward?

Isabeau's kingdom was in disarray, and he had injured her badly.

She wasn't dead. Yet the thought of going after her seemed unutterably wearying. Her histrionics were so tawdry. She had enemies enough in the world... she and Oberon's Dark Court were still at one another's throats. They could kill each another. He no longer needed to be a part of it.

Besides, the sword he bore wanted to go back to its holder. He could feel the pull from where it was sheathed in its scabbard. Its job was done.

So he let it be enough.

He rode back to the lake and offered the sword to its Lady. As he threw it, and her arm emerged, he whispered, "Thank you."

She caught the sword by the hilt and held it straight. His last sight of it was as she drew it down into the water. When the sword disappeared from view, somehow he knew he would never see it again.

What was past could finally lie in the past. It settled into its grave with one last sigh. He hoped he had brought it a measure of peace. Now, what he had to do was make amends for some of the things he had done. It didn't matter if he had done them while acting under the influence of the geas. Some wrongs needed to be put right.

Riding to the closest crossover passageway, he went to Earth. For the next several days he traveled along the Welsh Marches and removed all the cloaking spells he had placed on crossover passageways, both those leading to Lyonesse and those leading to Avalon. He couldn't do anything to repair the passageways he had ruined, but he could at least open the ones that were still useable.

As he worked to clear the last passageway, a huge black stallion with fiery hooves galloped to up him. The horse reared and changed into Robin, who eyed him warily.

"This is a surprise," Robin remarked.

Morgan raised an eyebrow. "I could say the same of you."

"I took your hunter's spray to your cottage, but of course, you weren't there." The puck eyed him curiously. "I found the castle ruined, and the town all but empty."

"Indeed." Morgan turned back to complete his task.

When he was finished, Robin asked, "I no longer sense the darkness on you. So you are free from Isabeau's control?"

"It would seem so." He rubbed his chest, which ached, but not because of the mortal wound Isabeau had given him. It ached from what had come after.

After a moment, Robin asked, "Where is she? What happened to Sidonie?"

"I don't know," he whispered.

She became something else. She wrapped chains around me, and freed me at the same time, and I grew outraged and left.

I left the best thing that has ever happened to me.

The thought ate at him in the night. Where had she gone? What was she doing? The news of her kidnapping had hit all the major newspapers and television channels. He scoured each story for clues, but there were none, just a professionally prepared news release in which she thanked her fans for respecting her privacy while she recovered from her ordeal.

He and the puck stood awkwardly together, in the middle of the sunlit clearing where the passageway shone clear and bright again.

Then Morgan turned to face Robin. "I am attempting to right a few of the wrongs I committed in Isabeau's name. All the crossover passageways are now clear again. Your king has fallen under a spell of mine. I would be glad to reverse it, if they would let me."

Robin laughed. "They would all, to a knight, die before they let you anywhere near Oberon. But I will pass on your regards and the message."

Morgan nodded, unsurprised. "Modred is dead," he told Robin. "Isabeau is alive and in hiding. I don't know where. I did manage to wound her, and she no longer commands the Hounds. I do. Tell this to the Dark Court as well—I mean them no harm. I never did, and I will take no further action against them as long as they leave me and mine alone. I'm done, puck. Do you hear me? I wash my hands of the war between you and the Light Court."

Robin smiled. "That was everything I had ever hoped for, sorcerer." Then his smile died. "When you find her again, would you please tell her a thing from me?"

Morgan didn't have to ask who Robin meant. He already knew. "What?"

"She offered me forgiveness once, even though, she said, she knew I did not want or need it. Could you please tell her I ask for her forgiveness now, even though she has already given it?" As he watched, Robin changed into the horse again. "After all, what would we have if we didn't have forgiveness?"

Morgan rubbed his eyes. "Good-bye, puck."

"Good-bye, sorcerer." The horse paused. "Despite all that came between us before, I say fare thee well."

Forgiveness.

Forgiveness might be given, even if one has never asked for it.

Raising a hand, Morgan watched the horse gallop away. Soon the puck was lost in the distance.

Morgan still wasn't done. He had a culling to do, and when he reached the Hounds' encampment outside Shrewsbury, it was bitter, ugly work.

By the time he, Harrow, and a few trusted others had finished, he had cut the number of Hounds from nearly eighty down to just thirty-two. When the last of the murderers and the criminals had been killed, he went off by himself and vomited until he had nothing left in his stomach.

Forgiveness was hardest to give to oneself. Even when he knew the geas had compelled him to do things, he still remembered doing them. But nobody could walk that road of forgiveness for him. He would have to find his way by himself.

He disbanded the rest of the Hounds and sent them off to live their individual lives, and then, when he lifted his head from all the wrongs he had worked to set right, he saw nothing ahead of him. Nothing, but what he chose for himself.

I order you to go find joy wherever you may, with whomever you may—to find love, if you like, with someone clever, kind, and educated while you sightsee all the beauty in the world.

Oh, Sidonie, he thought, while the pain in his chest swelled to overflowing. How could you chain me and then just give me up?

He couldn't do it.

He couldn't just walk away, and his inability to do so had nothing to do with the geas and everything to do with what they had shared for such a brief time.

I order you to follow your heart and your best impulses.

So he did. He cast a spell of finding that had brought him across the country, to this private farmhouse by the moors. And when she saw him, what did she do?

She ran away, and kept running.

What the hell?

Had he injured her that badly?

Leaning his forehead against the door, he said, "I know you can hear me. I know just how good your hearing is now. Sidonie, please don't run away anymore. We need to talk. I need to talk to you."

He paused to listen, but nothing happened.

Well, something *happened*, but it didn't seem to have any connection to him. He could hear her footsteps as she walked away. They went up a flight of stairs. She had retreated to the upper story.

Bewilderment mingled with pain. Her inexplicable behavior was unlike anything he had imagined when he'd thought about finding her. He had never felt at such a complete loss before.

He did the only thing he could think to do. He kept talking.

"Even though I want very badly to come in, I would never force open a door you closed on me," he said. "But I need to talk to you, so I'll wait here until you're ready. It's okay if it takes some time. I'll be patient."

A window overhead opened. As he looked up, Sidonie threw a paper airplane out. It sailed downward in loops until it nose-dived into the grass.

Walking over, he picked it up and unfolded it.

Scrawled across the blank page, she had written, *Please leave. I'm afraid to talk to you. I'm scared something I might say will trigger the geas.*

Ah. That.

Understanding illuminated everything.

Folding the paper with care, he tucked it into his pocket, turned, and sat on the porch stoop. Leaning his elbows on his knees, he looked over the acres of green pasture where a flock of sheep grazed.

"I love you," he told Sidonie. "I think I fell in love with you during one of my visits to you in the prison. It was when you snuggled against my side. You said, 'I can't really trust you, can I?' Yet you still put your head on my shoulder. Do you remember?"

Above him, she whispered, "Yes."

The single, tentative word shot hope into him. Lacing his fingers together, he looked down at his hands and thought, Be easy. Don't blow this.

"I thought, how could you possibly do that? How could you reach for me, when I tried to warn you away? But you didn't have many choices down there, did you?"

She sighed. "I had that choice. Nobody compelled me to do it. I understood I wasn't supposed to trust you, but I did anyway."

"You were in an impossible situation," he said. "They should never have done what they did to you."

"They should never have done what they did to you either." Her voice was soft and held so much sadness, he wanted fiercely to put his arms around her, but he couldn't. "*I* shouldn't have done what I did to you. I knew it, and I did it anyway. You were dead, and I-I couldn't—"

Her words cut off abruptly. Hurting for her, he clenched his fists and waited, but she didn't continue.

Bravery, he thought, was facing the impossible and saying, What's next? Which was exactly what she had done.

"When I think of how you confronted Azrael, I'm speechless," he told her. "And when I think of what you managed to win from the god of Death, I'm in awe. Here's the thing, my love. If I had faced what you had faced—if I had seen you killed, I would have done exactly the same thing as you did. I would have done anything I had to do in order to keep you. Anything. I realized I would do that the first time we made love."

"But the one thing he offered was the one thing I

knew you couldn't accept," she whispered. "I took it anyway, because I needed to know you were somewhere in the world, even if you weren't with me."

The pain in those simple, whispered words was so clear, his eyes dampened. What a desperate choice she'd faced.

"I'm here to ask for your forgiveness," he said.

"*You?* What do I have to forgive you for?"

Leaning forward, he put his head in his hands. "When I awakened, and you told me what you'd done, I reacted badly."

There was a small silence. "Well, for God's sake, you had your reasons. You had died." Her voice broke, but she picked up again quickly. "Died and then woken up again to discover you were still under the geas. I'd say you get a pass for reacting badly to that, Morgan."

He chuckled as he wiped his eyes. "Okay, but I still hurt you, and I can't take that back. I wish I could." Standing, he stepped back from the house to look up at her. She had crossed her arms as she leaned on the windowsill, and she looked so vulnerable and beautiful at once, he wanted to claw his way up the side of the house to her. "I'm sorry it took me a few weeks to work through it. I had a lot of baggage I needed to clear out of the way, and a lot of years of struggling against the geas. Those years taught me I wasn't supposed to trust anyone who held me in their control, but I trust you anyway."

Her gaze flared wide, and her expression came to

life, but not with the kind of emotion he had hoped so much to see. "You—trust me?" she repeated bitterly. "How could you be so stupid? *I don't trust me!*"

Chapter Twenty-Four

I T TOOK A second for that to sink in. He demanded, "Why not?"

"When I saw you walking down the street toward me earlier, the first thing I wanted to do was order you to stay!" she shouted. "That's why I ran! That dumb god never should have offered it to me. You can't trust me with the geas. But I also don't ever want to see you look at me the way you did back in the great hall."

"Please believe me, if I could take that back, I would." Frustration gnawed at him. She still kept her distance. She still wouldn't walk down to open the door for him.

But she had opened a window.

Striding away, he turned back to the house and took a running leap at the window. As he grabbed hold of the windowsill, she stumbled back. Quickly, he hauled himself inside. When he straightened, she sat on the edge of a bed, staring at him, both hands clapped over her mouth.

Kneeling in front of her, he gently pulled her hands down. "Stop denying what we both want. Don't try to push me away anymore. I know now that you love me, and that's why you let me go. You thought you were doing the right thing, and hell, at the time, you probably were. I needed to absorb what had happened. But I'm here now, and I want you more than I've wanted anything in my life."

Longing filled her gaze, along with a lingering reserve. She stroked his cheek. "What if I activate the geas? What if I accidentally say something it takes as an order—or what if I actually give you an order? Go to the store, and get some milk. Pick me up a sandwich on your way home. Order a pizza for tonight, will you? People say things like that all time."

"I don't know. I don't have all the answers." Giving in to what he had been wanting to do for a long time, he pulled her into his arms. The rightness of her body aligning with his brought such relief, he sighed and laid his head on her shoulder. Her arms tightened around him. "If you activate the geas somehow, I'll tell you to cut it out, and you'll stop. We can't live our lives in fear of it."

Her breath shuddered, and she tightened her arms. "We could if you left. You could have the entire world—everywhere except for where I am."

"I don't want the entire world." He pressed his lips against her neck. "I want you. I'm not going to lie to you, Sidonie. I think it will probably get messy sometimes, and I know we'll make mistakes. Neither of us has lived a normal life, and even when people have the best of intentions, they still hurt each other. But do you know what that damn puck said to me the other day?"

She nestled against him. "What?"

"He said, 'What would we have if we didn't have forgiveness?'" Closing his eyes, he breathed in her scent. With her becoming a lycanthrope, it had changed. It was deeper, wilder, and it resonated with all the wild places inside him. "We can make this work. We have to make it work. I want you too much to let go, and I will do anything I have to do in order to keep you. Anything."

"I want you too, so much," she whispered.

He murmured in her ear, "Then take me."

✧　✧　✧

TAKE ME, HE said.

It had been so impossible. Now could it really be that simple?

Pulling back, Sid searched his face. She saw nothing but love and determination.

"That whole resurrection thing is totally on me," she told him. "But this one is on you."

Laughter, like fire, lit his gaze. "I'll take full responsibility," he promised. "You can throw this back in my face every time we have an argument."

"I'll plan on it." Sudden tears flooded her eyes. Their separation was still too close and raw for her to joke very much.

He saw the tears, and his expression changed.

Cupping the back of her head, he cradled her close. "*Shh*," he murmured. "We're good. It's all good. It's so much better than I could have hoped for."

"I love you," she said. "I love you."

"I love you too, darling girl. With all my heart." He cupped her face and kissed her softly.

Not many men could pull off "darling girl," she thought hazily, but somehow when Morgan said it, it sounded warm, natural, and right.

He pulled back. "Hard as the past few weeks were, the time to reflect has been good for me. I've been thinking a lot about the orders you gave me in the great hall."

Anxiety flooded her expression. "I screwed up, didn't it? Did I screw it up?"

"Not in any way." He pressed his lips to her forehead. "But the more I think about it, the more I find the way you phrased things intriguing."

She touched the lean line of his jaw. "I was trying to set you free completely."

"I could see that, but at the time I was too close to living under Isabeau's control to believe it. I thought anything you said could be countermanded if you changed your mind, but the way you phrased things stuck with me. You said, *I order you to rediscover what it is like to live a life of your own choosing. I order the geas to rest forever and never compel you to do anything again. These words I speak are paramount. Nothing I can possibly say at any point for the rest of my life will ever override the orders I give you right now.*" He paused, his gaze lively with curiosity and speculation. "And I can't help but wonder—you were trying to turn the geas into something written in stone, and not to be revisited. What if you managed to do it?"

She blinked. "Is it possible? I want so much for it to be possible."

"I haven't felt a hint of compulsion since you stopped me from leaving in the great hall," he told her. "And if it's one thing I know, it's what the geas feels like when it activates. So... we'll never know if you managed it unless we try it. Give me an order, and let's see what happens."

Her stomach twisted and she recoiled. "I can't."

"Yes, you can." He took her by the shoulders and looked deeply into her eyes. "We need to know what we're going to be living with so we don't run into any surprises. And you need to listen to me when I say this—when you give me the order, anything that happens is okay."

What he said made sense, but she still hesitated. "Are you sure?"

"Absolutely." He smiled at her. "I'm okay. *We're* okay. So go ahead and do it. Order me to do something. I want to know what's going to happen."

"Well, okay..." She cast about for something to order him to do, but all she really wanted was to get back to the kissing part. Feeling self-conscious and awkward, she ordered, "Kiss me."

Amusement flashed across his face. Pulling her into

his arms, he rocked her as he laughed and laughed. Then he tilted her face up and kissed her with such evident enjoyment, she didn't know whether to be dismayed or pleased.

Winding an arm around his neck, she whispered against his mouth, "Is this bad? I can't tell if this is bad. Did the geas make you do it?"

Lifting his head, he told her, "First, let's get one thing straight—I will always want to obey any order you ever give me like that. Please give me as many orders to kiss you as you'd like. And secondly... I didn't feel a thing from the geas. Not one damn thing, you clever love."

Excitement and hope soared. "Are you saying it's gone?"

"Not gone. I wouldn't say that." He grinned. "We can keep testing it with other orders to make sure, but I think as long as you hold the control of the geas it might very well be tied off for good. And since Isabeau had cast the spell using Azrael's Athame, it makes sense he would be the only one who can transfer the geas to anyone else. I think we're as stable as we'll ever be."

The relief was immense. She sagged. "Thank God."

"Yes, and thank *you*." Cupping the back of her head, heat replaced the laughter in his expression. "I think I need to obey your order some more."

A smile broke over her face. She lost it quickly as he kissed her again. Her lips moved under his, while she pressed as close to him as she could get.

Nothing had changed between them. All the fierce burning was still there. The soft, healing kiss changed rapidly into raw demand. Prying her lips open, he plunged into her mouth with his tongue, driving into her with the force of his hunger.

That felt so good, so necessary, and *it had been so damn long* since he had done that, she moaned and feverishly began to unbutton his shirt while kissing him back.

He pulled back, his face flushed with intent, and tore out of his jacket. As he took over the job of unbuttoning his shirt, she stood to strip off her sweater, jeans, and shoes. She was just beginning to pull off her bra, when he stopped. Still kneeling, he wrapped his arms around her legs, turned his face into her stomach, and held her tightly.

The emotion in that wordless gesture made more tears spring to her eyes. Growing still, she stroked his hair. He pressed his lips to her skin, and she caressed his temple and the side of his face.

Pressing kisses along the edge of her panties, he murmured, "I trust you. I love you. I believe in you."

The words filled all the empty corners in her soul. As she began to kneel too, he stopped her. Easing her panties down, he pressed more kisses along the edge of her pelvis, then nuzzled at the juncture between her legs. Desire coiled through her in a gush of heat. When he slipped two fingers along the petals of her sex, she felt the strength leave her legs.

"Morgan, I-I can't do this standing up," she stammered.

He looked up quickly, humor flashing across his face. "Are you sure?" he asked, stroking her.

Pleasure rocked her back. She gasped, "I'm sure."

Coming to his feet, he pushed her back, back... until her shoulders met the wall behind her. "What about now?"

She looked from one side to the other. There were so many pitfalls, and nothing at all to prop her up on either side. "I don't know."

"Let's try," he coaxed as he undid the fastening of his slacks and stepped out of them. The humor still lingered in his expression, along with the building heat, and the combination was so damn sexy, she felt weak at the knees.

"I'm warning you, this is not a stable situation," she told him, shaking.

"So I can see." Standing nude in front of her, he rubbed her arms. "What can I do to help?"

Greedily she spread her hands across the expanse of his chest, running her unsteady fingers through the dark, crisp hair that narrowed to a thin strip down his abdomen, to his erect cock. Grasping his erection in both hands, she sank to her knees.

Breathing hard, she murmured, "This feels a lot steadier."

He laughed. "That's not what I had in mind."

"But you're not going to argue, are you?" Slanting a

sidelong look at him, she opened her mouth and took him in.

Everything felt so much more intense as a lycanthrope. His scent, the scrape of his fingernails across her skin, the roar of his magic that he no longer bothered to conceal. She felt giddy with it, with him, as she opened her throat to take him in all the way. His cock jumped as she suckled at the tip, then swallowed his length, and pulled back to caress the head again.

"I'm beginning to see your point about the unstable situation," he muttered. Cupping the back of her head, he fucked her mouth. His muscles were tight, his skin hot.

Closing her eyes, she gave into the moment, the salty taste of him and the hot, hard glide of his erection against her tongue. His thrusts became shorter, more urgent. Willingly, she opened up to it, stroking the long, taut length of his thighs and cupping his tight sac at the root of his cock.

Suddenly he pulled out fast, swearing. She looked up at him in disappointment. "No!" she complained. "You said, Take me. I was taking you. You don't get to pull out."

His breath shuddered audibly in his throat. Caressing her cheek, he gritted, "Coming in your mouth sounds like the hottest thing ever, but... not this time. I need to look in your eyes."

As soon as he said it, she wanted it too. She needed to see his soul housed in his body—that vital connection she had fought so hard to save.

"I'd like that," she whispered.

She rose to her feet, and, taking her hand, he led her to the bed. When he sat at the foot, she moved to straddle his lap, facing him. As she wrapped her arms around his head, he nuzzled her breasts, kissing first one then the other. With one hand, he stroked at her sex, while he stroked her back with the other.

She felt so loved and desired, pleasure lit her from the inside, turning her incandescent. When he gripped his erection and positioned it at her opening, she pushed down, taking him in deeper each time she moved against him. Soon she had him in as deep as she could get.

Grasping her by the hips, he thrust up in time to her rhythm. The pleasure spiraled higher, hotter. She couldn't take him in hard enough, deep enough. She needed—she needed...

With the ball of his thumb, he found her clitoris and rubbed, and the explosion that rocked her was so sudden and sharp she sobbed aloud.

Watching her closely, he moved steadily, providing the right pressure and the right penetration to help her spiral higher. "Give it to me again," he urged against her lips. "Sidonie, it's been fucking weeks. I've been tight and aching the whole time, and I thought you might never want to see me again."

Her shaking lips moved under his. "I felt the same way. I need you the same way."

"It's okay now, my darling girl. Don't strain for it. Let me bring it to you."

Trusting him, she hung on to his shoulders, letting him caress her while she flexed on his lap. He was endlessly inventive, nipping at her lower lip, sliding a finger inside her along with his cock.

She lost herself in total sensuality, drifting with the play of their bodies, until he grasped hold of her firmly and picked her up. Without withdrawing, he turned to lay her out on the bed, coming down with her and settling between her legs.

It was the simplest position of all, entirely pleasurable and comforting at once. She reveled in his weight, in his penetration, stroking his back and murmuring wordlessly as he kissed her. He picked up the rhythm and the strength of his thrusts, and she rose with it, until he drove at her, hard and steadily, and when he stopped to grind against her, he hit it just right, and she climaxed again.

He rocked with the waves of pleasure, then thrust hard, and hard again. Bowing his shoulders around her, he shuddered with his own completion. She stroked his shoulders as she watched him.

She didn't think it was possible to love him any more, to feel any more, but then in the middle of his own climax, while she could still feel him pulsing inside, he looked deep into her eyes.

"I'm yours," he whispered. "Don't ever doubt it. Don't doubt me."

That moment.

Tears slipped out the corners of her eyes as she took it in.

"No," she promised. "I never will."

THEY SPENT THE next few months at the farmhouse, taking their time to get to know each other and exploring the moors. When they'd had enough time together so she could unclench a bit, she remembered she needed to warn him about their yearly obligation in Azrael's Wild Hunt.

He took it better than she had expected. "If that's the price it took for me to come back to be with you, it will be entirely worth it," he told her. His features filled with the curiosity she was coming to associate with any time he became acquainted with something magical and new. "Besides, it should be interesting."

She snorted. "I guess you could say that."

On more mundane matters, they were both terrible cooks, but Morgan was more patient at trying to figure out recipes. Sid couldn't be bothered.

"I don't like to cook, and I don't like to clean toilets," she said. "And I'm more than happy to pay someone else to do those things."

Morgan had little to no interest in television shows other than the news, but he was a voracious reader. Sid dabbled at both.

Morgan insisted she swear a pact to avoid any news about Isabeau or Oberon. "I'm done," he said as they sprawled on the bed one lazy afternoon. "I'm out. I was done so many years ago. It was never my conflict to begin with, and I don't want to know anything more about it."

"Of course," she agreed, resting against his chest. "Part of me feels like I should have been more blood-thirsty about going after Isabeau, but you know something? When it came down to it, most of me didn't want to give her any more of my time."

"I understand." He hooked one arm behind his head. After a moment, he added, "But I had to kill Modred. He's the one who killed my king, from the time I was human. I couldn't... not kill him."

Lifting her head, she stared at him. He was watching the ceiling, his face pensive.

"Did it help?" she asked gently.

He sighed. "You know, it did. I worried it wouldn't, and I would always be looking back at a past I could no longer reach. It was worse when I was at Isabeau's court, because I could never get away from it. Being forced to interact with her and Modred was like rubbing salt into a wound that never healed. Now everything feels different. Cleaner." With a shrug, he added, "I don't know how to put it any better than that."

She pressed a kiss to his pectoral muscle. "I'm just glad you feel like you can move on."

He grinned. "I'm starting to have thoughts like, What am I going to do with my life now? And how do you start a new career when you're past middle age?"

That caused her to burst out laughing. "You can literally do anything you want. Thirty-seven is not middle-aged!"

He cocked an eyebrow at her. "When you've been thirty-seven for... Oh, never mind. I'm not going to share *that* number with you."

"You could always pick up your old instruments and start playing again."

"No," he said, after a reflective moment. "That belongs in the past too. Besides, I would far rather listen to you."

"Well, don't try to force anything," she murmured. "You have all the time in the world, and something will occur to you."

"I'll tell you one thing right now." He rapped a knuckle gently against her head. "Whenever you're ready to go on tour, you're not going to use Vince's security company again."

"Oh, no?" She hid a smile. She had a feeling she knew what was going to come next.

"No," he replied in a firm voice. "I'll take care of your security. Me, along with some of the other Hounds."

Even though Morgan had disbanded the thirty-two surviving Hounds, several had already asked to come back to him. Unable to settle into their former lives, they missed the structure and community of the pack. Morgan had been noncommittal up until this point, but now she knew he meant to take in everyone that asked.

"They need you," she said.

"Well, I need you," he told her. "So they can help me guard you and make sure you're safe."

"Lately, I've been daydreaming about starting a small, independent music label," she confessed. "But I'll be honest, the whole idea of the business side of things is overwhelming. That's what I pay Rikki to handle. I just want to write songs and play the violin."

He was silent for so long, she lifted her head to check on him. He was still watching the ceiling, but now his eyes were narrowed and his expression had come alive with interest.

He said slowly, "How would you feel if I looked into doing it? It sounds like the kind of challenge I might enjoy, and I like the idea of supporting independent musicians. Some of the Hounds would be good at management. Others could focus on security."

Rolling onto her back, she went into a full body stretch. "I think you can do anything you want to, even that."

When October came, Sid felt it was time to tackle going home to New York. "We don't have to stay, if you don't want," she told Morgan. "But I've got an apartment I'm paying a fortune for, and right now it's just gathering dust. I've got to figure out what I'm going to do with it."

"Let's go," he said immediately. "I'd like to spend some time in New York. Besides, there's someone there I would like to see."

"Okay!" she said. "I'm game if you are."

Within a couple of days, the travel arrangements were set, and they had packed up all their personal belongings. They flew into the Newark airport and took a car service to Sid's apartment.

She stared out at the early evening during the drive. The trees had begun to change, and the fall colors were brilliant. The smells were complex and exciting, and everything felt both familiar and strange at once.

Her apartment was located in a high-rise building, and it felt like a disappointment. She remembered it being spacious and comfortable, but as soon as they walked in the door, she knew it wouldn't do.

"This is too closed in for me," she said, walking over restlessly to the wall of windows to look out at the view. "Sure, the view is great, but you can't open any of these windows. This is going to make me crazy."

Morgan set the last of the luggage on the floor and joined her. "So we'll look for something else," he said with a shrug. "It's an attractive enough place, but I've dealt with being a lycanthrope for far longer than you have. I think you still need room to roam."

"Yeah," she muttered. "I do too."

Morgan had made arrangements to meet with the person he wanted to see that evening. She had overheard snatches of an intriguing phone conversation while she had been taking a shower, so after they hauled the luggage into her bedroom, she asked, "Do you want me to disappear when your person arrives?"

"Please don't feel like you have to," he told her with a relaxed smile. "But you might be more comfortable if you took an evening walk."

That settled it. She wouldn't leave now if the building were on fire.

Instead, she got to work unpacking while Morgan sat at her dining table with a glass of scotch and looked out over the city.

Soon there was an imperious knock on the door. Abandoning her chore, Sid stepped into the doorway of the bedroom to watch Morgan answer it. He stood back, holding the door wide.

A massive man prowled in. Close to seven feet in height, he dominated the apartment as soon as he set foot inside. He had raven black hair, dark bronze skin, fierce gold eyes, and he carried an invisible corona of Power that made Sid take an instinctive step back.

Dragos Cuelebre, Lord of the Wyr demesne in New York, had come to call.

"Hello," Morgan said. He still sounded relaxed, even friendly.

Dragos's eyes glittered hard as gold coins. "What are you doing in my city?"

"Well, I have a girlfriend now," Morgan replied. "Also, I thought you might like to know that I'm no longer bound by a geas to obey Isabeau."

"What?" Dragos rapped out.

The Wyr Lord's body language carried so much

leashed aggression, Sid launched out of the bedroom. Sticking out a hand, she hurried up to him, "Lord Cuelebre, I'm Sidonie Martel. It's an honor to meet you."

Dragos's eyes narrowed. "You're the musician that went missing in the UK. You'd been kidnapped."

He made no effort to shake her hand, and feeling awkward, she dropped it by her side. "Yes, sir, that's right."

Dragos turned his deadly gaze back to Morgan. "Did you do that?"

"Me? No—oh, no. That was someone else entirely." As Morgan turned to the dining table, he shot Sid a vivid, wry glance. "Have a drink with me, Dragos, and give me the chance to apologize."

"I'll skip the drink," Dragos said. "Get to the point. Convince me why I shouldn't burn you to a crisp."

Morgan spun back again, but before he could say anything, Sid leaped in. She told the Wyr Lord, "Whatever he did in the past wasn't his fault. Isabeau had him trapped in a geas. He didn't have a choice about any of the things he did."

Rubbing the back of his neck, Morgan murmured to her, "We should probably just have that printed on cards, so we can hand them out wherever we go."

Dragos angled his head as he considered Sidonie. The force of his attention was difficult to bear, and he looked... He looked like...

Hot gold eyes captured her. *Tell me the truth*, the

Wyr Lord whispered in her head. *Let me see it in your mind.*

Caught in his spell, she was helpless to stop the flood of images she gave him. In the space of a heartbeat, she gave him everything. The kidnapping, her imprisonment, the moments of heated tenderness with Morgan, the confrontation with Isabeau.

Her bargain with Azrael.

Abruptly, the connection snapped off, and she felt immersed, in Morgan's familiar magic.

Shaken, she staggered. Somehow Morgan had come to be standing by her. He put a steadying arm around her, and when he stared at Dragos, he looked as dangerous as she had ever seen him look.

"If you try anything like that again," Morgan growled. "We will become enemies in truth."

"Stop," she whispered to him, putting a hand on his chest. His muscles were rigid, and he was *furious*, but making an enemy of Dragos Cuelebre was the height of insanity. "He shouldn't have done that without asking, but he also didn't hurt me. If seeing my memories helped in any way, let's just let it go."

Dragos's eyelids lowered over his hot gold gaze, hiding their expression. "I'll take that drink after all," he said suddenly. "While you tell me why you're here."

"We're looking to relocate," Sid said, while Morgan fought a battle with his temper. "I'm no longer human since I've been kidnapped, Morgan's no longer bound to Isabeau, and we have... how many is it now?

Eighteen lycanthropes who used to be Isabeau's Hounds who need jobs and homes. This is my old apartment. It won't do—we're not all going to fit…"

Her lame attempt at a joke went over like a lead balloon as the two men glared at each other. Taking the scotch bottle, Dragos tipped it over the empty glass waiting on the table. Taking the glass, he drained it and set it back down.

He said to Morgan, "You endangered my mate and unborn son back in Hollywood."

"Under Isabeau's compulsion," Morgan replied tightly.

"Yes, I saw that was the truth." Dragos crossed his arms, and his stance relaxed. "Okay, I'll let it go."

Morgan shot a look at Sid that still sparked with temper, but, she saw, it was less than it had been before. He gave the Wyr Lord a nod. "That's good to know."

Dragos considered them, gold eyes narrowed. "Tell me why I should let lycanthropy into my back yard. It's a communicable disease."

"Yes, it is." Morgan nodded. "But it's a treatable one, if the victim who was bitten gets medical treatment right away. My Hounds are decent men. You can interview each one, if you like, and I'll personally vouch for every one of them. And none of us go into a mindless frenzy at the full moon. I can't say we won't defend ourselves if we're attacked for some reason, but we'll take full responsibility for cleaning the situation up—and we won't spread the lycanthropy virus. I give you my word."

Sid's new truthsense was just a baby bud on the vine, but even she heard the rock-solid sincerity in Morgan's voice. She smiled to herself. That sincerity had gotten her through the darkest time in her life.

"Say I accept your word on that particular issue," Dragos said as he considered each of them. "You're not Wyr, but you shapeshift, and you're very dangerous. You can live in my demesne if you swear fealty to me and live by Wyr laws. The same goes for any of your Hounds that wish to relocate. Those are my terms."

Sid felt compelled to speak up. "We owe fealty to one of the gods. Will that interfere?"

Dragos shook his head. "As long as your god doesn't cause you to break any civil laws, your fealty is no different from a dozen different religious practices scattered throughout New York."

She exchanged a glance with Morgan, who gave her a slight, private smile. He turned his attention to Dragos. "Agreed. We'll accept your terms."

A corner of Dragos's ruthless mouth lifted. "I think it could be very useful to have a sorcerer of your Power and skill owe me fealty."

Morgan narrowed his eyes and smiled. He countered, "I think it might be useful to have a dragon owe me a favor or two."

Dragos inclined his head and strode for the door.

Just before exiting the apartment, he stopped and turned back. In that brusque manner of his, he said, "I visited at Isabeau's court a long time ago. It was before you were there."

"Yes, she spoke of it once or twice," Morgan replied with a frown.

Dragos tilted his head. "I'm curious, what did she say? Did she ever tell you why I was there?"

Raising his eyebrows, Morgan replied readily enough. "She was convinced you wanted a Powerful artifact she had in her possession, called Azrael's Athame. She later used it to cast her geas on me. She said she always kept it hidden the times you were at court, but I don't know where. She would never reveal her hiding places to me. By the time she captured me, she had become obsessed with the fear of losing it, or it being stolen, so she ordered me to make a gold chain that was unbreakable. Whenever I was at court, she wore the Athame on the chain. I don't know what she did with it when I was absent."

Dragos's eyelids lowered, hiding the expression in his gaze. "Whatever happened to that artifact, do you know?"

Morgan smile held a wealth of satisfaction. "It has gone back to its original owner."

"I see."

With that, the Wyr Lord nodded to Sid and let himself out.

It was as if a fierce desert sun had gone behind

clouds. The apartment seemed much cooler and bigger than it had before.

Morgan swung around to face her, his expression filling with concern. "If I'd had any idea he would pull that stunt, I would never have met with him near you."

"Forget it," she muttered absently, her mind already on other things. "He was rude and invasive, but if you had done something that endangered his mate and baby, I'm not sure I blame him. He went straight for the weak spot in the room—me—and took what he needed to make sure you were on the up and up. Besides, you stopped him quickly enough." She frowned. "This might sound odd, Morgan, but I... I think he looks..."

His expression had eased as he listened to her. Rubbing her arms, he asked, "You think he looks, what?"

"I think he looks a lot like Azrael," she muttered. "It's hard to remember exactly. But he has gold eyes, of course, and Azrael has green."

"It's not so hard for me to imagine the dragon and Death might be connected," Morgan said dryly. "In any case, I'm glad to have that meeting behind me. Behind us."

She stepped closer so she could lean against him and tuck her nose in her favorite spot, at the hollow where his neck met his shoulder. "*Mmm*," she said. "What do you want to do now?"

He pressed his lips to her temple. She could hear

the smile in his voice as he murmured, "There's so much beauty in the world. What do you think about doing a little sightseeing?"

Breathing deeply, she took in his scent while delight at their future unfurled inside her like a flower. "I think that sounds absolutely perfect."

Thank you!

Dear Readers,

Thank you for reading *Spellbinder*! I hope you enjoyed reading about Morgan and Sidonie. I have, for many years, wanted to tell my version of what happened to the Merlin character in the Arthurian saga, and so this story is near and dear to my heart.

Would you like to stay in touch and hear about new releases? You can:

- Sign up for my monthly email at:
  www.theaharrison.com
- Follow me on Twitter at @TheaHarrison
- Like my Facebook page at
  facebook.com/TheaHarrison

Reviews help other readers find the books they like to read. I appreciate each and every review, whether positive or negative.

Happy reading!
~*Thea*

Coming Soon:

Lionheart

Available early 2018

Look for these titles from Thea Harrison

THE ELDER RACES SERIES – FULL LENGTH NOVELS

Published by Berkley

Dragon Bound

Storm's Heart

Serpent's Kiss

Oracle's Moon

Lord's Fall

Kinked

Night's Honor

Midnight's Kiss

Shadow's End

MOONSHADOW TRILOGY

Moonshadow

Spellbinder

Lionheart *Early 2018

ELDER RACES NOVELLAS

True Colors

Natural Evil

Devil's Gate

Hunter's Season

The Wicked

Dragos Takes a Holiday

Pia Saves the Day

Peanut Goes to School

Dragos Goes to Washington
Pia Does Hollywood
Liam Takes Manhattan

GAME OF SHADOWS SERIES
Published by Berkley

Rising Darkness
Falling Light

ROMANCES UNDER THE NAME AMANDA CARPENTER

E-published by Samhain Publishing
(original publication by Harlequin Mills & Boon)
*These stories are currently out of print

A Deeper Dimension
The Wall
A Damaged Trust
The Great Escape
Flashback
Rage
Waking Up
Rose-Coloured Love
Reckless
The Gift of Happiness
Caprice
Passage of the Night
Cry Wolf
A Solitary Heart
The Winter King

Made in the USA
San Bernardino, CA
10 August 2017